SUZANNAH ROWNTREE

The Lady of Kingdoms

Watchers of Outremer, Book Two

travel through time and space

Happy reading!

Suzannah Rowntree

suzannahrowntree.site

First published by Bocfodder Press 2019

Copyright © 2019 by Suzannah Rowntree

This novel is entirely a work of fiction. The names, characters and incidents portrayed in it are the work of the author's imagination. Any resemblance to actual persons, living or dead, events or localities is entirely coincidental.

First edition

ISBN: 9781710102024

Editing by L H Editing
Cover art by Seedlings Design Studio

This book was professionally typeset on Reedsy.
Find out more at reedsy.com

To Lilia.
Soix preux, cub!

Prologue

Miles of Plancy believed in miracles so long as they happened to someone else; preferably a saint, or anyone who could survive an encounter with the terrors of holiness. As for himself, he was already in the middle of a military disaster. Visions and portents were the last thing he needed right now.

His eyes must be deceiving him. Miles blinked, trying to wash the grit out of them. The rider he saw in the narrow desert ravine ahead of them simply *couldn't* be a Frankish knight.

In the sandy throat between the dun-coloured rocks ahead, the rider passed from left to right and then vanished. Mounted on a dusty white horse, a dusty white surcoat covering mail which, under the leaden February sky, reflected no glint from the struggling daylight, he might have been part of the rock. When Miles opened his eyes, the rider was gone.

A Frankish knight, here in Arabia? It was impossible. Miles was seven hundred miles from the nearest Frankish-held fortress. He knew better than to hope for a rescue. He must have been dreaming with his eyes open.

Miles glanced at the silent column of men behind him. Two hundred Franks—knights, sergeants, and seamen—not counting their Arab and Nubian captives. For three days they had trudged through the desert, praying for escape. Heads bowed. Feet dragged. He was the only one who had glimpsed the rider.

1

If they raced ahead to meet their rescue and found nothing, the men would be ready to cut his throat. If it was a Saracen ambush, they'd all die inside a few heartbeats.

Miles believed in miracles. Just not here. Not now.

He lifted his fist and croaked, "Halt!"

The column shuffled and creaked to a standstill. In the silence, the distant sound of thunder rumbled through the rocky gorge.

"Yakub," Miles said urgently, but one of the Bedouin guides had already thrown himself on the ground, pressing his ear to the rock.

"Horses," the man said. "Behind us."

"Devil take it." Miles' voice was only a dry scratch in his throat, his eyes reddened and itchy, his feet a mass of blisters. If an attack came, they would not last long, but in that moment of doom, he felt fleeting pride. He and his men had pierced seven hundred miles into Arabia, almost to the very gates of Medina, the burial place of Mahomet. In five hundred years, no Christian knight had set foot where they stood now.

They were just two hundred men, but they had delivered an insult the Saracens would never forget.

"Lances! Form ranks! Front rank kneeling, second rank standing, crossbows behind. Hold!"

Miles barked, striding towards one of the hand-carts they'd taken when they fled into the desert. Two prisoners were shackled to the cart, and with a clank of chains one of them stepped forward.

"If you surrender, your lives will be spared. Our law forbids the slaughter of captives."

Miles looked into the young man's old eyes. They had captured him on the Egyptian coast last month when they'd sailed into Aidhab, and since then Miles had become fascinated by him. He wore fine clothes and bore himself like a noble, but had refused to identify himself. Despite weeks of travel together, Miles had learned nothing about the other man, not even his name. All Miles knew was that the other Saracens were terrified of him.

Perhaps the man had influence with the Sultan Saladin. Perhaps he could save them.

Miles shoved his crossbow aside, and grabbed his battle-axe from the cart. No time to fumble for keys. "Hold still," he grunted.

Just one stroke, and the chain broke, leaving the young Saracen free to move away from the cart. Miles stepped after him, hands firm on the axe. "Give me your word you'll see us safe home."

The prisoner looked faintly amused. "Am I the sultan? I can tell you the law; I can't ransom you."

Miles glanced at his men as they rushed to unsling shields and load crossbows. Most of them were humble sergeants or footmen, and the few knights, like himself, were landless adventurers. "No one else is going to ransom us. So it might as well be you."

The Saracen smiled. "As God wills."

Miles grabbed the prisoner by the dusty finery on his back and propelled him forward through the hastily-forming ranks. Beyond, horsemen poured around the curve of the valley on their trail, banners flickering in the wind.

"Hold your bolts!" Miles shouted as he walked out to meet the oncoming tide of horseflesh and steel, shoving the prisoner ahead of him. *Six paces, and stand still. Try not to shiver; it looks bad.* Behind him, lance-butts thudded into the dry riverbed, forming a double horseshoe of spear-points against the stone wall of the valley—but it wasn't enough. Even with twice the number of men, the first shock of the charge would smash right through their thin defence.

A movement among the rocks above. Yakub and the other Bedouin who had guided them from the coast scrambled up the cliffs, running for safety. Miles didn't blame them: there was little love lost between Saladin's men and the desert wanderers. If caught helping Frankish raiders, their fate would be worse than his.

He gripped the Saracen prisoner more tightly as the horsemen thundered closer: a cohort of Egyptian light cavalry, flying the sultan's banners and shouting their war-cries. This was the first hurdle: whether they would even stop to let him speak.

Miles shivered in anticipation, but his prisoner was still and cold as ice.

3

Just in time, the Saracen trumpet screamed and the charge turned aside, surrounding the little Frankish redoubt and reining in. Within the blink of an eye there was an arrow on each string.

"Hold your bolts," Miles called again, this time in Arabic. He swallowed to steady his voice. "Which one of you is the leader? Let's talk like men of sense. Why should any of us die?"

A heavyset man in gilded lamellar armour kneed his horse forward. "You have attacked the Red Sea and destroyed the pilgrims' ships," he said harshly in a thick Armenian accent. "Should I continue? Surely that is enough reason why you should die."

Miles forced a laugh. "You misunderstand me, my lord. My concern is for your men as well as my own. I have a hundred crossbows at my back, already wound and aimed. How many of your men will die before they can draw?"

Strictly speaking, he probably barely had seventy crossbows back there, but negotiating with an enemy often required one to bend the truth.

"I claim quarter under Saracen law," Miles added. As the Armenian general hesitated, he nodded towards his prisoner. "This young knight tells me that the sultan's justice is to be relied upon."

"Then tell your men to lay down their weapons."

Relief washed over Miles, but he didn't permit himself time to savour it. "Wait! Your lordship is magnanimous, but I crave your patience a little longer. I'd also like to arrange a ransom."

"Whose?"

"His." Miles nodded to the prisoner he held before him like a shield, and hefted his axe with the sunniest smile he could muster. "Ours."

The Armenian scowled. "Whose?" he repeated incredulously.

"In exchange for our releasing our prisoners to you unharmed, I'd ask that you provide us a safe-conduct home to the Coast." Miles used the Saracen expression for the Christian kingdom of Jerusalem, ruled by Franks these last hundred years. "All two hundred of us. We would be happy to swear any oaths you require."

The Armenian reddened. "Are you mad? You have spat in the sultan's

4

face. It would be as much as my life is worth to release you. Be glad your lives will be spared. If you are a man of means, then no doubt your friends will arrange a ransom."

He had no means, and no friends. Miles tightened his grip, wishing the silent prisoner would weep, beg, show some fear for his life. "If you will not have compassion on us, then have compassion on this young man. Whose son is he? Your own, or another's?"

The Armenian barked a contemptuous laugh. "I have never set eyes on this man before in my life. Stop wasting my time and have your men lay down their weapons."

Miles shifted his grip on the axe and yanked the honed blade close to the prisoner's face. "You're lying," he snarled. "Give me a safe-conduct, or I'll kill him."

At last, the Saracen prisoner made a sound. A soft snort of contemptuous laughter. "The general is telling the truth. He does not know me."

Miles didn't know whether to believe the young Saracen, but his hands were shaking. He evidently could not intimidate the prisoner into revealing himself, and if that was so, there was no point in killing the prisoner.

"Saints," he almost sobbed. The Saracens had them surrounded. Maybe he should command the attack, go down in a blaze of glory. No, that wasn't fair on the men. "Throw down your weapons," he croaked, lowering his axe.

His men were all too ready to surrender. He heard their bows and spears hitting the ground before the Saracens moved forwards, streaming around Miles and the prisoner to shepherd the Franks away from the stockpile of weapons.

The prisoner shifted slightly, reminding Miles that he still held him by the scruff of his robe. Miles tightened his grip. "A boon," he growled.

"What do you ask?"

Miles let go, allowing the young Saracen to face him. Once again, Miles was struck by the gravity of the man's expression. Though nearly as young as Miles himself, he seemed decades older, and completely uninterested in Miles, save as a curiosity.

"I'm a bastard. I have no land, no money, and no family. No one is going to ransom me." Miles reached for his dagger. "If you won't ransom me, then I beg you, kill me now."

He stood there, fumbling wearily with the catch on the sheath, and the Saracen looked at him with detached amusement.

A tattoo of galloping hooves echoed suddenly between the ravine walls.

It was just one horse and Miles barely paid attention to it, until panicked shouts erupted from behind him. "Bows! Bows!" someone was yelling in Arabic. Miles turned.

The rider skimmed down the ravine from beyond, ripping through the unprepared Saracen flank like a boar ripping a hound's flank. White horse. White surcoat. Miles' jaw dropped as the lone rider burst into view, sending one luckless Saracen warrior after another flying from their horses' saddles.

The Frankish knight.

Miles stepped forward, his heart climbing into his throat. Waiting for the rest of the relief force.

No sign.

The solitary knight threw his horse into a nimble turn and leaned from the saddle to snatch the reins of a newly unburdened horse. Then his spurs struck and the pair of them headed straight towards Miles. The knight's arm went back, hefting the lance, and the weapon flew.

Miles yelled in surprise. The young Saracen beside him recoiled a step a moment before the spear bit quivering into the sand where he had stood.

For an instant the two of them stood staring at the weapon.

The young Saracen's eyes widened. Surprise, recognition, and hunger chased each other across his face; and then he dove for the spear.

Miles felt an instant's jubilation to see the Saracen so dumbfounded, and snatched the spear from the sand before his erstwhile prisoner could reach it. "No, you don't," he laughed, and turned, tossing it into the Frankish knight's outstretched hand.

The knight threw his horse into a snorting, staggering stop. Sand and tiny stones flicked up, stinging Miles' face, and the Saracen lifted his arm with an exclamation to shield himself.

The knight threw him the spare horse's reins. Catching them and rising like a bird to the saddle, Miles didn't hesitate to ask why. With Miles mounted, the knight lowered his spear and charged back through the shouting mob of Saracens.

Miles followed as the knight cut an effortless swathe through the melee. *Crash. Crash.* Enemies went down like ninepins before that deadly lance. To Miles' surprise, the knight wielded the spear butt-first, as though willing to bruise but not kill.

A few Saracen arrows rattled against his armour and stuck in his mail hauberk. Miles swung his axe, but the enemy was already scrambling out of their way. On his right, he glimpsed blurry pale faces watching from within the Saracen encirclement. His men! His fingers tightened on the reins. Maybe—

Heat and pain blazed along his ribs and Miles glanced down with a noise of shock to see a bloody crossbow bolt sticking from his hauberk. Pain made starbursts in his vision as the hot trickle of blood seeped through the padding beneath. He grabbed his saddle horn as dizziness clouded his vision; for a few heartbeats it was all he could do to stay in the saddle. By the time his head cleared they had broken through the encirclement and his rescuer had grabbed his horse's halter to guide them towards the empty ravine ahead.

The moment was gone. He was too late, too weakened to do anything for his men. Already, galloping hooves echoed behind as they raced up the dry gulley.

"They're following us," Miles gasped, putting a hand to his wound.

In their headlong blur of speed, he neither heard nor saw a response from the other knight. They rounded another bend in the ravine and Miles' heart sank as he saw the gorge wind on into the distance, narrowing as its walls rose higher into the mountains above. Instead of following the rocky trail, however, the strange knight reined their beasts aside into a hidden cleft of the rock.

Still clasping his ribs, Miles slid from the saddle and found himself in a sheltered space between a mound of boulders and the valley's wall. Despite the chill of winter, the clammy scent of horse sweat was almost suffocating as they backed their horses deeper into the cleft.

Beyond the boulders, the thunder of enemy hooves rolled closer and passed them. Miles leaned dizzily against the rocks, willing them to fall and hide him as the riders came into view galloping up the valley. All the Saracens had to do was turn around and they would have a clear view of the fugitives...

No. Think about something else. This knight, for instance. Who could it be? He wore one of those new helms with a plate to protect the face. White surcoat, white shield with a brass boss, no device, not even a cross.

The hair rose on the back of his neck. There were stories. Unknown knights on white horses. The armies of heaven, appearing to help win victories or escort shattered armies safely home from disastrous campaigns, only to vanish when the safety of Christian lands was reached again. The White Watcher.

Maybe this *was* a miracle.

A stealthy sound from behind made Miles turn his head to see that the horse and rider alike had vanished. Had his guide departed to his own celestial realm? But then there were footsteps, and the knight reappeared from between the boulders, beckoning him further into the cleft.

Miles got up unsteadily and followed. The passage went on and vanished into the black mouth of a cave; his horse looked out from the shadows with liquid brown eyes. Miles turned to look down the valley towards the enemy scouts. Just in time. The Saracens had reined in, apparently realising their quarry had escaped.

Miles shuffled back, into the darkness.

The knight came and stood next to him. For the first time, Miles noticed the stranger's stature and build—slighter and shorter than he'd expect from an angel.

"Who are you?" he whispered.

The knight went on looking up at him. At this range, Miles could see a glint of eyes in the shadow behind the face-plate—but in the dark, no more.

Further back in the cave, someone snickered. Miles turned and spotted a Bedouin holding the two—no, three—horses, chuckling to himself.

So, not an angel, then.

And most likely not a pilgrim from the West, since this knight knew enough to hire a Bedouin guide. Most pilgrims thought all Saracens were good for nothing but sheathing blades in.

A native, then. Someone born and bred in the kingdom of Jerusalem, someone who knew that the Saracens were as multifarious as the Franks.

"Why don't you speak?" he insisted.

The knight lifted off his helmet.

"I didn't want to miss the look on your face when you saw me."

It was a woman's voice. A woman's laughing, sweat-streaked face that emerged from under the face-plate, curling tendrils of black hair escaping from under her mail coif and clinging damply to her forehead. Miles' mouth fell open in sheer amazement.

"*Marta!* Marta Bessarion, as I live!" For a moment, words failed him. "All the way out here?" he croaked at last. "Alone? Dressed as a knight, and fighting like Hercules? *Have you lost your mind?*"

She smiled up at him with the laughter he knew so well, and peeled the steel coif back off her hair. "Don't look so shocked, Miles. God shields the just."

"It *is* a miracle." He shook his head. "Tell me you didn't come all the way to Arabia just to pull me out of the lion's jaw."

She quirked her eyebrows. "You must admit you *needed* the help."

"Yes, but…" He gave up. This was Marta Bessarion, after all. "How did you *get* here?"

Laughter glimmered in the back of her eyes. "That, my friend, is a *very* long story."

9

Chapter I.

Jerusalem, AD 636

It was partly the nightmare, and partly the summer heat. Marta woke in the night with her skin prickling, and fought the sheet off with a sense of suffocating panic. It made no difference; there was no relief from the thick, dry heat. The filmy curtains covering her window and open door hung slack and lifeless, but she got up anyway, and went outside.

Her father's house in Jerusalem was built around a green courtyard with an arched loggia running the ring of the second storey. Usually this was a pleasant and breezy place even in the heat of summer, but tonight, thick cloud sealed the day's heat to the earth.

A movement caught the edge of her vision. Marta jumped and turned. A white shape stood motionless at the other end of the loggia. It was too dark to see more. For a little while she held her breath and looked at it, until a whisper reached her.

"Marta?"

Mother. "Yes?"

Her mother came closer, still no more than a pale blur against the deeper darkness. "Your father's coming home. We have to get ready."

He's coming home. Marta didn't ask for more. Sometimes her mother was…*right* about things. Something told her this was one of those times, and inside her, a knot that had been clenched tight for weeks slowly relaxed. "Ready, how? For what?"

"We're going away."

Her heart sped. Father was coming back, and they were leaving Jerusalem at last. "Home? To Jamnia? Is the war over?"

Two years ago, when the heresiarchs from Arabia first began raiding Palestine, her father had closed the villa on the coast and shifted the whole family to the safety of walled Jerusalem. In the aftermath of a costly war between the Roman empire and the Persians, Syria and Palestine were weakened and depopulated, in no condition to fight a new invasion. It had taken Emperor Heraclius two years to coordinate a response worthy of the Roman empire but, finally, he had done it. Forging an alliance with his old Persian enemies, he amassed a mighty army and sent it south to confront the heretics. As the praetorian prefect of Palestine, Marta's father had rounded up all the men that could be spared from the garrison of Jerusalem before marching to join the army. More than two weeks ago, she had watched from the city wall as John Bessarion rode away. There had been no news since.

"Is it over?" Marta prompted when her mother didn't reply. "Did we win?"

"I don't know," Rahel Bessarion said tightly. "How soon can you be ready to leave?"

Again, Marta felt a sensation of suffocation and dragged her forearm across her forehead, blotting the sweat. *If we had won, we would not be running away.*

"By dawn. How many servants?"

Rahel spoke tentatively. "I think we take Joseph."

"And?"

"And you children."

It took a moment to fit her mind around the idea. Never in her life had the Bessarions travelled anywhere with fewer than twelve servants. It sounded like an adventure—like the heroes of old, David or Odysseus, leaving home to fight monsters.

"I can be ready in the quarter of an hour."

"Bring only as much as you can carry. I'll wake the others," her mother said. She reached out and touched Marta's arm. "I could be mistaken."

Marta didn't think so.

Five smooth stones and a sling—that's what Saint David took with him to fight the giants. In the absence of a sling of her own, Marta took her plainest tunic, her warmest shawl, and the knife her brother had bought for her last birthday. With its carnelian pommel and its etched steel blade, it was very pretty, but it was also very sharp.

Only minutes had passed, but when Marta slipped out her door again, the whole house was lit and busy. The pony-cart had been brought out, and somewhere, littlest sister Elisa was wailing from being woken rudely in the night.

A lamp burned in her elder brother's room. Marta paused on the threshold and saw him sitting motionless on his bed, his face buried in his hands.

"Lukas? What's wrong?"

He lifted a haggard face. "We lost," he whispered.

She didn't quite understand his tragic expression. "Did Mama tell you where we're going?"

"I don't want to go." He dropped his face into his hands again, his voice muffled. "I want to stay and *fight*."

Marta shook her head. Lukas seemed to take the invasion personally. Of course, the war *was* hard. People were losing their homes and families and livelihoods—some of them for the second time in a generation. At fourteen years old, Marta was old enough to remember the final years of the last war, but heroes weren't supposed to complain about things like that.

The sound of hooves in the courtyard interrupted her thoughts. Marta leaned over the parapet. "It's Father," she called softly to Lukas.

In the steady torchlight, John Bessarion was a huddle slumped on his horse's back, the man and animal both crusted with dirt. He had gone to war with three personal servants, a cart of belongings, two spare horses and a troop from the garrison, but now only one spearman rode behind him.

Lukas joined her at the rail. "Saint George," he breathed, and Marta knew that despite their mother's news and the obvious inference, he had hoped against hope for victory.

Their mother met John in the circle of torchlight as he stiffly dismounted. Across his back, a spear was slung, hampering his movements, but he waved away the servants who ran forward to take it. Instead he pulled their mother into his arms and looked up with red-rimmed eyes to beckon them down into the courtyard.

"Abba, what happened?" Lukas was breathless as they skidded to a stop in front of him.

"I have prepared, but I don't know what for, John." Rahel's arms were locked around his waist, her voice muffled against his chest.

"She said we had to go," Lukas added.

John didn't answer at once. "Where are the little ones?"

Already the nurse was bringing them downstairs: three year old Elisa, still half-asleep, and six year old Paulus with his knuckles stuffed into his eyes. The servants formed a silent, whispering circle around them, and John beckoned them closer. "The rest of you as well."

They shifted nearer, murmuring like a roost of frightened hens. He looked around at them, and Marta swallowed.

Her father was afraid, too.

"I will not dissemble with sweet words," he said wearily. "There was a battle north of the River Hieromices, which is also called Yarmouk. We fought the heretics for six days and lost. The Roman troops have fled to Antioch. Syria and Palestine stand undefended."

A stunned silence fell on the courtyard.

"There are now only two things standing between us and the armies of the heretics," he went on after a moment. "The Jordan river, and the grace of God. You must prepare yourselves."

His voice shook a little as he spoke, and that seemed to loosen their tongues. One of the servants gave an inarticulate cry of despair. Someone else called upon Saint Michael. One of them cried, "Is that why you are leaving us?"

"I will return to you, I promise. I am going only as far as Antioch to ask the emperor for reinforcements. If all goes well, I will bring back an army to defend the city."

"Take us with you!" one of the servants begged.

Lukas pushed forward. "How did we lose? The emperor's army was so strong."

"It was God's will," Rahel answered softly.

"You *always* say that."

"Have you packed?"

For a moment, his jaw bulged. Then he turned and stormed upstairs towards his room. Rahel sighed. "Put the children in the cart, Marta. I'll go and speak to him."

Marta did as she was told, then turned to see that her father was swaying wearily as he leaned on his spear. She ran into the house for a cup of wine, and brought it out to him. "Drink this, Abba. Are you hungry?"

He started and took the cup. As he turned, the torchlight more fully illuminated the spear. It was a thing of severe and lethal beauty: a lance of dark, polished wood, a tip of black steel with silver lines rippling through it. Marta's hand crept out to touch it.

"It's beautiful," she whispered.

Her father jerked it away just as her fingers brushed the wood. "It is *dangerous.*"

Lukas stomped downstairs again, clearly still in a mood, but with a bundle of belongings under his arm. "And if the emperor won't help us?" he wanted to know. "What then? Are we just going to run away?"

"Then we will go to the Syrian Watchers." John rubbed his eyes wearily. "Their council is meeting at Oliveta above Antioch within a few days. If the emperor will not help us, then maybe they will."

The Watchers! Marta touched her forearm, where, like the rest of the family, she carried the Watchers' Mark inked into her skin. Although her father was the Presbyter—the elder—of the local Watcher's council, she had never been to a proper meeting. Though they were ordinary laymen and women, Watchers were sworn to defend their people against the divine wrath. Watchers fed the poor. Watchers built hospitals. And if all else

14

failed and a miracle was needed, Watchers worked those miracles.

Was a miracle all that could save them now? Despite her fear, Marta felt a prickle of excitement. She had never met a Portentor; Watchers with the gifting to work miracles were rare these days.

The answer seemed to convince Lukas, because he threw his bundle into the back of the cart and took the reins of the horse which had been saddled for him. Their mother came back downstairs with the servant, Joseph, carrying a larger bundle. As Joseph helped Paulus and Elisa into the cart, the other servants pressed close, weeping, to say farewell.

"I won't leave you to face this alone," her father promised them. "If I live, I will come back to you. *If I forget thee, O Jerusalem, let my right hand forget her cunning!*"

That was how they left their home—in the dead of the night like thieves, the torchlight burning steadily in the still hot air and the sound of their wheels almost deafening against the paving-stones.

Marta expected her father to lead them directly to the Jaffa Gate. Instead, he turned them towards the Church of the Holy Sepulchre. The high walls of the houses around them blotted out what little light filtered through the stifling clouds. The city was dark as hell and almost as hot and rancid. Lukas rode ahead of the cart, next to their father, holding a torch to light the way. He hadn't spoken or looked at any of them since they left the courtyard, but Marta was glad he had come. She wasn't afraid of going to Syria, but she knew that if the heretics came to Jerusalem, Lukas would find a way to be in the middle of the fighting.

By the time they reached the Holy Sepulchre, Paulus and Elisa had snuggled down with their heads on their mother's lap. Careful not to disturb them, Marta crept forward to sit beside Joseph. The party circled the basilica and entered the courtyard of the Patriarch's palace beyond. Like their own house, this one was brightly-lit. Hooded servants closed and barred the gate hurriedly when they had entered.

At once the Patriarch hurried from the shadows to greet them, flanked by some of the priests of the Sepulchre. As the bishop of Christ's own city, Sophronius was by far the most important man in Jerusalem; in fact one of the two or three most important men in the whole world, second only to Emperor Heraclius and possibly the Patriarch of Rome. Usually she only saw him from a reverent distance. Tonight, he hurried up to them, the torchlight etching deep lines in his aging face.

"You're sooner than I would have expected, Prefect."

John Bessarion flicked a glance towards Rahel, but gave no explanation. "Do you have them ready?"

Two of the priests came forward bearing a chest. It was followed by a succession of other objects, some locked in boxes and others shrouded by canvas, some of them large and awkwardly shaped. Into the cart they went, filling up the small space around Rahel and the sleeping children.

A moment later the priests stood back. Sophronius said, "Godspeed, my son, and a safe voyage."

So they would travel by sea.

Once again they clattered through the narrow stone streets, now headed west to the Jaffa Gate. Marta had kept her head decently covered while they were in the Patriarch's presence, but now she unwound her *palla* and pressed a hand to her chest to halt the slow unpleasant trickle of sweat. Ahead of them, Lukas lifted the torch high enough to shed a little light into the cart. Marta slipped softly from her seat and peeled back a corner of the fabric that covered the Patriarch's goods. Gold and precious stones winked back at her, until Rahel caught the covering and yanked it down, shrouding the treasures from sight.

"What is it?" Marta whispered.

Her mother glanced around them, as though afraid someone might overhear. She herself seemed a little shaken by the sight, her voice barely audible. "The True Cross."

Marta's skin prickled. None of the relics from the Holy Sepulchre could possibly be more precious. The gold and jewels were the least part of its value. Desperate men would kill for something like that. "Why do *we* have it?"

Her mother shook her head. "If the city falls, this must be kept safe. They are sending it out of the city in secret. If it was known, the people would despair."

Outside the city, the night was a little less dark and the road was visible as a pale ribbon through the orchards and olive-groves of the Valley of Hinnon. They halted a moment, and John Bessarion dismounted, tethering his horse's halter to the back of the cart.

"My eyes are too heavy to keep open any longer," he explained. "Keep watch, Lukas. You know what to do." Still holding the spear, he burrowed in among the relics.

Joseph clucked softly to the horses and they started off towards the west. Feeling her eyelids grow heavy, Marta cleared herself a little space in the cart. It took her ages to get to sleep, for the cart rumbled and jolted and there were too many limbs and relics in the cart already. The spear itself jounced against her knee, but at last she slipped into an uneasy sleep.

In her dreams, Marta heard a voice wailing in the distance. At first she could make out no words, but then it was as though the voice wailed in her very ear:

Who will redeem me from this servitude? Will no one free me from this prison?

She jolted awake. At the same moment, her father sat up with a grunt. "Who called?"

"No one called, John." Her mother's voice was quiet and soothing.

The night was still and silent, the only sound horse's hooves and rumbling wheels.

"It must have been a dream," he said, lying down again.

Sleep did not come for Marta again.

Chapter II.

"As Watchers, our calling is to do justice with mercy, showing peace and humility to all men." John Bessarion paced a few steps into the centre of the Syrian Watchers' Council. "Some of us run hospitals, some adopt foundlings, all of us feed and clothe the poor. I did these things also. And yet, as the emperor's prefect, I was expected to coerce and destroy."

It had been a long day's travel, and Marta's attention was only half on the words being said. She shifted Elisa to her hip and surveyed the uneasy faces around her. In Antioch, the emperor had refused to help them. Now, in Oliveta, the Watchers were looking more and more uncomfortable as her father went on.

"I have sinned," John said. "All of us have sinned in doing these things. In the eyes of God, the heretics have committed no crime, no strife, no sedition. And we have murdered them."

"Presbyter John, what proof do you offer for this imagined crime?" demanded one of the Syrian Watchers.

"The wrath of God. I said that God fought against us in the battle. I will tell you who else fought against us. In the moment of our need, a division of our cavalry went over to the enemy. Monophysite heretics each one, not a man among them who would not gladly strike a blow against the Empire.

"The Watchers are founded on this truth: that each man will reap what he has sown. We sow justice in order to reap justice. We sow mercy in order to reap mercy. We remember that righteousness and justice are the foundations of God's throne, who will judge each of us according to his deeds. But what have we sown? Violence and hatred, and we will reap the same! We must change our ways if we are to save our homeland."

There was only silence in the aftermath of his words. Marta noticed the sweat beading their foreheads. Surely they felt the force of her father's words. Surely they would do what was necessary to save Jerusalem.

One of them, shinier than the others, swallowed and moved forward. "The Presbyter of Palestine has given us much to think about. I suggest that we postpone future discussion until the next Council."

"*Next* Council?" Lukas shoved forward, his fists clenched in frustration. "We came here for help! We're in the middle of an invasion!"

John caught him by the elbow and whispered in his ear.

The Watchers didn't even seem to notice the interruption. "That's an excellent idea," one of them said hurriedly. "If there's no dissent…"

"*I* dissent!" Lukas bared the Watchers' Mark on his arm. "Don't you understand? We don't have the time to delay. By next year's Council we'll probably be *dead.*"

Again, they sweated and squirmed, but refused to answer.

"Nevertheless, this is an issue that shouldn't be decided hastily. I support an adjournment."

"Then it's decided. Let's move to the next item on the agenda…Call the Messenger!"

Unlike her brother, Marta said nothing, but her cheeks flamed with heat. Were these the Watchers she had heard such great things of as a child? Was this all the miracle she could hope for?

Maybe I could do a miracle on my own. As soon as the thought came her cheeks flushed, this time with embarrassment. Who was she, to think of working portents? Few Watchers were granted a gift, and those who did usually had a quieter calling—Counsellors or Comforters.

Next to her, Rahel turned to take Elisa from her arms. The Watchers had called for the Messenger, but the only Messenger here was her mother. As Rahel carried her youngest child into the midst of the Watchers, Marta watched the mortifying realisation creep across the Watchers' faces. They had tried to silence the Presbyter of Palestine, but now they would have to

19

hear from his wife.

"Let me forgo the Message tonight." Rahel put Elisa on the floor in front of her. "The child will speak."

Retreating to the shadows where Marta stood, Lukas grunted with understanding. "Clever," he whispered. "If Elisa gives the Message, there will be no question of meddling."

Dispiritingly, Elisa burst into tears.

The Syrian Presbyter looked dubious. "Are you sure of this, sister?"

"I have the right to appoint my replacement, Presbyter. I appoint Elisa Bessarion."

"Very well." The Syrian Presbyter, president of the council, cleared his throat. "Elisa Bessarion, I name you Messenger for the Council of Watchers. If you have the words, speak."

At first the chubby, dark-haired child remained still, her face buried in her mother's skirts. Some of the Watchers grumbled, but Rahel held up her hand. The room quieted—and in the hush, Elisa spoke.

"Heart of stone!" She still kept her hands knotted into her mother's skirt, but she lifted her head to stare at the Watchers. Elisa's voice was unchildish, relentless. "Even the ancient Jews must release their slaves at the end of seven years, but you have kept yours years upon years with no recompense, no reparation. There are even some that you have maimed in anger."

Marta's scalp prickled. *A miracle.*

"If you will not confess your sins, they will be exposed before all." Elisa pointed a chubby finger at each of the Watchers in turn. *"You* have dealt cruelly with the strangers which God has sent you to welcome and protect. *You* have dealt treacherously with your wife. *You* have made false accusations of heresy for the enrichment of your own coffers."

Faces reddened. The stench of sweat was heavy in the air.

"You have the witness of your own hearts against you. You have had warning after warning and you have refused to heed them. Therefore the guardianship of these provinces is taken from you and given to John Bessarion and his heirs, in whom there is no deceit. The Council of Watchers is disbanded, and the land has vomited you out."

The voice ceased. Silence rang like a bell. After a few moments, an exhausted Elisa began to cry again, and the spell was broken. At once the Council began to shout.

"What's happening, Marta?" Paulus pulled on her hand, his forehead creased with worry. Marta pulled him closer, wishing she could block out the angry voices. No one had taken the war, and their flight from Jerusalem, as hard as Paulus had. Elisa was too small to understand, but Paulus was just old enough to know that his world was falling apart and even his parents and elder siblings were afraid.

"I should take Elisa home," said Rahel.

John nodded. "Lukas, will you...?"

Her brother was only too willing to leave: Marta could read the impatience in every jerky motion as he escorted Rahel from the church. She lifted Paulus into her arms and shook her head when her father looked at her. "I'm staying with you, Abba."

"Marta...you don't have to do that. Go home."

She only smiled at him. Actually, she did have to do it. She had no desire to lift her voice and be heard, no argument that could save her father from the Watchers' wrath. She just wanted to stand next to him, so that he wasn't alone when his brothers tore him to shreds. He was the one who had taught her to stand on the truth, no matter what. She put her shoulders back, and together they turned to face the council.

The Presbyter of Syria had gone red in the face. "Bessarion, I never would have dreamed it of you, but I must ask: did you tamper with the Messenger?"

Her father's eyes widened in pure shock. "My daughter is *three years old*. Her mouth cannot even form half the words you just heard from her lips."

"Be reasonable, Presbyter. After hearing what she said, can you really expect us to believe that?"

John blinked. "Why not consider the possibility that she may have spoken the *truth?*" Voices tried to override him, but he was almost shouting now. "As Watchers, we defend our people from the wrath of heaven. If there is no need to repent of our sins, then how is it that our land lies at the point

21

of conquest for the second time in a generation?"

"God's ways are inscrutable," someone said.

"Inscrutable? He has left us with his veritable word!"

"Who are you to interpret them?"

Marta watched them in astonishment. Recalling the looks on their faces while Elisa was speaking, her confusion heated into anger. They *knew* they were wrong. They just didn't want to admit it.

Maybe Lukas was right to leave, after all. Maybe they all should have left.

"My friend." It was the Syrian Presbyter again. "This is not seemly. I think we must ask you to leave."

John's shoulders slumped. The Council hushed, and the echoes that had reverberated through the belly of the small basilica finally had the chance to fall silent before he spoke again.

"Please." He sounded defeated. "I beg you, *please* imagine for a moment that you might be wrong. God is gracious. We can still have the miracle we need—but only if we are willing to change our ways."

"I understand, Presbyter. You have given us much to discuss."

The Syrian Presbyter spoke soothingly, but Marta and her father were barely halfway to the door when the Watchers folded themselves into a tight little knot, hissing agitated words to each other.

"Sedition", said one.

"Schismatics", another whispered.

Outside the basilica, the stifling summer heat had dissipated a little, leaving the night clear and warm. Paulus lifted his sleepy head from Marta's shoulder, leaving a damp patch where their sweat had soaked through her tunic and palla. "Are we going home now?" he asked.

Marta looked at her father inquiringly. All he could say was, "We're going back to the villa."

That seemed to satisfy Paulus. "My arms are getting tired," Marta told him. "Down you hop."

The basilica door opened onto a courtyard with a tessellated pavement. They had barely crossed it when Lukas pelted through the arch and almost ran into them. With one look at his face, Marta knew something was wrong.

"Mother's had a vision," Lukas gasped. "Heretics. A raid!"

Instantly, John wheeled around and rushed back to the church door, rattling the handle. "Heretics! Heretics! Raise the alarm!"

"Marta, what's happening?" Beside her, Paulus looked pale and began to tremble. Marta squeezed his hand, miserable that she could give him no other comfort.

Behind her, John's eyes were wide in disbelief. "They've locked us out."

Lukas' mouth fell open. "But we're *Watchers*. We have the Mark!"

Their father came back to them, reaching out with a trembling hand. "Take Paulus and run for the hills. Find your mother, go to Antioch and get a ship for Constantinople. *Don't return.*"

"What about you?" Lukas objected.

"Don't wait for me."

"Abba, no," Marta whispered.

Lukas was bristling. "First we ran away from Jerusalem. Now we're running away from Syria?" He clenched his fists. "I'm staying with you. I want to fight."

Marta's stomach turned over. "Shh. Listen."

They all heard it then: the sound of hoof beats, rolling towards them.

"Lukas, I'm not staying to fight!" John put both hands to his head. "I'm staying to give you a chance! Take your siblings and go!"

Marta reached for his arm. "No. Not unless you come with us."

"Where's Mama? Is Elisa all right?" Paulus' voice trembled.

"Don't be scared, chicken." Her own voice wasn't too steady, either.

Their father put one hand on her shoulder and one on Lukas'. "I know who this is, I know why he's here. I know he won't stop until he finds me."

At that instant, something beyond them seemed to catch his eye. John stiffened, looking towards the courtyard arch. Marta turned, pulling Paulus closer.

A man in a black cloak stood under the courtyard arch, watching them silently. How long had he been there? Marta's scalp prickled, and under folds of her palla her hand stole to her knife.

"Abba?" she whispered.

Beyond, in the town, doors slammed and people shouted. Inside the courtyard, the man in the cloak spoke in accented Greek. "I am not here to fight, John Bessarion. You know why I am here."

"I know." Her father moved forward, putting himself between the newcomer and his children.

A sword glimmered in the starlight. "If you are wise, you will surrender the weapon without resistance."

The weapon. Marta knew instantly which weapon he meant, and a flicker of excitement ran through her. The spear with the rippling blade. What other weapon was there? She hadn't seen it since Antioch, though: she assumed her father had sent it to Constantinople with the other relics.

Lukas moved, sliding a hand to his belt where his own knife hung. He caught her eye and she knew he meant to try to rush the man in the archway. Did he want her help? Marta didn't have the same training that her brother did, but she had grown up with him, and the two of them had been on many rough-and-tumble adventures.

Miracles don't happen unless you give them a chance. Marta tightened her hand on her own knife and gave him a tiny nod.

"Lukas," their father snapped. "Don't be a fool."

It was already too late: more shadows flowed into the courtyard. Lukas pressed his lips together briefly, then let go of his knife. The stranger's men silently surrounded them, levelling their spears at the Bessarions. Their eyes were watchful, but it was Lukas they watched, not Marta.

Quietly, Marta eased her own knife out of its sheath, thankful for the palla that disguised her movements. With everyone's attention on the men, she felt strangely as though she didn't exist. As though she could take Paulus' hand and walk out of the courtyard, and no one would even see them.

"The weapon. Where are you hiding it?" The man in the black cloak turned back to her father, his voice dangerously calm.

"Knowing I held such a thing, do you think I would willingly put it in the hands of my enemies?"

The man's voice was soft, but outside, in the streets, came the sound of screams and prayers. Paulus buried his face in her skirts, his body wracked with shivers. Marta put a hand on his head, wishing she could block out the sound.

"You have not destroyed it," the heretic leader said.

"Perhaps I might," said John. "Perhaps it is too dangerous a thing to exist."

"You will not. You need it too much."

"But you do not," John countered. "The armies of your heresiarchs have conquered Arabia and most of Syria. The armies of the orthodox flee before you. So what brings Khalil ibn Hassan through miles of enemy territory, with only a handful of men to retrieve it? Answer me that. Then, perhaps, I will know how to answer."

The heretic gave a hard smile. "He who has the strongest weapon holds power over men. Such a weapon belongs in the hands of the believing. But you spin out the time to no purpose, John Bessarion. Lead me to it."

John did not answer. He only smiled back at the heretic. Sweat glistened on both men's faces as they locked eyes. There was no outward sign of battle, but the hairs on Marta's neck prickled. She set her jaw and prayed, calling upon unseen armies.

The smell of blood hung in the air.

Khalil's mouth tightened. "Kill his children," he breathed.

The spear points edged closer around them. Her father's resistance snapped. "Touch them and I promise you'll never find the weapon!"

The spear points halted. Oliveta was wide awake now, shouts and screams echoing in the night air. There was a scuffle at the door of the basilica as the Watchers, hearing the commotion, tried to get out. More raiders swarmed to the door, barricading the Watchers inside.

A messenger whispered in Khalil's ear and he straightened, folding his arms with something like finality. "The town has been searched. There is no sign of the weapon. Tell me where to find it, and I'll spare your children."

"Don't tell him, Abba," Lukas hissed. "Whatever it is, that weapon should belong to *us*."

25

"How can I trust you to keep your word?" John asked their captor.

"You can trust me to kill them if you refuse."

Again, Marta felt that unseen battle. Again, it was her father who conceded defeat.

"It isn't in Oliveta. I left it in the heart of Antioch. Look for it in the great basilica, if you dare!"

At those words, Khalil's mask of urbanity shattered and he lunged forward, spitting curses. Paulus' arms tightened around Marta's waist, pinning her shawl and her knife-hand to her body. For a sickening heartbeat she could do nothing but stand, frozen, and watch as Khalil attacked her father, still snarling with rage.

Weaponless, there was nothing John could do except fold to the ground, shielding his belly and head as best he could from the heretic's maddened attack.

Even Lukas was crying now, but Marta felt only a remote and frozen anger. As though from a distance, she heard the church bells ringing the alarm. The sound seemed to bring Khalil back to his senses and he staggered back, breathing hard.

Marta loosened Paulus' grip, freeing her knife-hand.

Her father got to his elbows, his voice barely more than a gasp. "Rage all you like. It will not open Antioch's gates to you."

"No." The heretic breathed deeply. "But I have prepared for this hour. Have you?"

Marta tensed as the archway darkened with bodies. The people of Oliveta stumbled fearfully into the courtyard, prodded on by the raiders' spears. More heretics broke open the door of the basilica and dragged the Watchers out. Torches flared, shedding a bloody light over the courtyard as more and more frightened, crying people were herded in.

For the first time, the light revealed the heresiarch's face. Marta was surprised to see how ordinary he looked—younger than her father, with a well-kept beard and the feline grace of a warrior.

"Rage may not get me into Antioch, but power will." His gaze swept across the shivering people. "Those who inhabit the waste places, the silences of the desert, know that there is power to be found in destruction. But the ritual requires blood and perversity. I do not know if there is enough in this whole town."

Marta's gut clenched. He was going to kill them all.

Please, God, let this be her miracle.

Marta slid a foot forward, flicking her arm straight with a smooth, controlled motion. The knife left her hand, travelling in a flash of blood-red light.

Khalil twisted aside and the blade cut through empty air before clattering harmlessly on the tessellated pavement.

In the same instant one of the guards struck the back of her knee with the butt of his spear. Marta collapsed with a gasp of pain. The heresiarch picked her knife off the stones and stared at it in amazement.

For the first time since he had entered the courtyard, Khalil looked at her—looked at her with a terrifying fascination, as though she was a singing stone or a talking animal. Marta recoiled.

Then, as one of his men handed him a brush and pot of white paint, his attention slid away from her again.

The tessellated pavement beneath their feet radiated out in colourful geometric patterns of tile and glass from a central medallion. Using the paint, Khalil began to trace a sigil upon the ground, a four-edged pattern with a point towards each cardinal direction. Within it he drew ancient symbols and words in an incomprehensible flowing script.

Marta shivered as a crackling roar sounded from beyond the courtyard and light flooded the sky. *The town—they're burning the town.*

"Lukas," she hissed, "where are Mother and Elisa?"

He wasn't listening to her: in the red glare, his eyes were wild with fear.

Marta dropped to her knees to look Paulus in the eye. "Listen," she whispered. "There's nothing they can do that will hurt us, you know that? You can't see them, but there are angels around us right now." She gave his shoulders a little shake. "Look at me. They're going to take care of us, all right? It might be a little frightening for a minute, but you just remember the angels."

27

His little face was screwed up with fright, but he dragged in a brave sniff and said, "Like Saint Daniel in the lions' den?"

"Or the three children in the burning fiery furnace."

He nodded uncertainly. Then the raiders tore him from her arms.

Khalil had finished his pattern and his men wrestled each of the Bessarions to each of its four points. Marta, at the south, faced Paulus, at the north. Lukas was on her left and John on her right.

The sorcerer moved into the centre of the sigil, cutting off her view of Paulus.

Their hands and ankles were bound, immobilising them. Khalil bent over each of them in turn, marking them on the forehead with a finger dipped in paint, speaking in that quiet, calm voice.

"There are many djinn in the deserts and the mountains, from the hairy jackals that inhabit lost cities, to the Pestilence by Day and the Destruction by Night. For a sacrifice, they will give me the power to destroy Antioch…"

He raised his voice.

"Kill them all."

The world erupted in blood and fire, in screams and the sorcerer's steady chant. True to his word, Khalil had summoned something: and…*something*…had answered.

She had told Paulus that they were surrounded by angels, and as the slaughter unfolded, she saw coming down like a whirlwind creatures of shadow and steel, the hard feathers of their wings chattering in the hellish air. Marta felt her blood freeze in her veins. Angels, certainly, but not the kind she had hoped for.

It was the fallen.

They surrounded Khalil, but only one of them was able to touch him: a monster, a harpy, with red lips and wings of black steel. Just as the creature settled on the sorcerer's arm, *something* happened. The creatures of air and darkness screamed in glee. Lukas shouted for Paulus and Khalil's chant changed to a scream. And then—

Nothing.

And then—

CHAPTER II.

And then she woke in a gulley on a hillside.

Chapter III.

Marta erupted out of lush greenery with a yelp of alarm and sat chest-deep in yellow spring flowers, looking around her in bewilderment. Olive trees arched above her. Near the crest of the hill was a small fortress built of honey-coloured stone, a banner fluttering from its towers.

"Abba?" she called.

No answer.

"Paulus? Lukas?"

Marta got to her feet. There was no sign of her family. She staggered downhill, leaving a trampled path through the spring growth. A little further on, the trees thinned, allowing her to see green plains stretching towards distant blue hills and nearby at the foot of the slope on which she stood, a fair-sized village.

The sky was grey, the air humid, and each blade of grass and wildflower glowed with intense colour. Marta swallowed; it sounded like a sob.

Last night it had been the end of summer in the mountains above Antioch. Today it was spring, and she might wager she was home again somewhere in the coastal plains of Palestine. Those ahead of her could be the Galilee hills.

Maybe she was dead. She had always thought heaven would be rather like home.

Marta had never really feared death, but now quiet dread crawled up her throat. If this was heaven, *where was everyone else?* Her parents, siblings, the

30

people of Oliveta? She closed her eyes and saw fire and blood painted in the dark behind her eyelids. At the time she had watched it all as though from a great distance, but now, on this quiet flower-laden hillside it crashed down on her like a wave. She lifted shaking hands to her face and felt tears between her fingers. That steadied her. If she could feel this way, she couldn't be in heaven. Marta took a deep breath and pushed the horror away, promising that she would let herself feel it later. First she must find out where she was.

She was still gaining control of her thoughts when a figure came riding down from the fortress. Marta's first instinct was to duck back into the shadows under the olive trees, but it proved to be a man riding an ass. His vestments looked strange and he was unusually pale, like a foreigner from the north, but his tonsure and the crucifix around his neck convinced her that he must be some sort of priest. Emboldened, Marta pushed through the grass onto the road.

"Father," she called timidly, then stopped. *What day is it? Where am I?* If she asked the questions on her tongue, she'd sound like a fool. Instead, she tried to sound casual: "What village is this, again?"

The foreign priest reined in and looked her up and down. Marta swallowed, wishing she'd stopped to rake her fingers through her hair or rearrange her palla. She must look like a vagabond.

The priest spoke, but she didn't understand a single word.

"I beg your pardon," she faltered. "Don't you speak Syriac? What about Greek?"

Neither raised a flicker of understanding in the priest's eyes. He said something in a different language to the one he had initially used, but again, Marta couldn't understand. Her face reddened. "Never mind. I'll find someone local to ask."

Although the priest seemed to accept that they couldn't speak, he beckoned to her to follow him towards the village and would not move on until she reluctantly fell into step beside him. At the foot of the hill, the village seemed small but prosperous, built in a solid ring around a central marketplace: Marta spotted a bath-house, an oil press, a small basilica and an inn. Next to the inn was a long, low stone building that was full of rhythmic clacking.

The priest got off his donkey and waved her after him into a dim antechamber where a tough-looking old matron sat making marks in a ledger. With her darker skin and oval features, the woman looked as though she might be one of Marta's own people.

"Do you understand me?" she tried in Syriac, then Greek.

The hard old woman merely shrugged, and said something to the priest in his own language.

To Marta's horror, tears pooled in her eyes. She had come home, and she was a stranger. Was she going mad? What *was* this place? What had happened to her family? Were they lying dead in Oliveta?

Her stomach chose that moment to complain loudly. Marta pressed her hands against her belly. When they looked at her, she whispered, "I'm sorry. I'm *so hungry.*"

The old woman looked at her with flinty eyes, then bent under the bench that crossed the room, and thrust a small hunk of coarse bread at her. Marta took it reluctantly, and glanced at the door, but the priest stood blocking the doorway. Well, maybe, if she stayed, they would find someone who could speak to her. She took a mouthful of bread and chewed it slowly, listening to the old woman and the priest as they talked. Finally the man went away and the old woman beckoned her towards a curtained door leading into another room.

The curtain was lovely—a bolt of slubby silk with the warp and weft dyed in green and mulberry, so that together they made a colour you could not be quite sure of understanding. Beyond, the long stone building was dim and warm, lit by a few barred windows high along each wall. About twenty women sat there, weaving. Marta watched them in fascination. The looms she was accustomed to stood upright, requiring slow, careful work threading the warp and then tamping the new threads into place. These looms were placed horizontally. Treadles at each woman's foot lifted or depressed the required threads, making it possible to throw the bobbin quickly back and forth. A single straight bar tamped down the newly-woven thread with smart, rhythmic clacks.

The women did not stop weaving, nor did they look up as Marta followed the old woman into the room. They stopped at a loom where a black girl sat weaving a plain bolt of fabric. The old woman spoke, and the Nubian got up and moved to a different loom without sparing a glance for Marta. She sat down at the silent loom and quickly went on weaving.

The old woman motioned to her to sit down at the loom. Marta understood. She must do some work for the bread she had eaten. "If I do this, will you give me somewhere to sleep tonight?" she asked, but the woman had already walked away.

The horizontal loom was easy to use, and Marta had always had a knack with cloth. That first afternoon, she wove with a will, anxious to repay whatever she owed, letting the rhythm of the loom ease away her fear. What had happened to her was not a catastrophe; it was a miracle. She had survived. She must have faith that her family had survived—or if they had not, that they had gone on to something better.

She believed in miracles, and this was her own. But oh, she hoped she wouldn't be alone for long. As soon as she'd earned her bread, she would go in search of her family. That night Marta slept alongside the other women in their cramped bunkhouse behind the workshop.

The next morning, she discovered that she was not allowed to leave.

The workshop had two exits. One door led to the bunkhouse, a tiny room with thick walls. Its only openings were the narrow barred windows high up near the ceiling, and at the back of the room, an opening into a latrine. *That* was too small to let her through, even if she could have stomached the thought of diving into the fetid darkness.

The only real door out of the workshop was the thick, heavy door which the old woman guarded on the other side of the silk curtain. It always remained locked, except when the old woman came in to deliver new thread or to take away the finished bolts of cloth. Food was delivered through a hatch.

When Marta hammered on the door to be let out, no one answered. She turned to the other women as they began their day's work, and caught a look of pity in their eyes as they lowered their heads. The sight struck renewed fear into her heart and she beat on the door again. "Ho! Let me out!"

No answer.

The old woman must be ignoring her. Desperate, Marta turned to the other women in the room. She knew she didn't speak their language, but still she rushed to the nearest loom and pushed up her sleeve, revealing her Watcher's Mark. "Please. I'm a Watcher," she pleaded. "Can you—can *anyone* help me?"

The tired, unkempt woman stared at the Mark for a long, long moment. The pity left her face and her lips ironed shut.

Marta turned to the next weaver. "Please?"

Open hostility flared in this woman's eyes. Suddenly, she spat. Saliva hit Marta's tunic and slid down it. The weaver turned briskly to her loom and pumped the treadles, ignoring her. Around the dim room, the other women followed suit.

Marta fought tears as the looms clacked into motion. *I'm here,* she thought. *I'm alive. There will be a way out. Miracles aren't mistakes.*

Behind her, the food hatch slammed open. Through the opening, the old woman yelled at her, motioning towards the loom. Marta rushed to the hatch. "Please, you have to listen—"

But the hatch slammed shut before she reached it. Behind, the looms clacked without ceasing.

Marta refused to despair. Instead, she backed away from the hatch and sat at her loom. Around her, the weavers slid hostile sidelong glances at her. Marta took a deep breath, composed herself, and picked up her bobbin.

The looms stopped only to let the women pray. Five times a day, at dawn, noon, mid-afternoon, sunset, and night, they washed using sparing amounts of water and knelt on the floor, facing south. Not to be outdone in piety, Marta followed suit, pressing her forehead against the dusty stone floor and praying for the safety of her family.

Let them be safe. Let some miracle have spared them, too.

Lord God, please don't let Paulus be alone and frightened, like...like I am.

That noon, the women flocked together, whispering and exchanging suspicious looks. Nobody smiled at Marta anymore, or even looked at her. That night, when the food came through the hatch, the old woman distributed nothing for Marta, and none of the other weavers would share.

The second day of Marta's stay was a Sunday. She could hear the bells ringing at the basilica across the square, and the voices of the villagers as they attended Mass, but none of the weavers could leave.

By the fifth day, Marta was ready to scream from sheer loneliness. Each time the old woman opened the door to the shop, a burly, unpleasant-looking man stood in the doorway with his arms folded, watching them. There was no way out.

I am a slave, Marta realised.

The thread on her loom blurred as tears came to her eyes. For a moment, she stopped weaving, sniffling softly. It made an awful kind of sense. She had come here destitute, penniless, plainly-dressed, and speaking a language none of them knew. A stranger. A vagrant. And they had put her to work.

Hearing the loom fall silent, the old woman shouted something through the hatch. Marta blinked the water from her eyes and looked at the cloth she was weaving, a dull, featureless blue the colour of the midnight sky.

She sniffed at it with loathing. Horrible, cheap, blank colour! At home in Jerusalem, she'd woven tapestries as bright and glorious as a mosaic.

Someone brushed past her—the Nubian, carrying a basket of coloured threads which the old woman had just handed through the hatch. One of them glittered with gold and Marta instantly knew what form her rebellion would take. She moved so quickly the other girl didn't see her, whisking the thread-of-gold bobbin out of the basket and dropping it hastily into her lap, between her knees.

Her fingers shook as she thumped her loom back into action. Blue cloth. Gold thread. There was a pattern in her mind already.

The Nubian girl began setting her loom for a new piece of fabric, squinting at a colourful pattern marked on a piece of papyrus. It was a tedious job, taking hours, and as the sun went down it became slower. By the time of the evening meal, the girl had still not noticed the gold thread's absence.

That night, Marta got up quietly and wound the gold thread onto spare shuttles. She didn't need a pattern: she already had it in her mind. The next morning, she began to weave.

The gold thread ramped across the dull blue wool in a delicate tracery of starbursts and spirals that glinted in the dim morning light. Marta moved with new purpose, weaving faster and faster as she built new memories in her fingers. At the other end of the workshop the Nubian girl continued to thread her loom and Marta, watching her, wove even faster. The gold thread's absence would be noticed sooner or later, and Marta wanted to finish her own cloth before that happened.

She had woven a length of spangled cloth almost the height of a grown man before the girl noticed that anything was missing.

At the hatch, Marta heard her soft voice speaking to the old woman, apologetic. The old woman became shrill. After a moment, she burst into the workshop, scolding. Marta braced herself for discovery, but the old woman didn't waste a glance on the weavers or their cloth. Instead she searched beneath the looms, then slapped the girl's face and vanished into the bunkhouse, where she could be heard throwing their bedding about and muttering under her breath.

The Nubian stood where the old woman had struck her, beside Marta's loom. Like the other weavers, Marta had learned to keep her head down and her feet pumping the treadles whenever anyone from outside came into the workshop. But the Nubian was standing right next to her loom; and she had gone very still.

Marta stole an upward glance.

The girl looked from her spangled cloth to her face and Marta froze, her loom stuttering to a halt. Understanding lit the girl's dark eyes. Abruptly, she turned and went back to her own loom.

Marta began to weave again. When the old woman returned to the workshop, the other girl was finishing the sett of her loom. The old woman scolded her a little longer, then finally retreated through the door to the front shop. For a while after, they heard her searching outside under the windows. Evidently, the old woman believed the thread had been stolen; it did not occur to her that it might be *used*.

That evening they were kept working until the failing light made it difficult to continue. Then they collected their daily ration of bread and boiled salt mutton from the hatch. As usual, the other women sat in the workshop, chattering in their strange language, but Marta followed the Nubian girl into the tiny bunkhouse.

As she expected, the girl had nothing to eat at all. Because of what Marta had done.

Silently, Marta held out her own food.

The Nubian gave her a long, suspicious look and then accepted it. But as Marta turned to leave, the girl said something, ripping the food in half and offering a portion of it back to her.

Marta lifted her hands and backed away.

Stubbornly, the Nubian put the spare food on her blanket and began eating the half she had reserved for herself. As she lifted the half-ration of meat to her lips, the girl's loose sleeve fell back, and Marta's heart jumped. She could not speak, so she reached out gently, pulled the girl's arm towards her, and turned it over, running a finger over the pattern of raised scars she found there.

A double cross. A Watcher's Mark unlike any she'd ever seen.

Marta looked up into defiant eyes and let go, backing away. "Don't be afraid!" she said quickly. "I'm a Watcher too. Look!"

She shoved her own sleeve up to the elbow. Even in the darkness of the bunkhouse the black tattooed mark was stark against her pale skin: an *I* and *X* superimposed on each other, the symbol used by the Watchers of Syria and Palestine. For the second time that day, Marta found that her eyes were wet. "We're sisters," she said, in a strangled voice. She pointed to herself. "Marta."

"Marta." The girl looked dazed, and pointed to herself. "Persi."

Chapter IV.

After three days of shared food, the gold thread ran out. Marta dared to sit still for a minute or two after she had finished, watching the afternoon sunlight play across the sparks and whorls she had woven.

By now she had discovered something else about Persi: like Marta, she loved colour and pattern. Together, in the spring twilight, they sat together making coloured patterns from tiny offcuts of thread, and stumbling towards each other in the new language Marta was beginning to learn. She had discovered very little about her new friend. Persi was, perhaps, the most skilled weaver in the workshop, entrusted with any particularly complex cloth. She was quiet, keeping all her feelings locked deep down inside where they could not show on her face. But sometimes, Marta caught her staring at the open sky beyond the barred windows.

She wondered how long it had been since Persi felt the sun on her skin, or the wind on her face. She wondered how long it would be until she felt those things again, either.

She might not have her family, but at least she had a Watcher. Though she was barred from the starry sky, inside the workshop, she had made her own. Carefully, Marta snipped the finished fabric from the frame of her loom. She dared not carry it past Persi for one last look. Instead, she folded it neatly, took it to the hatch and pushed it through.

Marta held her breath.

The old woman boiled through the door, a guard at her back, and shook the fabric at Marta with her voice see-sawing into high registers of indignation. Marta could guess what she was saying: good thread-of-gold wasted on a piece of cheap worsted. Who would buy it? Who would wear it? Marta had wasted both the gold *and* the wool.

She stood silent, looking at the floor until the woman had finished and slammed back through into the front shop. The guard thrust a basket of thread towards Marta: more cheap worsted, this time mulberry-coloured and just as uninspiring as the blue.

Marta sighed, carried the basket to the loom, and began to thread it, wondering how long it would be till she *or* Persi would get more food.

Marta found herself blinking back tears again. She still had so many questions. What had happened to her family? How did she come to wake up in this strange place, surrounded by people who didn't speak her language?

Worst of all was how *powerless* she was. She was trapped here in a tiny, airless, sunless prison. There was no way out. There was no way home. In her place, Saint Sampson had thrown down the temple he was chained within. Marta stared at the door, tempted to try something similar. If she had a gifting, if she was a Portentor…

Excited chatter broke through her thoughts. The looms fell silent as the weavers jumped to their feet. Marta blinked, assuming it was time for the afternoon prayers. Yet instead of flocking to the water-pots to wash, the women crowded to the small high windows in the workshop's long eastern wall.

For once, the old woman didn't yell at them.

Marta lifted a questioning eyebrow at Persi. The taller girl grinned and made a stirrup from her hands, boosting Marta to a height where she could see out the window more easily.

Outside, the afternoon sunlight streamed through the village square. It was market-day, and the space was crowded with carts, booths, and livestock. At the inn next door, a party of travellers had just dismounted, and were talking to each other in big, carefree voices or calling for cups of wine. Marta's mouth opened in amazement at the sight of bright banners, burnished armour, and colourful tunics. They were evidently warrior-nobles, but to Marta's eyes they seemed as outlandish as a flock of exotic birds: tall, handsome people, their clothing a riot of different colours and styles. One man wore a Syrian-looking turban and robe; another the closer-fitting tunic and trousers of the far north, but woven in brightly-coloured silk rather than dun wool and fur.

Some of the riders were women, and as Marta watched, two of them strolled below the bars of her window and entered the front shop. Their voices hummed pleasantly through the hatch. They were shopping.

Unlike Marta's mother, who wore flowing tunics and shawls with hair pinned up, these women wore their hair in knee-length plaits woven with ribbon, and their dresses were laced tightly to their bodies, pulling fine silk or linen in tiny folds around their waists. Marta stepped down from Persi's hand, wishing she could tell her friend what she'd seen.

Beyond the door, the old woman was busy with the rich guests, leaving the weavers free to gossip about the travellers. It was like an instant holiday. Persi, who was tall enough to see through the windows on tiptoe, winked at Marta and put her nose in the air in an imitation of the noble shoppers.

For the first time since she had arrived in this strange place, Marta laughed.

As the workshop door suddenly opened, the weavers stilled and every head swivelled fearfully to see what would happen next. The old woman paused in the doorway and pointed. Her guard shouldered past her, striding purposefully towards the women clustered by the windows.

Towards *her*.

Marta gasped, backing away, but the guard's hand closed painfully tight on her upper arm and dragged her forward through the door and into the front room.

The door slammed behind her, and Marta looked up into the eyes of the two rich women standing at the counter.

Unfurled in front of them was the blue-and-gold cloth.

The younger and plumper of the two women was evidently very noble, her dress dyed a vivid and expensive royal purple, a diamond set in gold hanging from a string of pearls at her neck. She fingered Marta's fabric and asked a question in the language Persi was trying to teach her. One of the few words Marta caught was "cloth". *Did you weave this?*

"Yes," Marta hazarded in the same language.

The plump woman in purple traced a spiral with her forefinger, and said something in an undertone to her attendant. Both of them looked impressed, and Marta stood a little taller. The shape she had used was one her father had taught her to draw when she was still very small, the Golden Spiral. Any learned person would know it at once.

The lady asked another question, but this time Marta could only shrug, not recognising any words. At that, the old woman began to chatter away again, bobbing up and down in polite bows. The noble lady shook her head, arguing with her as though they were haggling over something. The cloth? The old woman charged out from behind her counter, grabbed Marta's right hand and shoved the sleeve up, pinching the flesh hard.

Oh. They were haggling over *her*.

Marta felt almost dizzy.

Two paces to her right, the shop door stood open onto the sunny square; a curtain shifted lazily in the cool breeze that came through the opening. She could *smell* the fresh air. Marta licked her lips, her blood humming with the urge to run. The guard had let go of her, but she still sensed him standing behind her, just within arm's reach. She couldn't risk a glance behind to see whether he was watching her or the noblewomen.

Marta drew a long silent breath and darted for the doorway.

Behind, the guard shouted in surprise. He shot out his hand to grab her—and missed. Marta swung through the door and instantly collided with another man—a man so tall that her eyes were only on a level with the jewelled gold chain decorating his chest.

"Oof," he said from somewhere above her head, as he dropped the spear in his right hand.

Marta rebounded from the man's mail-clad body, lost her balance and sprawled in the dust. The man staggered backward, his feet scuffing up a little cloud of dust—and settling in the dirt in front of her eyes was *the spear*.

She would never mistake that black, rippling blade; that dark, oiled shaft. It was her father's spear, the weapon for which Khalil had destroyed

Oliveta, and each detail was stamped in her mind like her own mother's face.

Her hand fastened around the shaft, and it was as though the weapon knew her, too. With the heft of it in her palm came a surge of strength, confidence, daring. In a heartbeat Marta was on her feet, the spear levelled at the man she'd charged into.

Not Khalil. This man was too old, too clean-shaven, much too tall.

The old woman's guard burst out of the shop, shouting. Marta swung the point to face him and he threw up his hands, skidding to a stop.

The nobleman grabbed for the spear with an insistent command, but Marta smacked his knuckles with it, eliciting a shout of pain. She backed away for a few steps, then whirled and raced away from workshop and inn and all. Behind, her hunters gave cry. Then came the sound she dreaded: hooves pounding into motion.

Marta took stock of the situation as she wove among carts and booths, veiled women and pungent shepherds. The village was a solid ring of stone houses, butting up against each other for easy defence. A single road bisected the village, providing only two narrow gaps between the houses at opposite sides of the square. One of those gaps was behind her, beyond the inn—and the armoured men searching for her. The other was on the far side of the village, scarcely visible through the crowd.

The place was a trap, and as the disturbance spread, someone ahead was sure to catch her. Just then, her eye caught a gate to the left. Marta vaulted it and leapfrogged from the cobblestones of a little courtyard to the bed of a cart, and then onto the tiles of a low pitched roof. She paused, breathing hard, to glance back. The armed men below waved their arms and shouted at her to come back in words she didn't understand.

Oh, no she wouldn't. She'd trusted the priest and the old woman, and look where that had got her. Blood hammered through her body. She *had* to escape. She had to find out what had happened to her family.

Ahead, the shed butted up against the side of a house, a single low storey with a flat roof. She rolled over the parapet and raced across it.

Outside the village to her left was a thick citrus orchard, and beyond that, rolling farmland. If she could only get into the shadows of those trees! But before she could find a way off the roof, the sound of hoofbeats returned. A single rider came galloping along the outside of the ring of houses, reining in when he saw her.

There was a strange contraption in his hand—some kind of short cross-mounted bow with a glinting bolt protruding from its stock. Recognising it instantly as a weapon, Marta recoiled from the parapet and raced down the length of the roof. The houses were all uneven heights, but their roofs were flat and it wasn't hard to hop from one to another. Still, hoofbeats echoed on the hard-packed earth beneath her. The horseman on her left raced ahead and turned, levelling his crossbow contraption straight at her.

She ignored his commanding voice and veered to her right again, bending almost double to present a smaller target. Back in view of the market, she scanned the crowd, then swung over the parapet and dropped between two stalls, almost putting her foot through a hen-coop.

She weaved through the crowded square, thanking her patron saint that so many people had come from miles around to attend the market. She took a breath and tried to look casual – as casual as a very dirty girl holding a spear could look.

Across the square, someone shouted and Marta whirled to meet the eyes of the tall nobleman. He and his followers were on horseback now, urging their way through the crowd. Moments ago, outside the inn, they had seemed indolent and carefree. Now they moved purposefully, unhurried as they converged on her.

One by one, the villagers turned to stare.

If these men thought she'd sit down and wait for them to catch her, they were wrong. The gap in the ring of houses was closer now, promising open country and, if God was kind, freedom. Marta ducked between two stalls and charged towards it—

Someone grabbed her wrist.

Marta swung around, dragging against him. The man gasped something at her, but he looked determined. Marta swept her sleeve back, revealing her Watcher's Mark.

"Please," she gasped. The man's eyes widened, but he didn't hesitate. A stall beside them sold clothes. He said something to the stall keeper, snagged a veil of black gauze from the table, and threw it over Marta's head. She was still battling the unexpected folds when he snatched the spear from her hand. Marta uttered a squeak of protest, but he only reversed it, point downward, and handed it directly back to her—now disguised as a simple staff.

As Marta's pursuers wove through the crowd trying to pick up her scent again, she and her rescuer turned and walked slowly in the opposite direction. To her relief, he didn't try to speak to her, but for the first time in days, Marta felt hope.

She didn't know where she was, she didn't know what had become of her family, but it still meant something, being a Watcher. There were still people who would help her.

The square wasn't a large one, and the soldiers spread out, scanning the crowd from atop their enormous horses. Despite her veil, Marta couldn't help ducking her head as the tall nobleman rode by just a few paces away.

Her guide led her by a meandering route, stopping finally at a sheep-pen a few steps away from the village gate. He held out a hand, and Marta returned the veil. "Thank you," she said, even though he didn't understand. Behind, none of the soldiers were looking her way. Marta broke into a run, a bright burst of citrus beckoning on the wind.

Freedom.

At the end of the short passage, the horseman appeared.

Marta skidded to a halt, tightening her grip on the spear. He called out and slid from his horse, letting its reins trail on the ground as he walked purposefully towards her. Marta wheeled, looking for a way out, but the horseman's yell had brought more soldiers scrambling through the square towards her. Walls towered on either side of her. The houses at this end of the village were two storeys high and built of stone, with no windows in the lower level to give her a foothold.

She was trapped.

What did they do to runaway slaves here? To thieves? As the soldiers neared, Marta backed against one high wall and sank into a fighter's crouch, her heart slamming against her ribs. She didn't want to find out. It was time to see if the rumours about this spear were true.

If they weren't, she didn't want to be taken alive.

Armour jingled as the horseman reached her. Marta stared: despite his tanned skin, the shape of his face was completely alien to her. His chin and cheekbones were raw and sharp, his hair blond as wheat. Another foreigner, and young, about the same age as her brother Lukas. For some reason, that gave her courage. If she could get past him—why then there was the citrus orchard, and a horse to carry her far away.

She tensed, and he must have guessed the thoughts going through her mind, because he lifted the crossbow and tutted at her.

Marta froze. At close range, the bow looked like a wicked little weapon, and while she might have a magic spear, she had no armour at all. Behind him, the other soldiers were closing in. Marta hissed a breath through her teeth, looking for a way out.

The boy spoke. As Marta's attention snapped back to him, he grinned at her coaxingly and gestured with his spare hand. She could not understand the words, but the rest of it was clear enough: *Be a good girl and put the weapon down.*

"I won't be locked up again," she snapped. Behind her, the tall nobleman and his men blocked the entrance to the village. They seemed to hang back cautiously, as though they thought she might be dangerous.

No doubt they knew all about this spear. That meant there was still a chance for her. Cautiously, Marta slid a foot forward, edging away from the wall.

The young rider motioned to her to put the spear down again, then put a hand on his heart and *winked* at her.

Come on. I'm a handsome fellow, you can trust me, Marta translated mentally.

She tensed, risking another glance at his friends. One of the soldiers had levelled another of those short bows at her back. Her shoulders itched, waiting for the impact. *Strife.* They'd kill her if they had to.

She couldn't trust these men—their lady had been trying to *buy* her.

The boy called out to the soldiers behind, and at a gesture from the tall nobleman the soldier behind her lowered his bow.

The boy in front bent down to lay his crossbow in the dust and then straightened, spreading his empty hands. *See? Nothing to fear.* He reached out, speaking soothingly, as though she were a nervous horse. *Come now. Hand it over.*

He'd given her a chance, and Marta intended to take it. She reversed the butt of the weapon and charged.

The boy was quick. As she lunged, his left hand fell to the hilt of his sword, parrying the spear-thrust as he drew backhanded. Still, the spear's butt struck his left shoulder, spinning him out of her way.

Even as he turned, he threw out his right hand and grabbed the spear just between her knuckles. Marta twisted the weapon from his grasp, but in those precious heartbeats he'd recovered his footing and forced her to face him again.

He passed his sword to his right hand, clearly not wanting to take any more chances.

The tall nobleman called out, his voice worried.

The boy laughed and shook his head, but he didn't take his eyes off Marta. She had the spear point facing him now, but she didn't know how long she would last, especially now that his sword was out. Enchanted spear or not, she wasn't trained to use weapons. All she had to go on was rough-and-tumble memories from her childhood with Lukas.

The boy didn't move, still trying to coax her, although he must have figured out by now that she couldn't understand a word he said. Behind, the nobleman and his soldiers edged closer.

It was just *one* boy! Marta lunged again and the boy jumped back, dodging the spear by inches. His sword flashed in a parry and Marta swung wildly. Spear and blade connected.

The sword shattered.

The laughter wiped off her opponent's face as Marta moved forward again, thrusting with the spear. She only meant to threaten, to drive him back far enough to give her a clear run for freedom. Instead, the blade punched through surcoat and chain mail, grazed against the boy's ribs.

He yelped with pain, a sound that swallowed up her own shriek of horror.

She should be running *now*. Instead she stood motionless, staring at the blood welling around the spear's blade. *Saints! Have I killed him?*

He staggered back, groaning. Too late, Marta recovered her wits. The onlooking soldiers now surrounded her, bows levelled. A dozen bolts and arrows pointed directly at her heart.

Marta swallowed and tilted her chin so that she was looking defiantly into the tall nobleman's eyes. They were hard as flint as he held out his hand and made what she knew was his final demand.

She was shaking all over, but she couldn't let go of the spear. "It's not yours. It belongs to my father!"

Surprise flashed in his eyes and he threw out a hand, barking a command to his men. Then, for the first time in days, she heard a language she knew.

"Your father's name?" He spoke in Greek.

Marta's mouth dropped open.

"Show me your left forearm," he demanded when she did not reply.

Dazed, Marta yanked her sleeve up to show her Watchers' Mark. "John Bessarion," she whispered. "My father is John Bessarion."

The nobleman swore softly, said something to his men in their strange language, then got down from his horse and came slowly towards her. Tentative. Almost reverent.

"You—it's *you*."

He *knew* her?

"You're the one we've been waiting for." She flinched as he reached out, but he closed her hands gently on the spear, his face utterly serious. "This belongs to you."

Chapter V.

The glass casement was open, letting in cool air and dawn birdsong. Sibylla stood silent, listening and watching.

The hillsides surrounding Jerusalem were green, speckled with trees. Slender cypresses formed ramparts on the Mount of Olives, and behind them, a faint blush of pink crept across the sky from the east. Above, a single black bird of prey circled lazily in the clear morning air.

Below her window the palace garden was empty, but beyond its wall, the city was just beginning to stir. In the Holy Sepulchre, Lauds would just be ending and the smell of meat and spices was already rising from the Street of Bad Cooking, awaiting the day's visitors. It was eighty-one years now since Sibylla's Frankish forefathers had settled in Jerusalem to guard the holy places and the thousands of pilgrims who came to visit them. With each year of peace, their numbers had increased, and now, close to Easter, the city was bursting with travellers from all over the world.

Soon the light would be strong enough that a man climbing out of her window would not go unnoticed, yet Sibylla could not bring herself to wake him. She relished this early morning silence almost more than when he was awake. Sibylla padded silently to the foot of her bed and knotted her slender fingers around one of the bedposts, looking down on him.

Guy was a small mountain of muscle and hair and odd, masculine smells: leather, horses, oil. His clothing, belts, weapons and lute were strewn carelessly across her floor wherever they had landed last night. Now he was snoring contentedly in her bed and taking up most of it.

The last time she'd had a man in her bed, it was so different. It wasn't that Longsword had been a cruel husband. He just…wasn't interested in anything she had to say. It was his disregard, more than anything else, that hurt. She was a king's daughter, trained for diplomacy and command. She had been younger then and thinner-skinned, fresh from the convent and so sure that God was just. Resistance or tyranny, that she would have known how to deal with. But crushing indifference? She'd had no defence against that. Saints, if he had only *laughed* with her—

But Longsword was dead, struck down within weeks of their marriage by an illness his western constitution couldn't handle, and all that was left of him was his son, sleeping in the next room. Should she have made a pretence of grief? The holy saints knew she'd felt none. When it happened, she had only been relieved that the stranger who owned her was gone.

When Guy had climbed her window last night, he'd fallen on the floor in front of her—the whole big, burly, six foot of him that could have crushed her like a sparrow—and he'd kissed the hem of her gown. Here, in secret, he had sworn undying fealty. To her! Not to her brother, the king. Not to a lord who could make him rich and powerful, but to her, because he loved her.

"Can you even *do* this?" she had asked, fascinated, as he had waited for her to clasp his hands. "I thought you still had a liege lord in the west."

"We won't ask him," Guy had said. He was on his knees, his hands lifted as though in prayer, and she knew she was his saint, his goddess. "You are more to me than he ever will be."

She knew he meant it. She knew that no matter what might happen next, Guy of Lusignan was her man, body and soul. He would obey her. He would serve her. If necessary he would even fight for her, and Sibylla found the thought intoxicating. His love was more than comfort and enchantment, though it was certainly that. It was power, and for the first time since her marriage, Sibylla felt like a force to be reckoned with.

In the bed before her, the snoring stopped and Guy reached out blindly. When he found that she wasn't beside him, he woke with a grunt, making the whole bed creak as he snapped upright.

Sibylla straightened, recalled to the present—and to her plans for the future.

"Be quiet." She spoke with concentrated intensity. "Remember, my women are sleeping just beyond that door. We have little time; the sun is rising, and Ramla is coming south to marry me."

Guy yawned, his voice fuzzy. "What? Marry you? Who?"

"Baldwin of Ibelin, the lord of Ramla," she repeated patiently.

"Ramla?" He scratched his head. "But what about that other fellow? That…French duke?"

"Duke Hugh of Burgundy is my brother's choice, and he has consented. But with the trouble in France, there's no chance he will be able to travel east this year, if at all. So Ramla rides to Jerusalem to demand a royal marriage. My father's cousins Tripoli and Antioch are with him. So is his brother and the queen-dowager. They will be too powerful for my brother to refuse, but even if he did, I could not choose according to my desire. He would never let me marry *you*."

"*Marry* you?" Guy repeated again, but this time she had shocked him into wakefulness. "Me? You're a princess of the blood, my lady. Who am I?"

"You are the only man who has ever vowed to serve me. Did you mean it or not?"

In answer he surged out of the bed and fell at her feet again. "To the last drop of blood."

"But you wouldn't marry me. Not even if my brother gave his consent?"

Guy shook his head, searching for words. "What we have…this secret…this is true love. If I married you, it would just be another grimy little political transaction. I would have to swear fealty to your brother."

"You swore fealty to me."

"That was love-fealty, not liege-fealty." He shook his head, his eyes shadowed. "I left all that behind when King Henry banished me from France."

"Then what *can* I give you?" Sibylla ran her fingers through his dark hair. "Tell me."

"You can love me for myself," he whispered. "I've never been good enough

50

for anyone else. Let me just be good enough for you."

She stilled. Guy was the only man she had ever wanted, *could* ever want. But the odds were against them, a thousand to one. "Don't you know? You are the whole world to me."

Beyond the intricately-carved wooden partition that divided her private bower from the living-quarters where her women slept came the unmistakeable sound of a door opening.

Voices.

"Then you'll do as I ask?" she whispered urgently.

"Always."

"Then take your things and *go*. And wait to hear from me."

As Guy swept his clothing into his arms and yanked a shirt over his head, Sibylla climbed back into the bed, smoothing away the traces of his presence and leaning back against the cushions. A timid tap sounded at the door and one of her women called, "My lady?"

Sibylla faked a yawn. "What is it, Sara?"

Her voice was panicked. "It's the *king*, my lady!"

From the voices, it was more than just the king. Minimally attired, Guy rushed to her bedside, seized her head and gave her one last, bruising kiss.

"My lady?"

Sibylla waved him towards the window. With her heart racing, it took a little more effort to make her voice sound sleepy this time. "Give me a moment, will you?"

Guy doubled his rope around the central pillar dividing the double-arched window and stepped out. Sibylla reached for a loose outer robe to throw on over the linen shift she had already donned, pulling the silk damask folds straight just as the rope slithered away from her window.

"All right, come in."

The door opened and people flooded her room. Sibylla's younger brother, Baldwin, entered first, walking with some difficulty, leaning on a crutch. Sibylla swallowed as she saw it. That was a new addition—his disease must be getting worse, weakening his legs. Such a shame. Once, he had been among the best horsemen in the kingdom. Now he would struggle even to sit a horse, let alone command the army as his office demanded. If war came, he'd have to appoint a bailli to lead them instead.

Sibylla's eyes narrowed fractionally. A successful bailliship could give the right man a decent claim to the throne. *Her* throne.

Behind the king, a monk of the Order of Saint Lazarus set down a folding chair and Baldwin sank into it with a stiffness that belonged to a much older man. Behind, his closest advisors—their mother and Uncle Joscelin—crowded into the chamber. Both stood at a respectful distance from the king. Each day they watched his leprosy worsen, and neither wanted to endure the same living death. Of course, Sibylla thought cynically, if they were to contract leprosy at their age, they were still more likely to die of old age than of the disease.

"Well, it's quite the family meeting." Sibylla accepted an enamelled glass of watered down wine from a waiting-woman. "To what do I owe the pleasure?"

The Leper King leaned forward. The disease had collapsed his nose and raised discoloured lumps across his once-handsome face, but it had not yet affected his eyes. Usually dark and bright, this morning they were clouded by worry. "Sister, the count of Tripoli and the prince of Antioch are coming south with an army. They know the Burgundy alliance has broken down and propose that you should wed with Ramla."

Sibylla feigned surprise. "With *Ramla?* What on earth?"

Her mother, Agnes of Courtenay, came to Sibylla's side and sat in the empty space that Guy had left on the bed. "The Ibelins are noble enough, but hardly a fit match for a future queen."

"They hate us, Agnes." Uncle Joscelin chewed his nether lip. "It's a ploy to get control of the throne and turn us out of the kingdom."

Not for the first time, Sibylla wondered if Uncle Joscelin was voicing his own opinions or his sister's. Certainly, she'd never yet caught him *disagreeing* with Agnes.

"You said they are bringing an army," Agnes said energetically. "Can we fight them?"

Baldwin blinked. "I don't *want* to fight them!"

"You can't afford *not* to fight them."

"Tripoli and Antioch are my father's cousins. The Ibelins are Watchers. Surely they should have *some* say in the affairs of this kingdom."

"It's not a voice they want. It's your crown," Agnes snapped. "Why would they cross your borders with a veritable army, unless they meant you violence? This is against all rules of lordly behaviour, and I tell you, you must fight them or give up the throne."

Baldwin's lips firmed stubbornly, but Sibylla could tell he was beginning to be afraid. "Uncle Joscelin?"

Sibylla hid a smile in her winecup as Uncle Joscelin, predictably, agreed with Agnes. "Even if they don't mean you violence, I'm afraid your mother is right. If you do nothing about this, you'll lose all credibility as a king."

Despite the rumours, Baldwin was a king, not a saint, and turning the other cheek was not something a king could do. He motioned to one of the servants. "Go and fetch my Constable."

As the servant departed, Sibylla silently sipped her wine.

"Why *Ramla?*" the king breathed, as though to himself. "Why would they do a thing like this for *his* sake?"

Sibylla cleared her throat. "That's easily answered. As Uncle Joscelin pointed out, they don't like the kingdom being ruled by the Courtenay side of the family, but they also don't want to be ordered around by a foreigner from the West. Everyone else in the kingdom is either too mean in status, already married, or too closely related by blood. Therefore, Ramla."

Baldwin stared at her. "Oh. How did you..."

"I use my head, brother."

Presently, the Constable was announced and Aimery of Lusignan entered. Guy's elder brother commanded the army, second only to the king himself. Like all the Lusignans, he was a man without roots, with the reputation of a troublemaker in his native Poitou, and he owed his position entirely to Agnes' patronage. Sibylla sometimes suspected her mother of being too openly partisan in her appointments, but she couldn't deny it was useful to have that kind of influence over one of the highest officers in the kingdom.

Aimery rasped his chin at a question that Sibylla, lost in her musings, had missed.

"No," he ventured. "They have already crossed our borders. If it's a question of battle, we don't have time to muster a large enough force—and that's assuming *all* the barons would stand by us. Those who are Watchers would almost certainly stand with the Ibelins."

"Saint George, defend us." Baldwin's alarm mounted. "We're defenceless. They could do whatever they like. How are we going to stop them, Aimery?"

The constable shook his head.

"They want a marriage," Sibylla began.

Agnes clicked her fingers in triumph. "They want a marriage. Forestall them. If Sibylla's married when they get here, there will be nothing they can do."

"They could still take the throne," Baldwin pointed out.

Joscelin lifted a hand. "No, my lord, I doubt it. The barons might take you off the throne if they could put another of your father's children onto it, but they won't abide a usurper."

"Another of my father's children? What about Isabella?"

Agnes frowned. "Isabella will have to be seen to one day. But she's too young to wed, only eight years old, and they will need a grown man to put on the throne."

"Their only real option is Sibylla," Joscelin added. "She'll have to marry. And fast."

The room was a babel of sound.

"But it's Holy Week already! No one gets married at Easter."

"That doesn't matter. The kingdom's at stake."

"Send for the Patriarch."

"But who?" Baldwin spoke as softly as ever, but still, his exhausted voice cut through the debate. "Whoever Sibylla marries will rule the kingdom after my death." He stared at his bandaged hands, his shoulders slumping. "William Longsword would have made a good king, but he is dead. Burgundy would have made a good king, but he is prevented from coming. Where do we turn now? I do not carry kings in my sleeves."

"There's the Marshal, Gerard of Ridefort. He's unmarried."

"He's barely noble enough. We can do better. What about Walter of Caesarea?"

"Caesarea is a Watcher. He's marching with Ramla."

"Devil take it," Joscelin muttered.

Aimery rubbed sleep out of his eyes. "What about one of the French?"

The brother of the king of France had been making a pilgrimage to the holy city, and was about to return home. Sibylla's fingers tightened on her cup, but she kept her voice light. "Not the old man, surely?"

Baldwin straightened, shaking his head. "No, but there's his son. How old is the boy?"

"Fourteen, my lord."

Still a year underage. But what were a few months when a kingdom was at stake? Sibylla did not speak as they looked at each other across her bed, as though daring each other to say it.

They would, she realised. They would marry her, a grown woman of twenty, to a beardless boy.

Her brother looked at her. "Sibylla?"

"Why ask me? I'm only the bride."

"I would not force you." His voice gentled. "It would be for the kingdom."

Sibylla looked him in the eye. "For the kingdom, my lord, I would do anything."

There was complete sincerity in her voice, and Baldwin nodded, evidently relieved to hear it. Sibylla sipped her wine again to hide the stubbornness lurking at the corners of her mouth. She *would* do anything for the kingdom, but that didn't mean blindly obeying the king.

A disturbance beyond the wooden partition drew Sibylla's attention to the door. After a moment, the Patriarch entered, and two attendant priests squeezed into the room after him. As bishop of Jerusalem—Christ's own city—the prelate occupied one of the most prestigious sees in Christendom. On ecclesiastical matters, his word was law. "You sent for me, my lord?"

Like the other courtiers, the Patriarch bowed but did not approach the king. Briefly, Sibylla wondered what it must be like to go through one's whole life never knowing human touch except for the deft ministrations of those who had made their peace with death.

She had patience with her brother, because the crown took a terrible toll on him. His illness had begun as a child, but in the six years since he'd inherited the burden of kingship, it had ravaged him to a weakened shell of his former self.

Yet, sometimes, she wondered. The weight of the crown was killing him, slowly, surely, horribly. Did he think her sacrifice should be as great?

"Send for the French king's brother," Baldwin said, and Sibylla jerked out of her thoughts with a sense of shock. The Patriarch was nodding.

"Irregular," he said, "but, given the present crisis…if the young gentleman's father is agreeable…"

Her mother reached out, found her hand, and patted it. Mechanically, Sibylla took another swallow of wine.

The Patriarch added, "Although I do wonder, why not simply acquiesce? Send to Ramla and offer him your sister's hand?"

"Do you jest?" Baldwin asked flatly. "Ramla is hardly noble enough to rule this kingdom."

"Perhaps not, my lord, but he's a seasoned warrior, he knows how war and diplomacy are conducted here…and the barons trust him."

"But *I* do not." Baldwin leaned forward earnestly. "Ramla is hot-headed and intemperate, unyielding in resentment and cruel to his peasantry. I could never give my kingdom to a man like that."

His kingdom, Sibylla thought with a flash of resentment. *What about his sister?* And that was the problem. She understood that the kingdom had to be more important to Baldwin than his sisters. But it was as though he never even *thought* of them. Had Ramla been noble enough and temperate enough, she would have been summarily handed over to him, regardless of her own wishes.

The Patriarch and Agnes immediately began discussing the details of the wedding. There was a certain procedure that must be followed, but the Patriarch would hasten matters where he could. A wedding could be organised within a few days, and once again, Sibylla would be sacrificed on the altar of the kingdom.

It seemed that the French lords were already at the palace, waiting to pay their final respects before leaving. Within minutes, the door opened again, and another of her serving-women appeared. "My lord, my lady, it's Lord Peter and his company."

Sibylla nodded dully. "Show them in."

As the French lords squeezed into her already crowded chamber, the other visitors shuffled back to make room for them. Then one of the priests tripped on something.

Finally.

"Dear me." The Patriarch froze, staring at something on the floor. Then he began to stutter a warning. "Ah-ah-ah, Brother Augustine—"

But it was too late. The little canon straightened, holding what had tripped him.

Guy of Lusignan's sword belt. Dropped last night and forgotten. Unmistakeable. Damning.

There was a moment's confused silence as everyone in the room stared at the sword.

"Did someone drop this?" the canon asked innocently, waving the gilded hilts.

Red with mortification, the Patriarch snatched the weapon. Constable Aimery recognised the sword at once, and his mouth dropped open.

Baldwin's eyes widened with shock, but he recovered quicker than anyone. "Clear the room," he said quietly. "Everyone out. Give me that, Patriarch. Forgive me, my lord," he added as the confused French lords were borne back into the antechamber amidst a stream of whispering servants and councillors.

Only Countess Agnes hesitated. *"Sibylla,"* she hissed reproachfully. "I *meant* you to have a prince!"

"Everyone, Mother." Baldwin's voice was hard, his bandaged hands curiously at home on the sword across his knees.

The door closed, leaving brother and sister alone together. Defiant, Sibylla drained her glass and crossed her arms.

Baldwin only looked disappointed, too weary for anger. "There will be no concealing this. By noon it will be all over the city."

"Concealment? Is that all you care about?" She tilted her chin. "And here I thought I would be blessed with a scolding for my corrupt life from Saint Baldwin himself."

He blinked. *"Saint Baldwin?"*

"Haven't you heard them call you that? *Finally, a chaste leper. It must be a miracle.*"

He looked down. "It's false, what they say about lepers."

"Oh, of course. You live like a monk because you're just that good."

"I'm not a saint, *or* a monk. I don't want anyone else to suffer this curse, and I certainly won't force it on the unwilling; that's all." He half rose, but as his crutch fell with a clatter on the floor, Baldwin seemed to remember that he could not jump up and pace the room as he would have liked. He fell back into his chair with a defeated sigh.

"I'm not a saint," he repeated, his voice hardening again. "I haven't the luxury of that. I'm your king, Sibylla. I have one job to do in this world—protect this kingdom until I can hand it over to a worthy successor."

"Am I not already a worthy successor?"

He didn't reply.

"Am I not?" she repeated. "You *know* I've been trained for it, just as you have. You *know* I have both the wit and the willpower to do it. You *know* the kingdom would be safe with me."

"You lack one thing, sister. The barons need a battle leader."

Sibylla was tempted to point out that he was hardly more fit than herself to lead men into battle, but the truth was that even if she had had the inclination to suffer the privations of campaign, she herself was weak and infirm, even for a woman. Subject to joint and muscle pains that baffled her physicians, her whole body weakened in times of anxiety. Pregnancy had almost crippled her; but for Sibylla, the worst thing was the fog that clouded her mind at such times, simple details sliding out of reach.

She could never do this alone, no more than her brother could. No realm could survive without a battle leader, and if she was to be a queen, it was plain that she needed a king at her side. Sibylla sighed.

58

"I hate it," Baldwin went on in a hard voice. "The crown. The throne. Do you think I would not hand it all to you if I could? I just want to be rid of it so that I can die in peace." He looked at Guy's sword. "Why must you make it so *difficult?*"

Here it was, the lecture on virtue. "Are you trying to tell me I'm ruined?"

"No! That isn't what this is." Baldwin leaned forward, his knobby hands tense on his knees, his voice dropping. "I know you, sister. You don't make mistakes."

Sibylla narrowed her eyes, trying to determine how much he suspected.

"Your mind is far beyond mine. If this sword was found, it was by your design. So put down your shield. Stop sparring and *talk* to me."

How well he knew her! Sibylla couldn't help a thin smile. "Very well. This is what will happen, Baldwin: two days from now I will marry, as arranged. To Guy of Lusignan."

His disfigured eyebrows lifted incredulously. "To *Lusignan?* This is *Lusignan's* sword?"

Somehow, his incredulity hurt her. "Who else?"

"But he's *nobody.*"

"He's from Poitou. A vassal of our cousin, Henry Plantagenet."

"Who *banished* him! He's a *manslayer*, Sibylla." Baldwin spoke between gritted teeth. "He murdered the earl of Salisbury."

"Watch how fast he's taken back into favour once he's the king of Jerusalem." Sibylla slid out of bed and reached for a comb. "Besides, a French alliance would be a terrible mistake right now. They'll be lucky to make it through the next five years with their kingdom intact, let alone send us the men and supplies we need to sustain ours. I'm telling you, Guy is our best choice."

"He's still a killer."

"It was twelve years ago, Baldwin. He was fifteen years old and it was his first battle!"

Baldwin was unmoved. At eighteen, despite his disease, he'd been in more battles than some Western greybeards could count. "By fifteen, *most* of us know it's wrong to stab a man from behind."

"Well, he's twenty-seven now. He's probably figured it out." Sibylla's voice was dry. "Does he not deserve a second chance?"

"Not at the expense of this kingdom."

"But it *won't* be at the expense of the kingdom." Sibylla tried to swallow her frustration. "Do you think I would have chosen him otherwise? Don't you trust my judgement at all? You said yourself that all I need is a battle leader. Well, Guy is more than capable of *that* job. I have the wits, and he has the courage. Between us, we can keep the kingdom safe."

Baldwin didn't answer right away. "Saints! How do you make it sound so rational?"

"Because it *is* rational."

His jaw worked, and she could tell it was a bitter pill to swallow.

She could tell she was winning.

"What better choice do we have? Burgundy isn't coming. France can't help us, even if they wanted to. And an army is coming to force Ramla on us at spear point." Fear shadowed Baldwin's eyes as she spoke, but Sibylla hardened her heart. "You might not want the throne, but do you want to be dragged off it and locked into Saint Lazarus for the rest of your life?"

"Merciful heaven, Sibylla…" Baldwin breathed. After a moment he shook his head. "Since you have chosen Guy of Lusignan, so be it." He reached down to retrieve his crutch and stood, shaking a little with the effort. "What I can't figure out is why Ramla thought he had a chance."

Sibylla shrugged. "Maybe he's ambitious, like all the Ibelins. Maybe he wants to step out of his brother's shadow. Maybe he thinks I encouraged him."

Baldwin cocked his head, something of the old bird-like quickness in his motions. "You *encouraged* him?"

Ah. Sometimes she forgot that her brother was, after all, no simpleton.

"You don't make mistakes," he said dazedly. "You planned this. You brought a war down on my head, just to force my consent to this marriage… Is that it?"

She gave him her blankest stare. "You seem to think I am very clever indeed."

Baldwin nodded towards Guy's sword, something between fascination and fear on his face. "Is there anything you won't do to get your own way, sister?"

Her own way? He thought she was doing this for *herself?*

That hurt. Some days, everything hurt.

"This kingdom is all the birthright I have," she whispered. "For the *kingdom*, I would do anything."

Chapter VI.

Marta was home, after all.

Sunset gilded the familiar Judaean hills. From the top of the hill where the foreigners—*Franks*, they called themselves—had camped, light and shadow streamed away from her, reaching towards Jerusalem, now less than a day's journey away.

Home.

And yet…not home.

She thumbed the shaft of her father's spear. Apart from the ancient hills, it was the only familiar thing here to greet her. The names went around and around in her mind. *Mama. Abba. Lukas. Paulus. Elisa.* She couldn't help wondering, fearing, hoping without hope. *Persi.* She hadn't even glimpsed her friend's face at the workshop window as the Franks had whisked her past to be mounted behind one of the servants for the next leg of their journey.

She was not in Oliveta anymore, that much she knew. She had woken in Cacho, a village of Caesarea. Which meant that somehow, she had travelled south nearly three hundred miles in the blink of an eye.

But that wasn't the only way she'd travelled. When the Watchers had met at Oliveta, it was six hundred and thirty-six years since the birth of Christ. Now it had been more than a thousand—one thousand, one hundred and eighty years to be precise. Thinking of it still made her a little dizzy, still trapped her breath in her chest when she tried to comprehend the enormity of it. There was nearly as much time between her and Oliveta as there had been between her birth and Christ's. Everything she knew—every*one* she knew—had been snatched away in an instant. No father. No mother. No siblings. Her heart shied away from considering it.

Later. She would feel it later, in the dark, when her tears would be private to her alone. Instead, she closed her grip on what she did have: her father's spear.

And a man she had never met who had waited so long for her.

She still didn't quite understand who the tall nobleman was—or why they had joined what appeared to be a small army marching south to Jerusalem for Easter. All she knew was his name: Balian, Lord of Ibelin and Nablus. He was married to the plump purple-clad noblewoman she had met in the weaver's shop, a Greek from Constantinople. And so they could speak her language.

That first day, Lord Balian had given her a hurried explanation that explained little, and left her mind reeling. Upon recognising her name, he had pushed up his sleeve to reveal a Watchers' Mark inked into his skin. It was a kind she had never seen before—a five-fold cross, the same emblem appearing on some of the banners carried by the army. "There's a tradition among the Watchers of Jerusalem," he had told her. "A prophecy handed down from my grandfather John…that one day a Bessarion would appear in the kingdom, and that the spear should be given over to him for his lifetime."

Him. "But I'm a girl," Marta had said, uncertainly. That had always been Lukas' excuse, whenever she wanted him to teach her the things he was learning in his warrior's training.

"It's your birthright, Marta Bessarion." Balian's eyes had crinkled, warmth in their depths. "In this kingdom, we don't deny a woman her inheritance; there are too few of us to let keen wits and valiant hearts go to waste. The spear is yours. You decide how it should be used, and by whom."

Since that first night, Marta had had no chance to speak to the tall lean nobleman, nor to his short buxom wife. Both of them were always busy, talking in the Frankish language to the other members of their party. At the end of each day's march they huddled together, speaking solemnly.

The men's fingers fidgeted uneasily on their swords.

Marta wondered what could possibly be worrying them. She could not speak to them, but she had watched these Franks and the land they ruled. Tall men and outspoken women alike flaunted Watchers' Marks openly. Under their rule, Palestine had thrived. The landscape, once ravaged by war, had healed. Farms, vineyards, olive groves and orchards quickened to life in the watchful shadow of dozens of new stone fortresses. When Marta and her family had fled Jerusalem, the countryside was depopulated, the people gaunt and anxious after thirty years of war. Now, just weeks—or rather, centuries—later, the labourers and herdsmen they passed looked stout and joyful.

If this was the future, it was a good one. She only wished she knew how she fitted into this picture, what role these new Watchers expected her to play. If she stayed with these people, would they lock her up to weave again? If she wanted to shoulder the spear and leave, would anyone stop her?

Jerusalem lay ahead of her in the hills, but even if she returned, would she ever find her people again?

"Marta!" someone called. As she turned, a boy came out of the camp and strolled towards her, waving.

"Miles," she responded warmly. The blond boy she'd fought and injured in Cacho was the only Frank who made an effort to be friendly—and he managed it too, despite his inability to speak her language. Marta pointed to his side, where his mail hauberk had been mended after she drove the spear through it. "How is it healing?"

He touched the wound and said something cheerful that she didn't understand, either. He stopped beside her, gesturing towards the sunset. "Jerusalem?"

Marta nodded.

Miles lifted an object he had in his hand, and Marta was intrigued to see a wax tablet and stylus. He made a crude sketch on one of the tablets—a female stick figure inside a house. He pointed from Marta to the stick figure, then tapped the house and said, "Jerusalem?"

(10)(5){}{}

Marta nodded enthusiastically. "Yes! Yes, I—I once lived in Jerusalem."
Miles grinned broadly and handed tablets and stylus to her.

She thought a moment, then drew a man and a woman, the woman holding a baby. She pointed from Miles to the baby, then tapped the man and said, "Balian?" *Are you Lord Balian's son?*

For a long, awkward instant, Miles just looked blank. When he finally did smile and shake his head, there was sadness lurking at the back of his eyes. Feeling obscurely guilty, she offered the tablet back to him, but he lifted his hands to refuse it. Instead, he said something she didn't understand, mimed taking a bite from a spoon, and beckoned her back to the camp.

Marta followed him over to the western side of the hill where the Franks' tents were pitched. Inside Lord Balian's tent, dinner had already begun and there was no space on the long benches at the foot of the table for Marta. She hung back, but Miles beckoned her over with a jerk of his head and shoved the others aside to make room for both of them.

Despite her shyness, Miles kept trying to draw her out. He tapped the inside of his forearm with an inquiring look. *So you're a Watcher?*

Marta nodded and shoved her sleeve back to show her Watcher's Mark. He inspected it with interest. Marta pointed to his arm, but he laughed a little and shook his head. *No, not me.* Instead, he pointed up the table towards the nobles and said something that contained the words *Prester Balian.*

It took Marta a moment to realise that *prester* must be a form of *Presbyter.* She stared at the tall nobleman with new respect. So Balian wasn't just a Watcher; he must also be the Presbyter of the Jerusalem Council.

Next to Lord Balian, his wife glanced up and caught Marta's eye. Though short and rotund, the Greek lady carried herself with dignity and dressed with splendour. The gold-embroidered ceremonial shoes Marta had glimpsed in her luggage suggested that, in Constantinople at least, she must have been of very high, perhaps imperial rank. She had not yet spoken to Marta, except briefly to compliment her on her fine weaving—but now she smiled, and Marta felt just a little bit more welcome.

A moment later the queen's eyes went beyond Marta to the open flap of the tent, and she half stood in surprise. "Isabella? What are *you* doing here?"

Marta turned. In the opening stood a pretty dark-haired little girl of eight years old. Despite being dressed for bed in a simple white shift and bare feet, she carried a fistful of red anemones. Till now, Marta had only seen the little girl from a distance, always with at least one nurse hovering over her. Evidently she'd found a way to give them the slip.

Isabella didn't seem even slightly abashed by the silence that had fallen over the tent. "I was picking flowers," she said airily in Greek, "and I found this old woman who said she had a message for Prester Balian." She turned and trumpeted, "Come on!"

The light darkened a little as the woman hobbled to the door of the tent. *Old*, Marta thought, *was an understatement*. Bent over a stick, her white hair contrasting sharply with her mahogany tan, the woman looked ancient.

Lord Balian got up from the table and moved forward. "I am Prester Balian," he began in Greek, but then caught himself and switched to his own language.

"I heard you the first time," the crone said in Greek. Her bright eyes probed the tent, looking at each face in turn. "My Message for you is this: you march against Jerusalem, but you little know what you're dealing with, Balian of Ibelin. You Watchers deal in power and politics, but it's all for your own benefit. What have you done to redeem this kingdom, to relieve the poor or free the captives? Count yourselves happy that King Baldwin has the favour of heaven while he lives." Her voice hardened. "You have until the king dies. After him, *the fire.*"

There was total silence in the tent. Marta's gut clenched. *No. Not Oliveta all over again. Not again—*

Lord Balian looked grief-stricken. "How long?"

"All I know is that if you fail, the fire will consume me also." She shook back her sleeve, revealing a withered and faded arm. "Lest you be tempted to doubt me, here is my Mark."

An emblem was inked into her skin, and Marta wasn't surprised to see that it was the Constantinople mark: whoever this woman was, she'd lived long and travelled far.

She'd lived *very* long, and Marta knew that the same question was on Lord Balian's mind: if the fire that destroyed the Watchers also destroyed the old woman, then how much longer did they have? Months? Weeks?

But already this wasn't Oliveta, for Lord Balian made three swift strides to the door of the tent and bowed before the old woman, thanking her for her Message. "If one man can do anything," she heard him whisper, "I will."

The rest of the meal was somewhat subdued, though Marta was quite sure that Lord Balian did not translate the old woman's prophecy for the rest of the tent. He came to her afterwards, cloaked and booted for riding, fidgeting with his gloves. "I suppose you heard all that," he said, fear shadowing his eyes. "What did you think of it? Was it trustworthy?"

Marta blinked at him, astonished to be asked her opinion, and more astonished to find that he could wonder at the Message's veracity. "I don't know," she said in a small voice. "Why are you asking me?"

He blinked at her. "Well, you're a Bessarion."

Marta reddened. Did that mean he expected her to have some special insight? Worse, did he expect her, a girl, to advise him, the Presbyter? She wanted to melt into the ground, but he looked so expectant, and she didn't want to disappoint him. "I heard someone deliver a similar Message to another Watchers' Council once," she said. "They didn't listen, and..."

There had certainly been fire—and worse. The memory was too horrible to repeat aloud. Marta took a ragged breath, and Lord Balian put a gentle hand on her shoulder. "If you believe her, I believe her."

"I believe her." Marta didn't know what else to say, until he started to turn away. "My lord?"

"What is it?"

He didn't know how beautiful it all was—this land, this *time.* "Please, listen to the Messenger. Do what she tells you."

He looked down at her with serious eyes. "I will. You have my word."

Something that had been pulled taut inside her relaxed. This wasn't Oliveta. Lord Balian would listen, would do what had to be done.

He smiled and began pulling on his gloves. Outside the tent, grooms were preparing horses. "My brother and I will ride to Jerusalem tonight."

Jerusalem. *Home.*

Marta's heart quickened. "May I come? Please?"

Lord Balian headed out towards the flap of the tent. "You should wait until the rest of us make the journey tomorrow, Marta. I think you'll find Jerusalem much changed since you were here last."

She hurried after him. "I know, but…it's still my home."

His voice was very gentle. "It's been more than five hundred years. What's the hurry?"

She gulped. "I don't know. I just…"

Maybe it wasn't just her. Maybe the rest of her family had travelled through the centuries, as well. Maybe some of them would be waiting for her—if she could only find her way home.

"Balian!" someone shouted from atop one of the horses. It was another Frankish lord: a battered warrior with thick, lowering eyebrows and a finger missing from his sword-hand. He was a little older and more heavyset than Balian, but now that Marta knew there was a brother, the family resemblance was obvious. He looked impatient.

Lord Balian, however, looked at her with sympathy. "Can you ride in that gown?"

Marta nodded.

"Then let's put you up behind Miles." Balian spoke a command and Miles, already mounted, kneed his horse closer and stretched out a hand. Marta stepped lightly onto his foot and swung her leg over his horse's withers with a soaring heart.

It would be a long, uncomfortable ride—but she was going *home.* If she only saw it, then she would be able to rest.

Chapter VII.

Balian sighed. "I'm still not sure this is a good idea, brother."

In the dim light of dusk, Baldwin of Ramla's teeth flashed in a grin. "What's wrong with you? Worried we'll be caught?"

Balian glanced around to gauge their privacy. His brother's squire and his own were riding far enough behind to have trouble listening to their conversation. As for Marta Bessarion, she did not yet understand enough Frankish. Still, he lowered his voice, ensuring none of them would hear. "That's not what I'm afraid of."

He couldn't shake the worry that had descended upon him with the old Messenger's prophecy, and his unease grew worse as they entered the massive David's Gate in the shadow of the great citadel. Holy Week found Jerusalem buzzing with pilgrims, and not just from the heartlands of Syria, Palestine, Egypt and Europe but also from further afield—from Gibraltar and Spain, from North Africa and Nubia, from Iceland and Russia, from Persia, Ind, and Cathay. Although sunset was only a rose-coloured memory in the west, the streets were still hectic with moneychangers and preachers, sherbet-hawkers and beggars, goldsmiths selling relics and sergeants rolling dice on the tavern doorsteps.

Among such crowded streets, the Ibelin brothers would go unnoticed. No. He was not afraid of being caught.

"Then try to keep up. Ah, how good it is to be in Christian lands again. Smell the gardens!"

Balian sighed and urged his horse closer. "This is very knightly, daring the king's wrath to see your lady, but no woman likes to be surprised by a suitor. What if she's indisposed? Gone to bed with a stomach-ache?"

"Gone to bed with a stomach-ache?" Ramla guffawed. "What a life your Greek queen must lead you."

Balian stiffened. "Sibylla is a royal lady too, not to be dealt with high-handedly. I think you'll find her equally mindful of her rights and privileges." *And less ready to waive them*, he thought. "Besides, it's Holy Week. She might be at church."

"You complain like a bad-tempered camel, Balian." They turned onto the Street of the Armenians, heading south past the massive stone bulk of the Tower of David. Beyond, a lower wall surrounded the king's palace and its pleasure-gardens.

"Here goes." Ramla grinned, turning his horse towards the gate.

Balian grabbed for the bridle, yanking his horse's head around. "There are *guards*."

"I know that." Ramla batted his hand away from the bridle. "What are you afraid of? They know us. We're barons of Jerusalem."

Balian glanced over his shoulder again, sinking his voice. "Yes, but we've come with an *army* and there's no chance the king doesn't know about it. Be prudent!"

"All right, O cautious brother of mine. How do we get into the palace?"

Balian had laid his plans as soon as his brother suggested the expedition. "There's a postern gate further down in the gardens."

"That will be guarded too."

"Only one man. Easier to bribe. I brought enough gold."

Ramla tipped his head. "Not a bad plan. Subtler than mine."

Balian snorted. "Subtlety has nothing to do with this outing, Baldwin." As Ramla went to move on, he caught his breath and took the plunge. "Listen: that old woman—"

"You're an old woman."

"That old woman said that God was being merciful to us—because of the Leper King."

Ramla shot a sideways glance at him. "God loves the Leper King? Well, that's hardly news."

Balian hesitated. Breathed a prayer. "Brother. Promise me you don't plan to depose him."

"What?"

"Promise me that this isn't a coup. Promise me it's only Lady Sibylla's hand you're after, not the kingdom."

Ramla shrugged, bemused. "If I get the lady's hand, I'll get the kingdom sooner or later, so what does it matter?"

"That old woman was a Messenger. She said, *After the Leper King—the fire.*" Balian leaned forward. "If there are hard times ahead for this kingdom, do you really want to be the man responsible?"

"Hard times, hah! We have our problems, but the kingdom is as strong as it ever has been. You shouldn't let the old wives scare you, Balian."

Balian swallowed, sinking his voice to a whisper. "I swore fealty to the Leper King, brother. If you make me choose between you, I *will* choose him."

Ramla looked back at him, his face unreadable in the shadows, until suddenly he gave a flashing smile. "Then you're in luck, so stop scowling. I only want the lady." Beckoning to the squires, Ramla took the lead down the twilit street. "This is not as mad as you think it is."

"No?" Balian wanted to bury his head in his hands. The only reason he was on this harebrained jaunt was to make sure Ramla didn't get himself into more boiling oil than absolutely necessary. "How well do you even know Sibylla? What makes you so convinced she wants to see you, let alone marry you?"

They reached the gardens across from the Armenian church of Saint James and headed through the arched gateway. Beyond, rows of spring greens and a heady whiff of orange-blossom greeted them. Because of the danger of siege, much land in the Holy City was dedicated to market-gardening.

Inside the gate, Ramla dismounted. "She wrote to me, Balian."

For a moment, speech left him. "When?"

"After the battle of Beaufort, when I was captive in Damascus. She told me that if I could arrange to pay my ransom, she would persuade her brother to let me marry her."

Balian stared.

"You said it yourself, my brother. Saladin demanded a king's ransom. Why else would he fix my freedom at such a price?"

Balian found his voice. "But she was as good as promised to the Duke of Burgundy."

Ramla grinned. "Nonetheless."

"But the Duke of Burgundy is…" Balian searched for words "…a *duke*. And what are we? Who was our father? Plain Sir Barisan, constable of Jaffa."

"Says Balian, Lord of Nablus, whom a princess of the Comneni found it no shame to wed with."

"There's no comparison. Maria and I married for love. King Amalric was dead and she was free to choose."

Ramla snorted. "You underrate yourself, Balian. Maria didn't marry you out of pity. She made damned sure she got her fief the best defender in the kingdom."

"You think so?" Balian couldn't help grinning. "Maybe I ought to have married Sibylla instead, and become king."

Ramla's voice was sincere. "Maybe it would have been better so. I'm not you, my brother. I don't have your gift for diplomacy, but I've seen more than my share of fighting. Whether Sibylla comes to the throne soon or late, she will need someone like me by her side. She realises that." He took a breath. "And, her letters were not devoid of—love."

As though embarrassed by the word, he reined his horse towards the postern gate that led into the palace grounds. Balian followed, his thoughts whirling. When he had heard that the count of Tripoli and the prince of Antioch would be riding to Jerusalem to put his brother forward as a suitor for the Lady Sibylla's hand, Balian had thought them half mad. He'd joined them because, after all, Ramla was his brother—and like Tripoli, he distrusted the Courtenay faction at court. Yet he'd never had much hope of their success.

Still, if the lady herself was for it…

Ramla dismounted at the gate, beckoning him closer. Concealing his face, Balian stepped forward, gold chinking between his fingers. A few moments later the gate swung open and they filed into the palace grounds amidst the cool murmur of water, the scent of herbs, and a shadowy display of orchid, poppy, and iris.

Balian turned to the squires and Marta, putting a finger to his lips and whispering for them to wait. Impatient, Ramla was already moving up the straight path towards the palace's façade. The hush of evening had fallen on the king's house, but lights burned in all but a few of the diamond-paned windows. Under the shade of a walnut tree, Ramla halted.

"Look," he murmured. "There's a light in her window."

"How do you know it's her window?"

"My informant."

"You have become a spymaster in your old age."

"A *lover*." Ramla pulled his hood deep over his face to conceal it. "Come on."

* * *

Sibylla was sitting up when Guy entered that evening, scanning some of the day's messages by the light of a gold-and-alabaster lamp.

"Oh, there you are," she said, leaning back in her carved chair and holding out a hand to him. "Mother is telling us we should make a wedding journey. Ostensibly to visit some of the shrines to pray, but really to show you off to the barons and the people." She wrinkled her nose. "There would be a lot of throwing money and going to church. What do you think?"

Guy came over and took her hand, but he seemed oddly reluctant to meet her eyes. "Do I have a choice?"

Sibylla searched his face before replying. It had been a busy four days; four days that had taken Guy from her secret lover to her husband and a count of the holiest of kingdoms. Until their wedding yesterday she'd had no opportunity to speak to him alone, and it was only now that she knew she hadn't imagined the restraint in his manner.

73

"Are you angry with me?" she asked coolly.

"Four days ago, when you asked if I would marry you…"

"You said you would do as I asked."

"I wasn't ready to be made a count and a king-in-waiting and God knows what else."

"Then you underestimated me." Sibylla couldn't repress a smile. "You'll have to learn that I have no idle talk."

"I had my brother Aimery locking my door and posting *guards* outside my window. Just in case I got cold feet."

"It's not as though you would have flown." Sibylla got up to face him. "You swore to serve me as love's Assassin." A tiny Saracen sect in the Syrian mountains, the Assassins were so devoted to their lord that they would throw themselves to their death on his whim. Sibylla approved; a ruler was nothing without loyalty. "You swore to die for me; will you not at least live for me?"

He sighed, sliding a hand under her hair, tracing her cheek with his thumb. "I told you I'm sick of playing politics. I'm sick of trying to please other people, of trying to be someone I'm not. I meant what I said the other day, when I said I was done being a lord. I never wanted to swear fealty to another king." His hand left her face. "But you left me no choice."

"That's because there *is* no choice," she said. "Do you want me to say I'm sorry? Because I'm not. The world you dream of doesn't exist. We all have lieges and underlings and there is no other choice. Your only choice is this: Will you play this game with me, and make them accept you as you are? Or will you run from it, and let them tread you underfoot?"

He looked at her with uncertainty in his eyes. Sibylla took his hands, raised each to her lips.

"Stop trying to please them. Why try to earn their love when you could command their fear? You're going to be a *king*, Guy of Lusignan. You're already my chosen husband. You no longer have to apologise for your past. For *anything*." She took a deep breath, knotting her fists into his silk tunic and pulling him closer. "Don't do it for the politics. Do it for love. Do it for me."

His hands slid around her waist possessively, but there was still a hint of doubt in his eyes. "Are you sure you chose the right man?"

Sibylla wanted to laugh. How many women were fortunate enough to marry a man they could love and trust as she did Guy? "I know you aren't a coward. Am I wrong?"

"I'm no such fool."

"Then we'll make them fear you. Together."

"Together." Guy pulled her close, angling her head to kiss her breathless.

A knock sounded at the door. Sibylla gave a huff of annoyance. "Come in," she called, but one look at the face of her waiting-gentlewoman brought her back to the present. "What is it, Alix?"

The woman pulled the door shut behind her and bustled in. "It's the Ibelins."

Sibylla swallowed. Last she'd heard, the coming host was camped between Jerusalem and Ramla, due to arrive tomorrow. They *should* have had a few hours' grace. "What have they done?"

"They've come *here*. Alone. They're in the antechamber now, asking to see you."

Sibylla blinked. "What, the two brothers?"

"Yes, my lady."

Guy growled, and Sibylla put a warning hand on his chest before he could speak. "How did they get in?"

"No one knows! What should I do? Call the guard? Warn the king?"

Sibylla shook her head, trying to think. They had had the nerve to come *here?* To take her by surprise, invade her privacy, and force it on her to make explanations? At least they were here and not making trouble somewhere else. Besides, explanations would have to be made sooner or later.

"Best if I handle this alone." A blue damask curtain lined the room's south-facing windows, looped back to let in the warm spring air. Sibylla turned to Guy. "Get behind the curtain. Don't come out unless I call for you."

His lips pursed mutinously and Sibylla laughed, standing on tiptoes to kiss them. "Don't rip their arms off *just* yet." He obeyed, and as Alix

75

whisked away the signs of his presence, Sibylla shook out the folds of her silk dress, adjusted the onyx signet ring which sat askew on her thumb, and smoothed her dark hair.

"Let them in, Alix."

The Ibelin brothers were tall as Flemings and dark as Syrians. Sibylla quickly marshalled what she knew of them. Balian—the younger brother, hanging back near the door—had two weaknesses. As the queen dowager's second, and much lower-ranked, husband, there were few decisions he could make without consulting her. Second, as the Prester of the Watchers, he was forced to maintain at least the appearance of justice and compassion in all his dealings. A man bound by a sense of fairness was predictable, and therefore easy to outmanoeuvre. She did not think that Balian would give her much trouble.

His elder brother, Baldwin of Ramla, by contrast, was everything the Leper King had said: hot-tempered and unpredictable. Everything depended on her ability to get him to see reason, tonight.

And if she failed, she must hope to channel his emotion in some way that would benefit herself.

Ramla pulled the hood from his greying head and knelt to kiss the hand she offered him. Sibylla said coolly, "This is a surprise."

He did not release her hand. "I am your true knight, lady."

Sibylla blinked; she had not expected an appeal to romance. Her voice was chilly, like a splash of cold water. "Come to the point, my lord. It is late, and I had retired."

"I have come to ask whether you will keep the promises you have made me."

"Promises? I made you no promises, my lord." On the contrary, she remembered being very careful not to pledge herself to anything.

Ramla's thick eyebrows gave him a perpetual scowl, but they drew down further as he got to his feet. "Do you deny that you counselled me to borrow money for my ransom—no matter the cost?"

"You are a seasoned warrior, one the kingdom can scarcely do without. Had he been in your place, I would have counselled your brother the same."

"Don't cozen me," he snapped. "I have put myself in debt for your sake. You promised to marry me, my lady. I am here to find out whether you will fulfil your end of the bargain." Ramla stepped forward, towering over her. Sibylla swallowed, sensing the violence simmering below the surface, but she didn't have to be afraid. Not now that she had Guy. Small and frail as she was, she stood her ground.

"We had no bargain," she said flatly. "And if we had it would have been broken the instant you entered this kingdom with an army."

"You…" Ramla's voice was thick with anger. *"You suggested it yourself."*

"On the contrary. When you asked me to marry you, I stated it as my opinion that my brother would not assent unless he was forced to it."

Ramla's jaw bulged.

Maybe she had been dishonourable, but she hadn't been *stupid*. She hadn't liked manipulating Ramla, as frighteningly easy as it had been to do. "You took the wrong meaning from my words. For that, I am truly sorry. If it's a wealthy marriage you need to pay your ransom, let me arrange something for you. The Constable's daughter—"

"To hell with the Constable's daughter," Ramla shouted. "Do you think a man changes mistresses as easily as gloves? It's *you* I love."

That startled her into honesty. Ramla, love her? Ramla, a man more than twice her age with whom she'd barely exchanged a few letters? "What *nonsense.*"

"Devil take it!" Ramla yelled.

Balian materialised at his brother's elbow, a warning hand against his chest. In the same moment, Guy burst out from behind the curtain, three inches of steel showing between hilt and scabbard. "Unhand her, *yokel,*" he bellowed, although neither of the Ibelins had laid a finger on her.

At the insult, Ramla's cheeks slowly drained of colour. Then he fumbled for his own sword. "Who are *you?*" he choked.

Balian closed a hand over his brother's wrist. "Not now, brother. We should leave."

Ramla looked at Sibylla, his face pulled into a grimace halfway between pain and disgust. "What, madam, not even a blush?"

Sibylla tilted her chin up. "Why should I blush? He is Guy of Lusignan, and he is my lawful husband."

She had never liked Ramla. She knew him for a bully, but she almost felt sorry for him then. He stared from her to Guy and back again, his hands clenched at his sides, utterly dumbstruck.

"Impossible."

"How so, my lord?"

"I should have heard of it."

"Hardly, since it was carried out very suddenly yesterday morning."

"Why?" He was not shouting anymore: he was the kind of man who would speak more civilly to a woman if there was a man standing beside her.

Sibylla shrugged. "You marched on Jerusalem like one who means to take the throne by force. What other choice did my brother have?"

"You convinced him I am a *usurper?*"

"My lord, *I* was not the one who gathered an army."

Ramla ground his teeth. "So this is my reward. After all that has passed between us." He pointed to Guy. "You have told us who this man is. Have you told him who I am?"

Sibylla turned to her husband. "This is Baldwin of Ibelin, the lord of Ramla, and the other one is—"

"There was talk between us of marriage," Ramla interrupted. "Talk! I put myself two hundred *thousand* bezants in debt to pay my ransom because of what this lady had promised me. I should not wonder if I were able to accuse this poxed sneaking marriage of bigamy."

"Do it." Guy snatched a glove from his belt. "Let's fight it out, old man."

Ramla smiled bitterly. "No fear of that. I would not have her now if she paid me every penny. One day she will serve you as she has served me, and as she served the duke of Burgundy before me. Come, Balian."

He stalked towards the door.

Sibylla did not recognise the feeling that had come over her at the lord of Ramla's words: she was shaking, her whole body tingling hot and cold by turns. If she could have strangled him, she would have done it cheerfully.

Instead, she said, "You will sing in a different key one day, when I am queen and Guy is king."

Ramla wheeled, ripping his sword from the scabbard. Balian grabbed at him with a cry of warning, but his brother only clenched the blade below the hilt and lifted it like a great shining cross.

"On my sword and my honour and my hope of heaven," he breathed, "this *puppy* will never be my king."

The door slammed shut behind the brothers, leaving a vast and echoing silence. Beside Sibylla, Guy was rigid. Her heart climbed into her throat. Devil take it—all those doubts that she had just convinced him to lay aside must be flocking back to him now.

She turned on him urgently. "Take no notice of him, Guy. Ramla is just one man."

But Guy growled deep in his chest. "I don't care if he's an army. I would make myself king for the mere pleasure of giving him the lie."

Chapter VIII.

In the hushed garden, Marta watched Lord Balian and his brother disappear through the shadows towards the palace. Miles and the other attendant held the horses, talking in whispers to the palace guard who had let them in. Once again, Marta felt frustrated at her inability to understand their words. She still had so many questions. Palestine ruled by Syrian-looking Franks? Watchers prophesying fire and destruction? Two lords and their attendants sneaking into the royal palace after dark? She *had* to learn the language.

"Miles," she said softly, tugging his elbow.

He turned to her with a smile that flashed pale in the shadows. "Marta?"

She tried a few of the words Persi had taught her, hoping he'd understand. "You—me—tongue."

To her horror, the other men greeted her words with enthusiastic hoots. The other attendant puckered up his mouth and made kissing sounds. Even Miles laughed.

Saints, couldn't she have been given the Watcher gift of Oratory? *"Frank* tongue," she tried to explain.

That didn't make it any better. Both the guard and the other attendant seemed eager to demonstrate that their tongues were genuinely Frankish. One of them tried to show her at close range, but Miles shoved him back with a sharp objection.

Marta backed a step, levelling her father's spear. Miles had his hands out, refusing to let either of the other men get to her. Still, the men were both laughing and wheedling, as though they thought it would be fun to make her kiss them.

The nerve! She had come here to find her family, not to have men pass her around. Behind her, the palace garden was a welcoming mass of shadows, trees, shrubs and herbs. Throwing a quick glance behind her to make sure that Miles still held the other men's attention, she slid noiselessly between two bushes and felt her way along the garden wall away from the hushed argument.

Marta felt better as soon as the voices were out of earshot. She went some distance before she found what she was looking for: a tall mulberry tree overhanging the garden wall. Her way out. Marta stepped lightly onto the round turf seat that surrounded its trunk, and felt for a bough, trying to figure out how to climb into the branches without losing the spear.

There was a movement on the other side of the tree, and a hoarse voice spoke abruptly in Frankish.

Marta froze.

A dark shape circled the tree and looked up at her, and Marta stopped being frightened at once: it was only a poor cripple, leaning on a crutch.

"I'm sorry," she whispered in Greek. "I shouldn't be here, I know. I'm just going."

After a moment's silence, the man sniffed noisily, and replied in the same language. "Who are you?"

It was almost impossible to see his face, but from the sound of his voice, Marta instantly knew he had been crying. The knowledge made her feel like even more of an intruder.

"My name's Marta. I'm sorry. I didn't mean to disturb you."

There was a creak, and a ray of flickering light shone out as he unshuttered a lantern. The light revealed a horrifying face, swollen and deformed with grotesque protrusions and a nose that had melted into his face like butter on a hot day. An open ulcer cratered the wrist holding the lantern.

A leper. No wonder he was weeping in the dark. Marta suppressed any reaction, pity warning her to let no pity show.

"Do you belong to the palace?" he asked.

"No," Marta said truthfully. And then, becoming curious: "Do you?"

There was a momentary silence. He blinked once or twice, and the corner of his mouth twisted in a smile. "I would to God I did not."

"Do they treat you badly, then?"

"No, it's…" He looked past her, into the distance. When his eyes focused on her again, he seemed to have abandoned that thought. "I won't be here much longer, anyway."

"Oh." Marta nodded. "I'm glad to hear that."

"I'm glad of it too," he said gravely. "I just…have some things to do before I go."

Too late, she understood his meaning. Again, something warned her not to react.

Marta wondered who the man could be. The lantern light revealed rich clothing and, to her surprise, a sword. A nobleman, then. That would explain why he was here, inside the wall of the city, instead of locked up in a leprosarium.

Sensing his need for company, she knelt on the seat. "How long since you…"

"The leprosy?" He said the word quite naturally. "Since I was a boy of eight. It was my arm that went numb first. Ten years ago."

That made him eighteen—it was impossible to tell from his ravaged face. Marta wanted to cry for him. Instead, she said, "What is it like?"

"It's like being dead while you're still alive." He spoke haltingly, not looking at her. "People treat you differently. My—the men have a whole repertoire of jokes they never tell if they think I might hear them, you know. As though I'm somewhere between a maiden and a saint. Others try not to look at you at all, as though you're too obscene to be seen in the daylight. As for the women, you know what they say about lepers."

"No?"

Again, the surprise. "Most of them are afraid of me. Lepers are supposed to be violent. Lustful." He smiled tiredly. "Frightened?"

Marta shook her head. "I could probably knock you flat without much trouble."

His startled laughter transformed his face, making it possible, just for a moment, to imagine who he might have been. "Does this martial maiden have a name?"

"Marta Bessarion. And you?"

"You really don't know who I am?" he countered

"It's a *very* long time since I was in Jerusalem."

He grinned teasingly. "Pardon me. I thought I was speaking to a very *young* maiden. You're a dryad or a peri, I expect, and secretly centuries old." He patted the mulberry tree.

It wasn't *entirely* wrong. "If I was the mulberry dryad, I'd know your name." On impulse, she added: "And what you were so unhappy about."

The humour drained from his face and he looked beyond her, into the dark. "It was nothing," he said. When she didn't speak again, one of his shoulders hitched. "My sister got married yesterday. A love match, although she tried to pass it off to me as an affair of policy. She'll have love, and children, and a long life." He swallowed. "No one touches me unless they expect to die."

There was nothing she could say in reply to that. For a moment, the only sound was the chorus of frogs croaking in some unseen pool. Wordlessly, Marta reached out to take his hand.

"No!" He jerked back, making the lantern swing wildly. "I won't condemn you to that! I wasn't asking for your pity."

Marta felt the colour mount in her cheeks and drew back. What an idiot! To show him pity, when she knew he'd hate it.

He took a deep breath. "Forgive me. I thank you for the thought." He steadied the light and looked at her more appraisingly. "I'm afraid I must ask what you're doing in my garden."

Marta hesitated, unwilling to implicate Lord Balian. "Trying to get out again," she said, and then something struck her. "This is *your* garden?"

This was some kind of palace. And the boy was no gardener.

"Well, I'm more of a caretaker, really."

"Who *are* you?"

He sighed, acknowledging his mistake. "My name is Baldwin, the fourth of that name to be king in Jerusalem. And seeing that you're trespassing in my garden—"

A *king.*

Strife, Marta thought. She didn't give him the chance to finish. In an instant, she climbed into the mulberry's branches and scrambled along them. Not daring to look back, she swung a leg over the wall and dropped to the ground on the other side.

* * *

The streets were quieter now that the glow of sunset had faded out of the west. At first, Marta ran, eager to get clear of the palace before the king raised the alarm. The streets hadn't changed much since her own time, and home called her across the city. As Praetorian Prefect, her father had the right to live in the Tower of David, but none of the family had liked the idea of being shut up within those massive, towering walls. Instead, they had gone on living in their own comfortable villa just beyond the Armenian quarter.

Was the house still there?

No hue and cry rose from the palace, but Marta didn't stop running.

The Jerusalem she remembered was shabby and depopulated. This Jerusalem was a chest of tiny jewel-boxes, a town of small alleyways and high walls concealing green courtyards, scented gardens, secret fountains, full of trickling water and the scent of cypress. Marta fled through it with a heart full of delight, longing to see it by daylight. On Temple Street, a lamp burned above a wide gateway in a wall of solid stone. Marta's heart jumped as she spotted it—a welcoming light to guide travellers home. She gripped the iron bars and looked through into the old familiar courtyard. In her father's time there had been potted trees on the cobbles and, more often than not, a wagon carrying a shipment of wine from the coastal estates. Now the centre of the courtyard held an open cistern filled with water and a fountain gilded by the torchlight.

Otherwise, the house was the same. Lights glowed from its doorways, outlining the loggia arches in flickering gold. Servants ran to and fro, and a woman's voice called out sharply in Greek to demand hot bathwater. Her hands tightened on the gate.

Home.

She didn't want to go any further, to break this beautiful hope.

Before she could emerge from her daydream, horses' hooves echoed in the street. Marta turned, poised to flee into the shadows, but it was only Lord Balian with his brother and attendants. Miles seemed relieved to see her, but the other attendant would not meet her eyes. The one called Ramla looked black as a thundercloud.

Lord Balian slid from his horse and hurried forward. "Marta, thank God. I was ready to strangle Miles for losing you. I see you found your way home."

He reached past her to knock at the gate. At once, a porter appeared and threw the gate open, welcoming him by name. Marta followed them into the familiar-yet-strange courtyard, her heart sinking. Servants emerged to lead the horses into the stables on the house's ground floor. Lord Balian's brother stormed wordlessly upstairs with his attendant at his heels. Another servant showed him into the room which had once been her own, and the door slammed behind.

There was a bitter taste in her mouth. No. Of course there were no Bessarions waiting for her here. It had been so foolish to hope. She stood numb and silent beside the fountain until Lord Balian came over.

"Marta? What's the matter?"

"This was *my* home," she whispered.

He dropped a hand on her shoulder, warm and comforting. "Then let it be your home still."

Marta looked up at him. Since Lord Balian had taken her from the textile workshop, all her thoughts had been bent on getting to Jerusalem, in the hope of finding her family again. But of course not. There were no Bessarions here, otherwise Lord Balian would not have been waiting for one to appear so that he could offer up the spear. She was the only one.

It was time to face the truth: there was no way back either. Black sorcery had brought her to this place and this time, and only black sorcery could take her home, or otherwise a miracle. She could not command miracles, and she had seen what happened to those who used sorcery.

She was alone.

Her fingers tightened nervously on the shaft of the spear, remembering the last time someone had offered her sanctuary. "My home, in return for what?"

"In return for nothing. I'll foster you like my own daughter."

She must have looked doubtful.

"There's no return," he insisted. "You are a Bessarion, and I am the Prester of the Watchers' Council in Jerusalem. It is my sacred duty."

"Thank you." She wished the words didn't ring so hollow.

He still searched her face in the torchlight, concerned. "Miles told me what happened in the garden. I'm sorry. I should have made it plain that you're a lady and ought to be treated like one. Were you frightened?"

Marta shook her head. "I had the spear."

"But not the training to use it. We'll have to find you a good husband; someone you can trust to wield it in your name." Marta's shock must have shown on her face, for he quickly added, "But there's no need to think of marriage at once. You must have the time to make your choice. Meanwhile, I'll call one of the women to get you settled in."

Balian beckoned towards the courtyard, but Marta hesitated and he dropped his hand again, watching her with quiet sympathy.

"You're a quiet thing, Marta. Do you have any questions about this?"

She bit her lip. *We don't deny a woman her inheritance,* he had said. She had watched Lord Balian and his wife, how he and the other high lords listened when she spoke, how the soldiers obeyed when she commanded. Perhaps he would not laugh at her if she asked.

"Might…might *I* be trained to use the spear?"

He looked surprised, but not aghast. "Why not? A little training in arms is good for any lady to learn. Of course."

"One more thing," she said, a little bolder now. "How much does it cost to buy a slave?"

"That depends on the slave. Do you want one?"

"One of the girls at the workshop was kind to me. Her name was Persi."

"I'll buy her for you. Anything else?"

"Someone to teach me Frankish." Cautiously, Marta allowed herself to hope. Was Lord Balian really offering her a new home, a new family? A place in this beautiful new world?

She might never know what had become of the people she loved, but Marta could make a place for herself here. If it lasted.

You have until the king dies, the Messenger had said. *After him, the fire.* If the Watchers failed, and the kingdom fell, she could not bear to live through a second Oliveta. She could not lose a second family.

What have you done to redeem this kingdom?

Marta took a deep breath.

Let this be her place. Let this be her mission.

Chapter IX.

"The Courtenays see us as a threat now. They won't forgive. They won't forget."

As Marta approached the armoury, Queen Maria's voice drifted up into the cool dark stairwell. The dowager queen spoke softly in Greek, and Marta knew instinctively that she was not meant to hear.

The Courtenays? Marta clutched her spear and edged closer, a knot of anxiety forming in her gut. Although Lord Balian treated her like one of his own children, she could not help feeling that a blade hung over her by a single thread. She had spent much of the past six months just trying to understand this new world, let alone find a place or a purpose. Thus, she felt compelled to master all the strange currents that flowed beneath the calm surface of her new life.

So much had changed in the last four centuries. Palestine as she had known it was racked with war and famine, a neglected province of the weakened Roman empire. But in the last hundred years of peace it had bloomed: new crops, orchards, castles, churches and marketplaces dotted the landscape. The burgesses had grown rich trading spices, sugar, glassware and soaps. Quite ordinary people dressed in gorgeous silk, and lived in fine new houses with running water and glass windows. Jews, Samaritans, Nestorians and Monophysites no longer met in secret for fear of persecution, and even the Saracens were permitted their own places to worship.

It was beautiful. It was right. She only wished her father was here to see it.

It was not always so. Old men and women spoke of a time when war was commonplace, leaving the towns decimated and churches destroyed, their rebuilding forbidden. Then eighty-one years ago, Franks from the west had conquered Jerusalem, setting up four realms dedicated to defending the holy places of Palestine and Syria and protecting the thousands of pilgrims who flocked to visit them. To this day, the prince of Antioch, the count of Tripoli, and the king of Jerusalem, with most of their vassals and many settlers, were descendants of Franks who had given up their patrimonies in the west and, in some cases, married easterners. Lord Balian had Syrian blood, and the Leper King, Armenian.

Yet in the far north of Syria, the Frankish county of Edessa had fallen, forcing its ruling family to find sanctuary in Jerusalem. The Courtenays. Suspected as foreigners, resented as interlopers, but firmly linked to the throne of Jerusalem. Politics in the kingdom had become a chess-game. On one side were the Leper King's mother and her kin, the Courtenays. On the other were his father's kin, the prince of Antioch and the count of Tripoli. Last Easter, when Lord Balian had joined Tripoli and Antioch in their march on Jerusalem, they had all but started a war.

Now, at the queen's words, Marta's gut tightened. Since the old Messenger's warning, Marta had expected something to threaten this new family. She simply hadn't expected it to come from the kingdom's internal politics.

Inside the armoury, Lord Balian replied in the same language. "At least Lady Sibylla managed to defuse the situation before it came to a confrontation. Sometimes I think she saved us from making a terrible mistake."

"But she *didn't*." The queen's voice was tight with worry. "It's no secret we tried to force a marriage on the king. For the sake of his own honour, he *must* retaliate."

"He's not vindictive, Maria. He knows we were only trying to secure the succession. Rest easy—it's been six months, after all." After a moment, Balian sighed. "There's nothing else we can do."

"*He* may not be vindictive," the queen said, "but the Courtenays have never forgiven me, and *they* are the power behind the throne."

By now, Marta was getting a grip on the tangled history of Jerusalem's royal house—a heritage forged by Frankish warlords and eastern princesses in the turbulent years following the western conquest.

Seventeen years ago when the Leper King's father ascended the throne, the barons had demanded he repudiate his wife Agnes of Courtenay, to whom they had taken a dislike even then. Frankish kings were not emperors: they must listen to their barons. So the marriage with Agnes was annulled and a new bride soon arrived from the court of Constantinople. Maria Comnena was own niece to the Greek emperor, a much more prestigious match than the discarded Courtenays, who had lost their land when the Saracens destroyed Edessa. But the new marriage hadn't lasted long either. Within a few years the old king had died, leaving Maria a dowager at twenty.

That was six years ago now. Queen Maria could have returned to the safety and wealth of her home in Constantinople, but if she had done that she would never have seen her young daughter again. Instead, she had stayed and married Lord Balian.

Behind Marta, a door opened and eight year old Princess Isabella clattered downstairs, disrupting the conversation in the armoury.

"Ah, there you are," said Lord Balian cheerfully, coming to the foot of the stairwell. "Ready for your first lesson?"

Marta and Isabella followed him through the dark, cool armoury and the shady peristyle beyond, into a blazing-bright courtyard lined with pockmarked white sand. Although it was October, rain had not yet arrived and the summer heat lingered. Marta blinked in the harsh midday light and twirled her spear experimentally.

It was time to learn to use it.

"I'm still not sure about this, my lord." Queen Maria emerged from the doorway, pulling on a black silken veil to shade her face from the sun. Beneath the veil, she wore a mail shirt and gambeson, incongruous on her short frame. "I should only look like a fool, trying to handle weapons."

"You aren't in Constantinople anymore, your Imperial ladyship," Lord

Balian teased her. "Nablus might be your dower fief, but it doesn't even have *walls*. You should know how to defend yourself."

"Defend myself? Surely you jest. That's what I married *you* for."

It was a good match, too. Lord Balian had become a great man in marrying King Amalric's widow. The youngest son of Ibelin now ruled the wealthy dower fief of Nablus in addition to the little fief south of Jaffa that gave the family their name.

Marta sighed. Nablus was beautiful, a jewel in Galilee, but she knew Ibelin. In her time it was called Jamnia, the site of her father's seaside estate. She shifted restlessly, making her mail jingle, and thought what a strange thing it was that Lord Balian should own both the old Bessarion properties, as well as her father's spear. Not even Lord Balian could explain it, but there was certainly some kind of connection between this family and her own.

Again, something pulled tight in her gut. She was here to help protect the kingdom, but she'd make sure nothing hurt these people either.

Lord Balian tossed a wooden practise sword in the air, caught it by the tip, and offered the hilt to the queen. "My mother, Helvis of Ramla, was once set upon by bandits as she made a pilgrimage from Mirabel to Saint Abraham. Thanks to my father's insistence that she have the proper training, she was able to hold her people together, repel the attack, and then pursue the bandits to their lair above Bethgibelin, where her people slaughtered them all and freed their slaves."

The queen accepted the sword gingerly. "She must have been a terrifying person. But in all earnest, my lord, I am wealthy enough to pay my garrison."

"And so I trust you always will be, my lady. But garrisons must be commanded by those who understand the use of weapons." Lord Balian turned to Marta, offering her another wooden sword. "Lay the spear aside, Marta. You must master a few basics first."

As she returned to the welcome shade of the peristyle, footsteps echoed in the dark armoury. Marta looked up with a little jolt of awareness. It was Miles, with the conspiratorial wink he kept especially for her and a collection of helmets in his arms.

"Try that on, my lady. I tried to find one to fit a dwarf like you." He jammed one of the steel caps onto Isabella's head.

Isabella giggled in delight. "I'm not a dwarf!"

"Oh yes? You'll need to grow a bit taller before I believe that, my lady." He turned to Marta. "Try this."

She leaned the spear carefully against the armoury wall and pulled the helmet on, finding that it was only a little loose. After six months, he'd taught her enough of the Frankish language to understand about half of his jokes. Most of the local Syrians didn't speak Frankish, but nor did they speak Syriac. Palestine had been ruled by the southern heretics so long that everyone spoke Arabic now.

She was learning that, too: it was the only way she could communicate with Persi.

Miles offered another helmet to the queen, who took off her silver circlet and settled the steel cap on above her veil.

"Not a word, young man," she warned.

"You look lovely, my lady." Miles reached over to adjust the wooden sword in her grip. "Hold it like this, not like that, or it'll fly out of your hand the moment you strike something."

The queen drew herself up haughtily. "My husband is my teacher, Miles of Plancy."

Lord Balian chuckled. "That's right, Miles, your pupils are over there."

"Work, work, work." Miles rolled his eyes. "Can't wait to get home to Kerak."

At first, Marta had supposed that Miles was Lord Balian's son. In fact, he was his squire—a young knight in training, whose primary job was tending his lord's horse and armour. His real father had been a powerful lord in the kingdom, but Miles' mother had been nobody—some chattel belonging to the Plancy estates across the sea. As a bastard, he would never inherit his father's lands or title.

Miles grabbed a wooden sword of his own and beckoned Marta and Isabella closer to the peristyle, a safe distance from Balian and the queen.

92

"You first, Marta. Try to hit me." He grinned, encouraging.

Marta hesitated.

"Oh, you won't hurt me. I'm made of iron. See?" He clanked his steel mitt against his helmet. "Come on."

Marta lifted her sword and tapped him on the designated spot.

"Ow!" he yelled, dropping his sword. *"Blessed* martyrs!"

Marta froze in horror.

Isabella chuckled. *"Miles.* Stop putting it on!"

Miles straightened and grinned. "That wouldn't have killed a midge. Come on. Hit me!"

He was teasing her. Marta blushed fiercely, gripped her hilt, and jabbed the sword at Miles' midriff.

"Oo!" He crumpled to the sand, groaning.

"Oh, no!" Marta dropped her sword.

"Arrrgh, you've killed me."

Isabella was in stitches and this time, Marta joined in weakly.

Miles leaped to his feet with a grin. "Lesson one, Marta. When we were fighting in Cacho, you froze up. You saw that you'd hurt me, and you let yourself miss an opportunity to run away. You were fortunate then, because we weren't trying to kill you. But you're going to have to train yourself not to apologise for hurting people. They will be ruthless. So you must train yourself to be ruthless, too." He handed back her sword. "One more time. As though you mean it."

Marta swallowed. "I don't think I want to be ruthless."

As he met her eyes, his suddenly became cold. "Remember those men in the garden in Jerusalem? What if I was one of them? What if I wasn't going to be satisfied with a kiss?" He stalked forward, lifting his sword. "Would you be able to stop me? *You have to mean it."*

Marta took a deep breath, set her jaw, and aimed a mighty buffet at the squire's thigh.

Miles moved faster than she could see. Something jarred her hands. There was a burn across her right palm, and then her fingers clutched air as the practice sword flew from her hand.

Marta staggered backwards into the peristyle, and Miles followed. Wind whistled on the wooden edge of his sword, forcing her back and back. Then he lunged, shoving her against the armoury wall and pinning her there with a stiff forearm against her chest.

Fear went through her like a spike, and Marta reacted on pure instinct. Her right hand closed around her spear and swept up the blunt end like a truncheon. Something like a thunderbolt shot through her, a terrible strength. The spear connected with Miles with impossible force, punching him backwards.

He slammed against one of the peristyle's stone pillars and crumpled onto the sand beyond. Isabella shrieked, not without enjoyment, and clasped her hands to her mouth.

Beyond, Lord Balian and Queen Maria stared.

Miles lay motionless. *Strife!* She'd sworn to *protect* this new family of hers, and she'd already nearly killed him twice. Marta dropped the spear and rushed to his side.

"Miles! Miles, speak to me!"

His face screwed up, pale with agony. "Can't…breathe."

"You winded him!" Isabella chuckled. "Serves you right, Miles! You're practically a *knight* and we don't know anything. That wasn't fair!"

He groaned again, rolling onto his elbow and putting a hand to his head, which had cracked against the pillar. "Your turn's…coming, parakeet," he gasped.

A shadow fell over them. Lord Balian. "Are you hurt, Miles?"

"Only my pride." Between words, Miles fought for breath. "Saints, Marta. Are you sure that was you? *Felt* like getting kicked by a horse."

"Lesson's over," Lord Balian said before she could reply. He stepped into the peristyle, picking up the spear. "I want you taken to the physician immediately, Miles. Make sure you don't have a commotion of the brain. My lady," he added, to Queen Maria, "will you—?"

The queen nodded, steadying Miles as he got up and following him into the armoury. Lord Balian shoved Isabella firmly through and closed the door behind them.

Marta swallowed, forcing herself to stand her ground as Lord Balian turned to her, balancing the spear on his palms. He'd been kind to her, but then so had the priest at Cacho before she found herself locked into the weavers' workshop.

"I'm sorry," she whispered. "I didn't mean—"

"Don't be," he said quickly. "I heard what Miles said to you. I saw what he did. You reacted appropriately."

"I hurt him. Again."

"Yes." He held out the weapon with a faint smile. "That's why we use blunts to spar with. But the Bessarion Lance is no ordinary weapon, Marta. With it, one man has the strength of ten."

She laid hold on the spear, but for a moment, he didn't let go. "We've always kept it a secret, even from our friends. Used it sparingly, only in battle where men do incredible feats and the fog of war blinds even our allies to what is happening. It's yours, Marta, but men might kill for power like this. Take care that it does not betray itself—nor you."

Chapter X.

"How old are you, Marta?" Isabella grinned up at her.

All morning, Marta had been accompanying the young princess in her lessons. Isabella was learning four languages—Greek, Frankish, Armenian and Arabic—as well as copying family trees from both sides of the Mediterranean. In the last few centuries, it seemed Marta had skipped over a complicated tapestry of history. Lord Balian himself had come to give them a little conversational Arabic, and now the two girls followed him through the palace's garden and up the loggia towards the queen's solar, where the family usually gathered for an hour at noon.

"I'm fourteen, my lady."

"Fourteen! That's old enough to marry. Do you want to be married, Marta?"

Marta's cheeks warmed. "I don't know." In the old days, she'd sometimes heard her mother and father discussing this or that young noble as a possible match for their daughter. The idea had always been rather alarming. Now, however, she found she couldn't help thinking of Miles. She would always think of him as a friend, first and foremost, yet she loved the way he talked with her and teased her, how generously he gave his time to train her. Even when she'd nearly killed him twice.

Maybe, if it was someone like Miles, she wouldn't mind.

She had hoped that Lord Balian hadn't heard the conversation, but the tall nobleman grinned at her as he stood back to let Isabella enter the open, airy solar. "I did promise to find you a good husband, Marta. What about the four young princes of Galilee?"

Marta remembered the princes from a recent visit. The eldest must be at least twice her age, and all of them had looked down haughty noses at her, before promptly forgetting she existed. Although Lord Balian treated her like a daughter, she suspected that to everyone else she'd always be the poor relation.

Still, she didn't want to seem ungrateful. "My lord, I...I didn't get to know them very well."

Incorrigible, Lord Balian winked. "I understand if you need more time to find your place here. But if anyone takes your fancy, let me know and we'll see what we can arrange."

Instantly, her thoughts returned to Miles. He'd often spoken of leaving Nablus once he was knighted. Maybe if she told Balian about him—

The thought died instantly. Maybe he wouldn't want her! Maybe Balian would laugh! Her face reddened just at the thought.

The queen's solar was a luxurious room, made cheerful with painted frescoes above inlaid marble half-walls and gorgeous carpets of red-and-blue dyed wool in patterns of intertwined birds and flowers. While Lord Balian headed outside again to look for the queen, Isabella grabbed a handful of dried figs from a faience bowl, then settled next to the diamond-paned window that overlooked the garden as she gobbled them. She beckoned Marta to join her in the window-seat and whispered conspiratorially.

"I know just who would suit you, Marta. Shall I tell you what letter begins his name?"

"No!"

"His name begins with *M.*"

Marta blushed. "Likely no one would want to marry me. I have no family tree."

"Neither does *he.*"

"Isabella, I'm serious. No."

"What will you *do* then? Will you be a nun?" Isabella grimaced. "You shouldn't do that, Marta. You like fighting too much."

Relieved to have changed the subject, Marta couldn't help laughing. "No fear! Persi and I have a *secret plan.*" True to his word, Lord Balian had bought the Nubian slave for her. He had been more than a little surprised when Marta instantly freed the girl.

With nowhere else to go, Persi had chosen to stay and work as her waiting-woman, but her heart wasn't in the work. Soon, however, she had suggested a better use for their time.

"Does it involve hitting things?" Isabella looked arch.

"A little bit." Marta wiggled an eyebrow.

Isabella flicked her fair hair over her shoulder, returning to the main subject. "Well, I don't have to worry about my family tree. My half-brother is the king! Every count in the kingdom will beg to marry me."

"Who has been telling you this, my daughter?"

Marta started guiltily. The queen dowager had appeared noiselessly at the door, and now she sailed in with a shimmer of fine silk. Lord Balian strolled after her with little Helvis perched on his shoulders. Behind, a nurse carried baby John.

Isabella shrugged, unperturbed. "Madame Anna taught us today about the lady Queen Melisende and her three sisters. Everyone wanted to marry them."

The little queen sank into her chair and beckoned to Isabella. "Come here sweeting, and talk with me."

Isabella ran up to her, smiling, and the queen kissed her. "It's true, my darling, but it is nothing to boast about."

"Why not?"

"Because high ladies like you and I do not marry to please ourselves. We marry for other reasons. To provide a strong leader for our people, like Queen Melisende or the Lady Sibylla. Or to make alliances between neighbouring princes, like I did in marrying your father."

"What about Lord Balian? You married him to please yourself."

"Liking and policy went hand-in-hand there, my darling." The queen smiled at her husband. "But not for you, that's the pity. Your brother will die one day, and he has no children. Lady Sibylla has made two marriages for the kingdom already. You must make another."

For the first time since Marta had known her, Isabella looked taken aback.

"Such solemn lectures for the rest-hour." Lord Balian swept two year old Helvis to the ground and sat next to the queen, putting an arm around her shoulders.

Isabella's frown cleared. "Tell us a story," she begged.

"Ah!" Lord Balian lifted his eyebrows. "Let's see, what will I tell you today?"

"There's Montgisard," the queen suggested. "You were there for that yourself."

Isabella clapped her hands. "I know this one!"

"Then maybe I should tell a new story."

"But Marta hasn't heard it!"

Balian laughed. "Montgisard, then." He pulled a small inlaid table close, unstoppered a bottle of blotting sand, and poured it in little heaps onto the table, drawing maps with his finger among the white grains.

"This happened in the third year of the reign of the Leper King, when most of the knights and barons of Jerusalem had gone away to campaign against the Saracens in the north. At that time, Sultan Saladin was living in Egypt. The moment our army left the kingdom, he gathered his own and headed straight to Ascalon. Do you remember who the lord of Ascalon was then, Isabella?"

Isabella had the answer at the tip of her tongue. "Humphrey of Toron, Constable of the kingdom."

"Very good. And why did Saladin ride towards Ascalon?"

"It belonged to the Egyptians for a long time." Isabella wrinkled her forehead. "And he wanted it back."

"But why was Ascalon important?"

"The Saracens used to land ships there and send men to raid the kingdom."

"Very good. So if Saladin could recover Ascalon, he had a way to raid the kingdom. Perhaps even begin to conquer it."

Isabella bounced in her chair. "But he made a mistake! Saladin went *right* past Gaza, and it was full of Templar knights."

The Templars—Marta didn't quite know what to think of them. Knights who took the vows of monks but did not give up arms, the Order of the Temple was dedicated to guarding the kingdom, garrisoning border fortresses or escorting bands of pilgrims to and from Jerusalem.

In her own time, no monk wielded arms. But Lord Balian said that it was just as holy to do works of mercy and even battle as it was to fast and pray, so long as it was for the defence of poor pilgrims.

It wasn't what she was used to, but Lord Balian was the Prester, so he must know. Besides, right and wrong didn't change depending on who you were, and if it was right for someone like her to protect poor people from bandits, why not a monk as well?

Lord Balian grinned and continued with his story. "Right again. So the Leper King gathered all the knights, barons, and Turcopoles that were left in the kingdom. We left the ladies to defend Jerusalem, rode to Ascalon as fast as horseflesh could carry us, and hid inside the city ready to defend it with our lives."

He grimaced. "Saladin was delighted! With most of our knights fighting in the north, and the rest shut up in Ascalon, he could do whatever he liked! We were so sure he intended to strike Ascalon that we never imagined what he'd do next. He turned aside and marched for Jerusalem herself."

"Why was that, Isabella?" the queen put in, quietly.

Isabella bit her lip. "Because he hates the Christians and wishes to defile the Holy Sepulchre?"

Lord Balian shook his head. "The reason is that if he doesn't make war on us at least once each year, he will lose his right to rule and worse, his hope of heaven. In his eyes, *we* are the infidels."

Isabella stared. "He thinks *we* are infidels? But…"

"Strange, but true." Lord Balian lifted a finger. "It's important to remember that even Saladin can be reasoned with. Bargained with. Won over. Some will tell you that the Saracens are no better than witless beasts, but I've met Saladin. He's just like us: he's a man with a soul, and he wants to save it.

100

"But in this case at least, there was no bargaining. Not with an army of twenty thousand headed towards Jerusalem. The Leper King sent messages to the Templar knights at Gaza, and at once they abandoned their city and flocked to join us.

"Now the hunt was up. Would we catch up with the Saracens before they reached Jerusalem? And even if we did, could we win? The Saracens outnumbered us three to one. Even with the Templars, we numbered fewer than five hundred knights. The rest were footmen—easy pickings. The king was barely more than a child, sixteen years old, and already weakened by his disease. So he put command of the battle-host in the hands of Prince Reynald, the lord of Kerak in Moab."

"Miles' wicked stepfather!" Isabella showed her teeth in a dramatic grimace. "Marta, guess what Prince Reynald did to the Patriarch of Antioch once? Tied him down in the sun and covered him with honey so the flies would nip him!"

"Oh, my," Marta said faintly.

Balian shook his head, laughing at his irrepressible stepdaughter. "The Leper King bandaged his sword to his right hand, lest his grip weary. He barely needed his reins, for he can govern a horse with his knees better than most men can with both hands." For a brief moment, Balian's smile fell away. "Saints, what a king he might have been!"

Once again, Marta thought of the boy she had met in the palace garden. What a contradiction he was: a king, leading an army into battle. A leper, weeping in the dark.

A saint, holding back the wrath of heaven.

Balian sketched battle-lines in the sand. "We caught up with Saladin outside the fortress of Montgisard. There, we took them utterly by surprise and pursued them until nightfall. All the plunder they had taken and all the captives from the villages they had burned fell back into our hands again. Many of their people surrendered to us. Saladin himself threw away his armour, leaped to the back of his fastest camel, and so escaped. Some saw my lord Saint George himself fighting for us that day.

"Now, Isabella. What mistake did Saladin make, to allow us so great a victory? Do you remember?"

Isabella screwed up her mouth in concentration. "Uh, he left the Templars at Gaza."

Lord Balian nodded. "That was part of it. But there was more."

"His men left their weapons with the baggage! When the battle started, they couldn't get at their spears and battle-axes."

"Right again. Marta, can you think why he might have made all these mistakes?"

"Oh...uh..." Marta felt suddenly nervous.

Queen Maria came to her rescue. "He underestimated his enemy."

"Exactly." Lord Balian nodded. "He left the Templars in Gaza; he left the king in Ascalon; he left his weapons in the baggage train; and mounting folly on folly, he failed to leave scouts at his rear. When we attacked, he had no warning."

Isabella scoffed. "What a fool!"

"Not so fast." Balian was intensely serious. "What have I been telling you, Isabella? *Never* underestimate your enemy. Saladin is very far from a fool, and next time he will leave *nothing* to chance. We should learn from his mistakes, not laugh at them. He surely will."

Queen Maria drummed her fingers thoughtfully. "Say the battle had gone badly. What should the ladies of Jerusalem have done when Saladin appeared at the gates?"

"Your mother's very wise, Isabella! Here we are speaking of battles in the field, when I should be teaching you to defend a city. All right, my lady, tell us what *you* would have done."

The queen's eyes unfocused as she considered her answer. "First, I should have posted scouts, so I should know that he was coming. Second, before he came I should send out messengers, in hope of aid. Third, I should admit the peasants within the walls, with their cattle and their goods. Fourth, I should send out a parley to Saladin."

"A parley!" Balian's eyebrows rose. "And what would you say to him?"

"First, I should offer him gold to go away and leave us in peace."

"Ha! Tell me, my lady, do you happen to be a Greek?"

"Pish," she said. "I'm a realist."

"Then *be* a realist, lady. You are a princess of Constantinople no longer. Would the Sultan of Egypt and Damascus accept any such modest sum as a lady of Jerusalem might command?"

Maria Comnena haughtily lifted her chin. "Naturally not, but we might haggle it over for days. Meanwhile, his men die of thirst and sickness outside the walls."

"You *are* a Greek." He laughed, undaunted by her frosty tone. "I beg your pardon. Go on."

"When that fails, we might hold out to him hope of surrendering the city, and waste more weeks in settling a price."

"And if the price is too high?"

"Then fight to the last drop."

Balian's laughter faded. "That is a desperate counsel. Especially in a land like ours. Gold we have, enough for our needs, if not enough to buy off the Sultan of the east. But men's lives…those are scarce, and therefore precious."

"What then? Would you have us surrender Christ's own city?"

"If there's no hope of holding it, then yes." Balian stared into his winecup. "Jerusalem is Christ's own city no matter who rules there. Let him entrust it to whom he will."

A servant slipped through the curtain that covered the door, and bent down to speak to the queen in a whisper. The colour drained from the queen dowager's face.

"Maria?" Lord Balian touched her arm. "What is it?"

The queen swallowed, fighting to regain her composure. Still caught up in the story, the children noticed nothing; only Marta saw the effort she made to keep her voice steady, and her whole body chilled with a sudden premonition.

"She's come herself, on an errand from the king."

"Who?"

"Countess Agnes." Queen Maria took a quick, shallow breath. "She never forgot."

Chapter XI.

Despite her nausea, Sibylla kept the silk curtains of her litter shut tight during her journey through the city streets. People exhausted her. At the best of times, she preferred not to leave the peace and quiet of the home she now shared with Guy, and this was far from the best of times. She was sick again—pregnancy was never easy for Sibylla, but then, as she always told Guy, dynasties didn't come cheap. The effort of carrying a child was no easier the second time, the pain often forcing her to spend most of the day in bed. Things were better now, but for a while she'd had trouble caring about anything enough even to *try* getting out of bed.

Sibylla gripped the wooden frame of the litter, hoping her stomach would settle before she had to use the brass bowl in the crook of her elbow. All the same, she noticed the silence.

It was six months since she'd married Guy. Franks or Syrians alike, the people of Jerusalem had little love for Westerners, but usually someone had a "God save my lady Sibylla!" for her, or a "Blessings upon you, little Lord Baldwin!" for her son with Longsword.

This time...nothing.

Forgetting her sickness, Sibylla twitched an edge of the curtain aside and glanced through. There *were* people in the narrow street; they were just watching in silence. As she peered through the gap, one of them lifted hands to trumpet: "Poitevins, go home!"

"Lecher!" someone else yelled.

Riding ahead of her litter, Guy turned towards the hecklers, his face reddening and his hand clenching on his sword hilt.

Lecher. Sibylla settled back into her litter with a sigh. She had been so sure that if anyone's reputation suffered from the discovery of Guy's sword in her bedroom, it would have been her own. No one expected a normal red-blooded knight to be chaste. So why did everyone blame *Guy* for seducing her into marriage? Did they think she had no mind of her own, merely because she was incapacitated by child-bearing?

Well, she could work with that. It was the *power* of a queen she wanted, not the fame, and she would wear the crown and seal the charters whether or not they saw her doing it. She only wished that Guy had not yet again been saddled with the blame for something that was not really his fault.

They came to a halt at last on the slopes of the Mount of Olives.

Guy opened the curtains and lifted her gently into his arms. "You look tired."

Sibylla had managed to keep her morning meal inside her, but now she wondered if it would have been wiser to have it out. She leaned her head against his shoulder, taking deep breaths to steady her stomach. "You look ready for battle."

"It's the Ibelin faction," he growled. "The Watchers. They still haven't forgiven me for snatching you out of their grip."

She smiled and left a kiss on his clean-shaven cheek. "Thank you for keeping your temper." A short way further up the slope, pavilions and the smoke of campfires among the trees marked where the other barons had gathered to begin the hunt. It was late October, and the heat had become less oppressive. "Is Chatillon here?" she murmured.

"He's here." Guy shifted her to a more comfortable position and strode up the hillside as easily as though she weighed nothing at all. "Are you sure you want to speak to him alone?"

"You've done your part. Enjoy the hunting. Chatillon needs to learn that I have a head on my shoulders and a will of my own."

"I've done my part? All I did was arrange this meeting."

"Which took some doing, believe me." Sibylla's voice was dry. "I have tried to buy him before, you know. It is wonderful what an interest he takes in my fortunes now that I have a husband."

"What do you always say? Strong alone…"

"…stronger together." Sibylla finished.

The olive-trees bore strange fruit: horns, hoods, and quivers. Beneath them, hounds sniffed each other and horses nosed the grass, while servants bustled to and fro serving wine and wheaten cakes to the lords and ladies sitting at table. Sibylla couldn't bear the smell of food, so she had the servants place her chair and cushions a little way from the table, looking towards the city across the Kidron Valley. The dry grass of summer was just beginning to show green again, and at the foot of the Temple Mount, the resident Templar knights had just ventured out for their day's training at the pells and quintain.

Guy lowered her gently into the seat, putting the footstool beneath her feet and helping to arrange the cushions comfortably at her back. Sibylla sank back with a sigh. Already, the fresh autumn air made her feel a little better, and the sight of Jerusalem on the hill opposite filled her with quiet pride. Eighty years ago, chroniclers recorded the city as dry and treeless. Now she was surrounded by pools, orchards, and olive-groves—both evidence and source of the kingdom's growing wealth.

Reynald of Chatillon did not come to speak to her until after the hunters had returned to lead the company in search of quarry. Chatillon's wife, Lady Stephanie, and his stepson, the handsome, stuttering Humphrey, went with them. As those who remained gathered into knots to talk, the battered old prince limped over with a glass of wine in one hand and a folding-chair in the other. "Well," he said as he subsided into it, "I hear you're breeding again, my lady."

Sibylla's lips tightened with distaste at his choice of words, but Reynald of Chatillon was too pig-headed to take any notice. Like Guy, Chatillon had come east as a young man. He had schemed, plundered and married his way into becoming the prince of Antioch. Then, when he'd had to hand over the princedom to the young heir, he had come down to Jerusalem and done it all again.

Now he was the lord of Transjordan, responsible for the kingdom's most dangerous frontier. He was brutal, he was cunning, and he was waiting for an answer.

He should be reminded that weakness came to everyone, in time. "I hear *you're* suffering gout again."

Chatillon grinned wolfishly, his voice dipping. "Tripe! Needed an excuse not to join the hunt. So, you wish to be queen, my lady?"

"Wish? My father was King Amalric. My grandmother was Queen Melisende. Wishing has nothing to do with it. I was born and raised for the throne." There was a moment's silence as Chatillon watched her appraisingly. Sibylla said softly: "I did not come to convince you of my right or ability, my lord. I only want to know your terms."

"If your claim is so secure, then why do you need *my* help?"

There was no point in being too clever. Sibylla answered with complete honesty. "Ramla has sworn an oath never to recognise Guy as king."

"And the other Watchers?"

"I'd prefer not to give them the opportunity to declare their opposition."

"I see." Reynald showed his teeth. "You say you're competent to rule: very well. Arrange something for me. Think of it as a test."

"Sounds fair."

Chatillon sipped his wine thoughtfully before continuing. "You have a sibling problem, my lady. Your brother is a dead man, but Isabella is also a daughter of Amalric, and a grandchild of Melisende."

"She is only eight years old. Hardly a rival."

Chatillon leaned back, his tone casual. "Now, perhaps. But a few years hence? Don't delude yourself! She was born 'in the purple'—while your father was king. And to the favoured wife. Some might call that a better claim than yours. The Watchers surely will."

Due to Queen Maria's remarriage, Prester Balian was the only father Isabella had ever known. If she became queen, the Watchers would effectively rule the kingdom, and Sibylla, as the defeated rival, would have to be suppressed. Sibylla laced her fingers over her belly. "I don't delude myself, believe me. I assume she has something to do with your terms?"

"The king nearly lost his throne at Easter. He doesn't want the girl under

107

Watcher influence any more than we do." Chatillon drummed his fingers on the arm of his chair. "As it happens, he owes my stepson a favour on account of old Humphrey's death saving his life at the battle of Banias."

"Your stepson? Young Humphrey?" As she suspected, Chatillon wanted a royal marriage for his heir. "Is he noble enough to marry the king's own sister?"

"She's third in line to the throne after you and your son—soon to be fourth—she doesn't need to marry a magnate. Besides, the king doesn't want Isabella with the Ibelins any more than you do. Once she's betrothed to Humphrey, she can be shifted to Transjordan, where I can keep an eye on her. And believe me, he's the one you want her married to." Chatillon spat derisively. "Done what I could to toughen him up, but he still prefers books to swords. Effeminate beggar."

"He sounds perfect. If you don't mind my asking, my lord, what's in it for you?"

"What's in it for me? My stepson married to the king's sister!"

Sibylla lifted an eyebrow, making sure not to betray her own suspicions. Once Chatillon had Isabella under his thumb, what was there to stop *him* doing exactly what he accused the Ibelins of, and ruling the kingdom through her?

Chatillon leaned closer. "The Watchers love me as little as they love your mother. The king won't distrust them forever. I need…a pledge. Some security for when they sneak back into favour."

So Chatillon felt insecure, did he? Sibylla folded that information away for future use, and considered whether she wanted to give this man a weapon like Isabella.

Yes, she decided at last. He was right about young Humphrey of Toron: she needed Isabella married to someone safe. Chatillon was old, and would not be a threat for very much longer. With both Tripoli and Antioch on the side of the Watchers, she and Guy *needed*allies.

Chatillon might feel insecure, but many of the barons looked to him for leadership, especially those who resented the Watchers' political meddling. Isabella would be dangerous anywhere, but in Chatillon's hands, at least she would be useful.

"I'll speak to my brother," she said.

* * *

Her conversation with Chatillon done, Sibylla saw no reason to linger. Pleading ill-health, she sent a servant after Guy to let him know she had gone, then ordered the servants to carry her back to the city.

She wasn't lying about how she felt: the smoke of the campfire had given her a headache on top of the usual aches and pains, and she knew she was coming to the end of her endurance. Still, now that she had gone to the effort of leaving the house, she should speak to the Leper King before she rested. If Isabella must be dealt with...

Unbidden, the young girl's face appeared in her thoughts. Isabella, with her dark curls, her round face, her ready smile. It was odd that she could remember the girl so clearly. For one thing, it didn't pay to lavish much attention on young children; death by misadventure or illness was always a little closer at that age. For another, Sibylla barely knew her half-sister. With different mothers, they had of course not been brought up together. Still, she had seen Isabella and her mother together at Easter, and couldn't help noticing the way they interacted, the way Isabella lit up when the queen spoke to her.

She cared little for her stepmother, yet she couldn't help imagining what it would feel like if someone took away her own son, simply because he was a political rival. As the sound of horses outside broke into her ponderings, Sibylla tried to shake the thoughts from her head. For the sake of her son *and* the kingdom, she could not afford to be sentimental. Yet still her sister's childish face hung in her thoughts, and Sibylla's resolve wavered. The sound of horses outside interrupted her musings, and Sibylla tried to shake the thoughts from her head. For the sake of her son *and* the kingdom, she could not afford to be so sentimental. Yet still, Isabella's childish, carefree laugh rang in her ears, and Sibylla's resolve wavered.

Cantering hooves overtook them and danced to a halt. Hearing Guy's voice, Sibylla twitched the curtain of her litter aside. "Guy?"

His horse moved restively, but he kept his seat with careless grace. "I received your message and came to see you home."

"I wasn't going home." They were in the Kidron valley, approaching the city gate. Sibylla glanced at the dappled shade in the olive grove of Gethsemane to the left. "Come aside and speak to me."

He dismounted, throwing his reins to an attendant, and they walked arm-in-arm into the grove. In the shadow of one of those massive, gnarled trunks, Sibylla turned and laced her fingers into Guy's.

As he searched her face, a tiny crease formed between his eyebrows. "He asked a steep price, then?"

"He wants Isabella as a wife for Humphrey."

For an instant the crease remained, then smoothed away. "Isabella? For Humphrey? Is that all?"

"It seems...unkind, somehow. Taking the child from her mother, handing her over to that old brute."

Guy's grip tightened. "What, like they tried to hand *you* over to Baldwin of Ramla?"

Sibylla guided his hands to her rounded belly. "But if it was *your* child?"

"I'd do whatever it takes to keep my child safe." He bent down, kissing her above the girdle. "I'd destroy the Watchers so they could never do this to *me.*"

"You think I should go ahead with it?" She stared, unseeing, at the blue horizon. A black bird of prey hovered with wings outstretched, unmoving, in the sky. "What will I tell my brother?"

His grey eyes were serious. "Tell him the Ibelins started this, not you. If they're too dangerous to be trusted with the girl, they have only themselves to blame."

He was undeniably right, and Sibylla sighed, the tension ebbing from her shoulders. For a moment, emotion had almost overruled sense; an indulgence she could not permit if she was to be a queen. "Of course. How foolish of me."

She headed back to the litter already rehearsing what she must say to her brother. "Don't bother to see me home," she told Guy. "I am going to the palace."

When Sibylla limped into her brother's solar, she was relieved to see her mother sitting opposite the king with a sheaf of papers in her hand, presumably going over some business. Although Sibylla often suspected Countess Agnes' political decisions of being short-sighted and partisan, she had a healthy respect for her mother's powers of persuasion.

Agnes jumped to her feet, all concern. "Sibylla! You should be at home resting."

"Nonsense, mother. It's just the baby."

The king looked anxious. "I would be happy to send you my own doctor…"

Sibylla sank into her mother's vacated chair with a sigh. She didn't like her brother's solar: she felt oppressed by the brightly-coloured frescoes painted on the plaster, the busy mosaics on the floor. When she was queen she would have the walls, at least, whitewashed. "Every doctor in the kingdom must have stared at my urine by now. They all say there's nothing wrong with me. What are you and Mother discussing?"

"Saints." Baldwin heaved a heavy sigh. "It's the new Patriarchal appointment."

The Patriarch that had officiated at her marriage to Guy had died only a few days ago after a short fever. Now it was the king's job to appoint a new bishop of Jerusalem. "Who are the candidates?"

"Well, there's Archbishop William." Countess Agnes looked disapproving.

"He's the obvious choice," Baldwin insisted eagerly, swivelling to face Sibylla. "He's served this family for three generations, all the way back to Grandmother Melisende. He's an educated man—he taught me everything I know. And he lives a particularly holy life—which is more than you could say for Archbishop Eraclius."

Agnes sniffed. "Eraclius is at *least* as learned as William…and, more importantly, he isn't a Watcher."

"What's wrong with the Watchers?" Baldwin shot back. "They build hospitals, give to the poor, and try to live holy lives. Sibylla, what do *you* think? Here's a petition from the kingdom's clergy, asking to have Archbishop William."

Sibylla took the petition from Agnes and ran her eyes over the names. It was an impressive list, but there was another detail that struck her. "Many of these signatories are also Watchers, brother."

"Should that frighten me?"

She laid the paper on her lap. "Baldwin, you might not have noticed, but last Easter when you nearly lost your throne to a coup—*all those men were Watchers.*" She counted them off on her fingers. "Baldwin of Ramla. Walter of Caesarea. Raymond of Tripoli. Balian of Ibelin, the Prester himself!"

"Archbishop William had nothing to do with that."

"Maybe not. But the fact is that no matter how the Watchers began, no matter what they *say* their purpose is, they've been controlling the politics of this kingdom for generations. They don't want any new blood in the kingdom—no more than when they forced Father to divorce Mother all those years ago. And now that she's in power again, they're determined to get rid of her and Uncle Joscelin, and if all else fails they won't hesitate to get rid of *you.*"

"I don't believe it," Baldwin said, but there was a shadow in his eyes.

"Then you haven't been paying attention. They will push you off the throne, and they will use your sisters as puppets. That's *exactly* what they tried to do at Easter." Sibylla nodded at Countess Agnes. "I agree with Mother. Even if Archbishop William *would* be a better Patriarch, we can't afford to give the Watchers any more power."

Baldwin stared at his bandaged hands. "William will be disappointed."

"Then tell him he can have the appointment," put in Agnes. "So long as he ceases to be a Watcher."

"I can't ask that of him! The Watchers are everything to him."

"*Really.*"

"Saints! All *right*, then." Her brother let out a shaky sigh. "As God is my witness, Sibylla, *I hate doing this.* I wish they had taken the damned throne."

Countess Agnes spoke gently. "You don't really mean that, my lord."

"No." He sighed. "I was anointed king. I have to do this until I find the right heir...or until it kills me."

The right heir? Sibylla thought, alarmed. For now, she let it pass. She and Guy were ready to rule; but Easter had taught her a lesson, too: the time was not yet ripe. "Speaking of the Watchers, have you given any thought to our half-sister?"

"To Isabella?" Baldwin looked startled. "I don't suppose *she's* planning anything."

Sibylla ignored his sarcasm. "Of course not. But since we agree that the Watchers are dangerous, surely we can agree that she ought not to be left in their care."

"Well, it's not as though I can take her from her mother. She's too young."

Now that she had made her decision, Sibylla found herself curiously unmoved by this argument. "Why not? We were taken from ours as infants. As it happens, Reynald of Chatillon was sounding me out today about a possible match between Isabella and young Humphrey. She's still a few years off marriageable age, but if there was a betrothal, it would be only natural to send her to Kerak for the duration."

Baldwin's voice sharpened. "You seem to have a lot of plans laid, Sibylla. Why doesn't Chatillon speak to me himself?"

"I have no doubt he will. He only asked me what I thought, and I said it had my approval. You can repay your debt to Humphrey of Toron and neutralise Isabella at the same time."

"Neutralise her? She's a child!"

"She's the last of our father's children," Sibylla said coldly. "That makes her dangerous. The Watchers tried to force me into a marriage of their choosing; what makes you think they'd hesitate to clap up some match for Isabella? Realms have been usurped in that way before now. Look at Aunt Alice in Antioch."

"Saints." Baldwin sank his head into his bandaged hands. At last he spoke, somewhat desperately. "Look, she's only a child. She needs her mother, not a *husband.* The Watchers may play politics, but they wouldn't force a marriage on an eight year old girl for the sake of power, and I won't do it either."

"It wouldn't be a marriage. It would be a betrothal."

"No! You already convinced me to hand the Patriarchate to Eraclius over William's head. Leave me with *some* self-respect, will you?"

"Self-respect? Since when is securing the throne something to be ashamed of?"

"Since when is dragging a child away from her mother securing the throne?"

"Since Easter, brother. Do keep up."

At her sarcastic tone, he flushed. Instantly, his voice changed, deepened with authority. "You forget your place, sister."

"Children," Agnes warned, but Sibylla felt herself go icy cold.

"I have not forgotten my place, but I think *you* have. *You* are king, not me. *You* should be protecting the kingdom, not me, and yet you shrink back from doing what must be done and call it self-respect? Why? Because you think you're a good man?"

"I'd like to be," he bit.

"Go ahead, then. Make William Patriarch. We all know he deserves it. We all know you owe it to him." She waited, but her brother didn't respond. "No? Didn't think so. Be a king, or be a saint, but for heaven's sake *commit* to one of them and stop trying to do the right thing with one hand and the smart thing with the other."

"Children," Agnes snapped.

Sibylla grabbed the arms of her chair. "It's all right, Mother. I should go."

"Sit down." Agnes' voice softened. "Baldwin, she's right. I know it's not what you want to be, but Jerusalem needs a king."

Baldwin got to his feet, grabbed his crutch and limped to the window looking out onto the garden. For a long time, he only stood there. Sibylla looked at her mother, impatient, but Agnes shook her head.

At last, her brother spoke.

"We're the children of kings, Sibylla. People like us may enjoy privileges beyond anything most people can dream of, but we also pay a price. Ruling a kingdom is hell. I've always told myself I don't want to shield my sisters from that; I want you both to be prepared." He thumped his crutch discontentedly against the floor. "Have it your way, then. Let Isabella learn the price of her high birth."

"For the good of the kingdom," Sibylla said softly.

Baldwin sighed. "For the good of the kingdom."

Sibylla went home with her victory sitting like lead in her gut. *I want you both to be prepared,* Baldwin had said.

Until I find the right heir, he had said.

Baldwin's claim to the throne was safe. But what about her own?

Exhausted and aching, Sibylla pushed the thought away, measured out a dose of a laudanum-and-hemlock-infused wine, and sank gratefully into oblivion.

Chapter XII.

"I know what this is." Queen Maria stood with shaking hands; her eyes darted sidelong to Isabella and then back to Lord Balian. "I have been afraid, ever since..."

"Maria." Balian caught her wrists gently. "Breathe. We can buy out of it if we have to."

"It's no *use.*" Her voice became a hissing whisper. "After what happened at Easter...She's too dangerous to leave with us. The Courtenays want us handicapped, and they will have *no* mercy."

"Maria," Balian said again, but this time it was his eyes that flicked towards Isabella. The queen dowager stiffened.

"Marta," she said after a moment. "Isabella has been working hard at her lessons all morning. Why don't you both have the afternoon off? Take one of the squires and go on an excursion."

With that, she and Balian hurried from the room.

Marta watched them go with worry churning her gut. Ever since she'd come here, something had been hanging over this new family that had been given to her so miraculously. Now it was happening at last.

She was surprised by the fierce protectiveness that rose up within her at the thought. Lord Balian and Queen Maria could never replace her own father and mother, yet Marta knew instantly that she would go just as far to protect them.

During the whispered conversation, Isabella had left her seat and was now half hanging out of the coloured-glass casement. "I can see Countess Agnes!" she squeaked.

Marta jumped from her seat and caught Isabella by the back of her tunic. "Don't fall out, my lady!" she warned, forcing herself not to lean out herself to hear everything she could of the conversation below. She needed a distraction, for both of them. "Come and see what Persi and I have been doing."

The palace at Nablus was three levels high, with sleeping quarters above and living quarters amidst. The lowest floor, half dug into the bedrock, was cool and dark, lit only by high narrow windows. Down here the horses were stabled, grain and merchandise was stored, and many of the lower servants had their sleeping-quarters. Marta led Isabella down a dark internal staircase until they emerged into one of these dingy storage-rooms where big bales of wool, ceded from Queen Maria's demesne, towered above them.

Clack-clack! Clack-clack!

"Do you hear that?" Marta whispered. "That's Persi hitting things."

They ventured between the bales to find a loom set up in the ray of light from one of the high windows. Isabella's face fell. "Weaving? Is that all? I thought you meant fighting. This is *servants'* work!"

Persi stilled the loom's treadles and put down her shuttle, laughing. In the six months they'd known each other, Marta had learned to speak Arabic and Persi, Frankish. Now the Nubian smiled, her teeth a white flash against her onyx skin. "In *my* country, they say that weaving is a very special kind of magic, my lady."

The web on the loom was made of fine wool dyed dark indigo. Brighter colours glowed against it like fire: blue the colour of duck's eggs, a bright saffron on the knife's edge between red and gold. Isabella couldn't help touching it. "That *is* magic. How far is your country, Persi?"

"Not too far, but far enough." She didn't go on. Marta knew that the memories were sorrowful for her friend. It had taken months for her to speak of it, and when she finally had, Marta knew she had been greatly favoured.

Persi was born in a city of scholars and pilgrims, Silimi on the Nile, but her parents had been weavers and she grew up amidst the clack of looms.

117

That is, until the war.

After Saladin took control of Egypt, a stream of fugitives began to arrive in Nubia, from Egyptian and Armenian nobility, loyal to the old regime, to peasants fleeing the harsh servitude their new sultan had imposed. They wanted to recover their land, and Nubia was the obvious place to turn for help. Persi had watched the alliance march north through Silimi to take Aswan…and then flee back with Saladin's armies behind.

As the northernmost town of Nubia, Silimi quickly fell to the Saracens. The occupation lasted two years before distance and harsh climate forced them to retreat. On the final day of the occupation, Persi's brother threw a stone and an insult at the Saracen general, but it wasn't him they took as punishment. It was Persi.

The story became vague after that. At some point, Marta gathered, Persi's skill as a weaver had been discovered. After some years in a textile workshop in Cairo, she was sold in the slave market there to an agent of the lord of Caesarea, who brought her to the textile shop in Cacho.

Isabella looked curious, but Marta knew Persi was reluctant to tell the story again. Instead she twanged the warp-threads, making the fiery cloth dance in the light. "I chose the colours and dyed the thread. Persi is weaving the kind of pattern they use in her homeland in Nubia. When we have finished the weaving, some wealthy merchant will pay a high price for this."

Persi nodded. "We use expensive dyes and finest thread. That helps us sell at higher prices and earn a fair rate for our work."

Marta beckoned. "Look at this, Isabella."

Beyond the loom was a table covered in scraps of paper. Each paper bore tiny grids, and Marta had used sparing dabs of coloured paint to pick out different designs. Some of them were Persi's Nubian designs Persi had described and Marta had coloured. Others were the products of her own imagination—abstract whirls and starbursts, geometric lines and ripples, sinuous birds and beasts.

Isabella's eyes widened. "Did *you* draw these, Marta?"

Persi stilled her loom and came over to join them. "These ones are mine."

118

"Mine are mostly just mathematics," Marta explained. The truth was that drawing the patterns made her feel better when she was missing home—her old home. Her father used mathematics to construct plans for buildings, and he'd taught Marta much of what he knew.

Isabella stabbed a finger at a pattern of birds. "I want a gown made of this one!"

Persi laughed. "Oh, yes? Can you afford it?"

"Mama can!"

The little girl's unwavering confidence made Marta's smile fade as she remembered the stark fear on Queen Maria's face. Children couldn't always be kept safe and happy. She closed her eyes, remembering her little brother Paulus, and the misery on his face as he was torn away from her.

In the hush, voices filtered through the iron grille over the window and Isabella's attention flashed away from her. "That's Mama," she whispered. An instant later she had scaled a tower of wool bales and knelt at the grate, peeking through into the garden beyond.

"Isabella," Marta hissed.

"They're talking about a wedding!" Isabella whispered over her shoulder. Then she stiffened, her eyes widening. *"Mine."*

Marta's stomach knotted. An instant later she was next to Isabella on the wool-bale, peering through the finely-wrought spiralled iron. Persi followed.

The narrow window looked into the garden. Between two raised beds of herbs, Lord Balian stood with his arms folded, staring at the ground. In front of him, Queen Maria faced another woman a few years older than Balian—slight, dark-haired, and strikingly beautiful despite her forty-odd years.

That must be Countess Agnes, the cast-off wife who had become the mother of a king.

"I knew you would have your revenge someday," Queen Maria said bitterly, "but I had hoped that whatever you did to me, you would spare my child."

Agnes smiled, and Marta immediately hated her. "You ought to have thought of that before you marched on Jerusalem."

"Let me take her to Constantinople," the queen said wildly. "We'll leave the kingdom, I swear it. We'll go so far away that no one will be able to use her. Please."

"The child belongs to the kingdom. Not you."

Agnes turned as though to leave, but Queen Maria stepped in front of her, still desperate. "I understand if I must lose her. But...*Kerak?* Was there *nowhere* else?"

"Chatillon is trustworthy. You are not."

Agnes took another step, but again Queen Maria stopped her. "Agnes," she said. No honorific. No title. The countess froze.

The queen stepped closer. Marta could only just hear her quiet voice. "You were never my enemy," she murmured. *"I* did not choose to marry Amalric. *I* did not choose to give him another heir. I have never knowingly harmed anyone in my life." She took a breath. "But I am not so old that I cannot begin."

Agnes' face was a mask. "You blame me?" she asked. "This was no decision of mine. Blame the king, if you must."

Queen Maria's fists clenched, but this time when Agnes stepped away, she didn't follow. Lord Balian looked up and followed the countess back towards the courtyard where her retinue waited, and still the queen stood there, staring at the herb bed.

Her face crumpled, and she whirled, rushing into the house.

Atop the bales, Isabella tugged on Marta's sleeve, looking up with a wobbling lip. "Am I going to live with Prince Reynald?"

Belatedly, Marta remembered that she was supposed to *keep* Isabella from witnessing this scene, not to help her eavesdrop. As the little girl's face crumpled, Marta wound her arms tightly around her, heart aching. *Not Isabella. Not her, too.*

"We'll see."

But Isabella was sobbing. "If I'm b-bad will he cover me in honey and let the flies nip me?"

"Of course not, chicken. You're a princess."

"He did it to the P-Patriarch!"

Marta couldn't speak. She pulled Isabella closer, and looked to Persi, hoping for comfort, but the Nubian girl looked just as unsettled.

"There's something wrong with that woman." Persi rubbed her eyes, looking dazed. "Something *very* wrong."

* * *

"It could be worse." Queen Maria stood at her window gazing out into the darkness beyond. Her face was still red from crying, but she was breathing deeply, determined to go downstairs and play the hostess as soon the signs of tears had passed. "Humphrey seems gentle and scholarly. And young, only six years older than she is."

Marta finished arranging the white silk veil over the plump queen's head and stepped back to admire the gauzy siqlatin fabric, with its delicate gold-woven border. Through the open window, the sound of talk and laughter signified that their guests were already gathering in the dining-hall.

Countess Agnes had given them no time to object to the betrothal and very little chance to draw breath, for within a week of her visit, Reynald of Chatillon had arrived with his wife and stepson. Tonight, the betrothal ceremony would be followed by a feast. Tomorrow, Isabella would return with her betrothed husband to his home in the distant Transjordan.

"Beautiful work, Marta. Thank you." Queen Maria touched the veil without looking at it as she tried in vain to argue herself into hope. "He will not be a man of many vices, I think."

Leaning against the frame of the window, Lord Balian frowned. "He will not be a man of many virtues, either. Since they arrived here yesterday I have tried to talk with him, but if it wasn't his mother answering for him, it was Chatillon."

"He's still only a boy."

"In a matter of months he will be fifteen, and a man. This is folly! If Isabella should inherit the kingdom, do you think the barons will follow that boy?"

"His grandfather—"

"Is dead. And it would be better for all of us if the Courtenay woman remembered that!"

Even after Marta closed the door behind her, she could hear Lord Balian's voice booming indistinctly from the next room, closer to anger than she'd ever seen him.

As for herself, she only felt confused. *The Courtenay woman.* Persi had disliked her on sight, although she wouldn't explain why. Marta had assumed it was the barely-suppressed sense of triumph she'd sensed rolling off the countess.

Yet Agnes had made it clear that it wasn't *her* decision to send Isabella to Kerak: it was the king—that soft-spoken boy she'd found crying in a palace garden. Everyone blamed Countess Agnes for ruining the kingdom, but Baldwin was the king, wasn't he? Sooner or later, *he* was the one who said yes or no. Which meant that this was *his* fault. No politics could justify taking a little girl away from her mother.

Not for the first time, Marta thought that she would like to ride to Jerusalem and give him a piece of her mind. Yet Lord Balian had already been to see the king, and it had not helped at all. Who was Marta to think she could do better?

She sighed and walked down the loggia to the room she shared with Isabella. It was time they both dressed for the ceremony. As Marta passed the top of the stairs from the courtyard, Miles came up them at a run and nearly barreled into her.

"Marta!" He caught her elbows, steadying them both. "I didn't see you there in the dark. May I see Isabella? Lord Humphrey had a trinket he wanted to give her."

Marta nodded sadly, and led the way to Isabella's door. Inside, the princess' nurse was combing her hair as she perched in silken damask splendour on a stool that didn't let her feet touch the ground. Marta's heart sank further at the sight of Isabella's dejected face.

"Miles has a gift for you, my lady."

"You do?" Isabella's gloom vanished.

Miles held out a little wooden box. "It's from Lord Humphrey."

Isabella scowled ferociously. "Take it back to him! I don't want it."

"Oh, come on." Miles shook the box, making an expensive-sounding rattle. "I'll wager it's pretty."

The nurse sized the box up at a glance. "It will be jewels, my lady. You should wear them tonight for the betrothal. Here." She put out her hand for the box.

"I don't *want* them!" Isabella shrieked. Then she slid from the high stool and rushed to Marta, winding her arms around her waist and burying her face. "I d-don't want to go," she wept. "I d-don't want to leave Mama…"

Marta jerked her head towards the door, signalling the others to leave them. The nurse obeyed, but Miles put the box on the stool and squatted down, stroking the little girl's hair.

"You won't be by yourself, you know. I'll be coming with you."

Isabella sniffled. "I don't w-want to m-marry that nasty boy!"

"Now then, he's not a nasty boy. He's a very nice boy. I should know, I've known him for years. He's my step—foster—sort-of-brother."

Isabella couldn't help a teary giggle.

"Look, little Isabella, I don't know what he is! My father married his mother after we were both born, before my father died and she married Prince Reynald. So he's my stepmother Stephanie's son. My stepbrother. He's nice, anyway. Very good-looking."

Isabella shifted her head to stare at him. "I don't want to leave Mama."

"But you want to be married, don't you? Countess Stephanie loves being married. She's been married ever so often."

Isabella wasn't fooled. "She had to. So that Transjordan had a lord to fight the Saracens." She seemed on the verge of dissolving into tears again.

"I know, I know. Just like you have to marry Humphrey so that the kingdom has a lord to fight the Saracens. Just like I'll have to marry an heiress so I can afford to eat Damascus apricots all summer."

"Don't *laugh* at me!" Isabella's arms tightened around Marta's waist, making her heart twinge with sympathy and remembered pain. "It's the Courtenays. They want to get me away from Mama and Lord Balian!"

"It's not the Courtenays, it's the king," Miles said, startling Marta with his perception. He went on reassuringly: "He'd never make you marry a boy who'd treat you badly. Trust me. Besides, you aren't going to marry him right away."

"Nurse says the king does what his mother tells him to do and he's too ill to know the difference!" The little girl burst into tears again, and Marta felt the hot tears seeping through her gown.

Miles muttered something under his breath and looked up at Marta appealingly. "She's not fit to be seen."

Marta shushed him and bent over Isabella, rocking her and waiting for her sobs to ease. A melody thrummed, first in her mind, then in her throat: the lilting psalm her mother sang as a lullaby.

Lord, hear my prayer, and let my cry
Have ready access unto Thee;
When in distress to thee I fly,
O hide not thou thy face from me.

The time for Zion's help is near,
The time appointed in Thy love;
O let Thy gracious aid appear,
Look Thou in mercy from above.

She sang of smoke, withering grass, and taunting foes, of drinking tears, and eating grief; and as she sang, Isabella's breathing grew calmer. Finally, Marta unwound the younger girl's arms from her waist and knelt down to look her in the eyes.

"Listen, chicken. Miles and I are going to make you a promise."

Isabella nodded, lifting a sleeve to wipe her eyes. Marta captured her arm and handed her a handkerchief instead.

"We can't keep Prince Reynald from taking you away." Not without setting off a war, anyway. Wild images of a midnight attack on the prince's convoy, just herself wielding her father's spear, danced through her mind and had to be pushed aside. That would only make trouble for Lord Balian. "We can't keep you in Nablus, but Miles is going to go with you and take care of you. He'll make sure Prince Reynald doesn't hurt you. Won't you, Miles?"

"I swear it," he said quickly. "Look, Isabella! I swear it." He whipped out his sword and kissed the cross on his sword's hilt. "I'll defend you from every enemy, my lady."

"And we're going to get you back," Marta added. "Remember that the world is round, and we never really leave home behind us. Lord Balian says we just have to wait until people calm down a little. He'll talk to the Leper King and arrange it somehow. You won't have to marry Humphrey, and one day soon your mama will go to Kerak herself and bring you home again."

Hope dawned in the little girl's face. "Do you swear?" She scrubbed her eyes with the handkerchief and turned to Miles. "Miles, do you swear? You'll take me home one day?"

"I'll do what I can, little Isabella."

"We'll never stop trying. Will we, Miles?" Marta looked from the tearstained little princess to the raw-boned squire, and a rush of pure affection went through her. She reached out, took Miles' hand to draw him into their circle. "We may not share the same blood, but we're family all the same. We'll go to the ends of the earth for each other. I swear it, Isabella."

"Family." Isabella grabbed Miles' free hand with her tiny paw. "Do you swear it, Miles?"

"I swear it, my lady. To the ends of the earth." He smiled down on her and kissed her little hand. "Are you ready to finish having your hair done now?"

Isabella sniffed and nodded. Marta kissed the tip of her nose and got up. "I'll send Nurse back in to finish you up."

Alone on the loggia, Miles hesitated before going downstairs. "Well done," he whispered.

She was glad the night was dark, so that he couldn't see the colour creeping into her cheeks.

"So you're leaving us."

"My time as a squire is over." He straightened, his teeth flashing in a grin. "I'm to be a knight."

"Thank you for training me."

"Don't stop practising: you're a natural. I've seen grown men handle a spear with less skill."

That made her cheeks burn in earnest. "Promise me something," she whispered.

"What is it, little Marta?"

She thought of all the things she would have said to her own mother, if she had had the chance. Or to Paulus and Elisa, her younger siblings. "Please...don't let Isabella forget us. Help her to remember that her home is here. In Nablus."

He reached out and swiftly squeezed her shoulder. "I swear it."

Next morning Miles rode away with Isabella, Prince Reynald, and his people. She did not see him again until three years later, in a ravine outside Medina.

Not quite the ends of the earth, but close.

Chapter XIII.

Arabia, AD 1183

"Marta Bessarion, as I live!" As close to speechless as she'd ever seen him, Miles stared at her through eyes glassy with pain.

He seemed to have forgotten how close they were standing to the Saracens who still milled in the ravine outside, looking for them. A crossbow-bolt protruded from his side and blood stained his linen surcoat.

"Are you badly hurt?" she hissed.

"Just a graze." Miles' foot slipped on the loose stones underfoot, jostling his wound, and he let out a stifled groan.

"Hush. You'll give us away!"

By now the Saracens were right outside their hiding-place. It was almost impossible to move silently in full armour, but the sound of calling voices, jinking armour, and hoofbeats outside allowed Marta to creep forward and peer between the rocks without being heard. A chill ran through her as a black shape moved into view: a Saracen rider waited just beyond the rock, close enough to touch with the tip of her spear. Man and horse were still as stone, silent as the grave.

All she could see was his grey-dapple horse and his dusty clothing, since his face was obscured by the rock. After a moment, a chill ran over Marta as she realised that he was *listening* for something. Had he heard them? She stilled, her grip tightening on her spear.

And then *she* heard it. Distant crying and wailing. Beyond the rock, the rider stiffened. Tensing to attack, Marta closed her eyes and whispered a prayer.

The rider kicked his horse into motion. As he did so, a hand closed on Marta's shoulder and she whipped in a breath and turned, bringing up her spear—

It was only Miles. She caught herself just as the spear-point grazed his breastbone.

Sidestepping the spear, Miles leaned past the rock and watched as the rider turned his horse and retreated to the scene of the Frankish surrender. The other scouts followed him. Moments later, the ravine had emptied and Marta relaxed her grip, trembling.

"Him!" Miles muttered.

"You know him?"

"Someone we captured raiding Egypt. Obviously a nobleman, but he wouldn't reveal his name, even when I tried to use him to bargain for our freedom. Odd."

Marta led the way back into the cleft of the rock where Omar waited with the horses. She stepped around him and pulled open one of the saddlebags, rummaging about for her medical supplies. "We'd best see to that wound."

The bloody crossbow bolt had done little more than nick him. A hand's breadth over, and it would have pierced his gut, dooming him beyond the shadow of a doubt. Marta took a long slow breath as the narrowness of his escape hit home: she might have lost another brother, and Isabella her only guardian.

Thankfully there was no barb on the tip. "Hold still and I'll pull this out," she murmured, handing him a leather strap to stick between his teeth.

He took the strap, but didn't clamp down on it yet. The ghost of a smile crossed his face. "How long has it *been?*"

Marta swallowed a lump in her throat. "Three years."

"Too long." His eyes crinkled, warm with affection. "Saints, Marta, where did you learn to fight like that?"

"From you, of course." She grabbed the bolt. "On the count of three, all right?"

"All right, all right." He bit down on the strap, and she counted dutifully to three and yanked. The bolt slid free, Miles groaned, and a moment later she had his hauberk and gambeson pulled up to wash the shallow oozing wound.

Miles winced as she gingerly sponged his side with wine. "You know, most of the time when the doctor says he'll count to three, he doesn't actually count to three."

"So what's the use of pulling sooner, if you're expecting it?" Marta lifted an eyebrow as she pressed a clean cotton pad to the wound. "I don't like to play with the truth for no reason. Hold that." She fumbled in the saddlebag for bandages. Beyond the rocks, a Saracen trumpet called and the slow sound of marching feet began fading into the distance.

Miles listened moodily. "God know what's going to happen to them. Poor souls..."

Marta's conscience stabbed her. She had been so selfishly focused on Miles that she had all but forgotten the other men. "I *ought* to have tried to rescue more of them...even if only one or two..."

Miles put a hand on her shoulder, and her heartbeat seemed very loud as she looked up into his kind grey eyes. "Don't blame yourself, Marta. We made our peace with this expedition. Bastards, exiles, human waste... We all knew there was no chance of ransom."

"Human waste?" Marta reached up to touch his hand, but their steel mitts met with a disconcerting chime. "Don't call yourself that, Miles. Even if Prince Reynald would abandon you, you still have other friends."

"The prince! We left him holding Eilat on the gulf—is he well?"

Marta tied off the bandage and stood, brow furrowed. "Of course he's well. Since sending *you* into danger, he's done nothing but relax. The moment the Saracens floated their ships on the Red Sea, they blockaded Eilat and the prince ran home to Kerak." She sighed. "Why did you do it, Miles?"

"Why? Saints, Marta! No Christian army has set foot in Arabia in *centuries.* And the Franks have *never* put ships in the Red Sea. Saladin never imagined we could. Who would have suspected that we would attack their pilgrim ships, threaten Mecca and Medina themselves? Saladin built his empire on the corpses of his own people, and if he can't even keep the pilgrims safe, then they'll begin to wonder if all that death was worth it."

His enthusiasm lifted Marta's eyebrows. "Oh? So harassing poor pilgrims is really a wonderful way to help them break free of Saladin's control? I'm glad you had the man who tortures patriarchs to explain that to you."

To his credit, Miles looked uncomfortable. "We didn't harass them *much*," he said at last. "I spared everyone who surrendered."

"So the prince came up with this harebrained scheme just to poke Saladin in the eye?" Marta sighed. "I'm sorry, I don't mean to give you trouble; it's just that Isabella *needs* you at Kerak. If you'd been captured..."

"That was my fault. I put my ships into harbour along the coast here and got myself blockaded by Saracen warships. We couldn't sail, we couldn't fight. We had to run." He shook his head. "I should have guessed they'd find a way to put warships on the Red Sea. But it's been five days afoot in the desert and I still haven't figured out how they got there so fast."

"Portage." Marta rummaged in the saddlebags again, coming out with twice-baked bread and dried salt meat. "They rolled the ships from the Nile to the Red Sea."

Miles took the food she offered him. "How do you know that?"

"Persi sent word."

"Persi? Whatever next? The two of you have turned spies now?"

Marta laughed, shaking her head as she unhooked a limp waterskin from the saddle. "Hardly! We're well-respected weavers. Persi is travelling to her homeland in Nubia to find her family and collect some samplers; the Makourian fashions sell well. Lord Balian thinks I am with her."

"You told Lord Balian you were going to Nubia with Persi? And you came to Arabia instead?" He stared at her again, as though what he saw fascinated him. *"Why?"*

Marta didn't answer right away, feeling a twinge of guilt as she stared at the saddlebag in her lap. She hadn't actually lied to Lord Balian, but she'd certainly let him believe something that wasn't true. "We made each other a promise, you and Isabella and me. Do you remember?"

"Of course I remember."

"I've already lost two brothers. I can't lose another." Marta had never told Miles the truth about her past. Even letting him see this much was daunting. "Isabella needs you too. Someday soon, Lord Balian will ask the Leper King for Isabella's return. When that happens, she'll need you more than ever."

He kept watching her, intent. "But all this way? Don't you realise what danger you're in, Marta?"

"I didn't have a choice. I made you a promise."

He gave her a sceptical look, and she laughed.

"I've taken every precaution. Look." She waved a black-and-burgundy tunic at him. "Bedouin gear, to disguise us with."

"Well, thank God for that. I thought you had ridden in here all by yourself with that iron pothelm on your head."

"Hardly. I travelled with Omar and some of his people."

The Bedouin was eating quietly from his own saddlebags. Miles stared at the guide's checked *keffiyeh* and kohl-rimmed eyes, and cleared his throat. "You're sure we can trust him?"

"He speaks Frankish, Miles."

Omar swallowed his mouthful and grinned. "I won't betray you, my lord. Mademoiselle there is paying me too well."

Marta raised an eyebrow. "Happy?"

Miles shook his head with a wry laugh. "Does nothing frighten you?"

How could she put the last three years into words for him? Three years of honing her skill on horse and foot until her father's spear almost seemed a part of her, as indispensable as a limb. Three years of stealing away from the Nablus palace in the grey light before dawn to seek adventure. Lord Balian wanted her to stay away from real war, to keep her identity a secret and the Bessarion Lance hidden, but there was work to be done that he simply could not do. It was she who had captured the bandits extorting grain from peasants, it was she who had made sure the headman of Kapheros stopped bullying his Samaritan villagers, and it was she who had appeared after the battle at Le Forbelet last year to shepherd the scattered and vulnerable foot soldiers to safety.

They called her the White Watcher.

A Watcher's mission was to do practical justice in everyday life. That was in her hands; Marta did not worry herself too much about the consequences. Heaven could take care of those.

She smiled. "Not much frightens me, no."

"What's the plan, then?"

"We ride back to the well where Omar's people are waiting for us."

"Not until nightfall," the Bedouin added. "The horses need rest. We'll need to ride hard all night to make it by morning." He nodded towards the ravine. "The rider beyond the rock. Did you know him, my lord?"

"The Saracen?" Miles nodded. "A captive we took in Egypt. He was a damned strange fellow. Looked noble, but sometimes he'd *say* things..."

Omar looked thoughtful, rummaging in his saddlebag for a knife and a block of acacia-wood. "Such as?"

"Oh, you know. The kind of thing you'd expect to hear from some old fanatic with barely a sound tooth in her head. That God loves the Leper King, but he'll abandon us once the king dies."

Marta stiffened. The old Messenger outside Jerusalem had said the same thing. *After the Leper King, the fire.*

The kingdom would only survive if its wrongs could be set right. Which was just one more reason why Isabella had to come home safely.

"Your king is a leper because of your sins." Omar's voice hardened and he dug his knife into the wood, flicking shavings against the rock. "That's a problem you can solve yourselves."

Miles said testily, "Why would God abandon us? We aren't *that* bad. It's not like we're Saracens. No offence meant," he added.

Omar grunted, clearly unimpressed. Whatever his reply might have been, it was forgotten as he looked out, past the stones, to the sky. Marta followed his gaze to see the black outline of a bird of prey riding the high heavens. Omar sat looking up at it, and his hands kept busy, whittling, smoothing, working as though their lives depended upon it.

"This place is being watched," he said. "Don't move into the open, either of you."

Marta didn't try to argue. When it came to the desert, he knew far more than she did. "Let's get some rest. We'll be safer once night falls."

She prayed that it was true.

* * *

"After that," Miles finished, "she was never allowed near the beehives again."

Marta wiped tears of laughter and gritty desert sand from bloodshot eyes. They had been riding half the night, following the brilliant throng of stars due north. The cold wind had blown sand into every fold and crease as it whipped across the flat grey expanse beneath their feet. Despite her afternoon nap, Marta's body longed for sleep. Stifling a yawn, she asked another question to keep herself awake.

"How was she when you left?"

"Nothing wrong with our Isabella. She's a blithe spirit."

"She must be eleven by now."

"Nearly a woman," Miles agreed. "But only acts like it about half the time."

Which meant that time was running out. "Are they kind to her?" Marta asked wistfully.

Miles hesitated. "Stephanie sees that she has everything she wants. The prince takes little notice of her."

Marta swallowed, imagining what a lonely life that might be. "That's not what I asked."

"Humphrey," Miles said after a moment. "Humphrey is kind to her."

"He'd *better* be."

Miles chuckled. "I verily believe you would ride him down and skewer him like a kebab if he wasn't."

"Only if he escaped you first."

"That's right! If he was unkind to little Isabella there wouldn't be much left of him by the time you arrived. You don't have to worry about her, Marta. Really. She's brave. She makes her own joy."

This time, her wistfulness was for him: "I wish you'd never left Nablus," she confessed. "Why don't you come back when Isabella does?" In the long silence that followed, Marta's heart plunged. "You don't want to *stay* with Prince Reynald, do you? He nearly got you enslaved!"

He sighed. "Kerak is the closest thing I'll ever have to a home and a family. I'm a bastard, Marta. Do you know what that's like? There's truly nothing lonelier. If I'd only been trueborn, I'd have lands, money, a title... I'd be able to do some *good* in this world."

"You have a home and a family with *us*, Miles."

She wished she could see his face in the dark.

Finally he replied, "Lord Balian was kind to me, Marta, but I've always known that if I stayed at Nablus, I'd never be more than a landless knight. At least at Kerak I have a chance to prove my worth. I'm already the prince's constable. Who knows? With this raid to my name, I might get a fief!"

"A fief?" Marta frowned. She couldn't imagine wanting to forsake the service of someone as wise and kind as Lord Balian, even for a fief. Still, perhaps Miles was right. A Frank of knightly birth, like him, wanted employment proper to his station, and Miles had been the offspring of a *great* noble.

So was she, of course, but then she had everything she'd ever wanted at Nablus: her father's spear, the training to use it, her loom and all the colours she would ever want.

"I'm sorry," she said after a moment. "I thought we were all so happy together at Nablus."

"We *were*." His voice warmed. "Marta Bessarion. I still can't believe you're really here. I swear, before you took off your helmet, I was sure you were either an angel or—who knows, with your face covered like that—maybe the Leper King! Never have I seen such tilting!"

Marta's cheeks burned as she rubbed her thumb lovingly along the shaft of her father's spear. "I've kept in practice."

"It's a miracle. How did you know I was in trouble?"

"It was a guess."

"And you guessed you'd find me at Medina? Come on, Marta, don't make me drag it out of you."

She tried to repress a smile. "All right. I knew Prince Reynald was planning a raid on the Red Sea because I heard Lord Balian discussing it with the queen. He said the Leper King was giving him money and craftsmen to build ships in the Transjordan. This was a few months ago, so I began to plan for it." She heaved a sigh and thumbed the lance again. "I thought, it's been so long since any of us saw Isabella, and we know we're unwelcome at Kerak. Lord Balian will be speaking to the king about it, so I wanted to send her a message. Tell her we still remember her, and we still want to have her back. So when Persi went to Nubia, I went with her as far as St Catherine's on Sinai."

Miles laughed again. "You rode off to Sinai like a knight-errant?"

She shook her head. "Like a burgess-woman, actually. We were able to get an escort of Templars most of the way. But I had my horse and my armour with me."

"All right: go on."

"I knew the prince would strike south to Eilat, and I meant to meet you there. By the time I arrived, you had already sailed, so I went back to Sinai and waited. When I heard that the prince had withdrawn to Kerak, I knew something had gone wrong. I rode into the desert again, to the nearest Bedouin tribe, and there's where I met Omar. They agreed to take me south. Early yesterday morning we met some relations of his who told us you were afoot in the desert and had hired some of their men as guides. After that it was easy."

Miles heaved a sigh. "It was still good luck that brought you at that moment. For that I vow a gold chain and the price of my best horse to Saint George. But only if he gets us home safely."

Marta's conscience struck her. "I'm sorry about the others."

"You couldn't have saved them; the Egyptians would have drilled you full of crossbow bolts first." There was a silence before his voice came out of the dark, empty and cold. "I suppose I ought to have stayed."

Marta stopped in her tracks. She had dragged him away from them without even asking. "Do you want to go back?"

"No. I won't risk putting them on your track."

"What will happen to them?"

"They'll live—as slaves."

"Then you must ransom them! Some of the monastic orders have funds for the ransom of poor prisoners. And there's always exchange, if you capture enough of *their* knights and sergeants."

"I can do that." Miles sounded relieved.

Marta yawned through a smile. "It can't be far off morning," she began, but then her horse stumbled and slowed, favouring a front hoof. She reined in. "Arrow has gone lame."

They'd been travelling for hours with barely a halt. When Marta dismounted, the animal stood with its head drooping wearily, lifting its foot with reluctance when she tugged at it. Touch told her at once what was wrong. She let the hoof fall and straightened with a sigh. "It's a cast shoe. Must have happened a while ago; the hoof is already ragged."

Neither of the others bothered to swear, although it was the worst possible news. After a short silence, Miles said, "Can it be fixed?"

"Not until we reach Omar's people," Marta replied.

Omar joined her and inspected the hoof himself. "It won't make it to the well," he said, straightening. "Open its veins and leave it."

"No," Marta protested. "I can walk."

"He's right," Miles said bleakly. "Even without a rider, after a few more hours on this ground it will be in agony."

Marta put a hand against the beast's muddy neck and closed her eyes, angry with herself for not taking better care of the animal. But Omar and Miles were right. The horse needed immediate rest and attention—and there was no way she could give them.

"Arrow," she whispered, "I'm so sorry."

Miles dismounted. "Do you want me to do it?"

"Please," she whispered.

The horse shuddered as Miles opened a vein, and Marta knelt down beside it, stroking its mane until it was gone.

After that, Marta took turns riding behind Miles and Omar. With one of the horses bearing a double burden at all times, they travelled more slowly.

Hours spooled by until one by one, the stars began to fade before the advance of dawn and the sky warmed to a clear, blue dome like enamelled glass. As the sun rose, it revealed a bare, scoured waste of rock and sand, broken only by dark scraggly shrubs.

In the grey light, Omar reined in. "The horses should rest," he said, his voice subdued.

Marta slid down from behind him, easing her aching body to the ground. "Might as well eat."

As they chewed on sandy bread, dry meat, and dates, Marta thought longingly of Nablus...nestled into the hills of Galilee, its white houses full of the scents of the soaps and perfumes made there. If she and Miles got back safely, she would spend a whole morning soaking in the baths before showing him the fine brocaded silks she and Persi were weaving, or else she'd take him to Ibelin, to the villa that had been her father's house before the Saracens came. They would wander the vineyards and pick grapes together, just as she and Lukas had done when they were young.

But Marta knew it would never happen, even if they did get back to the kingdom safely. Miles lived at Kerak now.

He grinned tiredly as she handed him food and collapsed onto the sand to eat it, letting his horse's reins trail on the ground. While they chewed in silence, Omar poured the last of their water into a collapsible leather bucket for the two remaining horses, then faced south to make his dawn prayers.

As the light grew stronger, Marta realised that yesterday's clouds had vanished in the night, leaving the air clear with a promise of unseasonable heat. She wrenched another mouthful of dried salt meat, and looked south.

In the distance, a dark mass shadowed their trail.

Instantly, she dropped the food back into her saddle-bag and stood up, straining her scratchy eyes. A flash of light flickered along the shadow's border. Lance-heads. Bits and bridles.

"Miles," she hissed.

Miles blinked and turned. "Holy angels, defend us. Get up, Omar. How far to these people of yours?"

Reluctantly, Omar sat back on his heels and stared south at the pursuit. "If we can see them, they have certainly seen us." His shoulders slumped. "It's no use. There must be at least two hundred of them. God have mercy."

Miles looked at Marta and shrugged. Neither of them needed an explanation: the nomadic Bedouin resented the sultan, and the sultan distrusted the Bedouin, especially given how willing some of the tribes were to cooperate with the Franks. If Saladin's men caught Omar and his people helping Miles and Marta, they could expect no mercy.

Marta dropped to her knees in front of him. "Our lives are in your hands, Omar. Even if they've seen us, they can't possibly be close enough to know who we are. As long as we reach the well ahead of them, we can hide our gear and disguise ourselves as Bedouin."

Omar's eyes flickered to Miles, and back to Marta again. "Do I have a choice?"

"Yes. If you choose, you may take Miles' horse as payment and go. We will take our chances."

Omar stared at her, astonished. "You'll never escape them on foot."

Marta had given her word, and now she must stand by it. "We'll wait for them here," she said. "You owe me no loyalty, and you have your own people to think of."

He hesitated, and his gaze went beyond her, into the sky. "It doesn't matter," he said dully. "They'll know I was here."

The black outline of a bird of prey hovered in the fathomless blue above them. Marta stood up, a chill running through her despite the day's heat. "That bird has been following us since the battle yesterday."

"It's only a stupid vulture," Miles cut in, irritated. "Are you taking us to the well, Omar? Or are we going to sit here until Saladin's men pick us up?"

Omar got up and made a bow to Marta, lifting a hand to lips, then forehead. "Since I am about to die, let me have the honour of dying in the company of a generous lady."

Marta almost felt light-headed with relief.

"How far?" Miles asked.

"Hours yet. At the pace we've been going, not before noon." Omar dug into his saddlebags, extracting his block of acacia wood. "Will you take the reins, mademoiselle?"

Marta looked at it, puzzled. "What are you carving? An amulet?"

"Something more useful," he replied, "a spoon."

As Omar had predicted, they did not travel fast. Slowly, the sun crawled up the sky to noon; slowly, the distant pursuit crept nearer. By midday the horses were stumbling from exhaustion, and the riders were taking it in turns to walk.

They had run out of water at dawn. Spasms plucked at Marta's muscles and she felt dizzy from the heat.

"How much further, Omar?" Miles called for the tenth time.

Omar, still whittling as he rode, spared a hand to point to the eastern hills. "When we're directly opposite the jackal-shaped rock, we will have arrived."

Miles squinted behind at the nearing pursuit. By now, they could pick out individual horses and camels, and sometimes hear lifted voices on the hot gusting wind. The Saracens didn't seem to be hurrying. Why should they? Their prey had nowhere to run.

Miles groaned. "We'll never reach it at this rate. Time to make a dash for it. Put that knife away, Omar."

"My lord—"

"Do it." Miles motioned to Marta, who had been taking her turn afoot. "Best if you ride with Omar; we shouldn't put two suits of armour on one horse."

Marta nodded, silent from sheer weariness, and clambered up in front of Omar, who stuck his wooden spoon back in the saddlebag and sheathed his knife. Miles dug in his spurs with a yell, and the two horses quickened into a choppy, unwilling canter. It lasted only a few paces and then both animals fell back to a walk. With a grunt of frustration, Miles raked his mount with his spurs. "Run, devil take it!"

Instead, it took a few unsteady steps before its legs folded beneath it.

Above, the black vulture screamed.

As his horse keeled to the dirt, Miles kicked his feet from the stirrups and jumped free, barely escaping being crushed beneath.

Then Marta heard the *buzz-thwap* of an arrow.

Behind her, Omar suddenly went limp, then tumbled sideways and hit the ground.

Marta's head was so fuzzy, her throat so dry, that no sound of warning escaped her: she could only watch, as though from a long distance. She half-fell from the Bedouin's horse, fumbling for the shield she wore around her neck. "They're shooting at us!"

"Can't be. They aren't within range." Miles staggered to Omar and rolled him over. The Bedouin's face was pale and clammy. "It's the heat."

Buzz. Thwap. This time, it was the last horse that gave a puff of exhaustion, and lay down as though it was too tired to go on standing. Marta turned to face their pursuers, lifting her father's spear for an overarm cast. But it was not the Saracens that met her gaze.

"Marta. Marta. What are you doing?" Miles staggered to his feet beside her.

"Don't you see him?" Marta choked.

"Who?"

Across the sand and through the midday glare, a terrifying creature stalked towards them. Tall and thin, its body was clad only in scales and hair. One huge eye was positioned at the centre of its forehead. The other blinked solemnly from the centre of its chest.

Miles edged up on her, reaching for her spear. "Marta, put that down. You're seeing things!"

"Don't!" She elbowed him aside.

Slowly, the hairy creature raised a short bow of horn and laid an arrow to the string. Marta shrieked and hurled the Bessarion Lance, putting every ounce of her strength behind it. The creature saw her coming and dodged, so impossibly fast it almost seem to blink from one place to another.

The spear struck the earth and stood there, quivering. The creature reached out a hand as though to take it, but his hand passed through the haft like smoke.

With something that might have been a shrug, he turned back to Marta and lifted his bow.

Miles grabbed Marta by her shoulders. "Look at me, Marta! There's nothing there. Focus—"

His grip was weak, but Marta couldn't get free of him. "Miles," she whispered, staring past him.

The hairy creature took aim again.

The ghostly arrow flew, striking Miles between the shoulder-blades. His eyelids fluttered. "Oh," he groaned, and slid soundlessly into the dust.

Standing over his body, Marta lifted her shield and drew her sword, but she knew it was futile. Her mind was a blank, her tongue paralysed as though in a nightmare. As the creature stalked closer, she backed away. If only she could remember her mother's prayers against devils—but all memory had fled.

A bolt of black fell from the blue sky, landing on two bare feet beside the hairy creature. Up close, the bird of prey that had followed them for two days proved to be a woman covered in black feathers, with claws for hands. When she saw Marta, she licked her red lips. "Look at this! A little Watcher, lost in the desert!"

Marta backed again, her lips trembling, as a fragment of her mother's prayer finally formed in her mind. "Lord God, send down a mighty angel—"

Again the horn bow sang. The arrow pierced straight through her shield and hit Marta like a fever chill, draining the strength from her body. The heat was suffocating. She slumped to her knees, catching herself with her shield, and stayed there, held upright by sheer willpower.

Beyond the two nightmarish figures, camels and horse-mounted war-riors drifted ever closer, shimmering like a dream.

She would be dead long before they arrived. Marta clenched her teeth, her breath coming fast. *Fair father God, accept my soul.*

The hairy creature lifted his bow again, his smile a mask of cold glee. The heat grew more intense, radiating through Marta's body, trapped beneath multiple layers of armour and clothing. She was going to melt...

There was a hiss in her ears like raging fire; heat shimmered from the white sand around her.

Then it localised, beating on her right cheek like a bonfire. Marta blinked as the hairy man and feathered woman stopped moving, staring at *something* beside her on the right. Something that radiated visible heat.

Something bad enough to put a look of slack horror on both their faces. With an effort, Marta turned her head.

It stood nine or ten paces away, but even at that distance, the white flame rippling down its scaled flanks with each motion of its six wings was hot enough to scorch her face. It was the size of an elephant and white-hot as a star, its long serpentine tail writhing and coiling like a long and restless flame.

A dragon, Marta thought with the very little mind she had left. *Maybe I am delirious.*

The feathered woman screamed. The hairy man snapped his bow up, aiming at Marta again, but the weapon shattered as he drew it. A crest on the dragon's head lifted and the creature spat a torrent of white flame at the two devils.

Though she stood to one side, the blast knocked Marta flat on the sand. Groaning, she rolled onto her stomach, trying to climb to her knees. The heat intensified. Tremors ran through the rock into her body. Then a hot, clawed foot ground into the rock beside her and Marta looked up into the scorching heat of the dragon's face.

The creature opened its mouth and a long, thin tongue slid out, touching her precisely on the forehead.

Burning pain lanced through Marta's head and she arced backward, screaming until oblivion took her.

Chapter XIV.

Marta returned to consciousness with a jolt and a wail, throwing out a hand that landed with a splash in a bowl of water and shocked her fully awake.

Someone reached out of the darkness and guided her trembling hand back to her side, speaking in a soothing woman's voice. With the touch, Marta found that she was lying naked under a thin sheet of wet cotton. More water streaked her torso.

Marta cracked her eyes open, wincing as her head throbbed. She lay on low flat cushions in the dim coolness of a tent pitched in the shade. A geometric tapestry of red, blue, green, purple and burgundy formed a partition above her, dividing the tent in two; this was obviously the women's side, as hearth, pots, and looms could testify.

Marta swallowed painfully. The skin on her face was tight and painful and her throat felt as though it had been packed with sawdust.

"Water," she whispered. "Please."

A face loomed out of the darkness. Framed with a black veil above and silver embroidery below, it was a kind, plain face, the eyes lined with kohl, the forehead with wrinkles.

"It is forbidden," the woman told her.

It took Marta a few moments to realise why. Arab hospitality forbade harming anyone who had taken so much as a drink of water in your tent. So, they were in the hands of enemies, and not friends.

The enemies who had chased them across the desert all day.

"Please," she repeated. "I don't mind if you end up killing me afterwards, really."

"It is forbidden. I'm sorry."

The woman had evidently done as much as she dared. Marta closed her eyes. "Where's Miles? And Omar?"

"Your companions? Beyond the partition, still asleep."

A little light drifted through the partition at eye-level, where a strip of gauze allowed those on the women's side of the tent to see and hear what was happening beyond. Before trying to get up, Marta felt among the cushions, her heart speeding as she tried to find what was missing.

"My spear?"

"Your weapons are safe."

Marta blinked at the woman, observing her black-and-silver robes, capable hands and brass bangles. "Are you Omar's friends?" she asked without much hope.

A shake of the head. "You are in the tent of al-Na'im Abdullah ibn-Abdul, sheikh of the Bani-Iaith."

Bani-Iaith. At least this was a Bedouin tribe, not a division of Saladin's army. Marta shook her head and got up on her elbows. "If you will let me have my clothes back, I will speak to him."

The woman's face flickered in surprise, but she only hesitated a moment. "The sheikh will return soon from his council-meeting." Instead of Marta's sweat-stained gambeson and trousers, the woman gave her a clean black robe, embroidered skull-cap and veil. Once dressed, Marta gratefully accepted a bone comb and a mirror of brass from the woman to tidy her dripping hair, which had evidently been washed as she slept.

When she peered into the mirror to part her hair, she paused, staring. A light shone from the polished surface: the spot on her forehead where the dragon had touched her.

Or was it a dragon? Marta reached up to touch the burn.

Send down a mighty angel, she had prayed. And that *creature* had appeared to save her, that…fiery flying serpent.

A seraph, she realised. An unfallen dragon. A holy creature of fire and justice.

144

The Bedouin woman held out a box. "Aloes for your burns."

Marta watched the light on her brow wink as she dabbed the slimy preparation onto her hot, tight skin. "How does it look?"

The woman turned her face towards her. "Red and painful."

Evidently, only Marta could see anything out of the ordinary. "Thank you," she said slowly.

The woman helped her don the veil, pinning it to the skullcap to hold it firmly in place. Then, carefully so as not to show herself to the strangers beyond, she drew back the partition to let Marta through.

The vestibule beyond was furnished with more rich carpets and colourful cushions. A flap was lifted to admit light too dazzling for Marta's sore eyes. She turned to where Miles and Omar lay, watched over by a pair of armed manservants. Their armour and weapons were nowhere to be seen.

"Where are our arms?" she asked the servants.

"Safe," one responded.

Safe! From whom? Marta staggered to the tent's open flap, a black-framed image of green and gold. Outside the tent, dark acacias and palm trees clustered around a sheet of sparkling water. Lush grass tempted her feet. High walls of rock enclosed an overgrown basin, full of tents, livestock and people.

Omar's well, at last.

"Marta?" Within the tent, Miles stirred. "Where's Marta?"

"I'm here." Marta felt her wobbly way back inside the tent again and knelt by Miles. Nearby, Omar rolled over and sat up, his hair and beard sticking out in every direction.

Miles reached for her hand, sounding relieved. "Marta. Are you all right?"

"I'm all right. Thirsty, though." Maybe, if she could make it to the pool on her own—

"You seemed to have a touch of the sun."

Marta swallowed. He hadn't seen the feathered woman, or the hairy man, nor the arrows they shot. He hadn't seen the seraph. "Really, I'm all right," she said in Frankish. "But these aren't Omar's people."

Omar smoothed his beard and then rubbed his dry throat, making a face. "My friends would have withdrawn when they saw these coming."

"They won't give us water and they've taken our weapons. I can't find my spear."

Miles paled. "No water? Devil take it."

A shadow blocked the tent's entrance. "Are you looking for this?"

A man in a sheikh's black robes and white *keffiyeh* stood silhouetted against the light with the Bessarion Lance in his hands. Forgetting her headache, Marta jumped to her feet and took two quick steps towards him. In a twinkling his hands firmed on the shaft and the blade pointed towards her.

Marta froze. "That spear belongs to me."

She half expected him to laugh. Most Bedouin women didn't even show their faces to strange men, let alone train with arms. But he only gave a polite shrug and spoke in good Frankish. "I have heard differently."

After a moment, he moved into the tent, revealing a pointed black beard and silvering hair in short braids that framed his face.

"Well met, Sir Miles of Plancy," he said. "Do you seek death, my friend?"

Miles' mouth fell open. "Saint *Michael*."

"No," said the sheikh, bowing deeply. "Al-Na'im of the Bani-Iaith. We have been following your tracks all day."

"*You* were following us?" Miles leaned forward, burying his head in his hands. "You couldn't have signalled? We killed a good horse running from you, and we were about to sell our lives—"

"You were *about* to die of the heat. And even if not..." The sheikh leaned on the Bessarion Lance. "There is a price on your head, Sir Miles. We'd just left Medina, escorting this caravan to Damascus, when our paths crossed with the Egyptians and their prisoners. The sorcerer al-Aziz has been in communication with the Sultan. Saladin shows no mercy. The law is to be disregarded in this case, and all Franks who have campaigned in the Red Sea must die. No one shall return to Jerusalem in safety to tell of what he has seen."

Marta made an involuntary sound of distress. Guilt haunted Miles' eyes.

146

"I was *promised* they would be safe."

"Nevertheless." The sheikh's beard stirred in a small hard smile. "The price on your head is a fortune. I have had to spend much time in council with the elders."

Marta's hands clenched on nothing but air. Miles' shoulders slumped. "Is that the way of it, my friend? The ledger speaks?"

There was a flash of teeth within the black beard, and an answering flash as al-Na'im extended the butt of the Bessarion Lance towards Marta. "The ledger *does* speak to the Bani-Iaith, but it speaks in Frankish. Prince Reynald is good to our people. He has made me rich for giving him news of caravans and the movements of armies. The Sultan is only interested in taking; he spills the blood of our young men in waging war on the house of Islam to his own glory."

The tension in Marta's stomach unknotted as she felt the familiar weight of the spear in her hands. Miles looked every bit as relieved as she felt. "You will see us safely to Kerak, then?"

The sheikh clapped his hands. "Mustafa! Bring water."

Instantly, the flap stirred and a young man entered with cups stacked in one hand and a water-jug in the other.

Al-Na'im smiled. "Were we in our grazing-lands in Transjordan, it would be sherbet cooled with snow of Hermon."

"It's enough," Miles said with fervent gratitude.

Marta closed her eyes as she tipped the cool, life-giving liquid down her throat.

"We'll deliver you safely to Kerak," Al-Nai'm said, "but it would be best if you did not leave the tent or show yourselves to the rest of the caravan."

"You fear for our safety, sheikh? Is it your own men you distrust, or these merchants?"

"I merely advise caution. Saladin is not a man to forgive such an insult as you have given him."

"You think he will seek revenge for what we have done?" Miles smiled faintly. "Saints, I would be angry too. All I did was beach my ships on the coast, and the people of Medina thought they were about to be besieged."

Al-Na'im shook his head, his eyes gleaming. "You have done worse than that, my friend. You have made the sultan look ridiculous. He already has much to do to pass off his empire-building as the defence of Islam. Now you have shown that he cannot even protect the pilgrims, and he'll have your name and the prince's written on his sword. I'll wager he appears before the walls of Kerak by the year's end, perhaps even before the heir marries."

Marta's attention had wandered as the men spoke. The tapestries and carpets in the tent were bold and colourful, and she had been examining them, wondering which dyes were used and whether she could wheedle the women into giving her some pattern samples before they returned to Jerusalem.

Al-Na'im's words jolted her back into awareness.

"But Saladin is still occupied with subduing Mosul, surely," Miles began.

"Before the heir marries?" Marta blurted. "Did you say Humphrey and Isabella will marry *this year?*"

"This is not commonly known?" The sheikh looked startled.

Miles cleared his throat. "Nothing is decided yet."

"But it's being planned." Marta spoke through lips that felt numb with shock. "They're going to marry Isabella to Humphrey and it will all be too late."

* * *

"I know you're there," Miles said.

Marta hesitated, shivering in her thin borrowed robe before padding across the grass to join him. The sun was long down, leaving only a thin sprinkle of stars to light the night, and Miles was little more than a dark silhouette against the pool's pale, shimmering water.

She was bone-tired and should have been asleep hours ago, but a question burned in her belly almost as fiercely as the raw skin on her forehead.

"They're planning the wedding, Miles! Why didn't you send word?"

He sighed and shifted on the great rock he sat on, making room. "It was only spoken of. There was no day named, nothing certain—I meant to pass word to Lord Balian as soon as there was."

"But she's still underage." Marta shook her head. "It's not just that Isabella's my sister: *nobody* should be treated like that. This is exactly the kind of injustice the Watchers are supposed to prevent."

He reached out and took her hand, drawing her down beside him on the rock. "There's time yet. Lord Balian will arrange something."

There was little room on the rock for both of them, and Miles' arm brushed against hers, warm in the cool night. Without thinking, Marta inched closer.

"Lord Balian had three years to arrange something." The words blurted out before she could stop them, shocking even herself. She'd never voiced a criticism of her Prester before. "He said the political situation was too delicate, that he needed to wait."

Miles seemed far away. "I suppose he knows what he's talking about."

"I did nothing," she whispered. "I wish…"

How could Balian let this happen? How could the Leper King do this to his sister?

They ought to be protecting the kingdom. Instead, they're leading us straight to destruction.

Her voice trailed away and Miles turned to face her. Although it was dark, she sensed that he was *looking* at her again, that crease between his eyebrows, as though he was trying to answer some question. He shifted, and his fingers brushed hers again before retreating. "Don't," he said. "If you wish too much, it'll drive you mad."

Still, no matter what Lord Balian had said, she *should* have done something.

Then the meaning of his words hit her.

"Miles, you couldn't have known they'd be executed."

He dragged in a sniff. "They were relying on me to get them home. Some of them were friends."

"You wish you'd stayed with them?" He didn't answer, and Marta felt wretched. "I'm so sorry."

He turned to watch her again. "Sorry for saving my life?"

"Sorry for forcing the choice on you. And the guilt." She shivered, trying to make sense of his last question. "Are you angry with me?"

"No. Never. You aren't to blame, and..." For the first time, emotion shook his voice. "I'm just so glad you came for me. That's all I feel. Am I wrong?"

"I don't know," she said, honestly. "But I'm glad I came for you, too."

He took a breath and looked away from her, his fingers lacing into hers. They sat side by side in silence.

Miles was right, she decided. One couldn't wish to change the past. One could only do one's best for the future.

Three years had passed. No one had done anything, and now Isabella was going to be married.

I have to stop it.

This is my mission.

Chapter XV.

Sails furled, the ship rocked quietly at anchor like a sleeping water-fowl. The Red Sea lapped incuriously at its hull, barely causing the lamps to sway inside the cabin, where a man sat in the narrow berth, lips moving as he pored over a tattered book. Since the Frankish raiders had been captured barely two days' journey from the port of Yanbu, a return to comfort among the ships of the Egyptian fleet had been easy to arrange.

He smiled thinly. The sultan's Armenian general had heard of him now.

There was scarcely a breath of wind, but the lamp suddenly guttered. Neither the door nor the window had opened, yet the man was no longer alone in the room. Unsurprised, he looked up, marking his place with his finger.

"Lilith," he said. "Well?"

Her pale face stared out of the shadows opposite him, white-skinned and red-lipped. She wore the darkness like a cloak. "We have failed," she hissed. "Qeteb was unable to kill the Watcher *or* its companions."

The book slammed shut. "And the weapon?"

"Picked up by the Bani-Iaith and returned to the Watcher."

The man swore. "What happened? Qeteb promised me he would end them."

"One of the Fiery Ones came down to protect them." The red lips curled. "Qeteb was powerless before it."

The man was silent for a moment; the news had rattled him. "That is...difficult to believe."

"But true. I could have told you the alliance with Qeteb would be useless."

Lilith drifted closer, the lamplight caressing the black feathers that covered her arms. "You should have remained with me. We both had more freedom then."

He laughed bitterly. *"You* had more freedom; I was trapped in stone. When I summoned him from the darkness, Qeteb did not make me his slave."

She spat angrily. "So you were once my slave, and now we are a triumvirate. What good has it done you?"

"It does my *people* good. You don't care who dies, do you? As long as you get blood. Don't imagine I don't know where you've been the last two weeks—following those Franks up and down the Red Sea feasting on the believers and pilgrims they killed." His voice shook. "On *my* people."

"You promised that if I abstained from their souls you would give me Franks to consume. So where are my Franks?"

"You shall have two hundred of them."

"Two hundred?" Lilith sputtered. "You muzzle me, you feed me scraps, and you expect me to help you?"

"Your appetite blinds you."

"And Qeteb has blinded *you* with his grandiose dreams, but he cannot defeat a single Watcher."

"And you would have done better?"

"I would not have brought the Fiery One down." Her eyes narrowed. "I would have whispered. Tempted. Seduced. By the time I was done, the Watcher would have been so corrupted that the Fiery One would not have known it as its own."

The man only snorted. "This is what you have been doing for the last hundred years, and with what result? The Franks retain their control of the Coast. Despite their arrogance and decadence, their king is protected. I cannot get in, not even to retrieve my spear."

"Have I not told you that their defences are growing thin? The Franks become more vulnerable every day. Once their king dies, there will be only a few weak Watchers left to maintain their defences. The eternal law works for me as well as against me. Let any of the creatures break it in one iota, and its protections will fail, and its soul is forfeit—to *me*." She licked her lips. "That is why Qeteb failed. He attacked too soon."

The man's eyes narrowed. "Neither you nor Qeteb can enter the kingdom—"

"Not ordinarily. Not freely. There are defences. But when a mortal creature forfeits its soul, I can always put my hand on it. Wherever it is."

The man snorted, unimpressed. "But only to claim what is yours. To whisper, nudge, suborn."

"There is no want of opportunity, believe me."

"It's child's play! Foolishness! You'll never destroy a kingdom like that."

"On the contrary," she said softly. "The mountains themselves are made from grains of sand. Soon the balance will tip. The Coast stands upon a knife's edge. The creature they call their king is dying, and they are killing it themselves with everything they do. And the heir..." She held out fingers tipped with curving black nails, more claw than hand. "The heir is already falling into my grip. I have already devoured its young, but I underestimated its cunning, its rage, its will to dominate. This one...this one is more than foodstuff. This one could be a weapon."

The man looked thoughtful. "Sibylla, the Lady of Jerusalem?"

"If we make our move wisely, we could control the throne itself."

"And the Watcher—where is she now?"

"It joined the Bani-Iaith."

He grunted and folded his arms, his eyebrows shadowing his eyes. "The Spear was so close," he said after a moment. "To *see* her—after all these years..."

"It *is* close." She drifted a little closer, her taloned feet not quite touching the floor. "Soon, soon. The heir will ripen. The king will die, and when it is gone..." She drew in a shivering breath. "Then, I will feast."

Chapter XVI.

As usual, Sibylla had the Damascene pottery merchant shown to her cabinet. This was a comfortable little room on the second floor of her house, containing a large desk and shelved ledgers to keep track of the revenues from her county of Jaffa and her charitable donations—among other things. Plain, whitewashed and brightly lit with a large window of clear glass, its only decoration was a large icon of the Virgin and Child that her great-grandmother, Queen Morphia, had brought as a wedding gift from Armenia.

The pottery merchant was neither a business venture nor a charitable cause, and so Sibylla nodded to him to close and bar the door behind him. He did as she directed, then stood before her desk with his thumbs stuck in his belt. He did not bow, and Sibylla instinctively understood that when she was alone with this man, he regarded himself as her equal. Perhaps he was, or perhaps he was just insolent. It didn't matter to Sibylla. She was more interested in his information.

"What news from Mosul, Kurosh?" she asked.

"The sultan has withdrawn from the area."

"Without receiving the city's submission?" At her informant's nod, Sibylla tapped a forefinger against her lips. This was good news. As long as Saladin failed to get control of Mesopotamia, he would be too distracted to make a serious effort on Jerusalem. "I take it your master was there to support Saladin—ostensibly, at least."

"My master's motivations are his own."

"Be that as it may, he might consider my offer." Sibylla fidgeted with the onyx ring on her thumb, tracing the Arabic engraving on its face. "Each year Saladin's power grows. It appears there is no end to his ambition. Your master could create a great opportunity for himself as well as for us if he was to...shorten...the sultan's career."

Kurosh smiled tightly. "He is not your errand boy. He will use the sultan so long as the sultan is of use to him."

Sibylla shrugged. "Naturally, he thinks he can saddle the lion, and ride without harm." She leaned forward. "Tell your master—whoever he is—that if he should ever change his mind about the sultan, he should speak to me. Here in Jerusalem we would be happy to assist."

"If you wish to forge an alliance, there is a thing my master wants. A toy, a weapon."

"Continue."

"It is a singular weapon, a little shorter and lighter than most Frankish lances. It has a shaft of ash and a blade of black Damascus steel, folded and hammered. Whoever owns it will have the reputation of a magnificent warrior."

Sibylla lifted an eyebrow. "Truly? Every man in this kingdom has such a reputation, and any one of them might have a Saracen spear in his armoury."

"This one was seen in Arabia lately. Carried in the company of the constable of Kerak."

That narrowed things down significantly. "I thought every man on the Red Sea raid was captured."

"Not the constable. Nor his companion." Kurosh fixed her with an implacable stare. "My master desires this weapon as he desires few other things in the world. If you can get it for him, you will put him in your debt forever."

Sibylla had no idea who the agent's master was—but she doubted that this thing was a laughing-matter to him. "What makes this spear so valuable?"

"My master does not unfold the book of his bosom to *every* passer-by."

Kurosh was good at keeping secrets, that was certain. Sibylla stifled a yawn. "I don't know this spear, and I am not your master's errand boy. That would be *you*, Kurosh."

"You refuse?"

"Oh no, Prince Reynald is a friend of mine, and I can easily ask him about his constable. But I am not happy with our bargain. Why should I pay twice for my information? I'll find you the answers your master seeks, *if* you answer my questions freely."

Kurosh only hesitated for a moment. "Very well."

"We know Saladin will attack the kingdom next. Where and when?"

He looked at her impassively. "I think this would put you in our debt again."

"I can do without your information," she said coldly. "Can you do without mine?"

It seemed he could not. That night, the merchant left Sibylla with plenty to think about. Why was the mysterious spear so important? Who was Kurosh's master, and how could she turn what little she'd learned to her advantage?

A tap came at the door, and Sibylla called, "Come in."

It was one of the domestic servants, carrying a taper with which to light the lamps. "Will you have light, my lady?"

Startled, Sibylla realised that dusk had fallen and the city's daytime commotion was hushed, allowing the splash of the fountain to be heard from the courtyard below. Outside on the loggia, some of the lamps were already lit.

"No," she said, "I have finished here. Go and light the lamps in my chamber."

The woman hesitated, fidgeting with something in her pocket.

"What is it, Miriam?" Sibylla asked sharply.

"Some of us pooled our money to buy you a gift, my lady." The woman withdrew her hand from her pouch and held out a tiny silver charm on a leather thong. It flashed in the light: an open hand with an eye in the palm.

Sibylla lifted an eyebrow. "You think I have the evil eye?"

Miriam gulped. "It isn't natural to lose so many babies, my lady, and we thought it couldn't hurt. They say the demon Lilith steals the lives of children before they come to light. If she is the one troubling you, perhaps this will keep her away."

Sibylla's heart constricted a little. Despite multiple pregnancies since her second marriage, so far she had only produced a single girl. She was not one to see demons in every shadow, and if anyone else had suggested she wear such a charm, she would have laughed at them.

Offered as a gift, it reached past her defences and touched her bruised hopes on the quick. Slowly, she reached out and accepted the charm. "Thank you, Miriam. I hope it makes a difference."

The servant bowed and left. Sibylla sat in the dark turning the charm over and over between fingers that barely felt it. Presently she slipped the leather thong over her head and ventured out of the cabinet to say goodnight to her son.

At six years old, little Baldwin was a pale, skinny child, nothing at all like William Longsword, his warrior father. But when he saw her, he sat bolt upright in bed. "Mama! Will you tell me a goodnight story?"

"Hush, my lord," the nurse warned. "You'll wake your little sister!"

"Of course I'll tell you a story." Sibylla sat on the edge of her son's bed. "I shall tell you a story of your great-grandmother Queen Melisende."

Little Baldwin lay back in hushed expectancy.

"Melisende was the daughter and heir of a king," Sibylla began. "After her husband died, she ruled alone as queen. She was a wise and foresighted woman, and her barons knew she was the best ruler the kingdom could ever have. But Melisende's eldest son grew impatient. 'I am a man now, and no longer a child,' he told his friends. 'Why am I not king instead of my mother?' So the ungrateful boy went to war with the queen."

"What happened?" Little Baldwin's eyes were wide.

"The queen's son stole her kingdom away from her. And, for a short time, there was peace. For a short time, the barons were happy with their young, warrior king. But it takes more than youth and battle-strength to rule a kingdom. Without Melisende's wisdom, the king was like a body with no mind, or a raid with no strategy. To save his kingdom, he had to call the queen back to his side. Melisende would have been justified in taking back her kingdom and gouging out her son's eyes, but she relented.

From then on, they ruled the kingdom together." Sibylla smoothed the covers over her son's tiny body. "The young king's name was Baldwin, too. Don't you think it would have been better if he had listened to his mother in the first place?"

A wide-eyed nod.

"That's why we have mothers. I know you'll be a wise boy, sweetheart." She leaned forward to kiss him on the cheek. When she turned to go, she found one of her women waiting at the doorway. Sibylla saw from the look on her face that Sara was worried about something, but as she emerged from her son's room, she was still surprised to walk almost directly into the arms of two sergeants in the royal livery.

"Countess," one of them said apologetically, "will you come with us to the palace? The king would have a word."

Sibylla didn't miss the sheen of sweat on their foreheads, or the crossbow one of them carried over his shoulder. A twinge of nervous pain ran through her.

What has Baldwin discovered?

Guy was in Jaffa on business, and naturally his armed retainers had gone with him. Apart from Sibylla and the children, there were only servants in the house. There was nothing she could do but go quietly.

"Bring my cloak," she murmured to Sara.

In the courtyard, more of her brother's men in the royal silver-and-gold livery waited to escort her to the palace. Sibylla's stomach knotted. *He knows about the pottery merchant. He knows I have an informant in Saladin's court.*

He knows I would never betray him.

Doesn't he?

Her brother's armed escort suggested otherwise. Although it was night, Sibylla draped a black veil over her head in addition to shrouding herself in the cloak. Best if this visit remained discreet.

It was almost night by the time they reached the palace, but the guards didn't lead her through the main gate. Instead, a postern admitted them to the garden, and Sibylla began to breathe a little more easily. The Leper

King's garden was his sanctuary; he would not meet with a suspected traitor here.

The guards marched her towards a bent fig tree. From its branches there hung a dozen lamps of coloured glass and among the networked shadows below, her brother sat in a chair with a rug over his knees to fend off the chill of spring. He looked up when he saw her coming, one dark eye reflecting the glow of the lantern. The other was a pale, blind milky-blue, withered by his disease. An ulcer crawled stickily up his neck.

Time was running out.

"The Countess of Jaffa, my lord."

"Sibylla," Baldwin said. "Sit. Please."

The guards shifted a chair to face the king and Sibylla dropped into it, unwinding the veil from her head. Her brother's man stood behind her, his armour faintly chinking. "Are your people going to breathe down my neck all night?"

"Leave us," Baldwin told them.

"Taking no risks, I see," she said acidly as the sergeants retreated.

"But you are."

Here we go. Sibylla folded her hands and waited for him to go on. Her brother heaved a sigh of exasperation. "Sibylla, that Saracen is an enemy spy. And he's been to see you three times in the last year."

"So you have me dragged from my home by a gang of hired cutthroats? He sells *pottery*, Baldwin. What next, are you going to investigate everyone in the city who's bought one of his finger-bowls? Stop every Saracen merchant entering the kingdom?"

"I may be going blind, Sibylla, but I'm not stupid. Nothing you do happens by mistake. You are the only person this man has visited on each of his three last trips to this kingdom. You are in communication with some very powerful people at Saladin's court. Why?"

"Why do you care?" she returned coldly. "Do you think I am a traitor, brother?"

"Sibylla. Answer my question. *Please.*"

She leaned forward in her chair. "Answer mine first. *Do you think I am a traitor?"*

"God help me, sister, I do not know *what* you are, or what you would not do to have your way. I might know better if you spoke to me more."

"You might know better if you *trusted* me better." Her mouth tightened. "Instead of spying on me and my visitors."

"I did trust you." His voice became huskier, as it did when he was agitated. "*Despite* your intrigues, I trusted your choice of husband. You said Guy would be a good leader. You said the people would warm to him. It's been three years, and—no, let me finish! It's been three years, and the barons still hate him as badly as they ever did. *What will happen* when they find out that you are spying for Saladin?"

Chills shot agonisingly through her body, and Sibylla gripped the arms of her chair. It was a moment before she could speak. "How dare you accuse me of such a thing?"

"I am not accusing you of that. I am telling you what the barons will think if they find out what you've been doing!"

"Why would they believe that? No one would be so stupid. I am King Amalric's daughter, I am your heir—why would I do such a thing?"

"Not everyone has your clarity of mind, sister."

Sibylla searched his face in the lantern-light, trying to determine whether he was being sincere.

After a moment he spoke again. "I'm *counting* on you, Sibylla. Each day...each day it comes nearer, the moment when I am gone and you are left. You could be the greatest queen this kingdom has ever seen, but you must not do anything to jeopardise the barons' loyalty. Guy is arrogant and ambitious and they already resent him. You must see to it that they don't come to resent *you*. Please."

Above, stars twinkled among the fig's branches. Sibylla stared at them, breathing slowly, and unwound her grip from the chair's arms. After a moment, she spoke softly.

"Every king should know what his enemies are doing. Tonight I learned that Saladin is retreating from Mosul, and that he will turn his attention to this kingdom next. He may be distracted by his ambitions in Mesopotamia, but he needs a victory against us in order to justify his wars against his own people. Are you ready to fight that war, Baldwin?"

Baldwin was silent a moment, then he sighed. In recent months, his disease had weakened him to the point that he could no longer walk. "I cannot. I will have to appoint a bailli."

Sibylla nodded eagerly. "Make it Guy."

There was an unwilling silence. "Guy?"

"You've said yourself that the barons distrust him. So let them see that *you* trust him, let him prove himself in battle. Better now than after your death."

Again, there was a silence. Baldwin's voice was distant when he replied. "Sibylla, I…"

A wave of frustration broke over her. "What is it? He's your natural successor; why won't you give him *any* responsibility? How are we to learn, if you don't—"

"Sibylla." He leaned forward, his one good eye burning with worry. "Guy's followers already go around every wine-shop in Jerusalem boasting that they are going to make him king. What am I supposed to make of that, hm?"

Sibylla stared. "Are—are you *jealous* of him?"

"I'm a little fearful, yes! It wouldn't be the first time someone has tried to throw the leper off the throne. What if he does as Ramla did, and tries to seize the kingdom?"

For an instant, Sibylla was almost angry. But the emotion seeped out of her at the sight of her brother's ravaged face and body. This wasn't just a question of what she herself wanted or deserved. "Would that be so bad, brother? You've been so ill. I know that above anything else, you want rest. Why not just give it up? Guy and I are strong. We're willing. We're *ready*."

His shoulders slumped, and she knew how badly he wanted to say yes. "God," he whispered, like a prayer.

She almost reached out and touched him. "Let us help you. Let us shoulder this burden for you."

At length he looked up at her. "You and Guy may be ready, but I don't know if the kingdom is. If I make him my bailli, will you swear not to receive your informant?"

Sibylla kept silent, running through the possibilities in her head, weighing up benefits and disadvantages.

"I'm willing to give Guy his chance, but…this kingdom is divided, Sibylla. I don't know if you realise that. For the last three years I've felt as though I am standing on a rift that could open at any moment, plunging us all into the abyss."

Her calculations finished, Sibylla shook her head. "Are you talking about the Watchers? I can convince them to try this." Although she and Guy must be careful. Even if they agreed to a Lusignan regency, the Watchers might see it as an opportunity to bring them down.

"Of course you can. But don't be overconfident, sister. Do you understand?" Baldwin leaned forward, his voice now little more than a scratchy whisper. "One false step, and it will mean war."

Chapter XVII.

Jerusalem's eastern gate admitted Marta and Miles to a city seething with life. Marta blinked at the crowds lining the Jehoshephat street. "What's the occasion? Surely it can't yet be Lent."

Miles nodded towards a stream of people emerging from the massive grey church of Saint Anne, their foreheads streaked with grey. "It's Ash Wednesday."

Marta shook her head, speechless. It must be the beginning of March. She'd been away for two months.

Gingerly, she touched two fingers to her own forehead. The burn mark was healing. The fiery pain that tormented her at first had now dulled to a constant ache, but it was still there, the scar puckering across her forehead where others wore ashes. "Ash Wednesday. That means the Watchers' Council will be meeting. If we hurry, we'll be in time to tell them about Isabella."

"I never thought I'd see this place again. So many others didn't." Miles shifted in his saddle, looking uncomfortable. "I should report to Prince Reynald. If he finds out I've spoken to the Watchers before himself, I doubt he'll be happy."

"Does it matter?"

"I made a promise to Isabella, remember? I can only keep it as long as I'm in the prince's good books."

Marta barely thought of that. If she was honest with herself, she coveted every heartbeat of this brief time with Miles, the last few weeks of their journey all the more precious for knowing that they must come to an end.

And now the end was here.

"Please, Miles. The Watchers might not believe just one person, but if *you* come with me..." She'd been gone for months, and she would have to do some explaining. "I don't want to face them alone."

He watched her thoughtfully for a moment. "All right. For you, little Marta."

"I'm not little," she said, embarrassed.

He looked her slight frame up and down. "You are," he said with conviction. "You are tiny and adorable. Where is the Council meeting, then?"

Marta blushed so violently she could barely untangle her tongue. "At the Temple."

Sometime in the last five hundred years, someone had built an octagonal church over the site of the old Jewish Temple. As always, Marta went in wishing that her father could have seen it. It was Greek architecture, like the churches she had grown up knowing, but for some reason there were no human faces, no stern Pantocrator hovering within the tall dome. Instead it glittered with mosaics and gold, all in geometrical patterns.

The morning's Mass was over, and a hum of voices sounded from the south side of the church where the great Watcher lords and ladies sat: Lord Balian, Queen Maria, Count Raymond of Tripoli, the grand commander of the Order of Saint John. As Marta led Miles towards the gathering, faces turned towards them, one of them dark as a starry night. Persi's face split in a smile when she saw Marta and she lunged forward, pulling her into a deep embrace.

"God be thanked, I feared the worst," she whispered in Marta's ear. "When I got back from Nubia and you were still gone..." She stopped with a look of surprise. "What happened to your forehead?"

"It's a long story. Look, I found him," Marta whispered back, jerking her head towards Miles.

Persi shot Miles a half-smile. "I still think you're mad."

Marta laughed and stepped back, squeezing Persi's elbows. "I have news for the council."

Despite her lowered voice, Marta's arrival had not gone unnoticed. Seeing her, the Watchers murmured in surprise and stood back, opening a path to the inner ring of chairs. At their head, a chair squawked as Lord Balian stood up suddenly.

"Marta! *Where have you been?*"

Marta wanted to melt into the floor, but unless she was going to beg pardon for what she'd done, she would have to brazen it out. She grabbed Miles by the hand and charged forward until she stood in the centre of the ring of Watchers. "Prester Balian, we have news from Kerak. They're going to marry Isabella to Humphrey by the end of this year."

An audible gasp came from Queen Maria, who sat at Balian's right hand. The other Watchers began muttering among themselves.

Lord Balian shook his head, bewildered. "You've been at *Kerak* all this time?"

"Only for one night, on the way back." Marta swallowed. "I went to Arabia, to find Miles."

Balian blinked, noticing him for the first time. "Miles of Plancy? Weren't you on the Red Sea raid?"

"I was its leader, my lord."

"We thought you had all been captured."

"We were." Miles looked down at her, smiling. "Marta snatched me from the lion's jaws."

As the Watchers began to clamour for details, Marta lost her nerve. Leaving Miles to answer the questions, she knelt beside the queen. "They're going to make her marry Humphrey," she whispered.

Queen Maria's eyes were haunted. "They can't make her do that. She's only eleven—she won't be of age until next year."

"Miles says it's true."

The queen caught her hand. "You spent a night in Kerak?"

Marta nodded. When the Bedouin and their caravan had turned east to skirt Transjordan on the road to Damascus, she and Miles had bid the sheikh farewell and entered Prince Reynald's domain. The prince himself was not at the castle, so after one night at Kerak, both she and Miles had ridden on, to Jerusalem.

"I didn't see Isabella," she whispered. "I asked, but Countess Stephanie..."

For three years Miles' stepmother had never allowed Isabella to see anyone connected with the Ibelins. Although disappointment pulled at the corners of her mouth, the queen nodded. "It's all right, Marta."

Miles must have finished explaining their adventures to the council, because Balian's hand descended on her shoulder. His voice was still bewildered. "Marta, you never told me you were planning *this*."

Was he disappointed with her? Yet as she looked up at him with all her words sticking in her throat, a grin broke across his face. "That's the bravest thing I ever heard of a young maiden doing."

"Preux," someone else agreed.

Marta blushed, no happier to be the centre of attention. "But what about Isabella?"

There was a brief silence.

"The king's health has worsened lately." The lanky, grey-haired man who spoke from another seat in the circle was the Leper King's cousin, Count Raymond of Tripoli. "The Courtenays must be desperate to have the girl safely wedded before he dies."

"And then who will be our king?" Ramla's perpetual scowl deepened. *"Guy of Lusignan?"*

The queen dowager buried her face in her hands. "She's still only a child."

"Buy out of the marriage," Walter of Caesarea suggested.

"Would the king accept that? The Courtenays still have his ear."

"There's only one way of stopping it without the king's permission," an elderly churchman put in. "No marriage can happen without the bride's consent."

Lord Balian snapped his fingers. "Chancellor, you're right. If she objects to marrying Humphrey, they can't force her to do it. Sir Miles, will you take Isabella a message?"

Before Miles could answer, raised voices echoed through the church, snatching away everyone's attention. The guards at the door had orders to admit only those who bore the Watchers' Mark, but now they were shoved aside. Footsteps echoed as Guy of Lusignan and Prince Reynald strode towards them at the head of a phalanx of armed men.

Chairs rattled as the Watchers rose to their feet. Sensing Miles stiffen, Marta put a comforting hand on his arm.

"I would speak to the Watchers' Council." Guy's voice reverberated through the high golden dome. "Will you hear me, Prester?"

Lord Balian settled his hands on his hips. "This is not a public occasion. Who told you we were meeting here?"

"I know everything it's my business to know. And since so many of my enemies are Watchers, that makes your council my business." The count stuck his thumbs in his belt, mirroring Balian's stance. Behind, his Poitevin retainers lined up with their arms folded, evidently aware of what an imposing sight they made. Next to Guy, Prince Reynald smiled around the scar that disfigured his cheek, and leaned on a walking-stick that might easily double as a club.

"I am the Prester of this council, and I am not your enemy," Lord Balian said quietly. "If you have anything to say to a friend, speak. Otherwise you are mistaken: you have no business here."

"The Leper King's illness is getting worse," Count Guy boomed. "He will need a bailli again by the end of the year. Sooner, if Saladin attacks. I'm here to offer myself for the post."

A dead silence fell over the room, until Lord Balian replied. "That is not Watcher business."

"No? But it's *your* business, Ibelin." The count swung around, searching for the other faces. "And yours, Ramla. And *yours*, Tripoli." He smirked into Count Raymond's shuttered face.

"Balian is right," the iron-grey count replied. "This is High Court business."

"It's everyone's business." Guy stared them each down in turn. "Haven't you heard the news? Saladin is retreating from Mosul. His men whisper together: how is it that the sultan goes to war with the lords of his own faith while ignoring the Christians of the Coast? Saladin must turn towards this kingdom, and soon."

"You seem to know a great deal about it," Lord Balian said. "Where do you get this information?"

"And even if it's true," Ramla put in, "why should we make you bailli?"

"Because *war is coming.*" Prince Reynald spoke in a low growl. "And the Leper King is no longer fit to lead us."

Count Guy shrugged. "I am to be your king. Make me your bailli, and I will prove that I deserve it."

In the silence, Caesarea snorted. "Why should this newcomer be our king? We want someone we can trust."

"My wife is the heiress of the kingdom. I will not let her be robbed of her inheritance."

"Jerusalem is not like France," Balian put in. "No one inherits the kingdom without the consent of the barons. We have the right to install a king of our own choosing."

Guy stared at them. "Then I suggest you *choose* the true heiress."

"The true heir is the one who can best defend the kingdom. That is our custom."

"I can defend the kingdom." Guy showed his teeth in a snarl. "And I can *take* it, too. Across the bodies of the whole High Court, if I must."

Prince Reynald sank his fingers into Guy's arm. "Count," he growled.

Sensing the violence in the air, Marta shifted both hands to her spear. At that moment, a blinding pain shot through her head. Darkness danced before her eyes, and when she took a breath and opened them again, Prince Reynald had stepped between Guy and the Watchers' Council, and the moment had passed.

"There need be no talk of taking. Or of war," the scarred prince growled. "All the count asks is the chance to prove that the one who can best defend the kingdom is himself."

"Thank you for making that clear." Lord Balian's voice was acidic, but polite. "If you and the count will be good enough to withdraw, we will consider it and send our answer within the hour."

"We'll wait on your summons." Count Guy looked determined. "You'll find us in the Templars' garden."

With his departure came an eruption of talk. "What kind of fool is he, to think we would agree to such a thing?" Caesarea snorted.

Lord Balian rubbed his chin, exchanging glances with Tripoli. "He has a point."

Balian's soft words silenced the debate. Tripoli nodded. "No matter how much we may distrust him, Guy is next in line for the throne. And he is determined to have it."

"We owe him at least the chance to prove that he's capable," Balian agreed softly. "Who knows? Perhaps he is."

"He's still an arrogant cockerel!" Caesarea grimaced. "I say we refuse."

Ramla shook his head. "No, *I* say we should let him. Let's make him bailli."

Lord Balian's eyebrows climbed. "What do you say, brother?"

"I say we should allow it." Ramla got to his feet with a sneer. "Let Lusignan play at being king. When he fouls it up, the king will *have* to listen to us. If we play the game right, we can get Guy cut out of the succession, *and* have Isabella married to someone of our choosing."

Pain pierced Marta's head again, and she stifled a gasp.

"That's not a bad idea." Caesarea seemed struck by the possibilities.

Lord Balian looked thoughtful. "No matter how it turns out, we can only be better off knowing what Guy is like as a leader."

"I say we do it." Queen Maria had been silent until now, but she turned to Balian with her mind evidently made up. "If there's even a chance of getting Isabella back..."

"Well then, we'll send for the count. Persi, would you go?"

She nodded and slipped away to the door. Marta blinked, struggling to conceal her pain, but gentle hands cupped her elbows. Miles.

"What's wrong, Marta?"

"My head hurts," she whispered.

She didn't quite see where he found the chair, but the next moment she was sitting down with Miles hovering above. "You should go home and rest."

She forced a smile. "No! I'll be all right, I promise."

169

Headache or no headache, she *must* speak to Lord Balian as soon as the council was over. Hadn't he asked her counsel, once or twice, when she'd first arrived in this time? She'd been loath to give it, because he was so much older and wiser than herself. Now she was beginning to think he might need it after all.

When Count Guy and Prince Reynald returned, Lord Balian cleared his throat. "We have made our decision. Those of the barons who are Watchers will not oppose you if you seek the regency."

Guy of Lusignan smiled, and it transformed his face. Watching, Marta understood what Countess Sibylla saw in him, even if nobody else did. "I'll inform the Leper King. You won't be sorry," he added as he left.

As Ramla and Caesarea exchanged smiles, another throb ran through Marta's head, and she stifled a groan. When her vision cleared, she looked up to see Persi kneeling beside her. "Marta, what's wrong? Your forehead—"

"I don't know—ow! Don't touch; it still hurts." She blinked, staring around at the disintegrating council. The meeting must have ended while her senses were clouded by the pain. "Where's Miles?"

"Went off with Prince Reynald. He said he'd come back to say goodbye."

Goodbye. Marta's stomach twisted with a lesser pang. She put it aside. "What about Lord Balian? I *have* to speak to him."

But he was already hurrying over to her. "Marta, what is it? Are you hurt?"

"I don't know," she said again. The pain was making it hard to think, hard to find the confidence to say what she must. She caught his hand. "Are you going to try to disgrace Count Guy?"

"What?" That note of utter puzzlement was back in his voice.

"Your brother wants to make him bailli so that he can ruin him."

"Oh, Ramla." Lord Balian shook his head with a wry laugh.

"You can't," Marta whispered. She'd never spoken to him like this before, but the old Messenger's prophecy rang in her ears. She couldn't bear to see this Watcher's Council fail as the Syrian Council had at Oliveta. "It wouldn't be right. Everyone will reap what he has sown, and if you sow

170

treachery…"

Balian dropped into a crouch so that he could see into her eyes. "Marta, hush. Every king has to deal with opposition. We're giving Count Guy a fair chance to win us over. That's all."

Slowly, the pain in her head began to subside. Marta pushed the hair back from her face. "A fair chance?"

"You have my word." Balian seemed more worried for her than offended. His eyes flickered to the scar on her forehead and away again. "Persi, could you take her home? She could do with a bath and a rest…"

Marta used her spear to lever herself out of the chair. She felt exhausted, but the headache was going. "I feel better," she said faintly. "Where's Miles?"

Persi's mouth thinned. "Oh, no you don't. You've already run across half of Arabia looking for that man. He can come and find you at home."

"I'm not *sick*, Persi." Marta gave a huff of laughter and shrugged her off. "I'll meet you back here soon."

She hurried across the floor of variegated tiles and emerged onto the high stone platform from which the Temple looked out over the city, its domes and towers punctuated by slender cypresses. The guard at the door pointed her left towards the Templars' gardens, and Marta descended the stairs to a lower level of the platform. Beyond the garden, with its fruit trees, herbs, and vegetables, rose the massive complex which housed the Templar knights.

Within the orchard, she could hear Miles speaking. Marta hurried towards the voices, then stopped as the words reached her.

"Am I to expect nothing, then?" Miles sounded bitter. "No credit, no reward? The mission was suicide. Which of your other knights would have agreed to such a thing?"

"What credit do I owe you?" Prince Reynald asked coldly. "I conceived the raid, the king provided the money and ships, and *you* led it into disaster, along with two hundred handpicked men. Reward you? I should have you whipped."

Miles' voice was thick with rage. "I am no peasant to be whipped."

"Then smile when you speak to me, boy, and enjoy what you have. Most bastards don't even get a knighthood."

Marta slid behind the foliage of a small lemon-tree as the prince stalked by, his walking-stick thumping on the gravel. Beyond the lemon-tree, Miles stood with his hands on his hips, staring out towards the Mount of Olives. Marta didn't move, unwilling to intrude.

"I know you're there," he said at last, turning.

Marta eased out from behind the tree. "I'm sorry, Miles."

The hurt in his eyes was not from her. "My father was the *lord* of Kerak, and what am I? A glorified lackey. He thinks he can treat me like dirt."

"He wants all the glory for himself." Marta shrugged. "I thought he might. He's just using you, Miles. Why don't you leave him?"

"Where else would I go? Your Watchers?" He gave a barking laugh. "I don't want to be Lord Balian's lackey any more than I want to be Reynald's."

"What *do* you want?"

"A fief! A chance to defend the kingdom like my father did." He stuck his thumbs in his belt. "Do you know why Reynald has such a good relationship with the Bedouin? *I* did that. *I* learned their language and charmed their sheikhs, and spent hours buffing out every detail of every agreement."

He was not just a warrior, a destroyer; he was a builder as well, and the knowledge made her heart warm to him. "See? You already do so much, Miles. You might not have the name and wealth that your father did, but you already work to defend the kingdom. And you'll *always* have friends who love you, like al-Na'im—"

"Not the kind of friends who can give me power." He shifted closer, his eyes burning as he looked into hers. "Listen. Reynald thinks I'm disposable, and he'll throw my life away if it suits him. I don't just *want* status and respect. I *need* them. Otherwise, I'm dead. Do you understand?"

Marta didn't know what to say, but to her terror, her eyes filled with sympathetic tears. Uncomfortable showing him so much emotion, she turned away, but Miles caught her wrist. Marta froze.

"You care." His voice was rough around the edges.

Now that this was in danger of becoming real, she was afraid. Afraid of letting him see her. Afraid of risking the friendship they'd rebuilt these last weeks.

"I've always cared," she whispered. "Let go."

Instead, he pulled her closer into his arms. A chill wind whistled through the fruit trees, but everything seemed to go still as she looked up into Miles' face. That watchful look had returned to his eyes, and Marta realised that he had been looking at her like this for weeks now, as though he had been asking himself some question ever since they met in the ravine.

A question that seemed to find its answer in the catch of her breath, the pounding of her heart even where it lay buried deep beneath layers of armour and padding.

He crushed her close and kissed her, banishing everything but this moment, this truth: that she had always cared, that despite distance and difficulty and danger she had fought for him. She had found him.

For an instant, Marta's heart stood absolutely still, her lips unresponsive to the gentle touch of his own, but as he drew back, his grip on her waist slackening, she realised with a little frantic sound at the back of her throat that she must make him *understand.* She grabbed the front of his surcoat and followed him, kissing him back in something between hunger and desperation.

He made a sound that made every hair on the back of her neck stand on end, chills shooting down her back. Suddenly, he grabbed her by the shoulders and pushed her to arm's length, breathing as hard as though he had just run a race.

"Holy Virgin, Marta, I didn't know…"

"I've *always* cared," she whispered. What was wrong? What didn't he know? Why was he pushing her away?

"This is all wrong!" His eyes were wide, stunned. "You're like a sister to me."

A moment ago she had been completely lost in this moment; now, suddenly, it was as though she watched from a very, very long distance. "What?"

Miles let go of her and stepped back. "I'll never forget what you did for me." His voice was far away. "Take care of yourself."

He put his head down and circled her, heading for the gate. Marta watched him go, still feeling as though her body was not her own. "Where will you go?" she called shakily.

He stopped, but didn't look back. "To Kerak. Why not? It's the best I've got."

No matter what had just happened between them, the kingdom was at stake and she had sworn to save it. "Please, Miles, don't forget to give Isabella our message. If she refuses to marry Humphrey, they can't make her do it. She can choose to come home."

"I'll tell her," Miles said, and then he was gone.

Chapter XVIII.

Marta collapsed onto the wall of a herb-bed and buried her face in her hands, thunderstruck and numb. Miles had rejected her.

You're like a sister to me. Marta cringed.

Then why did he kiss her at all? He must have at least been *curious*. What made him change his mind? Was it such a bad kiss? It must have been a bad kiss.

She almost wished she could never see him again.

"Marta! There you are!" As Persi hurried down the Temple steps, Marta stood up, rubbing her cuff across her eyes. "You should be in bed; you look exhausted."

"I'm sure." Marta gave a wild little laugh and picked up her spear. As she led the way back towards the platform where her horse—a wiry Arabian borrowed from the gracious al-Na'im— waited for her, she tried to think of something to say to distract Persi from what she'd nearly stumbled upon. "How was your trip? Did you see your family?"

Persi's face lit up. "God be thanked, I did. Each one of them was alive, and well."

A pang shot through Marta—dismay, sadness, and even a little envy, but she swallowed it all and kept her voice light. Persi had suffered at least as much as she, and her happiness could not be begrudged. "Even that pest of a brother?"

"He's carried a burden for eight years," Persi said after a moment's silence. "I hope it lifts now."

That had been an awful thing to say. Conscience-stricken, Marta stared at her feet. "I'm sorry, Persi. I'm being selfish. I always hoped you'd stay here, with me. But of course, now that you've found your family again—"

"No," Persi interrupted. "It was good to see them, and they'll always be my family, but there's no going back to the way things were."

Marta blinked. "You're staying?"

"Jerusalem is my home now."

She couldn't help it; a smile split her face. They stood at the head of the steps leading up from the Templars' gardens to a platform where the octagonal dome stood clad in blue-and-yellow mosaics. It was the beginning of spring, and somewhere on the green hill beyond the wall, a water-fowl was honking in sonorous content. "I can't blame you. This *is* the fairest of kingdoms."

Persi looked around them. Sighed. "Well, it certainly isn't the holiest."

She set off across the platform again and Marta fell into step beside her. "What do you mean? This is Christ's own city."

"And to some people, that means she is somehow exceptional. As though this kingdom, of all kingdoms, can do no wrong." Persi snorted. "Meanwhile men like Walter of Caesarea sit on the Watchers' Council, and no one says anything."

Though he was a Watcher in good standing and an ally of Lord Balian's in the High Court, Caesarea was also the lord who owned the textile workshop in Cacho.

"Jerusalem isn't perfect," Marta conceded. "But there's *hope* for us. We've already come so far! I remember a time when people used to live in fear of being arrested as Jews or heretics. These days, if someone asks you what your faith is, they're just trying to figure out what to serve you for dinner!"

"There's hope for everyone, even Jerusalem." Persi smiled at her. "But I believe my kingdom is just as capable of holiness as yours. Perhaps more, since in Nubia we take nothing for granted."

"But you'll stay? Even though we're nothing special?"

"Silimi is small, and has all the weavers she needs. With all the trade that passes through Jerusalem I can make better money, weaving finer cloth."

"That's another thing," Marta interrupted eagerly. "Do you know women

176

can buy land and inherit kingdoms here?"

"Not *all* women," Persi said soberly. "Yet, since you freed me, I've found more opportunities in Jerusalem than I ever did elsewhere. Opportunities to do my work, to *make* something of myself—but also to help others who need it." She swallowed. "Did you know that the women of my people are prized in Egypt as slaves? Their nobles find us...beautiful."

Marta shivered at the thought. "It could have been worse than Cacho, then." She retrieved her horse from the ring to which she'd tethered it.

Persi sighed and put a hand to Marta's cheek. "You have not seen the worst life has to offer, Marta."

The two of them set out down Temple Street into the city. Persi was silent for a while before clearing her throat. "So you rode all the way to Medina for the sake of one man."

Marta's cheeks warmed. "Miles promised to take care of Isabella. I couldn't let him die."

Persi grunted, unimpressed. "I hope he's worth it. Do you understand the risk you were taking?"

Marta lifted her chin. "I had nothing to fear. God helped me."

"Is it God you trust in, or that spear?"

Marta blinked at her.

"I understand, Marta. I *know* that sometimes you have to take these risks. I know you gave Miles your word. But spear or no spear, you are not invincible. And God helping you or not, you can still be hurt more terribly than you imagine." Persi stopped, catching Marta's shoulder, forcing her to look into her eyes. "Are you prepared for that?"

Marta shivered. A cloud seemed to have passed over the sun, and Persi was looking at her with haunted eyes. She swallowed. "I think so."

"Good," Persi said, but the shadows stayed in her eyes.

As they moved back into the flow of traffic, Persi gestured to Marta's forehead. "Were you going to tell me about that?"

Uncertain, Marta touched her brow. "I don't know if you'll believe me."

"A couple of times, at the Council, it was too bright to look at." Persi's voice hushed. "You've had to do with an angel."

"You can see it?"

Persi looked uncomfortable. "There's something I haven't told you." She took a deep breath. "I think I have a Watcher Gift."

"What? You do?" In her mind Marta ran through the Nine Gifts: *Counsellors, the wise who light our paths. Revealers, the discoverers of secrets. Comforters, the encouragers of the weary. Healers, the curative. Portentors, the miracle-workers. Messengers, the prophets. Perceptors, the discerners of spirits. Orators, the speakers in all tongues. Interpreters, the hearers in all tongues.* "Which one?"

"Perception," Persi said. "I first suspected it when I saw Countess Agnes, that day when she came to Nablus. Just as I could tell that you'd had to do with the angels, I could tell that she…hadn't. The blight wasn't obvious. But it was there. After that, I started seeing people with other sorts of signs. I've only seen one other with a light as bright as yours, though."

"You should have told me. Persi, that's marvellous!"

"I didn't know what was happening to me. I thought I'd go home to Silimi and ask my own people—if it was something they knew of. If it meant I was going insane." She let out the ghost of a laugh. "But I'm not mad. I'm gifted."

"Of course you are," Marta said loyally. She paused, her tired mind awhirl with all the different uses to which they could put such a gift. "Who was the other one, Persi? The one that shone like me?"

"Oh." Persi smiled. "It was the Leper King. He's had to do with angels too."

Chapter XIX.

Few pleasures remained to a man as sick as Baldwin. All his senses were leaving him; touch, taste, smell, and soon, sight.

Little remained to remind him that he was not already dead.

He leaned back in his chair, breathing slowly and listening to the sounds of evening. Cold air flooded his lungs, but frogs and crickets promised warmer weather soon. To Baldwin, the sound was foreboding. His disease left patches of skin deadened, unable to sweat. Then hot weather caused that dry skin to crack, forming raw and painful ulcers. How many more summers did he have to endure? Perhaps he could find an excuse to spend this one in one of the cooler coastal cities, like Tyre.

But only if he appointed a bailli—something he wished to avoid at all costs. The only choices were Tripoli, who had already tried to take his throne, and Sibylla's husband, who was clearly impatient to try.

Baldwin fumbled in his pouch for a lump of sugar and held it out on his bandaged palm, letting out a soft whistle. Hoofbeats wandered out of the shadows, and a soft, velvety nose leaned down to nibble it daintily from his palm. The war-horse, once his pride and joy, stood over him with hanging head, nuzzling his cheek.

Baldwin stroked the horse's neck. "I'm sorry, Pomers," he breathed. "I miss you, too."

A whisper of movement came from behind, kicking his heart to a gallop. Pomers shied away and Baldwin unsheathed his sword, twisting to face the intruder. "Who's there?"

His voice was almost gone now, little more than a tortured whisper. His legs could no longer carry him, and he only had one eye left to see out of.

"Don't be scared, my lord. It's me, Marta Bessarion."

"Marta Bessarion? You came back!" He sank back in his seat, breathing deeply in an attempt to slow his racing heart. Panicking at a footfall, how embarrassing.

Deciding that she was no threat after all, Pomers wandered into the darkness to crop grass, happy to make the most of his unexpected trip to the garden.

There was a smile in Marta's voice. "You remember me?"

"The girl who was unafraid of a leper, but ran away from a king? Of course I remember." He'd relived their conversation over and over in the years since he'd seen her; he remembered it as vividly as a flash of green in the desert. "What brings you back? How did you get in?"

She circled around in front of him, the lamplight falling on her face. Baldwin stared, fascinated. If not for the well-remembered face within her hood—the big dark eyes, the aquiline nose and the olive skin—he might have mistaken her for a boy. It was all fascinating. He'd never seen a woman in trousers before.

"I had to speak to you, so I climbed the wall."

"If you keep doing that, you'll be caught. And I... I'm not a well man. They don't tell me everything that goes on in this palace, you know. If something went wrong, I might not be able to help you."

"It's important." She didn't sound remotely afraid.

"I'm sure it is, but next time, come to the guards and give them your name. I'll leave orders that you're always to be admitted." That was one of the few pleasures left to him—conversation. And one that would do her no harm. He blurted out, "You *will* come again, won't you?"

Saints. He sounded like a fool of a boy, not a king of Jerusalem.

She was silent a moment. "If you like."

He scrambled to explain. "I mean, you don't have to come if you don't want to. But I don't often have the chance to just...talk to people who don't want anything from me."

After that, the silence was longer. "Oh," she said nervously.

Devil take it. "I'm sorry. Is there something I can do for you? Because I would be happy to do something for you. Really. I didn't mean…" He realised he was babbling.

"I came to beg a favour," she said when he stopped. "I'm a fosterling of Lord Balian, and I knew your sister Isabella before she was taken. I held her while she cried. I promised her she'd see her mother again." Marta paused.

"I'm listening," Baldwin prompted. *Saints,* he thought, *why did it have to be Ibelins?*

"Well, now I hear that they're going ahead with the marriage. But she's too young."

"I'm afraid I gave my word to young Humphrey."

"But she doesn't *want* to marry him. You can't force her to it without her consent."

"No, of course not." So this was why Marta Bessarion risked climbing into the garden of a king she'd already fled from once: out of love for his half-sister. Baldwin took pains to speak gently. "Truly, I honour you for your kindness. But Isabella is not like other girls. She will have to marry for the kingdom, and it might as well be someone who is kind and gentle with her, as they say Humphrey is. I think she will understand that."

Marta pushed her hood back to run a frustrated hand through her dark hair. "Three years ago, on the day I met you, I heard an old Watcher give a Message. She said that God gives you victories because he loves you, but that when you are dead, the kingdom will be destroyed. Last month, I was travelling with some Bedouin. They are saying the same things about you in Arabia."

"Rumours." Baldwin leaned into his chair with a sigh. "Everyone thinks I'm a saint because I don't keep mistresses or get bastards. I promise you, I'm just a leper."

"But what if it's *true?*"

"Please don't," he said harshly. "I've heard it before. God was angry with our sins, so he struck me with this illness. If I'd just do a little more penance, I'd get well. No! I tell you, it doesn't work."

181

Despite the fading light, he saw Marta's cheeks redden. "I wouldn't say anything so cruel! I meant about you being a saint. Listen. I'm going to tell you something that might sound very strange. In the desert, I met a thing like a great, white-hot dragon. It touched me on the forehead, and it burned me. That burn still pains me every time I think of doing something unjust, even when someone *near* me thinks of it."

It sounded every bit as crazy to Baldwin as she evidently feared. "Did you get a touch of the sun?" he asked, trying to be gracious.

"Well, yes. But the dragon saved us from a demon that pursued us, the Destroyer-by-Day. I think they call him Qeteb."

"I...see."

"Listen," she said, a note of desperation coming into her voice. "You and I both know that there is a world beyond the one we can see. Nothing like this has ever happened to me before. I was at the Watchers' Council this morning, and when something unjust was suggested, it was like a knife going through my head."

"You are a Watcher?" That shook him. Wherever Watchers were, prophecies and miracles were never far away.

Perhaps he was not a saint. But he began to think she might be. The only alternative was that she was mad—and he hated to think that of his only companion.

She put a hand to her sleeve. "I have the mark on my arm to prove it."

"I trust you. Go on."

"My friend is a Perceptor. She says that she sees a light shining from where the seraph touched me. She says she's only ever seen one other person with the same mark. *You*, my lord."

Nothing could have prepared him for that. "What are you saying? That I was...touched by an angel?" He almost laughed to hear the words leaving his lips. "I'm quite sure I would remember that."

She stepped swiftly closer, put a hand on the arm of his chair and knelt down to look into his eyes. "You said yourself that you've been sick since you were a very young child. Maybe you don't remember. But I think that you had something to do with a seraph—and now your conscience doesn't just prompt you: it *burns* you."

She was close enough to touch him, much too close for safety. Baldwin touched the tip of his tongue to his swollen lips. "I already told you, I'm *tired* of hearing that if I just tried to be a better man I wouldn't be so sick."

"I don't think that's how it works. Do you think the angels come down and bestow their kisses out of hatred? I think it was a *blessing*, to sharpen your conscience and make you a holy man. I know they say that lepers are violent and lustful, but you've shown them how wrong they are." She paused, her voice softening. "You've shown them a truly good man."

"Stop!" Baldwin spat. His maimed hands dug into his knees, shaking. He had long fought off the fear that his disease was a symptom of divine wrath, but even that was more bearable than the possibility that it might be a sign of divine favour. "God knows I try to do the right thing for the kingdom, but *no*. You're telling me I've been chosen to be a saint. That's not who I am. I am a *king*."

She smiled, her whole face lighting up. "Why choose when you can be both? A good man, *and* a king. It's so obvious. In all the stories, if the king suffers, then his land suffers. But really, it should be the other way around. If your land suffers because of injustice and ill-doing, then you suffer. That's fair, after all. *You're* the one who could stop them." She leaned nearer. "Even if it doesn't mend your disease, *you* could set the captives free. *You* could stop Reynald attacking the Saracen pilgrims. *You* could send Isabella home to her mother."

Each word was like a hammer-blow. "Stand back!" he exploded suddenly, and she recoiled, blood flooding her cheeks as she recalled who and what he was.

Baldwin sucked in a breath of pain. "God knows I do my best," he rasped. "What I do might not be pretty, but it's *necessary*. I can't run this kingdom on ideals alone! If I tried the kingdom would fall. *That* would be the real sin."

Her eyes widened with horror. "With reasoning like that, you could justify anything at all."

"Then what would *you* do?"

"The right thing!"

"You think it hasn't been tried?"

"I think…" Marta's voice trailed off and she stood still, looking down at him with a crease between her eyebrows. "I think you can't just try to do a *little* good. It would be like trying to smother a fire with your bare hands. If you want to win, you must stake everything."

Sibylla had said something similar once. "Including my kingdom?"

"Only if you want to keep it." She sucked in a breath. "Isn't that how it works in this world? *For whosoever will save his life shall lose it.* Unless something changes, we're going to lose the kingdom anyway. The sin in this kingdom will kill you, the divine protection will be withdrawn, and the time of the Saracens will come."

"I'm sorry, but I can't overturn this kingdom on fairytales alone. I have bigger things to worry about," Baldwin said tightly. "Like whether there'll even *be* a kingdom for the Saracens to conquer after the barons have finished killing each other for the throne."

"So we both agree that you need to stay alive." She stepped forward, eagerly. "Try it. Buy us the time we need!"

"I said no." Baldwin gritted his teeth together, ignoring the pain that shot through his jaw. "I think you had better leave."

Her lips tightened; then suddenly, she smiled. "I have faith in you, my lord. You'll do the right thing eventually. After all, a seraph kissed you."

She flicked her braids and ran for the wall.

The evening grew colder as night fell, but Baldwin didn't move from his seat or ring his bell for assistance. As usual, arguing had left him feeling sick and weak. Pain throbbed in his ulcers and all he could do was hunch over and wait for it to ebb.

Instead, it was the anger that left him. Marta Bessarion was naive and young and silly and *saints*, how he wished he had the luxury of being like that. Already he regretted telling her to leave. He'd never meant to quarrel with her, but she had to understand that what was right for a private person was not always what was right for a ruler. Now she would never come back.

He took a long, slow breath, trying to banish the pain. Once again, he thought of the life that was denied him when he was born to the throne. If he had never contracted leprosy. If he could have been an ordinary man with ordinary morals and an ordinary wife who knew with absolute certainty what was right and what was not. And perhaps, who sometimes wore trousers.

There was one thing the Syrian girl was right about: Reynald wanted to hold the wedding soon–just seven months from now, in October. Baldwin took another deep breath. This pain was yet another reminder that his condition had worsened rapidly of late. He had to set his affairs in order, and if Isabella didn't marry soon, she would be like a bottle of Greek fire tossed between the different sides, ready to smash and ignite.

With a grunt of exertion, the king reached for the bell at his side. He would send his permission to Reynald at once. As for Marta Bessarion?

She was wrong. She *had* to be wrong.

The alternative was too dreadful to contemplate.

Chapter XX.

Marta stood on the east wall of Kerak and stared across the mountain fortress towards the dying sunset. The limestone walls of the castle glowed red in the last light of day, and the hills of the frontier province unspooled before her, golden with dry grass and ripe grain.

This was Transjordan, the frontier province, where she had come to see Isabella marry Humphrey—or not.

Since her own disastrous attempt, Marta wondered if she had judged Lord Balian too harshly for failing to change the king's mind. Now Isabella herself was their last hope. She sighed. Maybe she should have gone to plead with the Leper King one more time—but he was so offended last time she spoke to him. She didn't understand why. Did people not have eyes to see? The Watchers of her own time had bloodied their hands in injustice, and they had fallen.

No more, she vowed. She wouldn't lose a second home because no one would learn from the mistakes of the past.

"Marta?"

At the waiting-woman's call, Marta hurried towards the queen's chambers, built into the wall nearby. She lingered for a moment at the doorway into the richly-decorated rooms, looking over her shoulder into the castle courtyard.

A frontier town like Kerak could boast few of the luxuries of Jerusalem, but no expense had been spared for the heir's wedding. Perched like a bird of prey atop an unassailable glacis ringed with ditches, Kerak castle hummed with music, murmured with speech, winked out sudden lights in the gathering dusk.

Too many people. Marta wished she was anywhere but here.

Beyond the heavy tapestry that covered the doorway, the queen looked into a glass hand-mirror as her waiting-woman settled a golden circlet hung with pearls over her filmy white veil. A tub of water, smelling faintly of jessamine, showed where the queen had washed in privacy—Marta and the other attendants had used the public baths downstairs.

Queen Maria set the mirror down. "Give us a moment, Helena."

Dame Helena and the others knew the queen had no wish to see her daughter wed. Perhaps they even guessed the queen meant to stop it if she could, but so long as they were in Stephanie of Milly's own castle, the details of her plan were limited only to those who needed to know.

The two of them.

With the room cleared, the queen fidgeted with a pot of carmine lip-stain. "I'll need you tonight, Marta."

"Eyes and ears?"

"And hands and feet." The queen stood, hooking gold-and-sapphire jewels into her ears. Silver laces criss-crossed her sides, pulling her bliaut into tight horizontal folds across her belly. A heavy train of silk pooled behind her; the fabric would have swamped most women of the queen's stature, but Queen Maria carried it with panache. "I want to see Isabella. You must find out how."

It was young Lord Humphrey who had welcomed them to the castle this afternoon. Two years of manhood had raised his stature and broadened his shoulders, but had done little to straighten his spine or louden his voice. There had been no sign of either his mother, Countess Stephanie, or of the young bride.

Marta put a hand to her ribs, remembering the hot tears shed the night Isabella was taken. "Surely the countess won't refuse you this time."

"Why should she change now?" the queen replied bitterly. She lifted her mirror again, dabbing at the corners of her eyes. When she lowered the glass, however, they were clear and resolute. "If she is wise, Stephanie will not relent tonight. What comes after will be your business."

Marta nodded. "Miles will help us, my lady." There were butterflies in her stomach at the thought of seeing him again. Part of her was afraid she'd throw up or faint or something stupid like that, but whatever might have happened between them, she didn't doubt he'd do his best for Isabella.

She touched the scar on her forehead, tugging her white veil forward a little to conceal it.

The queen dabbed stain onto her lips and pursed them at the mirror. "It was a foolish thing you did for him last winter. Foolish and dangerous, and we would have put a stop to it if we had known."

Which was why she would never have asked for permission.

"But I am glad for it, Marta, since it puts him in your debt. Make him remember. Make him repay you."

Marta took a deep breath. "He'll remember. He swore an oath to Isabella."

The queen adjusted the hem of her sleeves to allow her hands full movement. "Good. Do you have Stephanie's gift?"

Marta lifted the bolt of fine siqlatin, a design of her own making that interwove silk with gold. She and Persi had gained a reputation for fine weaving, and baronesses across the kingdom paid dearly for fabric made on the loom in the lower room of Nablus. As she followed the queen downstairs towards the castle's great hall, Marta hoped the gift would soften the countess of Transjordan—but somehow, she doubted it.

The great hall of the castle stood at the south end of the courtyard in the shadow of the massive keep. Inside, beneath high windows and acanthus-carved pillars, the hall seethed with guests, servants, and entertainers. The sight and sound of so many strangers made her want to turn around and run back to her own quarters, but Marta forced herself to follow the queen. She had work to do.

Slowly, they made their way towards the painted fresco at the head of the room, where Countess Stephanie and her son sat at the place of honour at the high table. Prince Reynald was not present: he was still in Jerusalem, trying to help Count Guy weather a political storm. Like so many of the Frankish women, the countess was tall and imposing, carrying herself with all the dignity of a great heiress who had buried a father and two

188

husbands already. She did not seem even slightly intimidated as Queen Maria stepped onto the dais and faced her across the table.

"Be welcomed to Kerak, my lady. Do you have everything you desire?"

"No." The queen dropped the single syllable like a block of ice. "There is a boon I must ask of you, my lady."

"Indeed? Shall I send for—"

"For Isabella," the queen cut in. "It has been three years since I saw my daughter. May I see her?"

Stephanie's voice was as hard as her face. "She is indisposed. A touch of the fever."

"Then I will go to her. She will want her mother beside her."

"When she is strong enough."

"Would you deny me?" The queen was losing her temper; her voice dipped. "You have no right. She is *my* daughter."

"And she is entrusted to *my* care."

"Will you use force to prevent me?"

Although their voices became softer, eyes and ears were turning to them from all across the hall. Beside the countess, young Lord Humphrey looked as though he wished the ground would open up and swallow him. Stephanie leaned forward a little and breathed one final word.

"*Yes.*"

All the queen's steel slammed back into the scabbard and she stepped back, her voice lifting to a pleasant conversational tone. Only Marta sensed her rage. "Another day, then."

Stephanie smiled, yet her eyes remained cool. "Yes. Another day."

But not, Marta guessed, until Isabella was safely married. Her own face was hot with indignation as the queen waved her forward. "I have a gift for you. Siqlatin, woven in my own household."

"A rich gift," Stephanie commented, and for the first time some real human warmth betrayed itself in her voice. *What's the matter?* Marta wanted to say. *Is there a corner of your heart you haven't turned to stone?*

As the queen made her way to her seat behind the high table, a female attendant took the cloth, which had taken weeks to design and weave.

189

Marta let it go with a pang. She never liked parting with her work, especially not to people she detested. But there was nothing to say. Marta backed away into the crowd.

Since Stephanie would not relent, it was up to her to find a way to Isabella. Marta ducked her head and slid through the crowd, a silent, meek shadow. Although her head was down, her ears were open. Gusts of talk blew past her.

"...the debacle in Galilee, surely?"

"But I don't see why he should have to resign. Was it such a debacle, after all?"

As she passed a carved pillar, Marta saw that the speakers were two churchmen—bishops, by their crosses and rings.

"The Leper King certainly thinks so," one retorted. "Two armies of that size, in the field for weeks, without ever coming to grips?"

"A fine tactical victory! You know the aim of war is to avoid pitched battle. Guy of Lusignan protected the kingdom, and with very little loss. Not the headstrong rush I'd have expected from him, but maybe he received good advice."

"Good advice?" The dubious churchman snorted. "Saladin walked into the kingdom and out again, and didn't even burn his fingers! I'm not surprised the king was furious. We look like fools!"

Of course, Marta thought, *the dispute between the king and his bailli would form the bulk of the conversation tonight.* She could not help wondering if the Watchers were responsible for this open hostility between King Baldwin and Count Guy. She frowned, touching her forehead. All she knew for sure was that the seraph's kiss was not hurting her tonight.

Ahead, Marta caught the sound of Miles' name and moved towards it.

"I don't like it," a voice boomed. "With all this raiding, the prince will pull down every vengeful Saracen on our heads, crying murder."

"Oh, there'll be full-scale war soon in any case. And not just because of Prince Reynald. Any credence Saladin has as a ruler depends on his ability to destroy us. When I was in Egypt last month—" The voice dropped out of hearing.

Marta shivered. All the more need to act tonight. She turned again, scanning the crowd, looking for Miles. As the prince's constable, he ought to be somewhere in the fortress—but perhaps he was still outside on duty. One of the sergeants on guard would know. She sidled through the crowd towards the door.

Conversation swirled around her.

"...said Count Guy was not fit to be king."

"...seen the town? What say we head down after dinner to drink wine in the Greek quarter?"

"Surely if she was underage, the church would put a stop to it..."

"...told me Saladin may forget for a while, but he never forgives."

"...failing again, and cannot sit a horse."

"...planning another raid for the next pilgrimage to Mecca."

"Another miscarriage, and otherwise only girls."

"Cooler weather in Tyre."

"Met him in Petra."

"Lady Sibylla..."

"The prince."

"Saladin."

Marta broke through the last cluster of voices, feeling suffocated. And then she saw him.

Miles.

He strode through one of the hall's arched doors, flanked by other knights, young and old. As their eyes met, Marta froze, fighting the urge to run and hide. Until this moment she'd been longing to see him again, but now they were surrounded by strangers, she wasn't so sure. She took a step back, just as he called her name.

"Marta Bessarion!" He grinned at the other knights. "Here she is—the damsel who wields a lance better than any man in Galilee."

Marta reddened. All her pots of scent and makeup, the trip to the bath-house, the ribbons braided into her hair, the masterpiece of grey silk damask she'd woven herself and sewn into a gown, and he greeted her as *the best lance in Galilee?* Skilled as she was with her lance, there was more to her than war.

A smiling crowd of knights had surrounded her and there was no escape short of an elbow to one of their throats. She darted a flushed glance around her and rose up on tiptoe to whisper in Miles' ear.

"Please, Miles. I must speak to you."

"What, now? It's dinnertime."

"Yes, now. Please."

He threw a glance around the room and sighed, nodding dismissal to his friends. Then he stepped back through the massive arch into the courtyard, beckoning her after him.

Outside, the darkness of late autumn cloaked the castle. Folding her arms as the cooler air struck her, Marta followed Miles upstairs onto the east wall.

"Give us some space," he told the sergeant they found standing guard at the top. As the man retreated, Marta walked to the crenelated wall and peered over. Here the height of the wall rose sheer from the brink of a precipice and at its foot, a smooth glacis of solid masonry sloped steeply into the valley below. Any besieging army would take one look at this side of the defences and give in.

Anyone losing balance here would hit the glacis first, then tumble down the unforgiving slope, unable to catch himself on the close-fitted stone. Marta pulled back, sickened by the sight in her mind's eye.

"Is it true, what they say about the prince? That when he executes a man, he locks his head inside a wooden box to…keep him alive longer…on the way down?"

"Who told you that?"

"Someone at Nablus."

Miles shook his head. "Don't believe everything you hear. That only happened once."

Marta's stomach knotted. "But it *did* happen." Her forehead ached with remembered pain. No wonder the king was sick, if such things happened in his realm. "How could you choose this place over Nablus? Lord Balian would *never* throw men from his walls."

"Only because Nablus *has* no walls. The law would allow any lord in the kingdom to do the same."

"Then the law is wrong." Clearly she had a lot of work to do, and not much time to do it in. That just made it more important to keep the Leper King alive, and in order to do that, she had to stop this wedding.

Miles hadn't taken his eyes off her since sending away the guard. Now, his words came out in a rush. "Look, Marta, I'm sorry for what I said—"

"You don't have to apologise," she interrupted, half terrified of what he might be about to say next. "I would be happy to be your sister."

The silence was horribly awkward, and she couldn't see his face properly in the dusk. "Are you sure?" he asked.

Her face burned with embarrassment. Of course he wouldn't want to be friends if she was always going to be languishing around after him. "As sure as sunrise."

"Well. I'm glad of that." Miles cleared his throat. "They'll serve dinner soon."

Marta came back to the present. "Where is Isabella? Is she well?"

"She's had a touch of fever, but she's mending."

Marta shook her head. "Poor Queen Maria. Can't you imagine what it's been like, these last three years—wondering if she was well, if she was happy, if she was lonely."

"No." Miles looked wistful. "Stephanie's the only mother I've ever known."

"And she might as well be cast in iron," Marta said bitterly. "Did you give Isabella our message?"

"I did, but it was months ago, when we first returned from Arabia."

"I understand." Worry gnawed at the pit of her stomach. "We have to see her, Miles. It's *wrong* that she should be made to marry like this. She's too young to say yes, and too weak to say no."

"You want to see her *now*?"

"Yes. Where is she?"

"In her own room. She'll be dining with her people, and then abed early, I imagine."

None of Isabella's former attendants had been permitted to attend her; Stephanie had provided her with a nurse and ladies. Just one more way in which the young princess had been isolated from her home and family.

"She sleeps in this tower." Miles motioned with his head and Marta glanced up at the tower reinforcing this side of the wall. Its great black bulk loomed over the light, airy rooms where the queen had been lodged. With its tiny window slits and thick walls, inside it would be cold and dark, more like a prison than a lady's bower.

It had a good view of one thing, though. The glacis where Prince Reynald carried out his executions.

She swallowed. "Miles, we have to get her out of this place."

A grin pulled at his mouth. "Why, are you planning a kidnapping?"

"I might."

"I'd wager you'd pull it off, too." He shook his head. "I don't know whether you're mad or magnificent."

Her face went hot. "I believe heaven assists the holy."

"So you keep saying." Miles gave a twisted smile. "I don't know much about theology, but that sounds like a doctrine that could get you killed."

"Maybe, but I'd rather die well than live badly."

"Mm-hm." Miles seemed unimpressed. "What's your plan?"

"Remember what Chancellor William said at the Watchers' council. No one can force Isabella to marry against her will. That's what we've got to tell her tonight."

"I see." Miles ran both his hands through his hair with a gust of laughter. "By all the saints, Marta. You are like a knight of romance. First you turn up to rescue me from Arabia, now you're in Kerak for Isabella. Where will we hear of you next? In Lebanon, in the mountain fortress of the Assassins?"

"Will you do it, though? Will you get us into the tower to see Isabella?"

The courtyard below had emptied as everyone took their places inside the hall for the feast, but Miles didn't seem to notice. He folded his arms and stared out at the eastern wilderness. The moon was too thin to cast much light, and only a few stars peeped through the clouds. There was nothing to see in the hills but darkness.

"Miles?" she prompted.

He didn't look at her. Just kept staring into the dark. At last he took a deep breath. "Marta, I can't."

"What?"

"I can't help you." He dropped his arms and turned to her. "I can't afford it. Since I lost my men in Arabia, I've been on quicksand with Prince Reynald. And even if the prince wasn't my only hope of advancement, this is the king's command."

Marta couldn't believe her ears. "But you *swore.* You swore to get her back."

"Believe me, I hate what's happening to Isabella as much as you do." He took a deep breath. "But I can't help you. And if you won't be warned, then I'll have to tell Countess Stephanie what you intend."

"What?" Marta felt a stabbing pain between her eyes—the seraph's kiss. She didn't know whether it was for herself or him. "You'd betray us? All we want to do is remind Isabella that she has a choice!"

"Hush, Marta! I'm sorry! I can't disobey the king!"

"But you can break your oath?"

"If that's the price of swearing foolishly."

"Then you are a liar as well as a fool! What eternal reward do you hope to reap for that?"

His voice lifted in frustration. "Marta, God doesn't care about things like this."

She was angry enough to spit. "I have seen a province conquered and a city burning because the Watchers thought so. Don't you realise you are playing with fire? Don't you realise the kingdom will be destroyed if we keep doing such things?"

"Well, I'm not a Watcher."

She might as well bang her head on a stone wall. "Well, then, I suppose you are free to lie and steal and kill as you like."

He didn't answer.

"I would have released you, Miles. You had only to tell me how your mind had changed. You never needed to—to—to *suck* the information out of me and then turn it over to our enemy!"

"See, this is where you're wrong." Miles' voice became cold. "You think you will win because you always do what is kind and good. And so you are honest and trusting and *foolish,* Marta. Prince Reynald will always win because he does what is clever and ruthless."

Tears spilled over and rolled down her cheeks, but they were tears of rage. Marta clenched her fists. "Is that what you think? Is it? Just watch me, Miles of Plancy! I *will* stop Isabella marrying Humphrey, and I'll do it without dirtying my hands." She took a long, shaking breath. "I can't *believe* I kissed you."

Miles started away from the parapet. "Marta, listen, I—"

Before he could say anything else, she flicked around and ran for Queen Maria's lodgings, slamming the door after her. She leaned against the wall, shaking as the pain in her forehead faded.

Miles.

Miles, her sworn brother, who she'd risked her life for. Miles, who'd taught her so much. Miles, who had been her friend from the very first moment he'd met her, when she was lost and frightened in the streets of Cacho.

All her anger drained away, leaving a terrible hurt in its place, like a wound she didn't want to examine.

Queen Maria, she reminded herself. She had to tell the queen that Miles had failed them.

Then they had to determine what to do next. Alone.

Chapter XXI.

Sibylla had known the Watchers would try to sabotage Guy's regency. What she didn't expect was the Leper King's response.

"I want to know what happened in Galilee," Baldwin rasped. "I want *your* side of the story, Lord Balian."

The tall lord of Ibelin shot an uncomfortable look to the corner of the king's solar where Sibylla sat listening. "Well, my lord, Saladin crossed the Jordan River and burned the town of Bethsan. Young Lord Humphrey and some of the Transjordan troops were quartered in Nablus, and he came immediately to join Count Guy at La Feve. On the way, he ran straight into a division of the sultan's mamluks and lost a hundred men."

The king refused to be distracted. "I don't want to hear about Humphrey. Keep on topic, my lord."

Sibylla shifted in her seat, wishing she could lie down, take something for the pain, and drift into oblivion. She was pregnant again, and a deep ache radiated up and down her spine, clamping her neck in a vicelike grip. Still, she was determined to witness this meeting if it killed her. In the two weeks since Guy had returned from the Galilee campaign, Baldwin's initial anger had only grown. Now, it seemed the Watchers hoped to have him removed altogether.

Ibelin cleared his throat and continued. "Ramla and I were already at La Feve with the count. Saladin sent out maybe a thousand troops to harass us. Some of us engaged them and they drew off. After that we advanced to La Tubanie and made camp...and there we sat in the wilderness for more than a week."

197

"And did *nothing?*"

"Saladin did his best to provoke a battle. Sent men to threaten Nazareth, and finally ascended Mount Tabor to pillage the Greek monastery. The local villagers had to drive them off, which they did with great honour. The day after, Saladin retreated across the Jordan and went to Damascus."

"But *why?*" Baldwin growled. "You had the greatest army Jerusalem has ever put in the field and you struck not a *single* blow against our enemy. Count Guy tells me that *you* were to blame."

A strained silence followed. Sibylla shifted again, permitting herself a cautious hope. Baldwin might be losing his last eye, but evidently he could see that the fault was not entirely Guy's.

Beside Ibelin, the iron-grey count of Tripoli shifted uncomfortably. "We advised Count Guy against it, my lord."

"We?" Baldwin repeated, his voice dangerously calm.

"Many of us. Myself. Ibelin and Ramla. Others."

The king's voice was like ice. "So it's true."

"My lord—"

Baldwin heaved himself to his feet, grabbing a table to keep himself upright. "This—poltroonery—was of *your* making?"

Tripoli replied stiffly. "When have you known me to show fear, my lord? It was not cowardice that guided me but my considered opinion. I advised him for the best."

"For the *best?*" Baldwin choked, trembling as his legs threatened to buckle under him. "Saladin roaming the kingdom, seeking whom he may devour. The Saracens burning Tabor unchastised. Those *peasants* showed more of the knightly spirit than you. God in heaven, Tripoli, you had best furnish me with good reasons why I should have so little regard for my flock!"

"Saladin is no mean enemy," Tripoli said doggedly. "He was strong in numbers and Count Guy is untried in warfare—"

"As was I," Baldwin interrupted, "at Montgisard. Why, think you, should a prince *have* advisors?"

Sibylla couldn't help enjoying the look on Tripoli's face.

"I advised as best I could. Saladin withdrew. Little damage was done.

The men of Jerusalem live to fight another day, when Saladin is in a weaker position."

Sibylla had told the king this herself: everyone knew that pitched battles were risky. You could never be certain which way a battle would go, no matter how strong your numbers, no matter what your element of surprise. If you were wise, you avoided them.

Not that she meant to remind her brother of this. Let the Watchers fashion a noose for their own necks.

Baldwin's knees buckled and he fell, exhausted, back into his seat. "Each year Saladin grows stronger," he whispered. "Each year he gains new territory. What will happen when he finally turns the full weight of his conquests against us?"

Sibylla cleared her throat. Time to play her final card. "My lord, rumour has it that Saladin's strength at Bethsan was not so great as my lord of Tripoli believed."

Baldwin stared. "What's this?"

"Guy tells me that for two days Saladin left his eastern flank unprotected. Our scouts were able to approach nearly to the camp itself. He proposed a surprise attack, but these worthy men refused to take part." She let her voice ring, then added: "Of course there would have been risk."

"Risk!" Baldwin shook his head. "Saladin was *there*. The opportunity was there. The *army* was there. Of course there was risk! Do none of you see danger except when it's breathing down your necks? Does no one ever look to the horizon? Why was this opportunity squandered?"

The silence was like pins and needles.

Sibylla looked at the other men, her lips thinning. "If you will not answer him, shall I?"

"You were not there, my lady. You know nothing of the case." Tripoli's voice was full of warning.

Until now, Ramla had been silent. He spoke now between gritted teeth. "Because it would have been Guy's victory. That is what the countess was going to say, and I don't care who knows it. For myself, I would not have stirred hand or foot under his banner if the whole kingdom was not at stake."

Baldwin drew a long breath. "Count Guy carries the full authority of a king of Jerusalem. Yet you admit that you worked to undermine him? I wonder you dare say this to my face. I beg your pardon, Sibylla. This, at least, was not your husband's fault."

"Thank you, brother." Sibylla's hope grew. Evidently, Baldwin was still willing to listen to her.

"What about you, Balian? Would *you* have ridden under the count's banner?"

The Prester looked uncomfortable but determined. "Into Galilee? I did. Into battle? No. I would not put my life or the lives of my people into the hands of any man who despises them."

"*Someone* must lead the army," Baldwin snapped.

Ramla jerked his head towards the king's cousin. "Why not Tripoli?"

Baldwin might have forgiven the attempted coup three years ago, but he hadn't forgotten. His voice sharpened. "Someone I can *trust*."

Tripoli bristled. "I thought you had pardoned me, my lord. Would you have me leave your dominion?"

"No, cousin." There was a silence, which Baldwin broke with a weary sigh. "Tripoli, Ibelin, Ramla. If you follow Count Guy, so will everyone in the kingdom. The succession will be safe. Jerusalem can hope to go on." He lifted his hands in a clumsy pleading gesture. "Can you not bring yourselves to follow him?"

"Ought we to?" Balian asked. "Is he a man of such virtue?"

"We already know him to be a murderer and a seducer," Ramla growled. "We knew that when he married the Lady Sibylla."

Baldwin looked exhausted. "It would be well for all of you to remember under what circumstances he became my sister's husband. It was *you* who forced me to it."

Tripoli was still gruff, hurt. "I wish you would believe me, my lord, when I say you had no reason to fear us. Not then. Not now. Not ever."

"*But I do fear you.*" Baldwin's voice cracked, and Sibylla couldn't help wishing she knew how a sickly and weak leper could silence a room full of wilful and powerful men like this. "I fear you most of all, because you care so little for the consequences of your actions. Is your grudge against Guy worth destroying the kingdom over?"

Ramla snorted. "The question is not whether the kingdom will be lost if we refuse to follow him. It's how soon it will be lost if we do."

Baldwin tried again. "He is Sibylla's husband, next in line for the throne. He will be justly offended if it is denied him."

"So you summon us and beg us to follow him because you think us more reasonable than him?"

"Guy is not an unreasonable man."

"No," Ramla sneered, "he can be reasoned into anything."

Sibylla glared daggers, but Ramla hadn't looked her way since he'd entered the room.

Baldwin noticed her indignation.

"You'll speak civilly or leave the room, Ramla," he snapped. For a while, no one spoke, and at last the king gave a weary sigh. "If I am the only man you will follow, I must go back into harness."

Sibylla stiffened. "What?"

"I am sorry," Balian said softly.

"I am *not*." Ramla was triumphant.

Tripoli frowned. "But do you have the strength, my lord?'

"I will *find* the strength," Baldwin said grimly.

"A moment, my lord." Sibylla stood up, holding onto the back of her chair to keep herself steady. "You're removing Guy from the regency? Your barons misbehave, and you penalise *Guy?*"

"Sibylla," he began.

She didn't care; she was so angry. If Guy became the man who was ignominiously removed from the regency, then how could he claim the throne? How could *she?* "Guy has done *nothing* wrong. You saw for yourself that it was the Watchers who tied his hands, and now they're using this to drive a wedge between him and you!"

"Leave us," Baldwin told the other men in the room.

When the other men had filed out, Baldwin sighed, his voice resigned.

"What would you have me do?"

"Give him more time. We can *do* this. Together."

"How much time am I to afford him?" Baldwin's voice hardened. "Guy has had three years to win the barons over. If he was any good as a king, if he was any good as a bailli, he would have been able to take *action* in Galilee, rather than submit to having his hands tied!"

It was like banging her head against a wall. "This is not just about Guy, brother. It's about me too. Do you forget that I am your true heir? That I have been trained to rule? Do you think me incapable?"

"Incapable? Sibylla, I *counted* on you. I promised myself the pleasure of living out my final years in peace, watching you rule this kingdom better than I ever could. Then you chose Guy and now…now I can't do that."

Sibylla pulled in a breath. "Listen, Baldwin. I am the rightful heir. You can't ignore that just because you disagree with some of my decisions."

"It wasn't just *any* decision. The choice of a consort—"

"But you would have trusted me alone?"

"Can *you* command an army in the field? Sibylla, right now you can barely stand."

"That's why I need Guy! Don't you see? *I* am the thought, and he is the action. I am the head, and he is the body. Everyone is looking for one perfect man to be king, but there's no such man in the world. Guy and I may be weak apart, but together, we're strong."

"I know, Sibylla." The pity in his voice made her squirm. "But there's more to ruling than ability. It takes honesty and gentleness—and Guy has neither."

"He's been honest and gentle with *me.* If Longsword had lived, I should have had to fight him for my kingdom, like Melisende did Fulk!"

"All the more reason why Guy should have been able to get the barons' loyalty as well as yours. I tell you there's no help for it."

"Is that it, then? You're going to cut me out of the succession?"

"No! No. Really, Sibylla, I'd rather it was you than anyone else."

"Then why not *tell* them so?"

Baldwin sighed. "Because it takes the barons to confirm a new king or queen, you know that. I can name my heir, but I can't force the barons to accept him. And I don't want to create that conflict." Baldwin looked into her eyes, his voice gentling for the coup-de-grace. "Sibylla, if you and Guy can't find a way to placate the barons, the best rulers might not *be* you and Guy after all. They might be Isabella and Humphrey."

Sibylla stared at her brother, not really seeing him. In the silence, a noise came from the loggia beyond the solar. A rustle of clothing. A slap of feet. A whispered word, sibilant and startling.

"News from Damascus, my lord." Prince Reynald of Chatillon burst into the room, breathless, as though he'd been running. "Saladin is on the move again. This time he's marching for Kerak."

"Kerak?" Baldwin froze.

It was the only revenge she knew how to get. Sibylla smiled maliciously. "Are you worried about Isabella? Oh, she'll be all right. Humphrey is there. I'm sure *he's* an able battle leader."

Prince Reynald shook his head grimly. "Humphrey? Ha! Humphrey couldn't lead a rat to a granary. No, my lord, I came here to take my leave. I'm riding to Kerak tonight."

Chapter XXII.

Believe me, I hate what's happening to Isabella as much as you do.

Marta wanted to get out on the training-field and hit something. Preferably Miles of Plancy.

Marta, God doesn't care about things like this.

Every time she thought of it, she wanted to scream. Just because everyone else thought it was alright to force a child into a political marriage didn't mean she was going to go along with it. Saints, even if she *wanted* to she couldn't go along with it—not with the seraph's kiss on her forehead.

Isabella would be married tomorrow.

Marta wanted to catch a horse, to gallop and never stop.

Instead, she swallowed and planted her needle cleanly and precisely in her hooped linen. The gold thread whispered through the fabric, making another tiny, even stitch in the colourful pattern. She was nearly done with the piece now, a special commission for the bishop of Nazareth's new cathedral.

Marta drew the thread firm and placed the needle again, letting the rhythm calm and empty her mind. With each stitch, the world became a little more beautiful, a little more peaceful. She could not force the king to change his mind. She could not beat Miles into repentance. Yet in a hundred years or so, when both she and he were gone, this rich work would still be lying on the altar in Nazareth.

Another stitch, and another. *The best lance in Galilee,* Miles had called her. That wasn't who she was. She was more than a warrior: she was a maker. If she fought, it was only for Isabella, for the altar cloth—for peace.

As the afternoon light faded, Marta shifted her stool closer to the glass-paned windows. The arched openings pierced the eastern wall, offering a glimpse of the arid hills beyond. There would be more light if she sat outside, on the wall itself, but she didn't want to risk meeting Miles just now.

Down in the courtyard below, a trumpet blew and urgent hoofbeats rolled. She lifted her head, curiosity piqued. After a few moments of confused shouting, the chapel bells began to ring, peal upon urgent peal.

The alarm!

Marta jumped, almost running the needle into her hand. Before she could reach the door, it opened and Queen Maria entered.

The queen was still a young woman, not much older than thirty, but her face was pulled tight with worry that deepened the lines around her mouth. With shaking hands, she held out a letter. "This just arrived from Jerusalem with Prince Reynald."

It read:

FOR THE HAND OF MY LADY, QUEEN MARIA.

Most beloved lady and wife, greetings. I beg you will not be cast down in any way but rely on the mercy of Christ, for the news has reached us that the Turkish Sultan with his full army has left Damascus and marches to Kerak. The prince has already departed with fifty knights and the King has sent word for the barons to muster at Jerusalem. I kiss your hands.

BALIAN OF IBELIN.

"Saladin," Marta breathed, feeling the blood leave her cheeks. What was it the Bedouin sheikh had said? *I wager you may expect him before the walls of Kerak before the year's end.*

"He will be here tomorrow at the latest."

Marta rushed to the door and burst out. From her vantage-point on the wall, she saw horsemen swarming the courtyard as Prince Reynald's small troop dismounted. A group of burgesses had run after him from the town and stood in the courtyard, heads together, gesticulating.

North of the town, a ribbon of black snaked through the hills towards the castle. Marta's heart jumped: for an instant, she thought it was the Saracens. Then she made out the herds of livestock. Peasants, fleeing their homes in Saladin's path.

No one had been willing to help them free Isabella. Now war was coming to Kerak.

Marta took a breath and scanned her surroundings, trying to put Lord Balian's siege-warfare lessons into practice. Built on a high ridge, Kerak was magnificently strong. Deep valleys carved the land along the east and west, rendering the walls on each side impregnable. South, the land fell steeply from the massive keep, defended by a steep glacis, a deep water-cistern, and beyond that, the great South Fosse. The only possible direction of approach was along the ridge from the north. That was defended by a stout wall with only a narrow postern for entry. Beyond the wall was the narrower North Fosse, which divided the castle from the town; and beyond the town was another limestone wall.

Was it enough?

The alarm bells fell silent and Prince Reynald emerged from the great hall, lifting his hand for silence. Miles stood on the prince's left and Lord Joscelin, the king's uncle, on his right. The seething courtyard hushed.

"You have no doubt heard that Saladin has invited himself to our wedding feast, with some twenty thousand additional guests, all of them armed and voracious!" The prince's voice was full of grim humour. "Well, he couldn't have picked a better time! We have enough food to feed an army! We have minstrels, tumblers, and jugglers! And steel enough to feed all the sons of hell! When our wine runs dry, we shall drink their blood! Let the feast begin!"

Marta's forehead throbbed with heat and she pressed cool fingers against it, shivering. "He must be sick in the mind," she murmured to the queen.

Below, one of the burgesses lifted a hand. "My lord, what are your orders concerning the town? May we place our wives and children within the castle?"

"No room," the prince boomed. "Get out and prepare to defend your homes! Off with you!"

"He's going to man the town?" Marta voiced the realisation aloud, in shock. The town's wall was long and low, far more difficult to defend than the castle wall.

Beside Marta, the queen hardly seemed to hear. "I hoped to take Isabella home with me," she murmured. "Now we're trapped here."

Recalled to the moment, Marta put her hand on the queen's arm. "Then let's do what we can. This uproar gives us our chance."

"Yes." The queen shook her head as though to clear it. "You know where I keep my gold."

Marta nodded, but Queen Maria's hand fastened on hers. "She's still so young. Will she have the courage to resist them?"

Marta remembered the stories Miles had told her. Isabella was irrepressible, full of life and defiance. Surely she was equal to this.

"Isabella is strong, my lady. We can only try."

* * *

Marta had attended weddings before, but she'd never been in a siege. As she slipped downstairs towards the castle laundry, she stared at the feverish bustle in the courtyard. Fugitives from the surrounding countryside had pitched makeshift shelters in the shadow of the walls, and the smell of the sheep or goats they roasted over their campfires mingled with the scent of bread, cakes, and pasties being prepared for tomorrow's wedding feast. At the foot of the stairs, Marta elbowed her way past jugglers in colourful motley, practising their tricks; on the other side of the courtyard, men in equally colourful livery sat around flaming braziers sharpening their swords. A burst of laughter from a knot of lords and ladies making conversation on the wall was cut through by the clank of hammers as the castle blacksmiths sweated to mend armour.

Marta pulled a black veil over her head before entering the service chambers behind the hall. Baths, ovens and laundry were built close to each other, the heat of the ovens serving to warm water for the other rooms.

Though the sun had set hours ago, lamps blazed in the kitchens and even the laundry was bright and bustling with tirewomen clacking in Frankish, Armenian, Greek, and Arabic as they sponged cloth-of-silver or cloth-of-gold gowns, some of which Marta had woven herself. Another knot of women worked cutting plain white linen into strips and rolling them into neat spools. *Bandages.* Her throat went a little dry.

Marta approached one of the women and said hesitantly, "I am looking for Heva."

She didn't even blink. "The princess' tirewoman? Over there."

Marta crossed the noisy room and saw a short Syrian woman plying an iron. "Heva?" she asked.

"Yes?" The tirewoman set the iron down and lifted the garment she had been pressing, shaking out the heavy folks. Marta's voice died in her throat. It was a silk gown, dyed purple and woven with gold, evidently meant to remind everyone that Lord Humphrey's bride was descended from the emperors of Constantinople.

That it was Isabella's, she had no doubt. It had been made to fit a child.

"Can I help you?" the tirewoman asked again, crisply.

"Oh." Feeling a little guilty, Marta dipped into her pouch and let a gleam of gold escape. "May I speak to you in private?"

Outside the laundry, she explained what Queen Maria wanted. Heva listened impassively and then said, "I was warned not to let any Ibelins interfere with my lady. It's as much as my neck's worth."

"Don't be afraid. Queen Maria and I will make sure no harm comes to you." Marta almost hoped there *was* trouble. It would be a relief to snatch her spear and do someone an injury.

Heva pointed to the pouch, evidently more interested in the gold than in Marta's offer of protection. "How much?"

"Oh." Marta dipped her hand back in, counting out eleven bezants. "One now. Ten more when we have seen the lady Isabella."

Heva snatched the gold coin and shoved it into her sash. "Get your lady, then, and meet me outside the east tower."

There was still the danger that the tirewoman would content herself with a single coin and report them. Still, unless Marta was going to try to scale the tower itself and climb through a window, this was the only way.

By the time Marta had fetched Queen Maria and met Heva at the tower, she was beginning to hope.

"I know *you*, Heva," the guard grumbled in Arabic, peering at their heavy veils, "but who are these? The countess has threatened to have my head if we let any of the nobs in."

Heva was carrying Isabella's wedding-gown, and the gold threads glinted as she shifted impatiently. "Oh, quit your bellyaching, Da'ud! This is my sister and her daughter. They've come up from the town with some valuables they want to leave with me for safekeeping, in case those Saracens capture the town."

Marta held out a fist, slowly uncurling the fingers to let him see the tiny gilt reliquary inside. "Please, we have nowhere else to leave our things."

"What is it?" the guard whispered.

"I bought it in the Street of the Holy Sepulchre. A fingerbone of Saint Sabas. Why don't you take it? It will bring you blessing, and I would rather a Christian had it than a heathen Turk. Only let us in."

He hesitated once, then grabbed it from her hand. "Now I will have the saint's protection in the siege."

Heva smiled. Just like that, they were inside the tower.

Marta bit her lip as she scaled the dark stairwell behind the queen and the tirewoman. They should have tried speaking to the servants before asking Miles to help them. He had so much more to lose: the high office he enjoyed, his only home. Wasn't it unfair of her to expect—

The tirewoman turned, raising a finger to her lips.

She opened a door into a big, dark room, studded with tiny windows that Marta doubted she would have been able to squeeze through if she had scaled the tower. The room was furnished with bright tapestries and an immense fire to stave off the autumn chill. Couches lined against the wall held sleeping attendants, but in the big canopied bed at the room's centre, a girl was sitting up, moving her hands in the light of the single lamp beside her bed.

Making shadow-puppets in the light, like the little girl she was. Marta's heart twinged as she remembered doing the same with her younger siblings.

Isabella turned her head and whispered, "Heva? Is that you?"

The tirewoman motioned them to wait by the door. "Could you not sleep, my lady?"

"Not a bit. I keep thinking of tomorrow. My stomach is so full of butterflies!"

Marta found the queen's hand beside hers in the dark, and gave it a squeeze.

"Who's that?" Isabella had caught sight of them.

"My lady, it's someone who has come a long way to see you. Hush, now. Come with me."

"Who?" Isabella repeated nervously as Heva helped her out of bed.

"Someone who loves you better than anything in the world." Queen Maria dropped her veil and stepped forward, letting the lamplight glow on her face.

"Mama?"

"Hush!" the tirewoman warned.

"Mama!" Isabella whispered hoarsely, then launched herself into the queen's arms.

Amidst the tears and whispers, Marta and Heva managed to shepherd the two of them into the next room, a large chamber which Isabella was clearly using as a solar. As Heva closed the door behind them, Isabella disentangled herself from the queen and threw herself at Marta.

"Marta! You're here too! Miles told me about your adventures in Arabia!"

Marta laughed, hugging her tightly. "How tall you've grown!"

Suddenly Isabella pulled back, her eyebrows stitched together in a frown. "You never came for me, Marta. You promised you would. You *promised* I could go home!"

The queen spoke. "My darling, we couldn't! Believe me, we tried."

"Countess Stephanie said you had changed your mind. That you didn't want me anymore."

Marta's gut clenched. "Oh, Isabella! That's not true. Didn't Miles tell you—"

Isabella's face screwed up in a ferocious scowl. "I hate Countess Stephanie! Do you know what else she said? She said you don't even want me to marry Humphrey!"

The queen froze, her breath caught in her throat, and a foreboding pang ran through Marta's head.

"She said you'd try to make me refuse him!"

Queen Maria cleared her throat. "Do—do you *want* to marry Humphrey, darling?"

A decided tilt of the chin. "Of course I want to marry him! I love him."

The silence was like broken bones.

O God in heaven, Marta thought. *We have come too late.*

Queen Maria's voice barely trembled. "Don't you want to come home, Isabella? Don't you want to see your brothers and sisters again? Helvis is growing to be such a little lady, and John is so clever for his age. And did you hear that you have two new siblings? Your little sister Margaret is two years old, and your baby brother Philip arrived just after Christmas."

"I love their names!" Isabella's face lit up. "Is the baby here?"

"Not this time, sweetheart. But if you marry Humphrey, you'll have to live here with him and Countess Stephanie. Wouldn't you rather come home to Nablus?"

Isabella hesitated, and Marta's heart jumped with painful hope. After a few moments, however, the little girl shook her head with an affectionate laugh. "Oh, Mama! I'm not a *baby* anymore! When Humphrey and I are married, then we'll come to visit you."

Her forehead ached, but that was nothing compared with what these people had done to Isabella. Marta stepped deeper into the shadows and pressed a fist against her mouth, trying to stem the tears.

Queen Maria bowed her head in defeat. "Then we will say no more about it, and you and Humphrey must visit us *often*. You won't believe how the children have grown. John takes after his father, but he has a little of your spirit, as well. I want you to be good friends." The queen chattered on, full of news and gossip and laughter, her voice bright and brittle as glass.

Marta felt as though she'd been kicked in the stomach. *Too little. Too late. I ought to have acted sooner.*

She was thankful when Heva returned a few minutes later, and the three of them ushered Isabella back to her bed. The young princess clung to her mother, refusing to let go.

"You'll be there tomorrow, Mama? To see me married?"

"Yes, Isabella. I'll be there."

"And you, Marta?"

Marta wanted to protest, but of course it was useless. She touched Isabella's cheek and did her best to smile. "Yes, Isabella. I'll be there if you want me."

There was no difficulty getting out of the tower. The same guard was on duty when they left, and after the frantic preparations of the afternoon and evening, the castle had fallen into an exhausted slumber. In silence, Marta paid Heva her ten additional coins, then followed the queen numbly back to their chamber.

Just outside the door, where they could speak in privacy, the queen halted, leaning her forehead against the timber. She made no sound, but her shoulders shook with sobs. Marta knew she should say something, that there was something people were *supposed* to do at such moments, but her mind was too numb to work.

"I don't understand," Marta whispered. "When they took her away, she was calling him a horrid boy."

"It's been three years." The queen took a shaking breath, fumbling for a kerchief to wipe her eyes. "We lost this battle the moment they took her away from us. In love! She's only a *child*, what does she know about love?"

Silently, Marta handed her own kerchief. It was the only comfort she knew how to give.

"I promised Agnes I would be her enemy if she took my daughter from me." The queen straightened, and in the starlight, her eyes glittered. "So be it. Agnes has had *her* revenge. Now I will have *mine.*"

A sharp pain drilled between Marta's eyes. "What do you mean, my lady?"

she cried, but the queen had already slipped through the door into her chamber, where her attendants lay sleeping. Questions would have to wait until morning.

Chapter XXIII.

When Sibylla had informed Guy of her brother's decision, he had been nothing daunted.

The little birds that can sing and won't sing, must be made to sing.

That had been his advice to her.

Sibylla had agreed, but before she could think how to make the little birds sing, she had suffered one of her periodic collapses. It was worse than ever this time, confining her to bed for several days in constant, unremitting pain, with only laudanum and hemlock wine for relief. The drug took away the pain, but left bad dreams in its place.

On the fourth day the pain eased, and Sibylla had herself carried to visit her mother. Normally the image of health, Countess Agnes had been ill too lately, with a persistent cough and an overabundance of bloody phlegm, and was still abed in her own solar. As Sibylla's servants carried her in and set her chair down, she was shocked to see how thin her mother looked.

"Sibylla!" The countess struggled to sit up in bed. "What's happened, girl?"

"I was about to ask the same thing," Sibylla returned. For a moment they only stared at each other, and then Agnes' face split in a reluctant grin. She laughed, but the convulsions racked her body and turned, at last, to more coughing.

"Look at us, lying in ruins," she whispered at last. Yet for all her laughter, her eyes were dark with understanding when she looked at Sibylla. "The baby?"

"Gone," she said flatly. "I lost it two days ago."

"Not this one, too." Agnes lay still, the black laughter drained out of her. "At least you have young Baldwin. And little Alice."

Sibylla didn't want anyone to feel sorry for her; she felt sorry enough for herself. How could she build a dynasty when so many of her children died? Young Baldwin was hardly strong, either.

Was she truly cursed? If a demon *was* troubling her, the servants' evil-eye charm had done nothing to help.

Refusing to let the grief swallow her, Sibylla pushed herself into anger. "I'll have another son if I must lie abed for twenty years."

"There must be some reason behind it." Agnes plucked fretfully at her silk coverlet. "It isn't natural for a woman to lose so many children. Promise me you'll see someone for it."

Sibylla smiled bitterly. "Who, mother? An apothecary, a priest, or a fortune-teller?"

"Anyone who will help."

"When you get well, you must find someone for me, then. Did you hear that Baldwin plans to remove Guy as bailli? We have until the next meeting of the High Court—"

"I'm not *quite* dead, Sibylla. Of course I heard." Agnes linked her hands on the coverlet. "The question is, what are you going to do about it?"

Sibylla shook her head. "I've been sick and miscarrying at home, or I'd have done something already!" She rubbed her temples. "With Guy removed from the regency in disgrace, we'll be at a terrible disadvantage in claiming the kingdom later. What if Prince Reynald tries to put Isabella and Humphrey on the throne? What if he convinces Baldwin to name them his heirs? What would *you* do, Mother?"

"Is Baldwin so set against Guy?"

Sibylla rubbed her chin. "After the Galilee campaign, Baldwin was angrier than I've ever seen him. He can be so emotional sometimes."

"The way *I* heard it, Guy responded in kind."

"Yes, but when a kingdom is at stake, you don't let personal dislikes get in the way of—of practical political realities!"

"*You* might not; but others do, or we wouldn't be having this conversation," Agnes pointed out. "Sibylla, you're very lucky that I might be able to fix this."

A wave of relief rushed through her. "You can?"

"I think I can." She was silent a moment, her voice tired. "One last favour for the king's mother."

"Last?" Fear clawed at Sibylla's throat. Somehow, she knew what her mother would say even before the words found their way out.

"I'm not getting well, Sibylla. It's the cough…it's been getting worse."

Everyone died sooner or later, but Agnes had been her best ally at court. Soon, she would have to forge her way alone. It would be like trying to fight without a right arm.

Sibylla herself understood a great many things, but she didn't usually understand people. She might predict what they would do, because the rational course of action seemed so blindingly obvious to her—but then off they would go and do something completely different, too stupid to know any better. Agnes was often as stupid as the rest of them, but she was somehow much better at convincing them to see things from her point of view.

Sibylla was still staring, speechless with dread, when Agnes spoke again. "Don't be afraid, Sibylla. Baldwin won't deny me one last favour. Go home and think it over, and choose wisely: it will be the last thing I can do for you."

Sibylla obeyed the first part of her mother's command, but the second was impossible. She had lost her baby, she was losing her kingdom, and she was about to lose her mother. Her mind wandered under a dark cloud, numb and overwhelmed.

Everyone died eventually. One day the world itself would die. What use was there in mourning?

I wonder how I will die, she thought.

Her litter had paused before the gate of her house when an old woman's voice pierced the stuffy darkness of the curtained space. "Lady Sibylla! Lady Sibylla! A message for you!"

Thinking she recognised the voice as one of her spies in the palace, Sibylla

216

twitched the litter's curtains aside with a hiss of annoyance. "Bring me that woman."

The ancient woman who approached the litter was ragged and unkempt, much older than her spy. "Who are *you?*" Sibylla demanded.

"You hope for a great inheritance, my lady," the crone wheezed, baring her arm to reveal a black mark inked into her skin. "They will take it away from you, and bestow it upon another."

Not a message. A *Message.* Sibylla drew back, understanding. "You are a *Watcher.*"

The old woman's mouth quirked with humour. "Not the kind who sits in king's palaces."

"I will have you whipped if you ever approach me again." Furious, Sibylla signalled to her guards.

Instead of recoiling, the old woman launched herself at the litter. "I came to warn you—"

Sibylla's guards grabbed the old woman and dragged her away. The woman's voice rose to a cracked yell. "Beware, my lady! Don't drink the hemlock!"

Her words cut off with a shriek and Sibylla clapped her hands shakily, ordering her litter through the gate and into the courtyard of her house. The old charlatan! It didn't take a supernatural gift to see which way the wind was blowing.

They will take it away from you, and bestow it upon another.

As they helped her into a chair and carried her upstairs to her own room, Sibylla's fingers fretted and fidgeted, tracing the engraving on her onyx ring.

They will take it away from you, and bestow it upon another.

On Isabella and Humphrey? On Tripoli? Or on anyone at all, so long as it was not Guy and Sibylla?

Alix waited in her solar, a cup of the laudanum-hemlock concoction waiting to dull her pain and ease her into sleep. *Beware. Don't drink.* The old fraud, trying to frighten her! Sibylla crossed the room in three strides and drank the draught in one gulp.

217

Sibylla sank into her chair, staring sightlessly out the window. So the Leper King feared there would be trouble if he forced Guy on the barons. Her jaw clenched. Nowhere near as much trouble as there would be if they tried to take her rightful inheritance.

She had tried playing by the rules. Appealing to the Watchers. Having Guy installed as bailli. Tried and failed, because her enemies had no scruples.

Well. Neither would she.

From now on, she would act as ruthlessly as she must.

She would make the little birds sing.

Chapter XXIV.

Marta knew she wouldn't sleep. Instead, she wrapped herself in her mantle and went out onto the wall to let the wind dry her tears. Leaning against the battlement, she watched the castle fall asleep for the night, campfires burning low in the courtyard, voices falling silent.

Far to the north between the black shoulders of two hills, distant pin-pricks of light showed where the Saracen army camped. Saladin might be coming to encircle them, but tomorrow morning, Isabella would lock her prison with her own hands.

It outraged every sense of justice, yet without some kind of miracle it was going to happen. Marta buried her face in her hands, trembling with an anger for which she could find no relief in action.

Slow hoofbeats sounded below. Across the courtyard, a light shone from the stable doors as a lonely rider dismounted. Marta caught a glimpse of a young man's silhouette, slight and weary-looking.

Humphrey.

He crossed the courtyard towards the living-quarters. Towards her. Marta didn't stop to think. Her soft leathern slippers made no sound on the stairs as she crept down. In the narrow, abandoned passage between the chapel and the wall she drew her dagger and rushed him, shoving him against the stones with the knife to his chin. The mark on her forehead burned, but Marta blinked tears of pain away, too angry to care.

Humphrey squinted down at her through the dark and said, "Oh, saints" in an exhausted voice that carried the fumes of wine. "Who are you?"

Marta's knife-hand shook, the moonlight jinking off its blade. "I'm

219

Isabella's sister and I want you to know that if you—if you hurt her..." Her voice trailed off. What *would* she do if Humphrey hurt Isabella? There was no lawful means of protest, except to the Leper King, and he had already refused to stop the wedding. What did that leave? Murder?

She was still trying to think of a viable threat when Humphrey snuffled. "Why does everyone think I want to marry Isabella?"

"You're *drunk*." Marta pulled back in disgust.

Humphrey slumped against the stones. "They said they'd make a man of me. I'm so *sick* of being made a man of. Always means blood and harlots and too much wine."

"Harlots?" Marta was scandalised. "How *dare* you?"

"It's all right," he mumbled. "I gave them the slip. Always works. Do you mind putting that knife away? It's giving me a headache."

Marta sheathed the blade. Her vast and aching anger would find no outlet here. "You don't want to marry Isabella?"

"Saints, no."

"But she's the Leper King's sister."

"She could be Helen of Troy for all I care." There was a reckless note in his voice. "She shouldn't be shackled to someone like me. I'm a *freak*."

Marta's lip curled. "How much wine did you drink?"

"I *begged* the prince not to make me do it." Humphrey's voice was raw with tears. "He gave me no choice."

The pain in his voice dissolved some of her animosity. "You *always* have a choice, my lord. No one can make you marry against your will. Tell them you won't do it."

Humphrey's jaw sagged. "Tell them *what?*"

"Tell them you won't marry Isabella. Tell them you don't want to. Tell them she's underage."

"I can't," Humphrey whispered.

"Of course you can! Just *tell* them."

"I *can't*." Humphrey's voice was jerky. "The prince will tell... Everyone will find out about...Gerard."

Marta stared. "Gerard?"

"He was my...tutor." Humphrey took a shaky breath, evidently close to tears. "The prince threw him from the wall when he found out...with his head locked inside a box."

Someone like me. A freak.

"Oh," Marta whispered. She had never suspected *this*, and now she didn't know what to say. "Oh...I see."

She'd heard of such affections, but she'd never tried to imagine what it might actually mean to live with such a secret. An indiscretion of this nature could cost Humphrey everything. The loyalty of his men. The respect of his peers.

His life.

"Oh," she repeated, helplessly.

"I shouldn't have a wife," he mumbled. "I'm a monster. Unnatural."

Marta blinked at him, and a cold chill went down her spine.

"No." If he believed that, then how would he treat Isabella? She grabbed his tunic and shook him. "No. You don't have to accept what they say about you. You still have a choice. You can remember that this violates both of you. You can treat her with kindness and respect. Or...or you can become a monster. Which is it going to be?"

Humphrey looked down at her. She couldn't see his face clearly in the dark, but she heard his breath even out, felt his muscles bunch as he straightened. "I won't...violate her," he whispered. "I can promise you that. They can force me to marry her, but they can't force me to touch her."

Marta's hands clenched in his tunic. Promises could be broken—she knew that all too well. But this was all she could do for Isabella now. "Do what you have promised, and you will make a man of yourself, Humphrey of Toron."

* * *

The day dawned cold, the sun's warmth swallowed in the roar of a late October wind. Miles of Plancy looked down from the low wall that surrounded Kerak town and shivered a little in his armour.

Beside him, Iven, a Burgundian, grunted as the Saracen army flooded the valley below. "The plan?"

Miles took a deep breath. While the great castle crowned a high ridge to the south, the town itself perched on a broad plateau. A wide road zig-zagged up from the valley to the town gate, providing the easiest mode of access. "These slopes should give them some trouble at least. So long as they focus their attack on the gate, we can focus our defence here, too."

In the valley below, the sultan's army divided, its cohorts spreading out to encircle the whole town.

Iven grunted again. "And if they *don't* focus their attack on the gate?"

Miles forced a smile. "Then we hope we aren't spread too thin."

A long silence stretched out like a held breath. On the road in the valley, a tent bloomed, and presently Saladin's eagle standard unfurled above it.

In the same moment, a trumpet screamed and drums pulsed.

With a sound that shook the hills, Saladin's army advanced.

* * *

The bright blare of trumpets sparked expectation amidst the tightly-packed crowd in Kerak's courtyard. In the silence after their sounding, Marta heard a distant commotion on the gusting north wind: the thump of war drums.

Saladin was here.

Her pulse quickened, but it brought little welcome warmth. Marta wrapped her woollen mantle a little more tightly around her shoulders. She had been standing wedged into the crowd near the church door for so long that her feet had nearly gone numb. A Syrian farmwife's basket was prodding her in the ribs and someone very close smelled as though he hadn't washed in a fortnight, but Marta didn't regret her choice to hide in the crowd. After last night she couldn't bear to walk with Queen Maria in the bridal procession.

She would watch the wedding, as she had promised Isabella, but she would not be a part of it. Not knowing how ruthlessly both bride and

222

groom had been exploited.

The doors of the great hall opened, spilling music into the morning air—the festive beat of flutes and drums. Guards pushed their way through the crowd, forging a path to the chapel. Around Marta, people jostled, craning their necks as the performers emerged from the hall wrapped in strands of music.

Behind them came the barons: tall, burly Franks, resplendent in furs and silks. A guard of honour—or perhaps just a guard—for the young man walking in their midst. Congratulatory shouts split the air as Humphrey walked towards the chapel, but he did not turn or smile to acknowledge them.

He looked rather as though he was walking to his own execution, but she could not quite bring herself to be sorry. To men like Reynald, even to the Leper King himself, Isabella was no more than a pawn to be sacrificed. Humphrey, at least, saw the living soul of her, felt the shame of what he was being forced to do.

On that drawn and desperate look hung all their tattered hopes for Isabella's happiness.

* * *

Saladin's army was as diverse as the lands he ruled. Fair-skinned Turks with their hair flying in long braids wielded short, powerful bows. Pale sunlight glinted off the slim straight swords and spears of Arab horsemen. Black mamluks and Kurdish sergeants trudged grimly up the road for the town gate, chanting a marching song. At first, Miles had tried to count them, but as they advanced to just out of bowshot of the wall, he had quickly given up.

There were enough to surround the town, and that was all that mattered.

"We'll need to man the whole wall," Miles decided. "Iven, I'll keep two companies here at the gate. But I want everyone else facing the enemy. No one is left in reserve. If we need reinforcements, we'll send to the castle."

But the old soldier wasn't paying attention. "What in God's name is that?"

Miles followed his pointing finger. Behind the massed ranks of attackers, skeletal wooden structures were taking shape, their components hastily assembled by sweating teams of engineers. Miles caught his breath as he recognised the machines.

"Mangonels," he breathed, as dread crawled up his spine. "Eight of them."

The trumpets sounded again. Whips cracked, and the massive siege engines rolled forward in awful majesty.

* * *

The crowd hushed, and Marta's stomach churned.

Last night it had been easy to think of Isabella as just a child. Now, as she emerged from the great hall decked out in the purple gown, veiled with gold and weighted down with jewels, she looked almost a woman and a queen. As the onlookers oohed and aahed, caught in the illusion, Marta's outrage nearly choked her.

Two lords escorted her, each holding one of her hands. On her right, the scarred and battered Prince Reynald, his armour glinting beneath his sweeping fur robe. On her left, the dark and sleek Count Joscelin, his smile an uncanny reminder of his sister Agnes.

Marta's fingernails bit into her palms. *What do the Courtenays have to do with Isabella? She is none of theirs. They have no right to dispose of her like this.*

Behind Isabella walked a bevy of noble ladies, glinting like precious metal in the thin sunlight. Countess Stephanie took precedence at their head—it was Queen Maria's place, by right, but the queen clearly could not bring herself to take it. Instead, she had exiled herself to the rear.

As the nobility passed, the crowd of onlookers fell into step behind them, flocking towards the chapel door where the bishop of Petra waited in the porch. Marta shoved through the crowd and slipped quietly into place beside the queen, touching her arm with sympathy. Queen Maria didn't move, staring rigidly as Humphrey and Isabella paused facing each other at the church door.

His hands shaking, Humphrey fumbled with the pouch of red samite that held the thirteen gold bezants symbolising Isabella's dowry.

The bishop cleared his throat. "My lord, my lady, kneel to receive the blessing of God upon this holy bond."

Yet the wind gusted, blowing away his words as he prayed, and all Marta could hear was the distant sound of war drums.

* * *

"What are they doing now?" Iven wondered as he prepared to lead his company west along the wall.

Miles narrowed his gaze at the white-robed mystics moving through the Saracen ranks. Fitfully, their chant drifted to his ears through the wind.

"They're praying," he said.

Iven snorted. "Think God is with them, do they?"

He whistled to his men and they marched on, two abreast on the narrow walkway that crowned the wall. Miles checked for the fifth time that his crossbow was wound, and checked once again to be sure. The excitement he often felt before a fight had been replaced by a hollow feeling in his gut.

Don't you realise you are playing with fire? Marta had said. *Don't you realise the kingdom will be destroyed if we keep doing such things?*

Maybe he should have tried to help her. Just in case.

He was almost grateful when trumpets screamed from the eagle banner, and the Saracen army surged up the slopes towards the wall.

"Wait for my signal!" he called to his company, lifting his crossbow. He narrowed his eyes, judging the distance as the Saracens crept within range. "And—*loose!*"

A storm of bolts flew towards the Saracen ranks, thinning them viciously before their own archers, with their less powerful bows, could get within range.

"Reload," Miles called. He drew breath for another order, but the words died on his lips as he recognised the long, notched poles the Saracens were planting against the wall.

Ladders. They had brought dozens of ladders.

He really should have tried to help.

* * *

Under her golden headdress, Isabella's eyes glowed as she looked into Humphrey's strained face. Marta's fists clenched in utter helplessness. If she had her spear and armour, she would be tempted to charge in and snatch Isabella out of their hands. But what then? The only way out of the castle was through the midst of a Saracen army—and Isabella would fight her every step of the way.

Humphrey took Isabella's hand and slipped the ring onto her thumb, his voice shaking as much as his hands. *"In nomine Patris."* He transferred the ring to her index finger. *"Et Filii."* Her middle finger. *"Et Spiritus Sancti."* He almost dropped the circle of gold, caught it, and finally got it onto her ring finger. "I marry thee, wife."

A stabbing pain shot between Marta's eyes, and she clamped her teeth on her sleeve to prevent a wail escaping her. Through tears she watched the bishop take Humphrey's hand and Isabella's, clasping them together.

"What God has joined together, let no man put asunder!"

The church door opened, and the bishop led the pair in for the nuptial Mass, with the lords and ladies flocking in after them. But Marta didn't move.

Wordlessly, she let her head tilt back and stared into the iron-grey sky against which all her prayers had rebounded in vain.

* * *

As the Saracens swarmed the wall, Miles' vision narrowed to a pinpoint focus. He strode to and fro, trying to meet the next challenge, the next ladder, the next enemy to gain a footing on the parapet.

He didn't see the engineers working feverishly at the great mangonels; didn't see the counterweights loaded, the great arm swinging.

226

He had no warning.

Whump.

The wall reeled as the missile hit, bursting open the battlement on his left and tossing the defenders away as though they were toys. Rocks and shards flew, rattling against his armour, stinging his cheeks. Miles recoiled. His vision expanded to take in the gap that had just opened in the wall beside him. The siege engines loading new missiles. The desperate struggle lining the whole wall.

He didn't know whether to believe Marta or not, but if God meant to show his displeasure, he could hardly be plainer than this.

Beside him a young sergeant froze in horror, staring at the broken men on the ground below the wall. Miles grabbed the boy's shoulder. "Bertrand. Take a horse and ride to the castle. Tell them we need more men. We can't hold the town." He swallowed. "Have the townsfolk retreat to the castle. I know what the prince said—but if these people don't move now, they'll be caught unsheltered in an iron storm."

The man nodded and bolted for the stairs, evidently glad to be relieved of his duty on the wall. Miles turned back to the melee and tightened his grip on his sword.

Chapter XXV.

The wedding feast was lavish, but a pall of silence hung over the great hall as the guests kept half their attention on the distant sound of Saladin's bombardment. Messengers kept stealing into the hall to drop a word in the prince's ear. One by one, the knights of Kerak left their places and did not return.

A tirewoman seated next to Marta leaned back to stop one of them as he passed. "What's happening, my lord?"

"Miles of Plancy is asking for reinforcements. Saladin's trying to get into the town."

Marta swallowed a bite of lamb too quickly as worry got the best of her. "Miles? Where is he?"

"On the town wall," the knight said. "Pardon me."

He rushed away and was hardly outside the door before Marta heard him calling for the company he'd brought with him from his own fief near Montreal.

When Prince Reynald himself stood, adjusted his sword-belt, and headed for the door, Marta could no longer stay in her seat. She got up, shooting a stealthy glance towards the high table. Queen Maria narrowed her eyes, but Marta ignored the warning. Instead, she ran up to the queen's chamber on the east wall and strained her eyes to the north. The town seethed with panicked citizens. Beyond those flat roofs and the limestone wall loomed eight immense siege-towers. Even as she watched, a gaunt arm like a long-handled spoon swung, and a stone sailed through the air.

Whump. The ground shivered beneath her feet.

228

The stone ploughed through one of the townhouses and threw up a plume of dust, adding to the pall that already hung over the town.

In the courtyard, hooves rolled like thunder as Prince Reynald led a division of riders towards the town. For a moment the double wall on the north gate blocked him from view. Then she heard the ringing of the wooden drawbridge as he crossed it.

Maybe Kerak deserved to fall, after the abomination that was Isabella's marriage. But maybe she could save it.

That was her job as a Watcher, after all.

Already plucking at the lacings of her gown, Marta wheeled and ran for the queen's chamber. She peeled off the fine grey silk and delved into her arms chest, squirming into gambeson, trousers, and hauberk. Coiling her two long braids around her head like a roll of padding, she pinned them in place before settling coif and helmet over the top.

A rap sounded on the door. "Marta?" It was the queen's tirewoman, Dame Helena.

Marta whipped the door open, nearly throwing the older woman off balance. "What is it?"

"Where are you going?" Helena hissed. "It's dangerous."

"So am I."

"The queen says that if it's that young knight you're going after again—"

Marta slid past, trying to hide her blazing cheeks. "Miles has nothing to do with it." Her forehead twinged. All right, maybe that wasn't strictly true.

As she emerged, the sound hit her like a wave. Screams, shouts, pounding drums and blaring trumpets. Marta had never heard anything like it. The town roiled with people fleeing towards the castle. Somewhere in the crowd, Prince Reynald's gryphon banner waved drunkenly in flight as his men elbowed their way back to safety.

The enemy must be inside the town already.

Marta raced for the gatehouse. By the time she reached the high wall that fronted the town, a steady stream of people was pouring in through the narrow gate and down the long dogleg passage between the double

229

wall: knights, sergeants, burgesses and beggars. Beyond, a deep fosse underscored the castle wall, a single narrow wooden bridge providing the only passage to safety. As the crowd fought to cross, some lost their footing and toppled into the dusty trench below with wails of fear and pain.

Beyond the town, the Saracen siege engines had fallen still, but their drums still pounded the advance. Marta raced up a stair onto the north wall, where a chain of narrow embrasures gave a sheltered view of the fosse and the crowd beyond. Up here, as below, confusion reigned. The sergeants who manned the wall seemed unsure what to do; contradictory shouts split the air.

Marta pounced on a crossbow that lay abandoned on the ground beside a quiver of bolts. It had been fired once and discarded, its user having no time to reload. Marta slid her feet into the stirrup and strained at the cord, but the effort was too much for her. As a sergeant rushed past, she threw an arm against his chest, halting him in his tracks.

"You load," she panted, slamming the bow into his arms. "I'll fire."

As he laid a quarrel to the groove, Marta scanned the town. By now Prince Reynald had pulled his men back into the castle, leaving the townsmen to defend their own retreat. Now, Saladin's mamluks advanced down the main street. A thin line of armed men retreated before them, trying to shield the retreat, but they were giving ground too fast. There was no time for the people beyond the ditch to file over the narrow bridge to safety. Marta stared in horror as the civilians crowded closer to the fosse, jostling more people over the edge in their desperation to escape.

"Here." The sergeant handed her the crossbow.

"Load me another," Marta told him, "and get the others shooting too."

It was one thing fighting with the Bessarion Lance, which she could always reverse to use as a blunt. It was another thing to shoot sharp and cold-blooded bolts. Marta took a deep breath, to steady herself. People were dying out there; and if the archers could hold off the Saracen advance, they might buy time for the townspeople's retreat.

Marta sighted down the stock, picked one rider out of the scrum and loosed the bolt. She didn't see if she hit her target, but she dropped the weapon and reached blindly. "Another!"

Footsteps clattered up the stairs onto the wall. Marta was already squinting down a new stock when Prince Reynald's voice cut through the clamour. "Keep those people moving! *Miles!* Miles of Plancy! Devil take it, where is he?"

Marta narrowed her eyes at the confused melee in the streets, trying to find a clear target. Her trigger finger twitched. Her bow sung. This time she was dismally sure she'd got her man; one of the riders jerked off his horse and as he did so, a gap opened in the melee, framing a Frankish knight still on his feet, facing the mamluk cavalry with that thin rear-guard.

Marta's stomach jerked. She'd know that battle-axe anywhere.

It was Miles.

He might disappoint her and disagree with her but he was *there,* standing between the people and the enemy: a shield, a wall, a life offered in another's place.

Nearby, someone answered Prince Reynald's question. "Miles of Plancy? Still out in the street, m'lord."

The prince swore. "I told him he was wanted here," he roared. "Get those crossbows in use. Where are our ballistae? Why am I surrounded by fools?"

Marta hoisted another crossbow to the embrasure, bracing herself to take aim. Along the north edge of the fosse, the townspeople had linked arms to keep themselves from tumbling over. The Saracens pressed close enough now that Marta could see their faces. They were in no great hurry; it was the town they wanted, and the more people that were shut up inside Kerak, the harder it would be for the defenders to feed and water them all.

Marta aimed and let fly, but her target moved, and the bolt skipped off his helmet doing no damage. Too each side of her, however, more hissing bolts began to fly, withering the enemy.

Her arms burned with the effort of lifting each reloaded weapon to the wall. As she wrestled the next to its place, someone nearby pointed and yelled. "That's him! That's Saladin!"

A man on horseback advanced down the town's main road towards them.

A canopy of silk was carried on four lances over his head by his mamluk bodyguards; gigantic shields carried ahead of the sultan protected him from arrows.

Marta lined up her crossbow, breathing slowly and willing her eyes to focus on that distant figure. After so much fine needle-work, her eyes needed a moment to adjust, but as they did, she found herself looking at a man's distant face—all that was visible of the sultan behind the shields.

With one bolt, she could save Kerak and who knew how many lives.

Marta breathed out gently and squeezed the trigger.

The bolt flew true, yet it never reached Saladin. Instead, it shivered into a puff of splinters in mid-air.

Marta straightened, feeling as though someone had poured ice-water down her neck. *Magic.* Someone—or something—was protecting the sultan.

Her sergeant pulled at her elbow. "Sir?"

Marta dropped the spent bow into his hands and wrestled a new one to the wall. Behind Miles, the crush was finally lessening as the townspeople streamed into the castle.

"Pull back," she muttered, "why don't you pull back?"

The sultan's advance halted. His mamluks dropped back, but only to gather for a charge. As Miles and his thin line of defenders braced themselves, Marta shot her bolt into the assembling charge and snatched for a new bow.

A thin yell rose from Saladin's army. The mamluks quickened to a gallop.

"Miles!" Was that scream ripped from her own throat? Marta shot into the oncoming tide and straightened. As the last of the townspeople jostled across the narrow wooden bridge, Miles and his handful of sergeants broke before the mamluk charge and raced for safety.

Marta lifted another crossbow to the wall, heart pounding as she tried to find a target. Given free reign, the mamluks ploughed through the town's last defenders, spattering blood into the dust.

At the bridge-head, Miles threw down his shield, caught a second axe from the ground and turned to face the enemy. His voice was unrecognisable as he howled instructions to the last defenders and burgesses. One by one they slipped past him and pelted across the bridge.

A mamluk levelled his spear at Miles and spurred his horse into a gallop. Moments later he slid from the saddle with Marta's crossbow bolt sticking out of his chest.

Everyone who would make it was now inside the castle—everyone except Miles. "Shut the gate!" His voice was a thin howl as he retreated onto the narrow wooden bridge with his axes sweeping the air before him. Now the Saracens could only come at him one by one. Marta swallowed, finding that her mouth was dry. *Thank God they have no—*

Ta-ta-tack. Three arrows sprouted from Miles' hauberk in quick succession.

She'd wondered where the Saracen archers were. Left in reserve, no doubt, since they were not shock troops. But now at least one of them had arrived. Marta jerked the stock of her crossbow up, searching for the bowman's hiding place. *There.* The top of his head peeped over a rooftop parapet in the town and he ducked as her bolt skipped across the stones next to his head.

Below, the arrows hadn't slowed Miles down. He had made it to the near side of the fosse, but the gate had already been closed, obedient to his commands. He sent one of his axes spinning into the ditch and whirled the other over his head, attacking the pegs which held the bridge in place.

Ta-tack-whing!

The Saracen archer was up again, loosing three arrows in quick succession. Two of the arrows sank into the gate just beyond where Miles sweated and grunted at the axe. The third glanced off his helmet. "Come on, Miles," Marta whispered under her breath.

Ta-tack! Another archer, on another rooftop. Miles staggered slightly as the arrows sank into his armoured body. Marta located the shooter at once, half by intuition. This one was less cautious than the first, and she got him in the throat.

He was replaced by a dozen more. They swarmed the rooftop, drawing their bows. Marta glanced to the next rooftop. And the next—

A whole army's worth of archers.

As she watched, the wind hissed like a snake. Marta recoiled behind the parapet as a hundred shafts smashed themselves against the stone. A scream on her left hand told where one of her fellow defenders had taken an arrow in the eye.

Grateful for the faceplate she wore, Marta scooped up her reloaded crossbow, turned, and loosed a bolt at one of the Saracen archers crowning the parapet opposite. But the attackers had the advantage now: although their short horn bows were less powerful than the Frankish crossbows, they could reload much faster.

Marta risked a glance at Miles. At least some of that volley of arrows was meant for him; he recoiled against the castle door, bristling like a pincushion. His grip on his axe slipped, and it spun into the ditch. In the same moment three Saracen footmen charged across the bridge towards him. Marta screamed a warning, levelled a reloaded crossbow and shot the foremost, toppling him into the ditch. One of his companions followed him an instant later as another bowman found a mark.

Now disarmed, Miles fell to his knees, grasping the shattered bridge-head. The third Saracen attacker yelled a war-cry, whirling his sword above his head. His blade arced down.

Miles let out a roar, heaving at the wooden bridge. Miraculously, the sturdy bridge lifted, slipped sideways, and spun into the ditch, taking the Saracen warrior with it.

Marta grabbed another crossbow from her sergeant, scanning the rooftops opposite for danger. A captain stood with the archers on one of the rooftops, lifting his arm for a signal. Marta let fly—and missed.

Another storm of arrows broke against the wall. Without the bridge to guard, Miles darted aside, taking cover in the angle of the gate. As soon as the rattle ceased, a shrill whistle sounded from Marta's right and a coil of rope snaked from the top of the ramparts. Miles caught it, threw a couple of coils around his wrists, and launched himself from the narrow bridgehead. The other end of the rope must have been attached to a counter-weight, for it retracted quickly, dragging Miles up and over the top ramparts.

The Saracen drums fell silent, their cavalry retreating towards the sultan's command post in the main street.

At her feet, the sergeant finished reloading her spare crossbow and handed it up, but Marta's arms suddenly felt like jelly. Pain sparked up and down her neck and shoulders when she tried to lift the weapon. Instead, she leaned it against the wall, where it had been a few short breaths ago when she had come to the wall. "Thank you," she gasped.

Her hands were shaking. How many men had she just killed? For *Prince Reynald,* no less?

No, she thought, *I did it for Miles. I did it for Miles, and for all the defenceless people who would have died today without the two of us.*

Overwrought laughter drifted from the very top of the wall. Miles did not sound as though he was badly hurt, despite the arrows he'd taken, and Marta fought back the impulse to go to him. Now was not the time, here not the place.

Archers still lined the rooftops opposite, but they seemed to have finished shooting, only their peaked helmets showing where they still lurked behind the parapets. Far down the street, a line of ballistae and catapults rolled forward through the abandoned town towards them. From the sultan's command point, a white flag unfurled to herald the coming of an embassy.

Saladin himself did not approach the walls. Instead, one of his amirs rode forward, halting at the ruined bridge-head. His voice rose to the wall, speaking in melodic Arabic.

"Prince Reynald of Kerak, if you will open your gates this day and give up your people, your animals and your treasury to our hand, we will spare their lives! But continue to resist us, and as God is our witness and our help, we will spare neither man nor beast."

Marta's attention was dragged away from the parley by a train of Syrian serving-men doggedly climbing the stairs to the wall beneath the weight of baskets and jars.

On the wall itself, Prince Reynald sounded almost amused. "And for myself?"

"Your own life is forfeit by reason of the intolerable insults you have rendered to the sultan."

Miles broke in, still in that fey mood. "Why limit your revenge to the prince? He did not ravage the Red Sea alone!"

The amir smiled grimly. "Also, the promised safe-conduct is revoked in the case of the knight named Miles of Plancy."

A shiver walked Marta's spine. By now all the men Miles had led on the Red Sea campaign were dead, publicly beheaded in the squares of Cairo and Mecca. Clearly, Saladin meant to have Miles' blood as well.

On the crest of the wall, Prince Reynald spat forcefully. "Do you think us fools or cowards, to offer such terms when we hold such a strong fortress? Tell your master I will give him sharp entertainment until the Leper King comes to open my gates. And on that day I hope to render Saladin such an insult as to wipe out all memory of what came before."

Braggart, Marta thought with distaste. Prince Reynald was outmanoeuvred, outnumbered and trapped. His only hope was the Leper King—and much could go wrong in the weeks before King Baldwin could muster an army and march to their relief.

"The sultan instructs me to offer a bargain," the amir said. "Let the knight Miles of Plancy give himself up to suffer the penalty for his crime, and we will depart."

A moment's silence, before Reynald's words drifted down from the battlements. "Well, Miles?"

Miles almost choked. "What?"

"You wanted to make amends for Arabia; now's your chance."

"You want me to give myself up?" Miles sounded furious. "I've done all my duty and more for you. Go ahead! Throw me to the dogs if you like, but have the guts to do it yourself."

"We'll think on it," the prince called to the amir. Marta thought she heard Miles mutter under his breath. Reynald went on: "My wife also has a message: she considers it shame that so distinguished a guest should travel so far to her son's wedding and go without food or cheer. Behold! A gift for the sultan's table."

Down into the ditch went the hampers, the mighty jars, the baskets of good things on the end of a dozen ropes—enough for a small feast in itself. Marta felt grudging admiration for Countess Stephanie's defiance: *We can afford to be lavish with our food and drink. Even to you. You cause us no concern at all.*

The amir beckoned to his men, who clambered into the fosse to collect the gift, stepping over the dead and dying to do so. "A courteous gift and worthy of a courteous response! You see that we have with us seven great mangonels. When your son takes his bride to bed, let them run a white standard up above their chamber, and the sultan will direct his machines against some other mark. Now, enough! We will speak no more, save with stone, steel, and fire."

He wheeled his horse and trotted for the shelter of the town, his people falling into line behind him. As though to signal the end of the truce, at once a hail of arrows drummed against the wall. The serving-men hurried downstairs to the courtyard again, their festive clothing providing no protection against missiles.

In the street, a ballista rolled forward and halted. As its team locked its wheels in place and began to load the immense crossbow mounted atop, a horseman rode forward from the sultan's position.

His face was hidden behind a veil of chainmail which hung from his helmet, but Marta recognised the grey-dapple horse and the great black bird of prey perched on his wrist. The stranger from the desert—the one who had stalked them in the ravine—and the feathered woman who'd hunted them through the desert.

He lifted his eyes to the top of the wall, and her mind rang with a thousand warning bells.

Miles.

Marta left her embrasure and bolted for the stairs leading to the crest of the wall. Halfway up the second flight she caught sight of Miles standing nose-to-nose with the prince. He'd managed to pluck the arrows from his hauberk, but his face was bloody and angry. As she watched, he wrenched his arm from the prince's grip and turned on his heel, stalking along the wall away from her.

"Miles," she yelled, and launched herself after him, trying to cut through the renewed clamour of battle. He hadn't heard her. *"Miles!"* she screamed, raising her voice an octave.

He turned, irritated at being interrupted. "Marta? What in the—"

A dart punched through his gut with enough force to fold him onto the walkway.

Marta shrieked his name again and flung herself to her knees beside him. He lay against the stone with his legs splayed, face ashen and eyes wide in shock. Blood welled between the fingers he clamped to the wound.

It was her fault. She had distracted him while he was standing before one of the crenels of the battlement. He'd turned to her, exposed.

"Miles," she gasped, not knowing what to do with her hands or her voice. She could use weapons, but she had no idea how to mend their damage. "Someone help him!" she screamed.

Chapter XXVI.

"Do you see anything?" the physician asked.

Baldwin had known this was coming for some time, but that didn't make it any easier. "A little light in my right eye, glowing yellow," he said. "Otherwise, nothing."

He'd lost the ability to blink, his eyelids losing strength first on one side, then the other. Regular application of salt water could only delay the process for so long as his eyeballs itched, burned, shrivelled, and died.

The light grew a little stronger, heat beating against his right cheek where some of his skin remained sensitive, not deadened and numb like the rest of it. The physician must be holding the lamp right next to his face.

"And now?"

"A little more light. But no forms."

The physician made a sound of assent. "The good news," he said with false cheer, "is that you'll keep your hearing. You may put some salve on those ulcers, Brother John, and bandage the arms."

He left, and Baldwin relaxed with a sigh as his attendant, a leper from the Order of Saint Lazarus, began the nightly process of salving and bandaging the ulcers on his chest, back, and limbs. Baldwin stared into the foggy dark, barely aware of the gentle hands touching him.

He was becoming a prisoner in his own body. Each day left him a little more distant from the world beyond his skin, a little more closely locked into this maimed and painful shell, far removed from the ordinary pleasures of life.

To produce the same effect, some men would retreat into the desert, go up pillars, live in caves on mountains and whip themselves. Hermits, stylites. Saints.

No. *No.* That wasn't what he was.

"I sent a message to my mother this afternoon." Baldwin's voice sounded loud and harsh in his own ears, for the disease made his throat stiff and painful. "Was there any reply?"

"It arrived while the physician was here, my lord. Would it please you to have me read it?"

The Lazarites had the care of his body; that didn't mean he wanted them to be privy to the affairs of the kingdom. Still, he could no longer read a message himself, and the countess was not well enough to visit in person.

"Read it," he barked.

There was a rustle of paper and Brother John cleared his throat. *"My lord—it was in our judgement for the best that she should wed a man without ambition or ability."* After a pause, he added, "That's the whole of it, my lord."

So it was true. He had been used—by Chatillon, by Sibylla, by his own mother, even. To make sure that Isabella could never claim the throne, they had convinced him to marry her off to Humphrey of Toron in the full knowledge that he could not—what was the expression Chatillon used?—couldn't lead a rat to a granary.

Abruptly he became aware that Brother John had finished bandaging him. "That will be all," Baldwin said, and when the brother seemed inclined to dispute, *"Leave."*

The door closed and Baldwin turned in his chair, placing one knobbed hand against a smooth surface that he knew to be the window overlooking the garden. If he still had the use of his eyes, he would have seen the fruit-trees, the pools, the herb-beds that bordered the palace in neat square beds.

But he would never see again.

The lamp still burned on a table near him and Baldwin leaned over, straining towards the light. On an impulse, he pulled the lamp closer, until his cheek touched the glass pane that shielded the flame. He held it there

240

one heartbeat, two, until the pain became unbearable.

He flinched away. This. This was proof that he was still alive, that he was not dead and dreaming.

No, he was alive. And he had just ordered his sister married to a man who would never be able to lead the kingdom, though he had bent and broken the law to make it so.

Sibylla had done this to remove a rival, and their mother had helped her. Baldwin slumped back in his chair, touching his scorched cheek. He could be angry at them, but right now he was more angry with himself. Why did he rely on their advice? Why hadn't he taken more care to ensure that Isabella's husband could lead men?

He wondered about Marta Bessarion—whether the young Syrian girl had known, whether she could have told him. But of course Humphrey's practical capability as a leader meant nothing to someone so sharply focused on questions of right and wrong.

Saints, what she must think of him! Selling his soul for an heir, and letting himself be cheated into the bargain!

Granted, the little Syrian had other things to occupy her at the moment. According to Balian, Marta was at Kerak with Queen Maria, surrounded by Saracens. If the castle fell, she was not noble enough to be ransomed, and knowing the danger she was in made his hands itch for weapons they could no longer hold. She might be foolish and naive, but she was kind and unafraid and reckless. He very badly wished her never to learn fear.

Perhaps if he'd listened to her that night in the garden, he wouldn't be in this mess.

Baldwin's thoughts chased themselves around in a treadmill within his head. He fixed his eye on the glow of lamplight and slid his left hand across the table until a soft rattle let him know he had touched the lamp. But there was no sensation in this hand, no feeling of heat. He withdrew it and sank back, burdened with weariness.

In his dreams he was a child again, six years old and lonely because his father was too busy to see him and his nurse had been sent away. He was hungry, and the new nurse did not have any food, but it was autumn and there were oranges growing on the big tree outside. He could see the shadow of the tree through the window in the moonlight, so he went downstairs and crept out a side door into the garden.

There was a red glow, like firelight, in the shadows. On bare and silent feet Baldwin walked softly through the grass between the herb beds, until he came to where the orange-tree grew beside a pool. The air grew warmer as he approached, and the light stronger.

A winged serpent was folded in heavy metallic coils around the foot of the orange-tree, its scales glowing with ember-red fire. The same red-gold light shone from the fruit on the tree.

Baldwin stopped, his heart beating. He knew this picture from illuminated capitals, from carvings, from glass windows. The Tree of Knowledge and its holy guardian; for this golden serpent was no fallen creature.

If it had been the Devil, he might have been less terrified.

The seraph lifted a head, down which yellow flames rippled, and said, "What do you want with the Eldest of Trees, mortal?"

"I was hungry," he whispered.

"You hunger no longer?"

Baldwin swallowed, and looked at that shining fruit, clustered high in the leaves. "I can't reach."

"I will fetch you one, if you wish."

Baldwin looked at the dragon. Rippling with flame, it looked hot enough to burn, if not solid enough to touch.

It lifted its head and a frill on its neck fanned out, blowing heat in his face. "You hesitate."

"Will—will you burn me?"

"I will burn armies, cities, and kingdoms; in time, I will burn you too, mortal."

Baldwin thought about this for a moment. "No, thank you," he said in his politest voice.

The creature bent closer. "The fruit will bring you wisdom. You will need it; you were born to be a king."

The heat scorched his cheeks, but it never occurred to Baldwin to run

242

back to his bed. Instead he touched his tongue to his lips and thought. If he *would* be a king one day, then it was also true that he would need wisdom. Something inside told him that it would be wrong to refuse such a gift, no matter how it burned him.

If you truly *knew* what was right and what was wrong, then your duty to act accordingly was so much greater, so much heavier.

He was only a child, but he was already too wise to refuse. "Then I had better take it," he said with a sigh.

The creature's flames brightened and it reared up, clutching one of the glowing fruits in its foreclaw. It looped to the ground again, offering the fruit. Baldwin put his left hand further into the shimmering heat that surrounded the winged serpent. As he took the fruit from the creature's grasp, his fingers touched the massive claw and pain shot like lightning through his whole body.

Baldwin startled awake in his chair by the window. A fuzzy glow in his right eye told him that the lamp was still burning, and for an instant he thought his whole body was on fire.

Dread clawed at Baldwin's stomach as realisation slowly dawned on him. He'd had this dream before.

Chapter XXVII.

"Gut wound," the surgeon said curtly. "He's going to die. Nothing we can do but keep him comfortable."

Marta's heart stilled. "What?"

"In a day or two, infection will set in. You'll have maybe a week to say goodbye. Use it well."

"But it's only a *tiny* wound! There must be something you can do!" Her fingernails dug into her palms. She couldn't lose more family—*she couldn't lose Miles!*

The surgeon stared at her flatly. "Excuse me, I have people I can actually *help.*"

He retreated into the infirmary without another word. The man had barely even glanced at Miles as they carried him in, but Marta swallowed her indignation. The infirmary was already full to bursting with knights, sergeants, and townspeople who'd suffered injuries in the retreat. The longer the siege continued, the busier the surgeon would be.

After the afternoon's fighting, her whole body ached. There was nothing she could do but try to rest, but a hollow pain thrummed behind Marta's breastbone as she picked her way across the courtyard towards Queen Maria's chambers.

If the infirmary was crowded, the castle courtyard was even worse. Wedding guests and their retinues, peasants and their cattle from the surrounding countryside, and townspeople from the settlement beyond the castle gates were all packed into the courtyard, leaving barely any clear ground to walk. Marta wove a coiling path amidst makeshift shelters, campfires, and livestock, trying not to step on anything—or anyone. She couldn't imagine how the place would smell within a matter of days.

Queen Maria stood with Dame Helena outside their chambers on the eastern wall. The older Greek woman held a pigeon, while the queen bound a scrap of paper to its leg with thread. A message to Lord Balian, no doubt. Marta stopped to watch as Dame Helena released the pigeon into the air. For a moment the bird circled above the castle, gaining height. Then it winged towards the west, a white speck against the cold grey clouds.

As the bird passed beyond the range of Saracen bows, pain shot through Marta's forehead.

Queen Maria's hand caught her elbow. "Marta? Do you need to sit down?"

Marta blinked back tears. "What did you *tell* him?"

The queen's voice was hard and bitter. "I have told him that Isabella is married."

"What else?

The queen pursed her lips. "The fewer people know, the better."

Despite her efforts, her tears spilled over. "My lady, *please.*"

"The pigeon's away. It's out of our hands now." But then she went on, her voice a whisper, almost lost on the wind. "I told Balian the time is come for our second plan. We couldn't save Isabella, and now we must move quickly to save the kingdom. Neither Humphrey nor Guy can be king. Our only hope now is to get Countess Sibylla safely married to someone else."

Marta whimpered.

"Marta? What's wrong?" The queen sounded frightened.

She fought back the blinding pain, grabbing for the queen's hands. "You'll force her to leave him? As *revenge?*"

The queen frowned. "It won't be revenge if Sibylla acts sensibly. She's ambitious. If cutting Guy loose is her only way to the throne, she'll do it."

"You can't do that!"

"I beg your pardon!"

Marta swallowed convulsively. "Forgive me, my lady, but this is *exactly* what they did to Isabella. Disposing of her life for their own convenience.

We're *Watchers*. We're better than that."

"You speak very freely." The queen's voice was clipped and icy. Nevertheless, she went on, as though trying to convince herself "We're outmanoeuvred. We tried playing by the rules, and Stephanie outwitted us at every turn because she was willing to be ruthless."

Marta stared blankly. "Miles said the same thing."

"This is not some kind of knightly joust: this is politics. There are no rules. There are only winners and losers."

Marta felt for one last hope. "Did you talk to Lord Balian about it?"

"Talk to him? It was *his* plan to begin with."

Marta's stomach clenched. It was so much worse than she thought. Her head buzzed. "But he's the *Prester*," she whispered.

They already stood on shaky ground. This could destroy the Watchers together with the whole kingdom. Unless...

Unless she could escape the castle somehow and plead with Lord Balian to find another way.

The queen's voice sounded far away. "It's not a good choice, but none of our choices are good ones."

Marta pushed her away. "I've heard that before, too." The pain in her forehead had faded to a slow throb, but it was still there, impelling her to action. Before the queen could speak again, she burst into the chamber, snatched up the Bessarion Lance, and clattered down the steps again, aiming for the infirmary.

* * *

It was evening by the time Miles awoke from his drugged slumber. They'd washed his wound with wine and bandaged it, but that was all.

He turned his head drowsily and saw her sitting by the side of his bed "Marta?"

Marta leaned forward anxiously. "Are you in pain?"

"Aren't you full of surprises?" His voice was husky. "You've been avoiding me for days."

246

Marta looked away. "I need your help with something. Are you in pain?"

"Seeing that my liege lord just offered to trade me to the enemy in exchange for his own hide, I'd say yes, considerable. What did the surgeons say?"

"They're going to let you die." Marta held out a glass of water, willing her hand not to tremble. "Drink?"

He took it with a hand that was steadier than hers. "Gut wound," he said, understandingly. "Well, I'm sorry, Marta. Looks like you went all that way to Medina for nothing."

Marta's stomach knotted.

"Better dead than maimed, I suppose," he added.

"If you were at the Hospital in Jerusalem they'd do something for you." Marta's hands clenched. "They have a *Healer* there."

Miles took a sip of water and lay back. "And if wishes were knights, we could do something about the army camped outside our gates."

He didn't understand. One of the apothecaries employed by the Hospital was a Watcher, with a Watcher's gift, and in her heart, she knew he could save Miles. Marta gnawed her lip, wondering how she was going to convince him to try this.

After a moment's silence, Miles blinked at her. "Wait. You wanted my *help?* Did I hear that right?"

She wondered if she was about to make another terrible mistake. "I have to ride to Jerusalem. I have a warning to deliver, and I thought you might help me get through the castle gate. Do you think you could sit a horse? If we rode south, we could be in Tafila tomorrow, before the infection sets in. And in Jerusalem three days after that."

For once, she seemed to have struck him completely speechless. It took him several moments to recover. "Marta, that's *insane.* Even for you. We're surrounded by Saracens. How would we get out?"

"The same way we got out of that ravine in Arabia. With a fast horse, God's help, and the Bessarion lance."

Miles huffed a laugh. "Oh that's right, you think God is on your side. Did you hear Saladin's emissary this morning? So does he. What makes him wrong, and you right?"

Marta thought of Prince Reynald throwing prisoners from the walls, of Lord Balian—of *Prester* Balian trying to repair injustice with further injustice. Of the Leper King dying in Jerusalem, and her bolt shivering to splinters before it reached the sultan. "What if he's *not* wrong? What if God really is on their side, blessing them with protection and victory? What if we deserve this bloodshed, and Saladin is God's angel of justice?"

Miles shivered. "You frighten me sometimes, Marta."

She leaned over the foot of his bed. "You *should* be frightened. Do you remember when we were in Arabia, the rider who nearly caught us in the valley? He was with Saladin today—and so were his servants. They have come to kill you, Miles. The walls of this castle will provide no protection against them."

For a moment, he seemed speechless.

"Then why save me?" he whispered at last. "I know what you think of me. Why not someone who deserves it?"

If she'd had even a thought of hesitating, that whisper would have decided her. A flood of emotion, carefully dammed back until now, washed through her.

"Because you're still the closest thing I have to a brother. What do you say, Miles? Will you ride with me?"

He hesitated. "What do you want in Jerusalem?"

"I—" Marta cut off as Dame Helena's voice echoed through the vestibule of the infirmary. "You haven't seen me," she hissed, dropping to the floor and rolling under his bed.

The lady's embroidered slippers flapped across the flagstones towards her. "Miles of Plancy?" Helena's voice was tight-lipped. "Have you seen Marta Bessarion today?"

"Why, is she sick? Hurt?" Miles responded with concern that Marta would have sworn was genuine.

"No, but…"

"Well, thank heaven."

"Do you have any idea where she might be?"

248

Miles' voice was thoughtful. "Until you came in, I would have *thought* she was with the Ibelin party. Maybe try the baths?"

Dame Helena withdrew, frustrated, and Marta crawled out from her hiding place to find Miles staring at her. "What are you playing at, Marta? I thought you were deep in the Ibelins' pockets."

"This is my own business." She folded her arms at him. "Are you coming with me?"

"Saints, Marta. I should be ordering you locked in a chamber with no sharp edges."

She tasted triumph. "That's a yes."

His face drained of humour. "I don't want to die. And if I do die, I don't want to die within a mile of Prince Reynald."

Marta let out a breath. "Good. Who can I speak to at the gatehouse?"

* * *

Marta timed the expedition for midnight, shortly before Vigils. As she and Miles made their way to the castle's gate, Marta was relieved to find that Prince Reynald had retired for the night, leaving the wall under the garrison's command. The walk from the infirmary left Miles white with pain, but although the gatekeepers protested, they obeyed his directions.

Two sergeants arrived from the stables, leading their horses, and Marta insisted that Miles be lashed into his saddle; she did not want to lose him in a moment of crisis. She climbed atop her own horse, rubbing its neck with soft words of encouragement. Although the extra weight might slow them down, she'd gratefully accepted the garrison's offer of a padded coat to protect the animal from arrows. There was nothing left to do but give the word.

"Let's go," Marta whispered, unslinging her spear.

She led the way at a walk down the long, narrow passageway between the double north walls. *Turn left.* Indistinct shapes ushered them into the darkness of the gatehouse, small but massively built. *Left again.* A small but very solid door faced them, made of oaken beams reinforced with iron.

"If this works, it'll be a miracle," Miles said.

Marta smiled. *"Now."*

Outside, there was a muffled thud as men on the wall lowered a new bridge to take them across the fosse. Then the door ground open and Marta nudged her horse through, across the bridge. Despite the rags muffling them, her horse's hooves thudded on the bridge like a drum.

The Saracens heard.

From a rooftop opposite, someone let out a piercing yell.

Marta clenched her fist on her spear and let out a yell of her own as she raked her spurs across her horse's thick coat. She'd picked this mount for endurance, not speed, but as it lumbered into motion, she knew the massive Frankish-bred beast would build up unstoppable momentum.

Answering thunder rolled behind her: Miles, huddled behind the cover of his shield.

They shot out of the forum, angling down the street that led past the town's cathedral to the gate. Marta dodged to her left as a massive black shape loomed up in the darkness. A ballista, surrounded by startled guards. She swung the butt of her spear like a truncheon to clear the way. In the blink of an eye they were past, gathering speed as they hurtled down the narrow street.

Yells, horn-blasts, and tardy arrows pursued them. Ahead, the road dog-legged between tenements and opened into another forum outside the cathedral. As they clattered out into the glare of flaming braziers, their luck ran out. A company of spearmen raced from the houses and strung across the square to meet them.

Firelight flickered from the points of their spears. Marta yelled again and drummed her heels against her horse's flanks, lowering her reversed weapon. Before the enemy could get their spears planted, she burst through the living barrier and careened across the square, galloping for the road that led to the town gate. Around her, the square seethed with horses and frightened, shouting men. Three arrows struck her in quick succession between the shoulders and stayed there, embedded harmlessly in her mail and gambeson. Everyone was running now, hastening to clear her path

250

rather than block it.

Almost everyone.

A mounted mamluk wrestled his horse into the clear path before her, mace swinging. Marta's heart jumped into her throat and she switched her grip on the Bessarion Lance from truncheon to razored point, unwilling to take chances.

As she charged, the mamluk twitched his horse aside at the last moment. Her spear-point merely nicked his silken tunic.

Then her head exploded with pain as he caught her with his mace on the back-swing.

Marta couldn't see. Her helmet was awry, the faceplate blocking her vision. Her horse shied, slid, and scrambled for footing on the cobblestones.

Air shuddered as Miles rushed past her. *"Marta!"* he yelled.

As her horse regained its feet, Marta ripped the blinding helmet from her head and emerged to find herself facing the direction they had come. Mere paces away, the mamluk swung back to meet her, still brandishing his mace. Marta dug her spurs into her horse and lowered the spear. Irresistible, it swept him from the saddle to the ground.

Within heartbeats she got her horse turned—and came face-to-face with something far worse.

He stood in the path between her and Miles. Just as she remembered, he was robed in black. Just as she remembered, the firelight cast shadows across his young, chiselled face. Just as she remembered, he was laughing, silently, terrifyingly.

"Khalil," she choked.

"Marta Bessarion!" He shook his head in delight. "I should have known it was you."

The air beside him shimmered. A hot, malicious breath of wind scorched Marta's cheek, and the feathered woman materialised at his side, baring her teeth and drawing a bow.

Khalil threw up a hand. "Lilith, *no!"*

Too late: the demon's arrow flew. In the same instant, Marta's forehead blazed with scorching light and there came a crack like thunder. She reeled in the saddle, her horse staggering back a few steps. When the afterburn cleared from her vision, the sorcerer was on the ground and the feathered woman had vanished. Wails of fright rose from the Saracens around them.

"Marta!" Miles screamed. In the street ahead, his horse was dancing with terror, struggling to get away.

On the ground before her, Khalil elbowed himself up, spitting blood. "That spear is rightfully mine, and I *will* have it."

Focused on escape, Marta only half heard him. She raked her spurs once more down her horse's flanks and thundered after Miles, leaving the Saracens' camp far behind.

Chapter XXVIII.

As the Bessarion girl's hoofbeats echoed into the night, a party of the sultan's mamluk cavalry rushed into the square, calling for their horses. Khalil climbed shakily to his feet, dabbing at his split lip, and turned to scan the chaos around him.

There was no sign of Lilith.

Scowling, Khalil elbowed his way through the frightened crowd, breaking into a run once he made it through the gate of the house he was occupying. In the second-storey room he used as an office, he sifted through the scrolls of paper and jars of powder littering the desk. "Lilith! *Lilith!* Stay with me!"

On the other side of the desk, half embedded in the wall, Qeteb faded into view. "Ooh, Lilith, hold my hand!" he mocked, before his voice deepened to a snarl. "Don't be pathetic! You don't need that lack witted hag. We're trying to build an *empire* and all she can think about is stuffing herself."

Khalil swore at the demon, finally locating the paper he sought. Despite his haste, he took a moment to straighten, drag both hands down his face, and breathe. If he didn't perform each part of the ritual with scrupulous care, he could open the door to something that would destroy him. He'd already paid with three hundred years of torment for the botched ritual at Oliveta, and he didn't plan to suffer any longer.

Qeteb drifted closer as Khalil set the herbs, the tinder and flint, the candles and the knife on the floor. Although night robbed the midday spirit of much of his power, Khalil saw hunger glitter in each eye. "Stay back," he said curtly, taking up a piece of chalk.

253

He worked quickly, drawing sigils, lighting candles, burning herbs, chanting. Qeteb roamed outside the wall of the sigil, sniffing at the ward's invisible wall, probing it with nose and fingers. The eye in his forehead was closed, but the eye in his chest burned with longing.

When Khalil slit his wrists open, the demon uttered an animal howl, pressed against the barrier. Shadows gathered in the corner of the house, pressing back the light. If the house's owners ever returned, their nightmares would drive them insane.

Repeating his summons, Khalil extinguished each candle.

When the light was gone, Lilith stood in the darkness outside the wards, opposite Qeteb. At midnight, she was as vivid and powerful as Qeteb was faded and weak. She shook herself, every feather ruffling complacently. "You called me back? Wise choice, mortal. You still need my help."

The hairy man's hackles raised, and he hissed at her. "You're a waste of blood."

Qeteb looked hungrily at Khalil's flowing wrists. Feeling dizzy, the sorcerer reached into his pockets for bandages, not daring to leave the protection of the sigil until the flow was stanched and the wounds wrapped tightly shut. "I need *your* help, Lilith? I think I would have done better tonight without you. Why didn't you *tell* me it was the Bessarion daughter who had the spear?"

Lilith bared her teeth. "Because I didn't *know.*"

"You've been watching the Watchers for the last *century*. You really expect me to believe you didn't *know* Marta Bessarion had turned up? She looks as though she's been here four or five *years!*"

"I am not made of meat," she hissed. "To me, you mortals are like smoke and water. I have neither eyes, nor ears, nor nose, to *know* such things."

Khalil could only take her word for it—but after a hundred years of dealing with these creatures, he thought he had begun to understand their limitations. "She was dedicated to you at Oliveta! She should have borne your mark!"

"Marks *fade.* They break. Sometimes they don't take at all; if the offering is—*protected.*"

"Protected." Khalil stepped forward, out of the sigil, breaking the wards. Qeteb and the shadows swarmed towards his spilled blood, but Lilith got there first, snarling them away as she bathed in the congealing liquid. Shadows flocked over Khalil's wrists until he plunged them into a basin of water, washing the last of the blood away. He remained on his feet, feeling weak and dizzy but knowing how dangerous it was to let either demon see it. "What happened when you shot her, Lilith?"

She rose from the blood, replete, glowing. "She *should* have perished. But it seems that the Fiery One from Arabia has kissed her."

Khalil's scalp prickled. *"Kissed* her?"

"She's under his protection. When I shot my bolt, there was—a reaction. It put me under a compulsion to depart. If you hadn't called me back…"

"I see."

"Useless hag," Qeteb growled.

Lilith snarled at him, fury transforming her, making her larger and more birdlike. Her eyes flamed yellow, her head flattening—

"Enough, Qeteb," Khalil said irritably. He turned back to Lilith. "You are telling me there's nothing you can do."

"It's not my fault." Lilith pouted, rippling back into woman-shape. "Who knew the protection would continue once she left the Fiery One's territory? It never used to be that way."

Khalil half leaned, half sat on the desk behind him. His head was light from the loss of blood, but he held on grimly, forcing himself to focus. If only he could enter the kingdom himself—but the protection on the Leper King extended to the borders of his realm, and Khalil was too closely bound to the two demons to survive an expedition behind enemy lines.

He saw the Bessarion girl in his mind's eye, as she'd been when she faced him in the square with the spear—*his* spear, the ibn Hassan Lance—clenched in her hand. She'd wielded the weapon as though she was born to it.

He was surprised to find that he was not even slightly envious.

He wanted that spear. He'd endured an agonising wait, centuries of frustration, to track her down. It surprised him to find that at the very last moment like this, his plans were changing.

"This is a task for mortals," he said. "I'll send a message to Kurosh. A moment," he added, as the djinn began to dissolve. "Lilith, where do you stand with the heir?"

The feathered woman's teeth showed in the dim light. "She is ripe," Lilith whispered. "And ready to fall."

Chapter XXIX.

Marta didn't try to outrun the pursuit she knew must be hard on their heels. Instead, as soon as the Sinai road led them up to the high plateau, she grabbed Miles' rein and pulled him off the path again, down a breakneck slope carpeted with acacia scrub. It was dark and the ground was rocky, so after a few paces she halted the horses and turned their noses uphill before hacking a branch from one of the bushes to erase their tracks.

She barely finished in time. Above, a band of mamluks trotted along the road, their colourful silken tunics glowing in the light of their torches. They passed Marta's hiding-place and dwindled into the distance along the south road.

Above her, Miles was still in the saddle, slumped over his stomach wound, his breath loud and agonised in the dark. Marta stared at the dwindling Saracen horsemen without seeing them.

Khalil, she thought. *The man on the dapple-grey horse, who wouldn't tell Miles his name. Khalil is here.*

Dear God, how can he be here? How can he say my father's spear belongs to him?

How can he be here?

Miles groaned, bringing her back to the moment. Marta yanked at the strap holding him to the saddle and eased him to the ground, cradling him in her arms. "Talk to me, Miles. Are you bleeding?"

"No," he groaned. He was clearly in agony, their headlong flight having put untold stress on his pierced gut. "I'll…I'll be fine. Just let me rest a moment."

The horses shifted uneasily, unhappy to be standing on a steep slope, but Marta grabbed their halters and shushed them, thinking furiously.

She had never expected to see Khalil again. She'd thought the demons must have killed him that night in Oliveta. She'd certainly never expected to find that, like her, he'd travelled through time. That he was *still* looking for the Bessarion Lance. She gripped the weapon more tightly, astonished to find that her hands were shaking.

Fear. She wasn't used to feeling that.

Miles seemed to be having trouble recovering his breath. "Saints, Marta. What *happened* back there? It looked as though you were struck by lightning."

"The seraph's kiss." Marta took a deep breath, forcing herself to stay calm. She was still under the dragon's protection. And she still had her lance.

"The *what?*"

She fell onto her knees in front of him. "Miles. Can you wait here for me? If I'm not back in an hour—"

"Holy Virgin!" He groaned, half in agony, half in disbelief. "What is it now? What are you going to do?"

Her hand was still shaking on the spear, but it was with determination and nerves, not outright fear. Her forehead was still tingling from the seraph's power. "I have to go back. There's someone in the Saracen camp I have to…" Words faded away as certainty replaced them. "I have to kill him," she whispered.

"Who? Why?"

"I can't explain."

"You want to ride back into the Saracen camp and challenge the sultan to single combat?"

"Not Saladin, someone else."

"Someone *else?*" His voice lifted into falsetto. "You want to ride back into the Saracen camp of twenty thousand trained soldiers, from whom we barely escaped with our lives, and challenge some complete nonentity to single combat?"

She rubbed her forehead. "He isn't a nonentity; he's a sorcerer, with demons for allies! Miles, *he* was the one who almost caught us in Arabia. *He* was the one who sent the hairy man and the feathered woman to strike us down. *He* was the one who directed the ballista yesterday when they shot you."

"*Stop it, Marta!*" He was as much in a panic as she was, his hand flailing to grab her shoulder. "Saints, I was afraid—Marta, I don't know *what* happened back there, but you aren't a saint and you aren't invincible! I don't care what you say kissed you; if you go back there, *you will die.*"

"I must. He's seen me now, he knows I have the spear. I've *seen* what he can do, Miles. He'll never stop hunting me." She took a deep breath. "I can do this. I have been blessed—"

"Marta, *please.*" His breath hitched in a sob. "Maybe this was a miracle, all right? Maybe a…a seraph really has blessed you. Who knows? I'm only a poor sinner. But if *I* was in that angel's boots, the last thing I'd want is for you to turn around and run right back into danger once I'd pulled you out of it."

Marta opened her mouth, then shut it again. Her head ached; she felt deathly tired all of a sudden.

For a moment there was only the sound of their laboured breathing in the dark. Miles sounded exhausted when he spoke again. "Come on, Marta. I can't make it to Tafila alone, and I thought you had a warning to deliver in Jerusalem."

Lord Balian, about to make a terrible mistake. Miles, counting the hours until death took him.

Khalil, still hunting for the Bessarion Lance.

Marta buried her face in her hands, feeling her pulse in her fingertips. Her head pounded with each heartbeat; the seraph's kiss, she belatedly realised.

"You're right." Her voice was muffled against her hands. The pain receded, only a little, but Marta felt more clarity. So long as the Watchers stood strong, Khalil could do nothing against them. "I must go to Jerusalem."

* * *

In the end it took five days to reach Jerusalem, not the four she'd hoped. When they remounted to continue their journey, Miles could not endure a pace any faster than a walk. By midday when they reached the tiny keep of Tafila, Marta was riding the same horse, supporting him upright in the saddle. By next morning, the wound had begun to putrefy. He was barely well enough to travel by litter, and their progress up the western shore of the Salt Sea became agonisingly slow.

It was a chilly November evening when she and Miles entered Jerusalem by the Jehoshephat Gate for the second time that year. Marta signalled to the five Turcopoles who had escorted them from Tafila.

"Take him directly to the Hospital and ask for the apothecary Benjamin of Borca. Tell him Marta Bessarion sent you." Leaning over Miles on the litter, she touched his feverish hand. "I'll come looking for you as soon as I'm done with Balian."

He lay flat, his eyes closed, and she didn't know if he'd heard her. She'd pushed the cavalcade as fast as she dared, but Miles had only worsened since Tafila, his gut distended with fluid. Marta's heart twisted into knots with worry. Even a Healer's touch might be unable to save him now.

Still, she'd done everything she could for him. Marta had other worries to deal with now.

When she knocked on the gate of the house on Temple Street, the gatekeeper stared as though he'd seen a ghost. "Is Lord Balian at home?" Marta demanded.

Breathless, the man nodded and gestured towards the upstairs room which Lord Balian used as a cabinet. She slid from her horse and threw him the reins. A light burned in one of the lower store-rooms, and the regular thump of a loom indicated that Persi was working late, but Marta's first duty was Lord Balian. She climbed the stairs wearily and found the cabinet door closed, a warm glow of lamplight shining in the keyhole. Marta thumped on the door until she heard Lord Balian's voice, and then let herself in.

260

"It's me, my lord."

Balian sat near the fireplace wrapped up in a fur robe, dictating some kind of letter to his chaplain. At her entrance, his jaw dropped and he started up. "Marta? What's happened at Kerak? Is Maria—"

"Still under siege, and just as safe as the rest of them."

"Thank God." He pulled her into a quick hug. "Wait—if the siege is still going, then what are *you* doing here?"

"I broke out five days ago. With Miles—he's badly wounded."

He stared at her. "You broke out? *Why?*"

"Because of the queen's pigeon. Did you get it?"

"Three days ago." Lord Balian glanced at the chaplain. "My thanks, Father. We will finish the letter later. Will you tell someone to bring up food and drink for the young lady? Have a seat, Marta. Oh, wait, Father—here, take this to pay for a thanksgiving Mass at Saint Giles'."

The door closed, shutting her into the warm familiarity of the cabinet, with its olive-green walls and red stripes adorning the coffered ceiling. She ought to be able to relax, but she couldn't bring herself to put down the Bessarion Lance, to sit, even to remove so much as a glove. The rings of her mail chattered a little with nervousness. "My lord, you mustn't compel them to divorce."

The words spilled out and Marta caught her breath, wondering how he would respond. He blinked at her, choosing his words more carefully than she had chosen hers. "You're speaking of Countess Sibylla and Guy?"

She nodded. "The queen told me that was in the message she sent. So I sneaked away and came—"

"Sneaked away? Was this how Miles got injured?"

"Oh, no." Marta didn't want to talk about their escape from Kerak; it was hard enough convincing Miles of what had happened. "Miles was wounded in the siege; we had no trouble getting out. But I had to warn you."

"Warn me?" He spoke slowly, more surprised than offended. "You used to *trust* me, Marta."

"I never used to think you'd do such a thing!" It made Marta's heart race, facing him like this, but she knew by now that speaking up was the only way to keep the pain at bay. "I told you what happened to the Watchers in my day. They were destroyed because of their injustice and oppression. I don't want to see another Watcher's Council slaughtered because they made the same mistake."

"Oh! And you think this would be injustice?" She could tell he was trying to look sympathetic. "I understand why that frightens you, Marta, but we need an expedient solution to the question of the succession. No one wants to see Guy become king."

Marta couldn't believe her ears. "You're the Prester of Jerusalem. Your *whole job* is to do the right thing when no one else will. I thought you understood."

"Dear girl, it's been done before. They made King Amalric part from Countess Agnes before they let him become king. Holy Church blessed it and the kingdom endures."

"At least King Amalric had a choice," Marta countered. "How much choice will you give Countess Sibylla? You can't force two people to break their marriage vows just because they're inconvenient for *you*. If that's not injustice, then what is?"

Lord Balian pursed his lips. "Holy Church would have to approve of it. If Holy Church approved of it, then it must be valid."

"Even Holy Church can make mistakes."

"Marta, it's our only choice." He ran his hand through his hair, letting her see the worry in his eyes. "I hear Isabella is married."

Marta gulped. "We couldn't get either of them to protest. I tried."

"I'm sure you did," he said gently. "But Humphrey has neither ambition nor support. Tripoli has no heirs of his body, even if we could get the Leper King to consent to name him his heir. The king knows we don't trust Count Guy. This is the only plan I could think of that he might agree to." He sighed. "Do *you* have a better one?"

Marta stared, speechless. She hadn't even thought of coming up with an alternative. Now, she scrambled to think. Name Humphrey heir? But if Humphrey became king, he would be a puppet, controlled by

Prince Reynald—a horrifying thought. Submit to Countess Sibylla and her husband? But they were hardly any better: it was said that the Kerak marriage had been Countess Sibylla's idea to begin with.

Watching her struggle with the question, Balian shrugged. "I thought not. Heaven bear me witness, Marta, I *tried*. I *tried* to think of another way."

The door opened, preventing her from answering. One of the servants set a tray of food on a side table and withdrew.

Marta's stomach growled helplessly at the aroma of roasted meat, soft cheese, and stuffed olives, but hungry though she was, she didn't feel like eating. *Not Lord Balian, too.* The kingdom was in more peril than she thought.

"Have you spoken to the king about it?"

"Not yet. I've an audience tonight."

"Tonight?"

He smiled faintly. "There's a High Court meeting tomorrow, to arrange for the kingdom's defence now that Count Guy is to be removed from the regency. If the king approves, we might debate the divorce in council."

There was nothing further she could say. Marta moved towards the door, then stopped. "When you found me, I was a slave in a workshop belonging to the Lord of Caesarea. Do you remember?"

"I remember."

"Those women stopped work five times a day to pray. I know what they prayed, because I prayed for it too. That God would come down and set us free. One day, I expect he'll hear those prayers, and answer them. I would not like to set myself against him when he does—when his patience finally runs out."

Lord Balian didn't answer, and when Marta looked back at him, he was paying very close attention to a letter.

Marta shivered. Lord Balian didn't know what happened when Watchers failed to heed warnings, when they failed to see justice done. She did.

Lord Balian didn't understand how beautiful and precious this kingdom of Jerusalem was, how fragile it might prove to be. But she did.

And if he wouldn't save it, she must.

She shoved the door open, stepped out onto the loggia, and was almost knocked over by Persi.

"Marta, thank God you're back. We're so far behind on the weaving, it's not even funny. The countess of Jaffa ordered a bolt of silk brocade to be finished by Saint Cecilia's day, and we aren't even done with that murrey silk for the princess of Galilee, and *that* was due on All Saints'."

Marta blinked at the Nubian girl. "Persi? Please—I'm sorry—not just now."

Persi's hands tightened on her shoulders. "You look exhausted. Have you eaten? They've been heating water for a bath."

"There's no time." She brushed past Persi and clattered downstairs, calling over her shoulder. "I have to go. I'm so sorry, Persi, I swear it's a matter of life and death."

Her horse had already been stabled, and it deserved a rest. Saddling another would take too long, so instead, Marta rushed out into the street, her legs feeling stumpy and slow after five days in the saddle. The city was quiet, its narrow streets not yet crowded with the Christmas pilgrims. Within ten minutes, she was knocking at the palace gate.

"I'm Marta Bessarion," she told the porter. "The Leper King said he'd see me anytime."

At least, she hoped he would, despite the discord of their last meeting. If she was denied, she'd have to climb the wall and try to get inside the palace some other way—the evening was so cold and wet that there was no chance of finding anyone in the garden.

Each bone in her body ached, but she had no other choice. If Lord Balian wouldn't listen to her, then maybe Baldwin would.

To Marta's relief, the porter nodded and waved her in. The steward who came to usher her upstairs to the king's chamber looked askance at her improper male attire, her scarred face and filthy, travel-worn appearance. Marta kept her countenance only by noting that the steward wore a coat dyed with a very inferior blue, but for the Leper King's sake she wished she'd had the time for a bath.

264

She needn't have worried. When the steward ushered her into the king's presence, she found Baldwin lying propped up in his bed with sticky ulcers crawling up his neck and arms. Behind his sunken nose, the pupils of both eyes had turned a blind and milky blue. He looked even sicker than when she'd seen him six months ago.

Once more, a yearning pity welled up in her heart for him. Once more, she reined in a fierce desire to touch him, the one comfort she could give.

His rasping voice was eager. "Marta? Is that you? I thought you were at Kerak."

As with Balian, she felt in no mood to explain. Not about the seraph, not about Khalil, and certainly not about the spear.

We've always kept it a secret, even from our friends. Now that Khalil knew she had it, he must be already planning how to get it back. A memory of Oliveta flashed into her mind for the first time in years, stark and nightmarish. In the last five days the conviction had only hardened: Khalil would hunt her as he had her father. Sooner or later, she must find him and destroy him; until that happened a part of her would always be afraid.

The king was still waiting for an answer.

"I was, but I got out."

"You got out." Baldwin's voice was flat and tired, but it sounded amused. "And there I was going to rush off with my army to rescue you. How did you do it?—Wait. Are you wearing *armour?*"

She only had a little time before Lord Balian arrived for his audience. "It's a long story, my lord."

"I love long stories. Who *are* you, Marta Bessarion?"

"Lord Balian's fosterling," she said with a sigh. "We don't have time, my lord. I came to warn you about something. Again. Forgive me."

He was silent for a little while and she knew he was remembering their last conversation, and not with pleasure. Marta's heart plunged, but Baldwin's next words shocked her.

"I am the one who should beg forgiveness. When we last spoke, I was ungracious. I..." The bandaged knob of his left arm moved restlessly on the coverlet. "I should have listened to you. I've barely met Humphrey...I didn't know my sister had chosen the boy specifically because he would not challenge Guy for the throne."

Marta thought of Isabella craning her neck to make her marriage vows, of the terror in Humphrey's voice when he told her how Prince Reynald controlled him. Her armour chimed as a shiver of anger ran down her spine. "You have done them both a very grave injury."

Baldwin was silent for a moment. "You were right in this too," he said softly, "that as a king I must choose rightly between good and ill. In this I have failed."

"I am not the one you should ask for forgiveness."

"No," he acknowledged. "But I wanted you to know that when you warned me again, you would be heard. What did you come to say?"

Encouraged, Marta ventured a few steps nearer the king's bedside. "Lord Balian said he's coming to see you tonight. I think he's going to make a suggestion. *You mustn't agree to it.*"

"What kind of suggestion?"

Marta had thought it over on her way through the rainy streets. "I'd rather not say, because I hope he won't," she confessed. "I begged him not to, and maybe he'll think better of it." Even now, she couldn't believe Lord Balian would actually *do* something like this, despite all his excuses. "Still, last I heard, he was going to ask you to compel someone to break an oath. *Please* don't say yes."

"How mysterious." He grinned. "And not very filial of you, Ibelin fosterling."

Marta's cheeks heated. She couldn't deny his accusation, but how could she help it? Her duty as a Watcher came before her duty to her family. Until now, she'd never dreamed that those duties might conflict.

Now that they had, there was only one thing to do.

"I'm only trying to keep him from making a terrible mistake. And you, my lord. Please don't say yes?"

Baldwin was silent a moment. "I can hardly promise to deny a man's request when I don't know what the request is." He watched her with his blind eyes and ruined face. "If I knew, perhaps I could suggest an alternative

266

that would satisfy the Lord of Ibelin."

Marta squeezed her eyes shut. *Do you have a better plan?* Lord Balian had asked her. And she didn't. She wasn't a diplomat or a politician. She wasn't clever. All she had to navigate this maze was a magic spear and a white-hot conscience.

She'd done nothing but fail until now. Yet there must be a reason she was here, miraculously, in this time. There must be a reason she bore the seraph's kiss on her forehead, and it was not so that she could *fail.*

"Just promise me you won't say yes at once. Promise me you'll put him off a day or two, while I..." she let out a sigh. "While I try to find an alternative."

"That sounds reasonable." He made a little huff that could have been a laugh. "But what are you going to do, Marta Bessarion?"

That was the problem. Marta hesitated. "I'll think of something. I'm...I'm not used to meddling with politics."

"Then you'll certainly surprise us."

"Thank you, my lord." Marta moved towards the door. "Lord Balian will be here any minute. I'd better go."

"Come back tomorrow at noon, and tell me how you've fared," he added. There was no laughter in his voice now. "If this matter is as weighty as I think it is, I would prefer to know your plans *before* the High Court meets."

In that instant the solution dropped into Marta's head, dazzling in its simplicity. Of *course* she didn't have the brain to solve the Leper King's dilemma. But she knew of someone who did.

Someone who had every reason to come up with an alternative.

Tomorrow, at noon. Marta's scalp prickled. *Was that enough time?* She swallowed and said, "I'll do my best, my lord."

Chapter XXX.

Night, cold and wet, had fallen. Marta returned to the house on Temple Street and paused in the courtyard, shivering in the chill wind. What was she thinking? This was a political conundrum that had puzzled the Leper King during his whole reign, and she'd volunteered to solve it within half a day!

Ridiculous.

A light shone from one of the windows next to the stables, making the windowpanes glow pale-green in the darkness of the courtyard. The door was closed, but Marta could still make out the steady *clack-clack!* of the loom.

Persi. Still hard at work. She'd *said* they were behind on the weaving.

She pushed open the door and went in. Persi glanced up at her, but didn't stop weaving. "What are you still doing up? You should be getting out of that armour and into your bed."

"You're one to talk." Her own loom stood silent next to Persi, still holding an unfinished bolt of blue and silver linen. The sight struck her conscience, but she ignored the buzz in her forehead. "Persi, did you say Countess Sibylla ordered some cloth?"

"Right after you left for Kerak. I agreed because of course we didn't count on a siege." Persi stopped the treadles and leaned her elbows on the loom, rubbing tired eyes. "Oh, and that's right, there was a siege. *What on earth are you doing here, Marta?*"

"I think Lord Balian might be about to do something terrible. I had to stop him."

"Of course." Persi sighed. "Have you always been this exhausting?"

"I used to annoy my brother Lukas, giving my pocket money to beggars and not letting him kill spiders."

"You let spiders have the run of the house?"

"Oh no, I'd release them into the garden, where they could be happy."

"So, what? Your eight-legged friends spun you a rope of silk, and you got out of Kerak that way?"

"No, I..." Marta sighed, knowing how Persi was going to react. "I charged out the front gate. Took the Saracens by surprise."

Persi looked aghast. "Alone?"

"Heaven was with me, and—"

"Saints," Persi muttered. The look on her face stopped Marta from saying anything else. There was a long silence in which Persi's eyes unfocused, looking at the murrey silk without really seeing it. "And nobody told you your idea was *insane?*"

"Well, yes. But it all worked out, didn't it? Here I am, not a bit the worse for wear."

"This time." Persi's voice was soft, faded, like an old tent.

Time was too short to debate it. "Did you speak to Countess Sibylla in person?"

"Yes, she chose one of the brocades. Now I only need you to make the cloth." Persi gestured at the murrey silk on the loom in front of her. "This is Princess Eschiva's. I can take care of this double-cloth, but I don't have your skill for brocade."

Marta nodded. In the years since they'd begun weaving and selling fine cloth, a natural division of labour had sprung up between them. Where Marta was shy and imaginative, Persi was confident, personable, and shrewd with money. While Marta was good at designing, Persi was good at selling. The business needed both of them. Too often, this year, Marta had left to undertake some adventure of knight-errantry, leaving Persi to bear the full burden of their work.

She would have to make it up to her, as soon as this crisis was over.

"I need to see the countess, tonight. Will you take me to see her?"

Persi threw down her shuttle and clutched at her hair, which was captured into dozens of tiny braids and gathered into two thick plaits that framed her face. "I can't take you to see the countess of Jaffa! *I don't have her cloth!*"

"I'll start weaving the moment I can, Persi. I will. I promise."

"I'm looking for another weaver," Persi said flatly.

Marta froze. "What?"

"Your heart's not in this, Marta. You keep running off with that spear, and we keep getting behind on our orders."

Marta swallowed. "Do...do you not want to work with me anymore?"

Persi's look of horror was reassuring. "No, Marta, you'd still be part of the business. It's partly your designs that bring us so many buyers. But this way, you could spend less time weaving and more making new designs. We could accept more orders. We could even start shipping fabric across the sea, to Constantinople or France."

Persi's enthusiasm was catching, and it made sense to expand the business rather than let it languish while she travelled. "Isn't there a weaver's shop in the Patriarch's Quarter? In the same street as all those Jewish dyers. Perhaps we could have some of the simpler designs made there."

"I know that shop. They use Saracen slaves." Persi's jaw firmed stubbornly. "We can't build our business at the cost of others."

"I didn't know," Marta said slowly. "Of course, free weavers would be more expensive."

"We could probably find someone among the silk weavers of Tripoli, but that's too far to travel." Persi stared at her loom. "If I could, I'd go back to Cacho; I'd buy that shop and tear that door open, and anyone who wanted could stay and weave for us as free women. But I did the numbers; there's no way we could afford it."

"Are there any free weavers in Jerusalem?"

"Not that I know of. I've begun asking around, and I've heard of some in Acre and Ascalon. The problem is that I can't get away from Jerusalem until these orders are completed."

Marta looked around at the half-finished designs that littered the room.

This is where she belonged—in the lamplight, making things, not destroying them. Looking down at her armour-cased body, Marta heaved a sigh. "I wouldn't be doing this if it wasn't desperately important. I promise."

"I know. That's why I want to find a way for you to do what you have to do. Just promise me one thing."

"Anything, Persi."

She stared up at Marta, a crease in her forehead. "Promise me you'll be careful. In this world it takes more than a magic spear to keep safe."

Marta grinned and dropped a kiss on her cheek. "Thanks, Persi. I'll be back to help you soon. Tomorrow, I hope."

Outside in the courtyard, a chilling rain continued to fall, making the stones slick with water. Marta ran numb fingers through her damp hair. She was still coated with horse sweat and mud from the road, her cold and sodden gambeson chafing her skin. Climbing up to her own room, Marta found a tray of food and a bath that was still warm. This time, she succumbed to both, and by the time she climbed out of the water, she felt three-quarters asleep. All the same, she pulled on a thick woollen gown, topped it with a sturdy mantle, and strapped on her stoutest shoes. *What now?*

Miles. She needed Miles. If he was still alive.

She was almost afraid to find out

The Hospital complex was not far—down the end of Temple Street, through the chicken market and past the twin churches of Saint Mary. Marta entered it from the back, through a narrow alley between a row of shops. The Hospital itself was a massive two-storey building wedged against the back of Saint Mary Major, its beautiful white façade arcaded with dozens of tiny arches. Here, the brothers of the Order of Saint John provided food, shelter, and medical care to anyone who needed it. The thought still staggered Marta a little. No matter who you were—pilgrim or native, Christian or Saracen, orphaned infant or ailing elder—there was a home at the Hospital for as long as you needed it.

Marta entered by the door in the church vestibule and asked the brother on night duty for Miles of Plancy. He motioned her to follow him softly through an immense room filled with hundreds of beds, dimly lit by only three or four lamps.

Miles lay in a bed in the corner, his hands folded over his chest, so still that for an instant Marta wondered if he was dead. After a moment, however, his chest rose and fell, his breath shallow and quick.

The brother consulted a wax tablet hanging on the wall above the bed. "We've confessed and anointed him, tapped his belly to remove some of the fluid, and will drain the rest tomorrow if he makes it through the night. We also gave him something to relieve the pain and help him sleep—I suppose that's why the apothecary looked in on him."

"Benjamin of Borca?" Marta asked hopefully.

"That's him. Are you acquainted?"

"He's a Watcher." *And a Healer.* She knelt by Miles, afraid to touch him. "He does look more peaceful. Is there any hope, Brother?"

Behind her, the monk cleared his throat. "I'm afraid we don't expect a recovery. I've heard of damaged guts being repaired, if a skilled surgeon treats them soon enough. But there's the putrefaction to contend with, and the fluid, which will kill him if it all rushes out at once. It may be too late to do anything but ease his death. I'm sorry."

"I understand." Marta's voice seemed to come from far away. "May I stay and watch him, Brother?"

"It isn't normally permitted to let women remain in the men's ward—"

"Please."

The brother hesitated, then came to a decision. "I'll send one of the sisters in to keep you company."

He marked the time of his visit on the wax tablet and continued around the ward, checking on the other patients who filled the immense room with soft sounds of sleep. Hesitantly, Marta reached out to touch Miles' wrist. The skin was still hot and feverish, and his pulse raced like a bird's beneath her fingers.

"Come back to me, Miles," she whispered. "I still need your help."

Chapter XXXI.

Marta jerked awake to a loud crash as someone dropped a tray onto the flagstones. She didn't remember curling up in the empty bed next to Miles'. Nor did she remember falling asleep, yet Terce was already approaching. Clear warm light shone in through the hospital's many high windows, dazzling after yesterday's rainy gloom. The nun who had come to sit with her last night was gone, and Miles was watching her from the pillow a few feet away.

"Looked like you needed that," he whispered.

"You made it," Marta breathed. She rolled off the bed and knelt down to feel his wrist. His pulse had slowed, his skin was cool. "Your fever broke."

He looked exhausted, dark rings circling his eyes, his cheekbones prominent from the days of enforced fasting. "Look." He pushed the covers down his torso. His stomach was still a little swollen, but when he wedged a finger beneath the bandages and lifted them, the wound didn't stink or ooze. If Marta hadn't known better, she would have thought it was only a day or two old.

"I don't know what they did to me, but it's a miracle." He looked up at her, wide-eyed. "If it wasn't for you..."

Marta blushed. "I only brought you here. The Healer must have laid hands on you."

A shadow fell across the bed and Marta pulled back as a young man in a shabby robe and turban approached. Marta recognised him at once as partly Syriac, one of her own people.

"Well," he said cheerfully, "*you* look better than you did yesterday, sir."

His sleeves were rolled up, revealing a Watcher's Mark on his arm. Marta stood up, touching her own left forearm in the casual gesture with which Watchers sometimes introduced themselves. "You must be Benjamin of Borca—the Healer."

"Sometimes," he said shyly. "But most of my work is pills and potions."

"I've never seen you at the Watchers' Council."

"To tell the truth, I don't normally attend. The great Watchers rule the kingdom, but the rest of us are just trying to make ends meet and do a little good as we find the opportunity. We have our own little meetings, where we discuss our own small affairs."

Benjamin leaned down to inspect Miles' wound. After peeking below the bandages, he pressed his palm to them, and for an instant his eyes fluttered shut, and his lips moved. A moment later he straightened. "I'm sure the doctor on duty will be making his rounds soon, but that's looking much better, and I see the fever's come down. I expect they'll want to tap the rest of that fluid and put some stitches in the intestine, but at least the putrefaction is reducing."

Miles' eyes widened. "They can stitch up my gut?"

"The learned Albucasis claims to have done it, using catgut. But you'll have to discuss that with the doctor when he comes."

"Huh." Miles put a hand to his stomach, his eyes a little unfocused with relief. When he looked up again, he was grinning. "So what do you think? Will I be able to play the bagpipes when I get well?"

"Not without taking lessons, sir."

"My oath! You really *have* heard it all."

"More or less." Benjamin straightened with a smile. "All the best, sir. Mademoiselle."

Benjamin shuffled away in the direction of his workshop, leaving Miles to stare up at Marta. "I mean it, Marta. You've saved my life. Again."

Marta sat down on the bed again, rubbing sleep from her eyes. "It was my fault you got hurt at all. I distracted you."

"I'm glad of it." Miles reached out, and after a moment's hesitation she let him take her hand. He squeezed. "I needed to get away from Kerak,

274

from Prince Reynald."

Marta's heart lifted. At least *something* good was happening today. "You won't go back to him?"

"He would have handed me over to the enemy to save his own skin. So, no."

"He couldn't have forced you to do it." With Miles out of his clutches, Marta felt she could afford to be generous towards the evil old prince. "You both swore oaths of loyalty and protection to each other. He'd have destroyed his reputation if he'd done it."

"Oh, he wouldn't have *appeared* to force me. He just would have found something to hold over my head until I would have skinned myself alive on his say-so. That was his way, you know."

Marta thought of Humphrey. "Yes. I know."

"I should have listened to you. He only ever meant to use me. He was never going to give me that fief. I suppose I'll just have to find someone who will."

Marta looked at their interlinked fingers. "My one regret is Isabella. You were all she had."

"She won't be gadding about with the constable now that she's a married woman." The cheer in his voice rang false.

"She isn't a *woman*." Marta closed her eyes, trying to hold back tears. She'd hoped to never fail her family again, but despite everything, it seemed that all she *could* do was fail them. "She's only a child—a child who's never been allowed to know her own mind."

Miles gave her hand a swift squeeze, his voice gentling. "I know, Marta. But there's little we can do for her now."

Marta sniffed. "I need your help, Miles."

He blinked and focused on her, putting a theatrical hand to his heart. "Unto half my kingdom."

She couldn't help a smile. "Tempting. What does this kingdom consist of?"

"A horse, a suit of armour, and as pretty a man as any in Jerusalem."

She grimaced. "Oh. About the horse. We left him in Tafila to recover from that ride."

"Well, that still leaves the armour and the man."

"The armour had to be deposited with the brothers, since patients who die here bequeath their belongings to the Hospital. And honestly, you didn't *look* as though you'd make it."

His grin was lopsided, like a mask that was sliding off his face. "Well, then…seems you'll just have to make do with the man."

Marta's heart bounded, but she tried not to heed it. No, he *had* to be joking. He cared for her like a sister, no more. She forced a smile. "Then half the kingdom is half the man, and how could I trust only half a man?"

There was a long, uncomfortable silence. Marta tried to let go of his hand, but his grip tightened, almost painfully. "Marta, I have to apologise. That night, when you wanted to see Isabella, I hurt you, I disappointed you…I said things no man should ever say to one who's pulled him from the jaws of death once, let alone twice."

Marta's face heated again. "I said some hurtful things too."

"You made me think," he said softly. "About you. About me. About *us.* You don't know how much I care what you think of me, Marta. For two days I was sure you were never going to speak to me again, and I could hardly bear it. But then you came to the infirmary…"

Her heart was running at a gallop, but she thought her voice was sufficiently gruff as she replied. "Of course I did."

"You would have been well within your rights not to."

"Don't be foolish. You're all the brother I have."

"It wasn't my first mistake." His gaze trapped hers, making her helpless to look away. "I promised myself, if I lived, I'd tell you this: that I've always known how you feel about me, Marta."

Oh, strife. Her throat was dry, and she couldn't have said a word if she'd tried.

"It wasn't until Arabia that I even took it seriously," he added. "I can be slow, sometimes. But I thought, oh, once this is over, I'll steal a kiss, I'll see if this is real. And it *was.* It was so real that it terrified me. I left you standing there, like a coward, and I ran home to Kerak." He took a breath.

"Won't you say something?"

"I don't know what to say," she said in a whisper. As her tears spilled over, she flushed even redder and scrubbed at them with her sleeve. "I just didn't want to lose you..."

"Just let me try again," he whispered. "I'm a bastard, and I can't offer you much, but I want you to be more than a sister to me, Marta Bessarion."

For an instant she was poised between joy and fear, terrified to wedge open her shy heart and let him see inside.

"Speak to me, Marta. Say yes."

She could show him that much. "All I want is you," she whispered. Her heart pounding, Marta knelt down beside the bed and kissed him. Whistles and cheers from around the ward reminded her that everyone could see them, but in this delirious moment, that didn't seem to matter in the least.

When she pulled back, Miles lay with his eyes closed and a dreamy smile on his face. "What, leaving so soon?"

"We'd be likely to start a riot," she said shakily. *Or a fire.* Her heart sang: Miles surviving the night, Miles getting well, Miles kissing her. But there were other things to attend to, and she'd wasted enough time. "I really should leave, but first, I need your help. I've got to see Countess Sibylla first thing this morning, and it's nearly Terce."

"Countess *Sibylla?*" Miles focused on her in astonishment. "Wait; is this the warning you said you had to deliver? To *Sibylla?*"

Marta fidgeted with the cuff of her sleeve. "That's what it's come to. Yes." If anyone could provide the king with the alternative he needed, it would be her. "I thought you might be able to give me an introduction, or a token, or a password, or something. Since Prince Reynald is such friends with the countess."

If Miles was going to die of anything, it would be curiosity. His face was a study in mystification. "What's happening with you, Marta? Hiding from Dame Helena, bursting out of Kerak to warn Countess Sibylla...I never expected *you* to change sides."

"I haven't."

"Saints, I wonder if Lord Balian sees it the same way."

277

Marta shrugged. "People change, but right and wrong never do. It would be more truthful to say that in this, Lord Balian is not on *my* side."

Miles stared at her blankly for a long moment. "Your side," he repeated. "I've said it before: I don't know whether you're mad or magnificent. But I'm beginning to suspect the second."

Marta lit up in a smile. "So you're on my side now?"

"I am. I'd be a fool to cross you. You, with your angels and your magic spear."

Marta froze, glancing around the ward. It took a moment to find the words. "Hush! You know about the spear? How?"

He rolled onto his side, lowering his voice. "I've seen how close you keep it. I've seen how you fight with it—like the Angel of Death himself is clearing your way. I taught you well, but not *that* well. So when we returned from Arabia, I asked some questions. It turns out the Watchers have been keeping Lord Balian's old lance a secret for a very long time."

"It belongs to my family."

Again, the intensity of his gaze held her captive. "I was wrong about you, Marta. I told myself you were a sentimental fool, but you're no such thing. Our escape from Kerak proved that. You might be the most powerful woman—no, the most powerful *person* in the whole kingdom." He swallowed, his eyes lighting with some grand vision. "There's *nothing* you couldn't achieve, if you set your mind to it."

Marta swallowed. "Miles, really, I'm just a weaver."

"And you just want to see Countess Sibylla about a silk gown, I suppose."

Marta sighed. He was right: she could not be *just* a weaver. The thrum of pain on her forehead prevented that. As long as power could be wielded to hurt people like Isabella, or the women in the workshop in Cacho, then her conscience would drive her to play this game of politics as earnestly as any high lord.

"You shouldn't let me tease you," Miles said ruefully. He glanced around the ward, and beckoned her closer. "Give us your ear—the password between Prince Reynald and the count and countess of Jaffa is *domina regnorum*. Means *the lady of kingdoms*, I take it. Sounds like you." He brushed a kiss across her lips.

"*Domina regnorum,*" Marta repeated under her breath. *The lady of kingdoms. Sounds like you. The most powerful person in the whole kingdom.* "That's not me," she added, soberly.

"I know, I was only teasing. It means Jerusalem herself, the fairest and holiest of all kingdoms."

Marta bit her lip, remembering her conversation with Persi outside the Temple. In Holy Scripture, the *domina regnorum* was not Jerusalem, it was Babylon. And God was going to destroy it.

She walked out of the Hospital, into the sunlight and the fresh sharp air that followed last night's rain. Every colour was washed bright, from the pale stonework to the greenery of the trees, from the brightly-painted carvings on the church lintels to the blood-red shock of late-blooming roses.

Jerusalem, the fair kingdom, which lay like a burden on her shoulders. As she walked towards Countess Sibylla's house, she prayed she would be able to save her.

Chapter XXXII.

"Sibylla! Are you listening to me?"

"H'm?" The sharp voice jolted Sibylla back into something like wakefulness. She sat at her mother's bedside, slumped in the high-backed wooden chair with slack muscles and drooping eyes. She couldn't feel the hands lying numbly in her lap, or the feet that protruded from the hem of her gown, or the worry that ought to be there at the sight of spots of blood on her mother's handkerchief.

Strange that she felt so hazy; Sibylla didn't usually take her hemlock potion if there was a chance she might need to leave home.

"Sibylla, pay attention." Countess Agnes repeated. Sibylla struggled to focus on her mother's face. "Baldwin is going to disinherit you."

Her lips were numb, but Sibylla managed to speak. "I know, mother. I've been trying to think of...some way..." Her voice trailed off.

"You're the rightful heir. Baldwin should *know* what happens when the women of his house are set at naught."

"I'm the rightful heir," Sibylla repeated, her mind still thick with fog. Her fingers twitched, and she clasped her hands together, touching the onyx ring on her thumb, tracing the engraving on its face. "My grandmother was Melisende of Jerusalem. My aunt was Hodierna of Tripoli. He should know better."

"Why not *use* it? Use Hodierna's ring, Sibylla. Before it's too late, and you're locked out of the succession."

Sibylla's hands stilled and she mused on this for a while. "Use it on whom, though?"

"Surely I don't have to spell it out." Agnes shifted her head impatiently on the pillow, and for an instant, Sibylla caught a glimpse of black feathers speckling her mother's arms.

Before she could ask again, Sibylla surfaced out of her dream and into genuine waking. Her head ached and her throat was dry, as often occurred after she'd used her hemlock potion. Her back ached fiercely, and this was evidently what had woken her, for the room was still hushed and dark despite the morning light peeping through her damask curtains.

Sibylla turned onto her side with a stifled groan. She already knew what today would bring, as clearly as though it had already happened. More pain, more bad news from her mother's sickbed, more of Baldwin's attempts to ensure that she never gained the throne. Today, the High Court met to discuss who would take up the regency once Guy was stripped of the post. The answer would, of course, be Tripoli. When the news actually came, she herself would still manage to be surprised and disappointed. More bad news, more pain.

She might as well not get up. After all, she already knew exactly what was going to happen, and how, and why. There was nothing she could do to stop any of it.

The onyx signet ring sat askew on her thumb. Sibylla couldn't help remembering her dream as she twisted it into place again, and a cold sweat sheened her skin at the thought. Well, there was *one* thing she could do, if she chose. The dream was right: there was no need to spell it out. Sibylla had many rivals, but there was only one king.

When Baldwin died, she could take the throne. Neither Tripoli, nor Reynald, nor even the whole Watchers' Council could stop an heir who was determined, ruthless, and right here in Jerusalem.

Sibylla thrust the thought down with a shudder. She would oppose her enemies ruthlessly if they tried to take away her rightful inheritance, but Baldwin wasn't her *enemy*. He was her king. He was her *brother*.

Outside on the loggia, whispering voices and shuffling slippers disturbed her thoughts. A shadow loomed on the other side of the door, listening. Her waiting-women must be wondering if they should disturb her over something. Perhaps the inevitable awfulness of today had been interrupted by something surprising.

Sibylla hated surprises, but it paid to keep abreast of them. She rang the bell next to her bed and eased herself up against the pillows. At once Alix slipped in. "Good morning, my lady. Should I send for breakfast?"

"Just tell me what's happened to put you in such a pother."

"Oh! Well, there's a…messenger, my lady, from Prince Reynald."

This *was* a surprise. "Name?" Sibylla asked laconically, as Alix pulled the curtains open, letting in an unwelcome shaft of light.

"Marta Bessarion, my lady."

For a moment, words vanished completely from Sibylla's mind. All she could do was look at the glowing coals of last night's fire. "Repeat that name?"

"Marta Bessarion?"

"I'll see her at once," Sibylla snapped. "Make up the fire, and hand me my robe."

Surprised, but too well trained to ask questions, Alix obeyed and vanished through the door. Sibylla got out of bed, pulling her thick furred robe around her shivering body and running her fingers through her hair to tame the black waves. She paused at the hearth, staring into the fire.

Kurosh's message from last night was long gone, consumed to ash within minutes of Sibylla receiving it, but every word was engraved on her memory. *The weapon my master seeks is in the possession of a woman named Marta Bessarion. Get it for him. Get the woman herself, alive, and your reward will be doubled.*

Last night, Sibylla had stared blankly at the words, trying to make sense of them. Marta Bessarion? The *weaver?* Why, she'd commissioned a gown's worth of fabric from the girl just last month. Sibylla touched her tongue to her lips. *Alive.* She couldn't imagine what for. Information? Power? Or revenge? No matter the reason, clearly both were desperately important to Kurosh's master, and she would be a fool not to learn why before she handed them over.

A scratch came on the door. Marta Bessarion followed Alix into the room and proved to be a young Syrian girl in a plain gown of rumpled grey wool; no obvious power or influence hung about her. Sibylla frowned, trying to figure out where the girl belonged. That she'd made a name as a weaver suggested she was of the burgess class, but then, the rumours of her knightly exploits suggested a higher status.

"Leave us," Sibylla told Alix, and when the door closed, she sank down into a chair and stretched her slippered feet towards the fire before speaking again. "You bring a message from the prince?"

"Not as such, my lady." The Syrian coloured. "But I do have to warn you about something, and the constable of Kerak gave me the password to get me in to see you. My name's Marta Bessarion."

Sibylla's eyes narrowed. "I thought you were an Ibelin fosterling. A Watcher."

"I am both. But I have my own conscience, too." Her eyes flickered around the plain but luxurious room, and Sibylla had the distinct impression that she missed no detail, however small. She touched a nervous tongue to her lips, returning her attention to Sibylla. "I believe the Watchers have asked the king for a divorce between you and the count."

For a long, long moment Sibylla didn't breathe. It was the very last thing she had expected, although now it seemed so clear, so obvious. She should have seen it coming. Devil *take* it.

She wiped her face clean of emotion and spoke in a very soft, controlled voice: "Why would they do that? Surely it would be less trouble if my brother named our cousin Tripoli as heir."

The Syrian shook her head. "The count of Tripoli has no heirs of his own, so it wouldn't be a real solution. The Watchers want a new husband for you."

"Who?"

"I don't know if they've thought that far."

Sibylla clenched her teeth. "And my brother? What does he think of this idea?"

"I spoke to him last night, before Lord Balian could see him. He agreed not to say yes until I'd had a chance to find a different answer. We have

283

until the High Court meeting this afternoon to come up with a solution."

We. This Syrian chit had a high opinion of herself. *He agreed not to say yes*—Devil take it! Baldwin would never give *her* so much latitude. His own sister! Who *was* this little Syrian? A jumped-up weaver? A protégé of the parvenu Ibelins? Baldwin would thwart her at every turn, but this *weaver* got admitted to his councils and granted boons?

To her horror, Sibylla realised that a sob was crawling up her throat. She got to her feet, almost knocking her chair over, and rushed for the door leading onto the loggia.

"My lady?" The Syrian was startled.

Sibylla blew past her into the loggia, dashed into the cabinet next door, closed the door behind her and leaned against it, breathing deeply in an effort to calm herself.

Divorce.

All this time, she'd been so focused on trying to keep the kingdom, she'd never imagined they'd try to take Guy from her instead. *How* did she fail to foresee this?

Because it is outrageous, she answered herself. With Isabella married and the king's health declining, they must be desperate for a solution. Tripoli was no doubt their preference, but Baldwin still didn't trust his cousin, and as the Syrian had pointed out, he had no heirs either.

So now, with Guy and Baldwin at loggerheads since the Galilee campaign, they would make their move. Sibylla pressed a hand to the hollow below her ribcage. By Saint Anne, it made sense. Baldwin was as filled with hatred against Guy as the Watchers were, and that gave them their chance. They would tear her from her husband's arms and force her to marry another.

And Baldwin would do nothing to stop them.

A knock sounded on the door. "Sibylla?" Guy called.

"Come in," she gasped.

"I saw you run in here," he began, venturing through the door. Sibylla caught and slammed it the moment he was through, grabbed him by the collar of his shirt and stopped his words with her kiss.

He made a sound of pain at her fierce onslaught, and pulled away for air.

284

"Sibylla, what's wrong?"

She had her arms locked around his neck, her toes hardly touching the floor. Feverish chills ran through her body. "We're alone," she breathed. "It's you and me against the whole world now."

His arms tightened. "As long as it's the two of us, isn't that all we need?"

"All we need," she breathed. "Guy, they're going to try to divorce us."

He froze. "Holy Virgin..."

His strength. Her wit. "We can overcome this," she whispered between kisses. "As long as we're together. Tell me, Guy of Lusignan: are you my man still?"

"To my dying breath, lady."

Her mind had begun to work again. Sibylla slipped from his arms, patting her hair smooth. "There's a Syrian girl in my room. Tell her to go away." *If Baldwin has anything to say, he should see me himself, instead of sending a go-between.* "I need to speak to my mother."

Guy obeyed, and Sibylla rang for Alix to bring a tray of food. She sat behind her writing-desk, staring at the onyx ring.

No. The problem was already too dire to be solved with the stroke of one knife, and besides, Baldwin was now the only person standing between Sibylla and the worst fate she could imagine. She let go of the black stone and reached for a piece of paper, scribbling a few words for her mother's steward.

It was only once she'd finished the note that she remembered she should have detained the Syrian girl. Saint Anne, she was becoming careless.

Chapter XXXIII.

The countess' chamber was austere but beautiful, its dark oaken furniture contrasting with whitewashed walls and snowy curtains. The only splash of colour was a red Persian carpet on the floor and a matching cushion on the vacated chair opposite the fireplace.

There was not much to look at, and Marta had almost decided the countess had forgotten her by the time the door opened and one of the waiting-woman looked in. "You're Marta Bessarion?" She barely waited for an answer. "You can leave now."

Marta blinked. "Where's the countess? Did she leave any message for me?"

"No." The waiting-woman gestured towards the door, her voice forbidding any dispute.

She was being sent away like a lackey, Marta realised. Her cheeks warmed, but she ducked her head submissively and followed the woman out of the white chamber onto the loggia. There was no sign of the countess as the waiting-woman ushered her firmly downstairs and across the courtyard to the gate. When the door of the countess' house slammed shut behind her, she stood motionless in the street with her stomach churning.

What had she just done?

She'd betrayed Lord Balian's secret plan to his enemy. He was wrong and needed to be stopped—but had she just done something terribly foolish?

What was Lord Balian going to say when he found out? Would he ever trust her again?

As for the countess—what would she do now? Marta had seen Sibylla's face as she rushed from the room, her barely-concealed distress.

Had she just started a civil war?

It was amazing how many questions you never thought of asking until it was already much too late. How foolish to assume that Countess Sibylla would be like Lord Balian or Baldwin—that they'd talk about the problem and, together, they'd come up with a solution. The countess was a stranger to her; *of course* she had no reason to share her plans.

Baldwin had asked her to visit him by noon. That was still a couple of hours away, but Marta couldn't bring herself to go home and wait. She slunk past Temple Street house with her head down and continued past the central markets to the royal palace. She had to tell the king what she'd done.

Like last night, she was shown into the palace immediately and left to wait in a frescoed antechamber that was already crowded with barons and courtiers. Marta held tightly onto the cuffs of her sleeves as she leaned against the wall, acutely aware of her shabby grey gown amidst the bright silks, jewels, and furs of the court. At first no one noticed her, but then the door to the king's solar opened and a servant emerged.

"The king's apologies, mademoiselle. He asks you to wait a little, until he's finished meeting with the Antiochene envoys."

"Thank you," she replied. As the servant left, she realised that nearly every noble in the room was staring at her, envy and disdain playing across their faces. It took all her courage to keep from running away then and there.

Soon enough, however, she was ushered into the solar, where Baldwin sat propped up in a chair, furs over his knees. "Is that you, Marta?" he whispered in a hopeful rasp. He paused to listen. "You're not wearing armour today."

"No, my lord."

"Wish I still had eyes. I don't think I've ever seen you by day." He gestured vaguely to a chair that stood opposite him. "Please sit. I've been waiting all morning to hear that story you promised me."

"Story?" Marta asked, startled.

"About your escape from Kerak," he prompted.

Marta stared at him, bemused. "But, my lord, the council this afternoon..."

He stilled for a moment, and although very little of his face remained mobile or expressive, she could feel the enthusiasm draining out of him. He managed something like a grin. "Well, drat it. I thought we might be able to distract each other from business for a while. What's the news, then? Balian told me what he wanted, and why. Do you have an alternative?"

Marta swallowed. "No, my lord. I'm sorry."

Baldwin was silent for a moment. As his shoulders slumped, she couldn't help noticing how thin he was. "It's all right. You aren't a miracle-worker."

Marta wanted nothing more than to slide her arm around those thin shoulders, to let him know that even if she couldn't help, she was with him. Touch was how she voiced the thoughts she could not put into words, and her heart was overflowing. But she couldn't do it: he'd think she was acting out of pity, and he'd be so afraid to pass on his disease.

"I'm afraid not." As she tucked her fingers around her elbows to stop them fluttering towards him, her forehead twinged. She blinked through the pain, and hurried into the confession she must make. "I, um, I've just been to see Countess Sibylla."

The Leper King made a startled noise. "I beg your pardon?"

It was just as bad as she'd feared. "I told her what Lord Balian was planning," she said. "I thought she would be better placed to find a solution than I am."

"Undoubtedly." Baldwin looked uncomfortable. "It's just...saints! What *kind* of solution?"

"I'm not entirely sure. She didn't discuss it with me." Was it the crackling fire on the hearthstone, or the awkward silence making her sweat? "Have I ruined everything, my lord?"

"Oh, please don't apologise," he said with a sigh. "I knew last night that whatever you did, it would probably be something...creative."

Creative? Marta sparked. "Whatever happens, it was only fair that

Countess Sibylla should know. It's her marriage, after all."

"Indeed. It's just..." He was silent a moment. "Saints. It's just that I should have been the one to tell her, I suppose. She's going to be angry that I didn't see her myself."

That hadn't occurred to Marta. "Maybe you can mend it by supporting her at the council this afternoon."

"Perhaps, but that still doesn't solve the problem of succession. The only way I can truly appease Sibylla is to make her queen and Guy king. I can't do that without the barons' support."

There must be some compromise. Marta frowned. How many hours until the council met? The countess had been surprised and upset by her news; she would need time to react, to think, to plan. Maybe, somehow, there was still hope.

"I'm afraid I've been a churl to you," Baldwin said suddenly, "putting all my burdens on you like this. I'm grateful for your help, truly." He gave a rush of wry laughter. "Sometimes I think you would make a better ruler than Sibylla *or* me."

Marta stared at him, horrified. "Oh, no, my lord."

"You'd make a good lady, though," he teased, "at least if Lord Balian can be trusted. He spoke of you last night. In fact, we sat before the fire like a pair of old women, and scratched our heads trying to think of a good noble match for you."

Not Baldwin, too! Her cheeks burned. "I'd rather you didn't."

There was a moment's silence before he asked lightly, "Is there someone else, then?"

There was Miles, and clearly she had to tell Lord Balian about him soon, before he thought to arrange her a marriage with someone else.

And before *that*, she owed him the truth about what she'd told Sibylla this morning.

She swallowed. "There is, my lord, but that's all I can tell you."

"There is?" She didn't know why he sounded sad. "What kind of man is he? Not too old, I hope."

"Oh no, my lord—he's about your age."

289

"And his occupation?"

"He's a knight." Marta's thoughts flew to the Hospital. "Or he *has* been. But he's very ill."

There was a long silence. "Marta," Baldwin said in an uncertain voice, "may I ask you something?"

"Of course," Marta said, but her gut clenched a little at the solemnness in his voice.

She waited, and silence unspooled. Because of the swellings on his face, it was impossible to tell what Baldwin was thinking, but he shifted a little in his chair, as though he was trying to find the right words. "Marta, do you…"

"Yes?" she asked after an unbearable moment of silence.

He shifted again in his chair, and then blurted, "Do you like oranges?"

Marta blinked. "My lord?"

"The trees are laden with them at this time of year. Feel free to take one when you go." He paused and added, rather defensively, "There's nothing special about them."

"Oh." Evidently, that was not what he had originally planned to say, but there was no point in trying to guess. Confused, she stood up and kicked a leg back in a curtsey, despite his inability to see it. "Thank you, my lord. I will."

"Visit me again sometime?" he rasped. "I still want to know how you escaped Kerak."

"I'll do that too," she promised.

She left the solar via the antechamber, ran the gauntlet of courtiers and slid out onto the loggia. Before she reached the head of the stairs, running footsteps sounded behind her and a panting manservant appeared with a basket of oranges. "A gift from the king," he said.

Marta accepted them, still mystified. She firmly refused the servant's offer to carry them home for her, and went out into the city with slow deliberate steps.

What now? All she could do was stand aimlessly in the street in the increasing certainty that her work wasn't done yet. She hadn't offered

Baldwin a solution. The question was still unresolved.

She could only hope that by now, Countess Sibylla would have recovered from her distress and laid her plans. Marta balanced her basket of oranges on her hip and moved into the street, thinking furiously. It was not yet noon. There was still time.

Marta turned left on the Street of the Patriarch and a few minutes later let herself into the Hospital. A tall man in a black robe stood at the foot of Miles' bed speaking to him, and Marta was astonished when he turned to greet her with a smile.

"Sheikh al-Na'im!" she exclaimed. "Peace be upon you!"

Miles looked tired, but cheerful. "Look who came to visit!"

Marta set down the oranges and straightened. "What brings you to Jerusalem, sheikh?"

"And upon you, peace. I've come to ask permission for my people to graze in the Leper King's land at Darum."

The coast south of Gaza was the smallest of the royal domains, little more than a small fortress watching the road to Egypt, and the king was always willing to trade pasture land for information on the sultan's troop movements. "I'm sure he'll be happy to oblige you. I suppose your usual grazing in Transjordan is not so safe this year?"

"For more reasons than one. I don't like to settle my people anywhere without a guarantee of safe-conduct—and Prince Reynald is somewhat occupied at present."

"Is Saladin serious about taking Kerak, do you think?" Miles put in. "Once we send our army, do you think he'll wait and give battle?"

"God willing, he'll raise the siege and retreat." Al-Na'im thought for a few moments. "In truth, I suspect that's what he'd do anyway. He would not embark upon the conquest of the Coast now, with his claims in Mesopotamia unsettled. But only God knows."

The sheikh graciously accepted one of Marta's oranges and departed. Once he had left, Marta turned to Miles, worried. "You look tired. What did the doctors say? How do you feel?"

Miles grinned. "They're going to tap my stomach again this afternoon, and then try sewing up my intestines. Lord Balian came this morning, wondering where you were."

Oh, dear. "What did you tell him?"

"Don't worry, I haven't given you away." Miles grinned. "I distracted him with the story of how we left Kerak." His voice dipped to a whisper. "How'd it go with the countess?"

Marta bit her lip. "Not too well."

"What's bothering you, Marta?"

"I…" She sighed, and took his hand, holding it tight. "You said you were on my side now."

"Always."

She brushed her lips across his knuckles. "I'm afraid of what she's going to do with the information I gave her. I hoped we would work together to find a solution, but instead, she just sent me away."

"Wait." A wicked gleam lit Miles' eye. "Information? You've been giving away Watcher secrets to *Sibylla?*"

"Hush!" Marta glanced around the hospital, worried.

"Does Lord Balian suspect?"

Marta shook her head. "I don't know. I just know that I need to salvage something from this mess I've got myself into. If I could convince Countess Sibylla to tell me her plans…"

"…then you'd have the chance to stop her if you disagreed with them?"

"Or at least convince her that there's a better way." Marta sighed. "I've started meddling in this business now. I have to see it through, but I'm no good at negotiating. There's Persi, but she…" Marta did not have the courage to face her yet. "Persi's busy. And you know the Courtenay faction so much better than I do. Help me."

"Of course." Miles rolled onto his back, staring intently at the groin-vaulted ceiling. "First, let's hear exactly what happened when you spoke to the countess."

Chapter XXXIV.

"I know you must have some plan in mind, my lady." Miles would have said the words with a charming smile, but Marta wasn't sure that was within her power. Instead, she just tried to look respectful. "Please let me know how I can help."

"Help *me?* And how do you propose to do that?"

Earlier that morning, Countess Sibylla's panic had been palpable. Now, she sat beside the desk in her cabinet with her hands laced tightly in her lap, her fingers pale with pressure. Marta swallowed. "Maybe I can convince Prester Balian to agree to your plan."

"Why would you do that? Do you expect a reward?"

"No, my lady. I only want to see justice done."

The countess' eyes narrowed. "Only a fool gives away information for free." She reached for a small casket, throwing the lid back with a bang. "Name your price."

Marta's face grew hot. "I mean it. I don't have a price."

"*Everyone* has a price. Money. Rank. A rich marriage, or a convent office."

The seraph's kiss began to burn, and Marta clapped a hand to her forehead with a yelp of indignation. That wasn't fair—she wasn't even *thinking* of taking the payment. "Please, my lady. I can't."

"How can I trust someone who won't take my money? If I'm not paying you, who is?"

"No one! I'm a weaver. I make my own money."

There was a short silence. Sibylla watched her closely, her eyes hard and

293

dark as sapphires. Then, with a bang, she closed the lid of the casket. "So. An honest woman."

Marta's forehead stopped tingling, and she lowered her hand cautiously. "I try, my lady."

"Join my household," the countess said. "Leave Balian to his own devices. I could use a reliable woman."

Marta shook her head, bewildered. "Can't you trust me without paying me?"

"I hear that you're something more than a weaver," the countess insisted. "You rode into Arabia earlier this year and rescued the constable of Kerak. The one who gave you the password, I take it. Where is he now?"

"Miles of Plancy is in the Hospital, my lady."

The countess gave a curt nod. "Is he your sweetheart?"

Marta didn't mistake the countess' razor-sharp focus for idle chit-chat, and her natural defences came up. Until Lord Balian knew, she couldn't tell anyone. "He's like a brother to me."

"And *my* brother?"

"My lady?"

"I'm told a Syrian girl of your description spent half an hour with him this morning. Tongues are wagging."

"Oh, dear, no!" Marta's cheeks flamed. "He's also like a brother to me."

"And Lord Balian is your foster-father," Sibylla said sarcastically. "Is there anyone in this kingdom you *haven't* adopted?"

Startled, Marta considered this. "No," she admitted. It was true. She had never chosen to be torn away from her family and dropped into this far future, but this had been the one choice she did have. She had taken this new life and new family for her own, and she would do anything to keep them safe.

Sibylla still looked suspicious, but she didn't press Marta further. "I went to see my mother." Her lips compressed into a pale line, and Marta realised she was furious. "I have a son, young Baldwin. He is nine years old and my first heir. My mother's counsel is that in order to be permitted my husband, I should resign my claim to the throne in favour of my son. That

294

he should become Baldwin the Fifth. That I should become no one."

Marta understood, and an immense burden rolled off her shoulders. That would neatly bypass not only Count Guy but also the count of Tripoli, while also holding out hope of a better king than anyone expected Humphrey to be. As such, it was the only compromise that both the Watchers and their opponents would accept. It was the alternative Baldwin had asked her for.

"It's perfect," she exclaimed.

"It's insanity," Sibylla spat. "My son is a *child*. He can't protect this kingdom. He can't lead an army. He hasn't the wit to know wisdom from folly. And to cap it all, once he was crowned we should *still* have to find a bailli. The only possible benefit to anyone is that because he is a child, the barons are confident they can control him."

Isabella had been treated just as badly, but Marta had enough sense not to say it aloud. Sibylla looked at her interlaced hands, and when she spoke again, her voice was emotionless again. "You believe the Watchers will accept this, then."

Marta touched the tip of her tongue to her lips. "I believe so, my lady. I'm sure your brother will."

"Oh, I thank you for the reassurance." The countess scowled. "I wonder, was this Balian's plan all along? Did he think I'd be so loath to give up my husband that I'd surrender the throne for him?"

Marta opened her mouth to protest, but doubt took hold of her. Did she really know Lord Balian so well?

She'd assumed the Watchers were righteous, again. She'd been proven wrong. Again.

Sibylla must have seen the thoughts chasing themselves across Marta's face. "Indeed," she said. The countess stared at a sheet of blank paper that sat on the slope of her writing-desk, a quill lying sharpened beside it. Waiting for orders. Waiting for a decision.

Abruptly, she shook back her voluminous sleeve, picked up the quill, and scribbled a single word on the paper. "They leave me no choice. I accept your help." She ironed the paper into a folded envelope, and thrust her sealing-wax in the flame of a candle. "I'll have my mother send to the king—he won't refuse her this last request. But you must talk to the Watchers. Convince them to agree, and you can name your own reward."

Marta was already certain that she didn't want to be beholden to this lady in any way. Besides, none of the things she truly craved were in Sibylla's power to give: the king's health, the kingdom's security, the Watchers' virtue. "Your thanks will be enough. Truly."

"Hmm." Sibylla looked sceptical. "You may go. Be sure you tell the Watchers that their choices are *also* running out."

"Yes, my lady."

"And, Bessarion."

"My lady?"

"My offer still stands. You need not suffer for what you have done today. If the Watchers cast you out, there is a place in my household for you."

Marta curtseyed and hurried away with her gut twisting. It had occurred to her that Lord Balian might be angry with her for what she'd done today, but would he really cast her out?

She sighed. All fears aside, she owed him an explanation, and there was no putting it off any longer. It was past noon, and the sundial in Sibylla's courtyard told her that there was barely an hour left before the High Court meeting.

She swallowed her fear and set off towards Temple Street.

It turned out that what she needed to steady her nerves was a little adversity. At Temple Street, she summoned up all her courage to tap at the door of Lord Balian's cabinet, only to find it empty. She searched all over the house before a servant informed her that he had already left for the palace.

Marta stopped by the kitchens to pocket a little bread and cheese, then hurried towards the palace. As she approached the Street of the Armenians, she heard a commotion and saw passers-by hurrying past the head of the street with bemused stares. Marta's pulse quickened, and she dashed around the corner to see a small crowd gathering outside the palace gate. There was a confused sound of shouting and hooting, and over it all a group of men were singing in rowdy, monotonous French:

CHAPTER XXXIV.

Never mind what the Polains do,
We shall have a king from Poitou!

Polains. It meant *colts,* a Western insult for the Franks of the East. Ahead, clods flew as the shouts got louder. *Not again,* Marta thought. Evidently, Count Guy's Poitevin followers had chosen this of all days to make trouble in the streets. Her hands reflexively patted her hip, but all she had was a brocaded girdle in place of a sword-belt.

The crowd effectively blocked the palace gates. As Marta slipped by on the opposite side of the street, she caught a glimpse of the red-faced Poitevins behind a wall of incensed Jerusalemites, arms linked, defiantly chanting their slogan. Some of the indignant natives were in livery; Marta glimpsed the Lord of Sidon and his followers laying about them with the flat of their swords in an effort to reach the palace gate.

Thankfully, Marta was nimble enough not to need a gate. She ran into the public gardens at the end of the palace grounds, found the postern gate unguarded, and climbed easily over the bars. With the commotion in the street, nobody was watching the garden, and it wasn't until she entered the palace courtyard that she found a servant to direct her to Lord Balian.

"He's meeting with the king, mademoiselle," the man told her. "If you'll wait in the antechamber, you'll catch him when he comes out."

The antechamber was empty this afternoon, and Marta debated whether she should just knock on the solar door and ask to be let in. She had no time to decide, however, for just as the servant showed her in, the door opened and Lord Balian stuck his head out. "Oh, Marta," he said, surprised. "Do *you* know what that infernal racket is?"

"It's the Poitevins again, my lord." It was the truth, and she could hardly say anything else, but Lord Balian's expression in the silence following her words made her heart sink. Count Guy was not making her job any simpler.

"If that's Marta, tell her to come in," rasped a familiar voice and Lord Balian beckoned her into the solar with a wave of the parchment he held in his hand. Baldwin sat propped up in the same comfortable chair where

297

she'd seen him a couple of hours ago, but something about his posture told her that he was cruelly tired, in pain, and determined to keep going anyway. "What are they singing out there?" he asked. "I keep hearing that tune."

Marta hesitated, instinctively aware that repeating the words would be a mistake. "My lord, they're just taunting the people."

"Guy has no business to let them do that," the king snapped. "Where is he? Send for him at once. Where's my mother's letter, Balian?"

As he returned from giving the servant his instructions, Balian shot Marta a shrewd look that made her feel rather uncomfortable. "Here, my lord."

"My mother asks me to have my young nephew crowned co-king, if I will insist on removing Guy from the bailliship," Baldwin told Marta. "She writes that it is her dying wish. I take it that this is her alternative to that other matter we discussed."

Under Balian's scrutiny, Marta blushed. "Yes, my lord, I believe it is."

"Naturally, that would cut Guy and Sibylla out of the succession altogether. Making a divorce more or less unnecessary— Devil take it, I can hardly hear myself think. Why doesn't Guy calm them down? What are they singing out there, Marta?"

He waited, and Marta realised there was no helping it. She cleared her throat. *"Never mind what the Polains do, we shall have a king from Poitou."*

There was a silence.

"Saint George," the Leper King erupted. "How dare they? What is Guy *thinking*, allowing them to do this? *I* am king in Jerusalem. This is tantamount to treason."

Marta risked a pleading glance at Balian, but his face was shuttered. He said nothing.

"My lord," Marta began at last, but a scratch sounded on the door and the servant poked his head in to announce Count Guy of Jaffa.

"Ibelin, Marta, you had better leave us," Baldwin said coldly. "Show him in."

Marta followed Lord Balian into the antechamber, where the bailli waited, dwarfed by the frescoes of King Solomon that adorned the walls. He said nothing, but smiled mockingly as he shouldered through the door into the king's solar and closed it behind them.

Outside in the street, the rhythmic chanting continued. Nearer at hand, Count Guy's voice murmured behind the solar door, not quite loud enough to distinguish words. On one wall, the young King Solomon knelt asking heaven for the gift of wisdom. On another, the old king forgot his wisdom, bowing before gods of his own making while his people were oppressed by harsh task-masters.

Marta stared at the vivid figures without seeing them. As soon as she'd found Lord Balian meeting with the king, she had guessed that he must know everything she had done in the last day. What unsettled her was his unreadable face. She swallowed hard and said, "Are you very angry with me?"

Even the calm in Balian's voice was forbidding. "Have you done something I should be angry about?"

That was very bad. Marta felt the sweat bead on her forehead. "I told Countess Sibylla the truth. I had to."

"So I gather." There was another silence, and for the first time, emotion broke into his voice. "Do you have any idea how badly that might have gone for us, Marta?"

"Yes, my lord." She spoke meekly, but was compelled to add, "But it didn't. And we have a workable option now."

"Don't think it hadn't already crossed my mind," Lord Balian said. "To cut Guy and Sibylla out of the succession by crowning her son. But I rejected that thought out of hand."

Marta stared at him, forgetting to be respectful. "You *rejected* it? Why?"

"Because two weak and incapable kings do not make one whole king." Lord Balian stuck his thumbs into his belt. "Because as the king's parents, Guy and Sibylla will still be the power behind the throne. They might even claim the bailliship. Or what if young Baldwin was to die? No. The only way we could get rid of Guy for good would be a divorce."

"She would fight for him," Marta protested. "And she would be right to do so. Is this what you want? To go to war in an unjust cause?"

Lord Balian was silent for a moment. Then he sank onto a bench and beckoned her to him, his face almost on a level with hers and deadly serious. "Come here, Marta. Look into my eyes and swear to me that you know this to be right."

"I know that to divorce them unwillingly would be wrong."

His gaze slipped past her, fixed itself on the door to the king's solar. The voices within had become agitated. "Guy is a madman," he said softly. "He believes that he can make enemies of all of us and still rule us. *Never mind what the Polains do...*"

Marta didn't know what else to say. She had begged and pleaded, to no avail. *You should have kissed Miles, or Persi, or someone who could actually do the job,* she prayed into the waiting silence.

Lord Balian looked back at her, his eyes thoughtful. "I went to see Miles at the Hospital this morning. He told me things that can hardly be believed."

Marta blinked at him, thrown off by the change of subject. "My lord?"

"He told me you charged out of Kerak by the front gate. That you fought your way through Saladin's whole camp. That a man who tried to stop you was struck by lightning."

"That wasn't me. The lightning, I mean."

"Oh, I know that. Miles thinks it was the Bessarion Lance, but I was its guardian for fifteen years. I know that it is a weapon, and that is all it is. It does not stop stray arrows. It does not put the bearer in the right part of the battle at the right time. It is not the favour of God."

Marta stared, astonished to find that he understood. Despite all this, he understood.

"I should have listened to you," he went on softly. "God must be with you, to do the things you have done. If you swear it's wrong to divorce them, then we'll have to take Sibylla's compromise."

Marta remembered the sting of the seraph's kiss. "It is, my lord. I'd stake my soul on it."

Balian bent his head for a moment and took a deep breath before looking up at her again. "Then I believe you, and I trust you."

"You do? Despite this?" Marta's voice shook as she gestured towards the voices echoing in the solar.

"That's what faith is, isn't it? *The substance of things hoped for.*" He reached out, took her hand. "Don't cry."

Marta scrubbed at her wet eyes with her sleeve and drew breath to speak, but a shout from the solar interrupted her.

"I'm damned if I'll apologise," Count Guy yelled. "You would steal my wife from me!"

Lord Balian jumped to his feet and threw open the door of the solar, his hand on his sword-hilt. Hard on his heels, Marta peered under the tall lord's elbow in time to catch a glimpse of Count Guy whirling to face them. The Leper King sat hunched up in his chair like a doll with the stuffing removed, but he didn't seem to be in any personal distress, and Balian's hand relaxed on the hilt of his sword.

"Don't be a fool, Guy." Baldwin leaned forward, clutching the arms of his chair. "This divorce was neither my idea, nor my intention."

Count Guy shot Balian a look full of bile before turning to confront the Leper King again. "In that case, *my lord,* you'd best make peace with the fact that I am the husband of the lawful heir, and that I *will* protect her interests. If you don't like that, then you'd best get rid of me."

He turned again and Lord Balian and Marta barely had time to get out of his way before he shoved past them, his footsteps echoing loudly across the antechamber as he headed for the door.

Marta ran to Baldwin, falling to her knees before him. He sank back into his chair just too late. She didn't mean to touch him: but as her fingertips brushed the bandages on his arm, pain burned through her, and something groaned in her ears like iron.

He shifted and she looked up into his swollen face. He hadn't even noticed her touch.

"Are you all right, my lord?" she asked shakily. Her forehead was painlessly hot, as though something had awoken its power. What did *that* mean?

"I'm perfectly well," he snapped, although clearly nothing was further from the truth. His teeth ground. "Arrogant, insufferable, high-handed *bully*," he spat. "Nothing but a hired cutthroat, and my sister *married* him."

"Does he know of the plan to crown his stepson?" Lord Balian was still poised by the door, as though ready to send messengers running in all directions.

Baldwin barked with laughter. "Oh no, we didn't make it that far. We were too busy debating the necessity of his keeping his followers from seditious rioting." His voice, ragged from overuse, dissolved into coughing; a moment later, his body was racked with it.

Marta jumped up. A jug of pure snowmelt stood on the table at his elbow, and she sloshed some of the icy water into a cup. "Here—drink."

"Don't touch me!" he gasped between coughs. "Strike—strike that bell."

Marta obeyed, and a few moments later, one of the king's leper attendants appeared. Calmly, the man guided Baldwin's hands to the cup, helped him grip it, and then counted his pulse while he drank.

"What time is it, Brother John?" he whispered when he could breathe without coughing.

"A little after two o'clock, my lord."

His shoulders slumped. "And we've kept the High Court waiting. Splendid."

Lord Balian cleared his throat. "My lord, that petition of mine…I withdraw it. I'm not going to present it to the council."

Baldwin didn't speak, and for a moment Marta assumed he must not have heard. But then he spoke. "My mother's compromise satisfies you?"

"Yes, my lord."

"Well. It doesn't rid us of this Poitevin upstart, but it buys us some time."

"Thanks to Marta," Lord Balian added.

"Yes—thanks to Marta." The king's voice warmed. "I think we owe you some recognition for your efforts, Marta Bessarion. Is there anything we can do for you?"

When Sibylla had asked her the same thing, earlier that day, Marta could only think of things that no mortal power could provide. Now, something else occurred to her.

"I'd like to get married," she said shyly, turning to Lord Balian. "To Miles of Plancy. Is there...do you think you could give us a small dowry, my lord?"

Behind her, there was a crash. Baldwin had knocked his glass to the floor.

Chapter XXXV.

True to the Syrian's word, Sibylla found the constable of Kerak in the Hospital of Saint John. The brothers warned her that he'd been drugged into a deep sleep that afternoon for surgery, but Sibylla had no time to waste.

Swathed in a black veil to conceal her identity, she could barely see inside the dimly lit Hospital. It was nearly Compline, and the sunset was fading quickly from the sky outside, thick water droplets forming on the windows. The night would be as cold and clear as the day had been bright and sunny; there was a nip of frost in the air.

It seemed wrong that the most disastrous day of her life should have been so clear and fair. True, the ultimate disaster was averted. Despite Guy's quarrel with Baldwin before the council meeting this afternoon, neither the king nor Balian of Ibelin had proposed a divorce to the High Court. Instead, it was decided that in two weeks' time, her son should be crowned king in the Holy Sepulchre, securing the succession before the army marched to relieve Prince Reynald in Kerak.

That was the price of today's victory. Since her brother first became ill, she had lived and worked and prepared for the day she would become queen. Now she had been forced to surrender that claim in exchange for a faint hope that she and Guy might be able to do something for the kingdom as bailli later on.

She had married Guy because she was sure he would be her strength, but today he had been her weakness—a weakness her enemies had ruthlessly exploited to refuse her the throne.

Well. She could be as ruthless as they and more.

The constable of Kerak lay in the far corner of the building, two empty beds on his near side providing all the privacy she could hope for. Alix trimmed the wick on the lantern that stood near his bed, causing the light to burn brightly enough for Sibylla to see that he was still asleep.

"Miles of Plancy." Sibylla put a ring of command into her voice, and he groaned before jolting into full wakefulness at the sight of his two veiled guests.

Dishevelled and still muzzy from his drugged sleep, he nevertheless managed a charming smile. "Ladies, I am at your service."

"Do you know me, Sir Miles?" Sibylla extended her hand for him to kiss. He took it, and his eyes flickered to the black onyx signet on her thumb.

He paused, caught his breath, and then brushed his lips lightly across her skin. "My lady. I do know you."

He was quick-witted and discreet then, as well as useful. Sibylla eased herself onto the bed across from him. "I need your help, Miles of Plancy."

He gingerly pulled himself to a sitting position, one hand curled protectively around his gut. "You have only to command, my lady."

There was no point in beating around the bush. "I need information. What do you know about the little weaver and her weapon?"

"My lady?"

His voice seemed puzzled, and she might have sworn it was genuine had she not already satisfied herself of his wits. "Don't bother fencing with me. You know exactly what I mean."

There was a silence. "Why do you ask?"

Under her veil, Sibylla smiled. It was good to feel powerful tonight; the little Syrian weaver might have ideas above her station, but it was good to know that the countess of Jaffa was still someone a penniless young knight couldn't afford to antagonise. "Let us say that the weapon and its owner are both highly valuable to someone I know of, and I wish to know why."

"Saint George," he breathed, thoughtfully. There was a very long silence, and then he said, "My lady, I'm really not the right person to ask. You should speak to the weaver herself."

So the Syrian had his loyalty. Yet it was clear that he hoped not to offend her by an outright refusal. Sibylla responded with words just as guarded: "I have spoken to her twice today, and I still have questions."

Another silence followed while he wrestled with his conscience. "Forgive me, my lady. Believe me, I wish I could help you."

Sibylla sighed. "As I wish I could help you. I know a little about you, Sir Miles of Plancy. I know you were born on the wrong side of the blanket. I know you have only ever been a lackey in the castle where your father once ruled. I know that if it had been left to Prince Reynald to save you, you would never have come back from Arabia alive." She stood up slowly, ignoring the pain that shot through her back and hips. "You're a man of wit and courage, Plancy. You could be so much more than the constable in another man's castle."

She'd taken three steps away from the bed when Plancy gasped, "My lady. Wait. I have left the prince's service. I am no longer the constable of Kerak."

"That was foolish of you."

Her tone was not encouraging, and he ran his tongue over his lips before continuing. "If I tell you what you want to know, will you take me into your service?"

"Perhaps." Sibylla returned to her seat on the bed and leaned forward. Time to strip off the velvet glove. "The weapon. What does it do?"

"It makes the wielder invincible. No one can stand before it." He took a shaky breath. "You've seen Marta. She's tiny. Yet I've seen her charge through a whole army of Saracens just using the butt-end. I don't know who it is that wants to buy the weapon, but the only people who might have seen it in action lately are the Saracens. My lady, if they get their hands on that thing, we're finished."

Sibylla's eyes narrowed. "An enchanted weapon? Are you romancing?"

"I've seen it with these two eyes, I swear."

"And the girl herself? Is she a witch?" That wouldn't ease the sting of knowing that the Syrian was closer to Baldwin than his own sister, but it would at least explain.

"Either that, or a saint. I haven't figured out which."

"Where did Ibelin pick her up?"

"I gather she grew up with noble people, but we found her in a textile shop near Caesarea." He shrugged. "That's all I know. She only ever spoke to Lord Balian about her past."

"Mm." Sibylla drummed her fingers on her knee, looking past Plancy to the stone wall beyond his bed. It was clear, of course, that she couldn't let Kurosh or his master have the spear. It was equally clear that such a thing could not be permitted to remain in the Ibelins' control—not that Balian seemed able to *control* the Syrian weaver.

But then, if Balian couldn't control Marta Bessarion, could Sibylla?

"I tried to buy her this morning. I was generous in my offer, but she refused to join my household."

"She likes to be her own mistress."

"So does everyone. What's her price?"

"As far as I can tell, she doesn't have one."

"*Everyone* has a price. Think, Plancy."

"You don't know her, my lady. Take my word for it: she can't be bought."

Sibylla was enjoying herself: Plancy was like so many men she knew, trying to keep his hands clean enough to satisfy his conscience, but weak and greedy enough to bend at the slightest pressure. She leaned forward, wishing her veil didn't obscure her view of his face. "Young man, you fail to grasp the situation. You say that this girl wields an invincible weapon. You admit that she is ungovernable, and claim that she is incorruptible. What choice does that leave me? I *must* have the weapon, and I'd prefer not to have to eliminate the girl. As it is, however, I'm seriously considering trading her to the buyer I spoke of, to appease his anger when I retain the weapon. If you care for this girl, you'd better come up with a way for me to earn her loyalty."

Plancy's horror was evident, even through the black mesh of her veil. "My lady..."

"As I say, I'd rather not have to do that. So how do I win her loyalty? *What is her price?*"

He swallowed audibly. "Me," he whispered. "She wants me."

Sibylla gave a puff of derision. "Every young man thinks this."

"Not with such proof as I have. She rode seven hundred miles into the heart of Arabia to pull me out of the sultan's grip. When I got a bolt through my guts, she single-handedly battled through Saladin's entire army to bring me to Jerusalem. She wants me."

"And you want her?"

He nodded, his voice tired and thin. "Yes, my lady."

Then the solution was the simplest in the world. "Then win her, and bring her into my service. I'll pay you enough to support her in comfort, and the sooner you get her with child, the sooner you'll wield the lance for yourself."

Plancy bit his lip, obviously uneasy with the bargain. "And you'll give me a fief?"

"The first heiress in my gift shall be yours," Sibylla promised. She leaned forward, her voice sinking again. "Serve me, and I will make you a great man, Miles of Plancy. Refuse me, and I will make sure that you never find patronage in this kingdom again."

She came away from the interview feeling exhausted, but hopeful. If she ever wished to rule the kingdom, she would need the power to crush any dissenting barons. Or better yet, the power to prevent them from dissenting in the first place. With the Bessarion Lance in her control, she would have that power.

Something, at least, was salvaged from the wreckage of this day. Something, at least, was won back from the cursed Watchers.

The exertions of the afternoon left her aching and tired, her brain buzzing with ideas. Once again, Sibylla drank her opium-and-hemlock wine, suppressing the pain long enough to fall asleep. Towards morning, she dreamed that she stood with her mother atop the Tower of David, overlooking the palace and its gardens: the patchwork of roofs, domes, and greenery that made up the city, the valleys carving their way around the walls, and the hillsides beyond, prickly with pencil cypresses.

"You could use the ring now," Agnes told her. Something was wrong

308

with her hands: they were like a bird's talons, the nails long and black and sharp. Sibylla blinked and, for an instant, saw a suggestion of black feathers. "There are two weeks before the coronation, Sibylla. Strike now, and all this might yet be yours."

"That would be premature." Yesterday she might have done it; she was the heir. Today she was not, and she could not risk bringing everything to a crisis now. Not before she had the Bessarion Lance.

Besides, she thought, Baldwin might be letting the Watchers use him, and he might be irretrievably at odds with Guy, but *he* wasn't the one who'd forced this ultimatum upon her. Deep inside, Sibylla couldn't forget the child he'd once been, the brother she'd loved since he was just a mound within their mother's belly.

"He is dying anyway," Agnes replied, although Sibylla hadn't spoken aloud. "He has suffered so long. Surely the kindest thing would be to give him rest."

Sibylla fidgeted the signet ring on her thumb. "It's too soon," she said at last. "The ring can be used only once. I will not act in haste, and waste a thing which my family has kept for generations."

Chapter XXXVI.

With Lord Balian and the Leper King gone to the High Court meeting, Marta headed back to the house on Temple Street. By now her feet ached from running to and fro in the city, but she couldn't make herself feel calm.

What on earth had happened when her fingers brushed Baldwin's arm?

Persi was still hard at work when she got home, the ceaseless clacking echoing in the workroom. When Marta entered, she let her loom fall silent and stretched gratefully. "Oh, there you are. Are you ready to start on Countess Sibylla's brocade?"

"I'll finish the blue first." Marta fingered the double-weave cloth stretched out on Persi's loom, reluctant to sit down to her own with its half-finished cloth. "You've woven so much since last night!"

"I'm nearly done. Princess Eschiva has been very patient, but some of the others have been less understanding." Persi rolled her shoulders and arched her back. "How's that altar-cloth for Nazareth coming along? If you remember, you were going to have it ready by Saint Cecilia's Day."

Marta grimaced. "Nearly done, but I had to leave it in Kerak." She moved to her own loom, walking her fingers across the royal-blue warp threads. *Kerak, which could fall at any moment. Kerak, which has no idea what dark forces are arrayed against it.*

Persi sighed, frustration in her voice. "I suppose if the castle falls we can kiss that order goodbye. All this war is murder on business." She slumped over her loom with a sigh. "Do you ever think of just leaving it all? Going away to some place that's peaceful?"

Marta blinked at the web on her loom. "No," she said truthfully. "Is there peace anywhere in this world?"

"I suppose not." Persi straightened and picked up her shuttle. "Don't worry, Marta. I'm not leaving you."

The clack of her loom began again. Marta sighed and drifted to the desk under the window, where Persi had laid out the pattern and threads for Sibylla's damask. The countess had chosen one of Marta's favourite patterns, a subtle interplay of grey and white. On paper the pattern was bland and uninteresting and until now no one had ever asked her to make it. The countess, it seemed, had seen past the bland paper to the shimmering opalescent web Marta had designed. She would finally have the chance to make this beautiful thing.

And yet she could not bring herself to start.

Khalil was at Kerak. Isabella and the queen were in danger, and Marta knew better than to hope that the lord of Kerak could protect them. Against the powers that Khalil commanded a man like Prince Reynald would be helpless. Marta chewed her lip. As a Watcher, Queen Maria might help, and there must be other Watchers among her entourage and the fugitives from the town…but in the end, could they really make a difference? Watchers hadn't helped Oliveta.

Despite her worry, she forced herself to sit down to finish the blue, commissioned by a Venetian merchant from Acre. She'd been working for two hours when hoofbeats echoed in the courtyard. Within a heartbeat Marta was up and hurrying for the door. "It's Lord Balian!"

He was dismounting in the courtyard, and his face lit up in a cheerful smile when he saw her. Marta's shoulders sagged with relief. "They listened?"

Balian nodded. "Young Baldwin will be crowned in a fortnight."

Her gut tightened. "So far away? But what about Kerak?"

"We'll march for Kerak the day after." Balian pulled off his gloves. "Don't despair. It will take that long to complete the muster, and Chatillon sent a pigeon to tell us he can hold out that long."

Lord Balian headed upstairs, leaving Marta standing in the courtyard. Prince Reynald might think he could withstand the siege, but he had no idea what he was dealing with. Khalil's magic could not be resisted by mortal means. Kerak needed Watchers.

She couldn't stay here.

The decision crystallised with a sense of relief. Marta thought of Persi, and her conscience stung, but neither Prince Reynald nor Queen Maria were equipped to deal with Khalil. He was her own responsibility, and she needed to face him.

She bit her lip and went upstairs to the room she shared with Persi. The Bessarion Lance was locked in a long chest, along with her armour and gear, newly cleaned and shining. Marta leaned the lance in the corner and shook out her hauberk with a soft jingle of rings. As she reached for her helmet, a shadow darkened the open doorway.

"Marta? What do you think you're doing?" Persi's voice was incredulous.

Marta whipped around, feeling her face heat up. "Persi, I..."

The Nubian stared at her armour. "Not *again.*"

"You don't understand. *He's here*, Persi. Khalil is *here*. He nearly stopped me leaving Kerak."

Persi's sharp intake of breath told Marta that she understood the gravity of the situation. "And you want to go *back?*"

"He saw me. He saw the spear. I have to deal with him before he grows any stronger."

"And how will you do that?"

Marta swallowed. Persi followed her glance, and her lips tightened. "Oh, no, you don't," she snapped, and the next instant she snatched the spear and slid out of the room.

Marta leaped forward, jamming the door open with her dagger hilt just as it would have slammed shut. Beyond the door, the taller, stronger girl yanked on the door-handle with her left hand, trying to knock the dagger free with the butt of the spear.

Marta kept her grip on the dagger and tried to wrestle the door open. "Persi! What on *earth?*"

"I'm trying to intervene, you cuckoo!" Laughing, Persi poked the butt of the Bessarion Lance at her, aiming for Marta's ribs in an attempt to force her away from the door.

Flattening herself against the wall to present a smaller target, Marta grabbed for the spear. "Persi, stop it! This isn't funny! Let me out!"

Persi stilled, and her voice sobered. "No, you're right. It's not funny."

The door whisked open, bringing them face-to-face. Persi twisted the spear out of Marta's reach and gripped it with whitened knuckles. "It's not at all funny to watch you run off again and again, risking your life on these hare-brained adventures."

Marta opened her mouth to protest.

"No," Persi snapped. "You listen to me, all right? I understand that you have duties as a Watcher, but you also have a responsibility to our business, to me and to the people who are paying you for cloth. And meanwhile you're off running crazy risks for this Plancy boy."

Her whole face felt hot. "I'm not doing this for Miles!"

"Oh, indeed?"

"He's not even *at* Kerak! He's here in Jerusalem, at the hospital!"

"Oh! You brought him with you, did you? Well, that's absolutely typical! Why do you keep risking your life for that boy, anyway?"

Marta huffed a breath. "I was coming to Jerusalem with or without him."

"And it nearly *killed* you." Persi struck her palm to her forehead. "Now you want to go *back?* You promised me you'd be careful!"

"I told you Khalil is there. He'll hunt me down—just as he hunted my father. He knows I have the spear."

"All the more reason to keep it right here in this room, where he can't get at it—instead of walking through Saladin's camp with it!" Persi shook her head, frustrated. "All he'd need is *one crossbow.* He wouldn't even need to get near you!"

"But Isabella's in Kerak," Marta protested, rubbing her forehead. "And Queen Maria."

"Queen Maria is a Watcher. If she doesn't know what to do, do you think *you* can save her?"

"I could try!"

"You don't have to try." Persi spoke each word in its own staccato sentence.

"Marta, the fate of this world doesn't ride on your shoulders. There are other Watchers. There are other warriors. You can let them fight their battles. You can *do your work* like you promised you would, and trust heaven for the rest." Her shoulders slumped, her voice fading to a whisper. "I don't want to have to bury you."

Marta's head ached, and as she put a hand to her forehead again her fingers brushed across the scar left by the seraph's kiss. The pain was so subtle that she hadn't noticed it. *Strife.*

Still, it was there, underscoring what she already knew: Persi was right. "I'm sorry. I just...I can't rest when I can see something going wrong in the world."

"I've noticed."

"What about Khalil?"

"You don't have to fear him. He isn't all-powerful." Persi's fingers loosened their grip on the spear. "You'll stay?"

Marta sighed. "I'll stay. As long as I should."

Chapter XXXVII.

There was one thing about being blind: sometimes, it was easier to see things when you couldn't look at them.

Baldwin lay in his litter before the high altar in the Holy Sepulchre, in the beating heart of the whole world. Under the Patriarch's lilting voice, reciting the coronation prayers, the assembled barons and burgesses fidgeted and whispered, making a froth of sound like the waves on the seashore. Faintly from the narrow streets beyond, fitful gusts of sound blew towards him on the winter wind. The clip of horse-shoes, the creak of hand-carts, the mournful cry of a hawker selling watered down wine to the packed crowds in the Street of Palms. As Advent neared, Jerusalem was filled with pilgrims, and today, thousands of them had flocked to the holiest of all places to witness the coronation of the nine year old Baldwin the Fifth.

Baldwin the elder should have been paying more attention. After his young nephew had taken his oath at the colonnaded entrance to the church, the boy had been led between the Tomb of Christ and the high altar to be prayed over by Patriarch Eraclius. In another moment he would take his seat on the throne next to Baldwin the elder's litter, consecrated with holy oil and crowned with his uncle's own hand. A heavy golden circlet made for a child rested on the Leper King's lap.

His own crown weighted his own head, making his temples pound.

It wasn't so long, after all, that he had knelt there in the choir listening to the Patriarch saying the same words over him. Like his nephew, he should have been listening. Praying. Filled with pure light as he rededicated himself to the noblest calling in Christendom.

Instead, his gut was a knot of black and seething resentment.

Poor child, he thought, *I wonder how long you'll last.*

His coronation had been his own death sentence. The stress of kingship had accelerated an illness he might otherwise have survived for decades. The crown had taken everything from him.

Even the chance to be loved.

The black mass inside him churned. It shouldn't have mattered to him that Marta Bessarion was going to marry someone else. How well did he know her, after all? She had her own people, her own lover, her own hopes and dreams. What could he offer her? A disease that would consume her as painfully and slowly as it had him? She surely wasn't noble enough for him to offer her anything more. No. He'd known from the start that they could never be anything but friends.

He still knew, but it made no difference at all to how he felt. She loved someone else. She was going to marry someone else, and his gut was full of broken glass and razor-sharp shadow.

He would never experience that kind of love; not with Marta, and not with anyone else. To embrace him was to embrace death, and he had no right to hope for it or even to want it. All he could do was hide it and hope that no one would notice.

Especially not Marta.

The Patriarch reached his Amen, and the jubilant tones of the *Te Deum* washed through the church. Baldwin caught the shuffle of feet as the Patriarch led the boy king to the nearby throne and helped him climb the footstool into the immense chair. The throne had almost swallowed Baldwin himself when he was a boy of thirteen, and his nephew was even smaller.

An expectant silence descended on the church. It was the moment of anointing, the moment that would consecrate his nephew as the junior king of Jerusalem. Patriarch Eraclius breathed heavily with concentration as he marked the sign of the cross in oil on the young king's forehead.

Would it be enough?

An invalid and a child. Together, the two of them could only provide the kingdom with political stability, and Jerusalem needed so much more than a pair of useless figureheads whose only function was keeping Guy of Lusignan off the throne.

Lusignan. Baldwin's jaw clenched as he tallied the count of Jaffa's trespasses.

If you don't like that, then you'd best get rid of me.

After that scene, he'd been sorely tempted to beg Ibelin to make his petition for a divorce anyway. Crowning the boy might block Guy from the throne, but it wouldn't dislodge him from the kingdom. Whether as baron or brother-in-law, Guy would always be a thorn in his side.

God knew he didn't want to deprive his sister of her rights. God *knew* he had the highest opinion of her abilities, but *what did she see in the arrogant Poitevin cockerel?*

If only Longsword had lived!

If only there had been some better option than Guy of Lusignan, when the choice was forced upon him!

"Vivat rex in prosperitate!" the prelates shouted, jolting him back to the present. *"Vivat rex in prosperitate! Long live the king in prosperity!"*

Baldwin's head ached, but there were hours yet in the ceremony. The Patriarch served the Eucharist to the new king, and then with some relief, Baldwin touched the small crown gingerly as the Patriarch lifted it onto the young king's head. He fell back, his own role in the ceremony finished. There.

He had handed his kingdom over to a successor.

Poor lad.

He'd met with his nephew a week ago, in an attempt to explain his responsibilities to him.

"Mama says I must be king," the boy had said. "But can't you make her queen instead? Please?"

"I'm sorry," was all that Baldwin could say. "I wish I could. Your mother would make a very fine queen."

And she would. That was what filled his gut with bile. Sibylla could *do* this—if only she would let go of Guy. His brilliant, capable sister—the sister he'd relied on to lead the kingdom when he was ready to give up the throne—had destroyed her chances and crippled her kingdom for the sake of Lusignan.

Now the barons filed past, putting their hands between the young king's and swearing fealty. Baldwin paid attention, but he didn't hear Guy's voice.

He cleared his throat. "Aimery."

Count Guy's brother, the Constable of the kingdom, stood nearby holding the royal banner. "My lord?" he whispered.

"Does your brother swear fealty today?"

A silence followed. Guy had been stripped of the bailliship this morning, but Aimery still held his office and was doubtless anxious to keep it. Cautiously, he said, "I don't see him in the church, my lord."

Part of him had hoped that Guy would be here, that he would accept this setback with dignity. Instead, it seemed that he had chosen to remain at home, sulking or scheming. Baldwin lapsed into silence, listening to the whispers and murmurs from onlookers.

He paid little attention to the rest of the oath-taking. His mind was too busy.

Chapter XXXVIII.

Despite the jubilant peal of bells and the distant cheers from the Holy Sepulchre, Marta shivered as she ventured out into the grey, raw November day. The tiny Greek church where she'd just attended Divine Liturgy stood not far south of the Hospital, and Marta wrapped her mantle more closely before setting off in that direction.

After two weeks of steady work, she'd finished her weaving backlog and was about to begin setting her loom for Countess Sibylla's brocade. Miles was still at the Hospital, recovering well from his gut wound and amusing himself trying to calculate how much money they would need in order to support themselves in their own home. Marta's only worry was Lord Balian.

He hadn't seemed very enthusiastic about her and Miles. That afternoon at the palace, he'd looked startled and promised to discuss the question of a dowry after the council meeting. But then...he hadn't. Not until yesterday, when he'd wandered into her workroom while Persi was out on a business call to the dyers.

"You could do better, Marta," he'd said, rather baldly. "Plancy has no name, no family, no fortune and no patronage. Even young Samuel Arrabi would be a better match for you than Miles."

Samuel Arrabi and his father were both vassals of Lord Balian's. The Arrabis were one of the few Syrian families that had become ennobled under the Frankish regime, and Marta liked them well enough.

Yet Samuel wasn't *Miles.* Miles, who'd offered her gentleness and friendship even before they could speak the same language. Miles, who'd stood up for her to his friends and taught her to fight. Miles, who was clever and kind, who made her heart jump just by entering the room.

"He's going to find a new lord," she objected. "And he's not unworthy just because he's a bastard."

"I want you to wait," Lord Balian said gently. "You're both young. Give it a year, and if you're still determined to marry at the end of it, you shall have your dowry, I swear it."

She had already waited three years; she wasn't sure what difference another one would make. Still, Marta had swallowed the words and accepted. Being Lord Balian's fosterling brought with it duties as well as privileges.

Persi had been plainer still. "Good," she'd said, when she heard. "Give him a chance to prove himself worthy of you. Last I checked, he was ravaging the Red Sea for Prince Reynald, and that's not the kind of thing a good man does."

By the time Marta reached the Hospital, the coronation procession was on its way down the Street of Palms towards the Temple, where the new king would lay his crown as an offering on the high altar. Everyone who was well enough had flocked outside or upstairs to watch the procession go by. Marta found Miles' bed empty, made with new linen, but as she turned to ask where he had gone, he walked up behind her and slipped an arm around her shoulders. His smile made her heart jolt.

"There you are! I was only waiting for you before I left."

He kissed her hand, and Marta linked her fingers through his. "You're leaving?"

"All packed up and released, and they've given my armour back, since it seems I'm not going to fall off my perch." He tugged at her hand, moving slowly not to aggravate his gut, and she followed him out of the Hospital and into the crowded courtyard. "Let's find somewhere quiet to sit. And something hot to eat."

Mystified, Marta followed him through the covered Street of Bad Cooking to collect hot skewered lamb. "Did you see the coronation?" he asked. "The brothers invited me upstairs to watch young Baldwin arrive

320

at the Sepulchre."

Marta shook her head. "Too many people. I went to Liturgy instead. Did you see the Leper King? How was he?"

"Same as ever. Bedridden."

Marta sighed. Weaving and visiting Miles had kept her busy during the week, but last Sunday, she'd gone to the palace to see Baldwin, conscious of her promise to tell him the tale of her escape from Kerak. For once, she'd been refused: the king needed rest and couldn't see her.

"Where are you going to stay now that you've left the Hospital?" she asked, eyeing Miles' new woollen clothes as he handed over an extravagant quantity of silver for a jar of Galilean wine.

"That's what we're celebrating. I've found a lord. I have a generous new money fief."

"Oh! Who?"

"Well, not a real fief." Miles led her up the Street of the Patriarch and into the gardens. While most of the land was fenced off into small market-garden plots, there was a little walled pleasure-garden with rambling roses and turf seats, all of them rather damp and cold. A summer-house tucked under a nook of the city wall provided shelter and dry seats. Miles put their wine-jug, dried raisins, and bread down on the bench between them, and swivelled to face her. "Still, there's a chance of getting my own castle later on. And in the meantime, I'd be able to support you in comfort—even without the weaving."

"That's wonderful, Miles! You didn't tell me you had all this planned!" Marta grinned at him around a bite of hot, spicy lamb.

He smiled more with his teeth than his eyes as he uncorked the wine jar. "I didn't want to say anything until it was certain. Didn't want to get your hopes up." He took a swig, then met her eyes. "As of today, I'm sworn to the count of Jaffa."

Marta swallowed a lump of lamb too fast. "Count *Guy?*"

He nodded, scratching his chin self-consciously. "It's not the best choice, I know. But it's a path forward for me—and it means we can be together." He looked at her pleadingly. "You're still with me?"

"Of course," she returned. "But you didn't need to do that, Miles."

His forehead wrinkled. "I thought you'd decided the Jaffas weren't so bad."

"Maybe they aren't," Marta admitted. "But I would have helped them stay together even if they were both *monsters*." She sighed. "Giving them help is one thing, but taking oaths to them is another. As far as I can see, Count Guy is arrogant and Countess Sibylla is ruthless. It was *her* idea to take Isabella away from us."

Miles looked at his feet. When he looked up, his face was completely serious. "I agree. Which is why I think we should both stay on their good side."

Marta laughed uncertainly. "Why, are you afraid of them?"

Again, his smile didn't reach his eyes. "Just thinking of our future, little Marta."

Something was wrong here, but Marta wasn't sure what. She took a deep breath. "I've been talking to Lord Balian. He wants us to wait a year, but at the end of it, he says he'll be happy to give us a dowry."

Miles blinked. "A dowry?"

"So, you see, you don't *really* need that money fief. We'd have to wait before we could marry, but then we could choose who to serve."

Abruptly, Miles got up and walked to the other side of the summerhouse, gripping the railing. His shoulders tensed; his head sunk. "A dowry," he repeated, as though in a daze. "Saints."

Something was *certainly* wrong. Marta put her skewered meat down and got up, wiping her fingers nervously. "What is it? Miles?"

"Saints," he repeated, and then spun around, his face red, his gesture large and reckless. "Yes! Why not? I *will* marry you, Marta Bessarion. By Saint George, it'll be the end of my hopes, but I'd rather have you than any fief in the kingdom."

For a long, breathless moment, Marta didn't know what to say. She felt as though her ribs had turned inside-out. "You *will* marry me? What is that supposed to mean? What else did you have in mind?"

His discomfort was evident, but it did nothing to set her at ease. "Love,

322

children, companionship." He shook his head with a grimace. "Marta, marriage is for—forging alliances and gaining land and consolidating power—marriage is the death of love. But I love you for who you are. I don't want to cheapen that."

Marta remembered a night long ago, and her gut filled with bile. "No, I understand," she said slowly. "How did you put it, that night when Isabella was betrothed? You have to marry an heiress so you can afford to eat Damascus apricots all summer."

He looked away from her with a sigh. "I didn't know you then. Or love you, as I do now."

"How *dare* you." Her voice cracked, rage boiling out of her. "How dare you speak to me of love, and ask me to share you with another woman?"

"But I *told* you I couldn't give you much. You said you only wanted me. I thought—"

"And children! How *dare* you?" She was shouting now. "You were a bastard yourself! And you want to make *more* bastards? You want to treat *my* children as heartlessly as *your* father treated *you?*"

He looked sick, as though she'd punched him in the gut. "No, Marta, I'm asking you to marry me!"

"Why, because you're embarrassed? Or because you can't get a better deal?" She took a sobbing breath, and to her horror, her tears spilled over.

"Marta, don't cry," he implored, starting across the summerhouse towards her.

"*Stay away from me!*" she shrieked. The cooling skewer of lamb lay on the bench next to her. She snatched it up and hurled it at his face.

Miles ducked, and the meat flew over his head. "Marta, for the love of God—"

She turned in a flurry of skirts and fled.

* * *

She should have seen it coming. Marta had always known she was neither rich nor noble enough to marry a knight, especially not one with Miles' ambition.

Once or twice before—on the walls at Kerak, or later, in the Hospital, when he spoke of the Bessarion Lance—she had been dimly aware of something inside him, an irresolvable conflict between them. Even when he left Kerak, it was only because he'd realised Prince Reynald would never give him his fief.

He cared for her. That was what tore at her heart; a traitorous voice in her head whispering that perhaps, *perhaps*, he'd yet choose her over his ambitions. He'd *agreed* to marry her, after all. He'd capitulated, even as he threw it in her teeth what he was giving up in doing so.

No. If he was going to resent her for destroying his hopes, then she couldn't marry him. A gift offered grudgingly was no gift at all, and she didn't owe him the smallest ounce of gratitude.

Persi and Lord Balian had to be told. Although Marta sensed their relief, they were kind enough not to show it, and didn't bother her with questions. When Miles came the next morning, she didn't have to speak to him: the porter turned him away at the gate.

"He said that if you change your mind, he's staying at the count of Jaffa's house, mademoiselle," the porter informed her hesitantly.

As she stared at her loom that afternoon, she felt as though she wanted to scream, run, fight. "Persi," she said, "let's not stay here."

Once dismantled, their looms fit easily into one cart, and Lord Balian was happy to send them up to join the rest of the family in Nablus. He was also happy to send Samuel Arrabi to escort them, for reasons which would have made Marta laugh if she'd been less heartsore.

Samuel was no friendlier than usual, thankfully, and he stayed in Nablus only long enough to collect a brace of homing-pigeons. The muster was complete, and the army of Jerusalem would leave for Kerak by the end of the week. Marta set up her loom, and lost herself in work.

December came in, but no word returned from Lord Balian at Kerak.

It was on the feast of Saint Nicholas, late in the afternoon, that news finally came.

Persi crashed through the door into the workshop, making Marta's heart jump with terror. A scrap of paper waved from her hand. "Marta," she gasped, "you have to go to Kerak. *Now.*"

Chapter XXXIX.

Kerak at last.

Balian dismounted, stretched the stiffness out of his knees, and threw his reins to his squire. He'd last seen the place during the time of Miles of Plancy the elder, and the castle had grown considerably since then. Prince Reynald had reinforced its walls, added a lower courtyard on the west side, and deepened the north and south fosses.

Saladin had retreated to Damascus at the royal army's approach, unwilling to risk pitched battle, but the outlying town still bore the scars of an army's month-long abuse. Man and beast had feasted on the flocks and grain, wasted the oil and wine. War machines still ringed the castle on all sides, now fallen silent. The north wall had been breached, and bodies still littered the north fosse at the point where the Saracens had made a half-hearted effort to get in. Inside the castle, gaps in the battlements showed where missiles had fallen. By now many of the people who'd fled to Kerak for refuge had returned to their homes, but the courtyard still looked shabby, littered with rubbish. Despite the scouring winter wind and the sweepers hard at work, it smelled worse than a farmyard.

Ahead, Tripoli dismounted. A High Court meeting held by the shores of the Salt Sea had named him bailli once it became clear that the king was not in good enough health to direct a battle himself. Now, the fur lining of his cloak rippled in the wind, making it look as though the count was shivering. Count Guy was no more comfortable. As he had done since Jerusalem, he sat his enormous Flemish destrier in morose silence.

The Leper King lay in his litter, armed snugly in mail-shirt and helmet.

Although his hands would never grasp weapons again, a sword lay beside him. His body-servants helped him to sit up as Prince Reynald and Countess Stephanie bypassed both the bailli and the former bailli to kneel before him.

"My lord, it is good to see you in Kerak."

"It is good to see Kerak still standing." The king spoke in a tolerably clear voice which carried well to the onlookers. "This is Saladin's retaliation for the war on the Red Sea, but don't deceive yourselves, my lords. To justify his wars against his co-religionists, Saladin will need to win a *real* victory against us. I may be blind, but this I can still see: one day, sooner or later, we must fight Saladin and break him, or never sleep quietly again in our homes."

The king seemed to have finished his speech, but no one raised a cheer. There was only a leaden silence in the air, and Balian indulged a little secret worry. It was true that Saladin was expected to justify his rule with holy war, but Balian had met a lot of Saracen warriors; he'd yet to meet one that didn't have a genuine cause for complaint against the Franks of the Coast.

How much of the coming storm had been stirred up by Prince Reynald's brigandage?

"Is my sister here?" King Baldwin asked. "Where is Isabella?"

There was a stir in the crowd, and young Humphrey of Toron led Isabella forward. It was the first time in three years that Balian had seen his stepdaughter. His first thought was how much she had grown; his second, how young she still was despite the wedding ring on her hand.

Without a word, Balian left his place among the other barons and circled to the Kerak side of the crowd, climbing into the shadowed portico of the great hall for a better view of the assembly.

He was still searching the crowd for a glimpse of Queen Maria when a hand fell on his shoulder. "Balian?"

He pulled her into his arms, into the shadows of the stone arches. "I'm sorry, Maria. I'm so sorry."

His queen turned drowning blue eyes to him. "I should have tried harder. I should have told her I forbade it."

327

"Don't," he said quickly. "We did what we could. At least she's happy with him."

"Sometime during these last three years, he got her heart."

Balian stroked her hair and nodded. "Marta told me all about it."

"There was nothing I could do," Maria whispered. "The countess didn't even have to turn her against me."

As his brother followed them into the portico, Balian pulled back. "Be comforted." Ramla flashed the queen a grin. "Young Baldwin is crowned, Guy is excluded from the succession, and the king is hatching a plan to deal with the Lusignan for good."

Queen Maria bared her teeth in displeasure. "Do you think this is about *politics*, Ramla? My *child* has been taken from me!"

For a moment, Ramla stared at her, abashed. Then his face hardened.

"No," he growled. "This is about honour. All of us owe Guy a rich revenge...and we're about to get it, too."

Far back in Balian's mind, a warning bell started to ring. "What are you talking about, brother?"

"Oh, nothing, nothing!" Ramla winked. "Right now it's just talk. But you'll see."

He strolled away with a smug grin, and Balian watched, mystified. What was the king planning?

* * *

That night, Prince Reynald hosted a feast to celebrate the end of the siege.

Certainly a feast was appropriate, but Baldwin could only recline at the high table and worry. Behind the cheers that had greeted the army on their arrival, he thought he had heard the sound of sobbing. Brother John told him that the town had been taken over by the Saracens; he couldn't imagine what it would be like to return to a home that had been used, most likely plundered, by enemy troops. It was primarily Chatillon's responsibility, but he hoped Tripoli was keeping an eye out for anything that might need royal contribution—oil presses or ovens repaired, cisterns rebuilt, granaries restocked. It was easy to imagine what kind of destruction the enemy might have wrought in withdrawing, because he had done it himself on a hundred raids. Yet because he no longer had eyes, he did not know what needed to be repaired *now*.

He might as well be dead.

No, he reminded himself. He still had value. He hadn't overlooked the fact that this afternoon, Prince Reynald and his wife had bypassed both Guy and Tripoli, making their bows directly to him. No matter how ill he became, he was still the king.

After the feast, the Lazarites carried Baldwin back to his quarters. The raucous sound of singing drifted up to him on the wind from a distant part of the castle, and Baldwin caught his breath as he identified the tune.

> *Never mind what the Polains do,*
> *We shall have a king from Poitou!*

"Saint *George*," he breathed, incredulous. "Does Guy still think he'll be king?"

Footsteps crunched into the courtyard, and Ramla's voice echoed loudly. "Seems like Count Guy's men are getting drunk with the garrison."

The distant chorus was cut short in laughter and did not begin again. But Baldwin was almost trembling in anger. "How *dare* they?"

Two pairs of footsteps halted by his litter. "Men are fools when they're drunk, my lord."

That was Balian, trying to soothe him. Baldwin clenched his teeth. "Thank you, Ibelin. I'll take that under consideration."

The old fear bit like an arrow-tip wedged into his armour. His brother-in-law was ambitious, utterly determined to be king and utterly disqualified for the office. As long as he remained in the kingdom, Guy of Lusignan was a threat. And Baldwin was tired of being wrongfooted.

"Speak of the devil," Ramla said. "Here's the Poitevin now."

Brisk footsteps came towards them, together with the tuneless under-the-breath whistling that Guy used when he was thinking about something.

He was whistling the song his men had been singing mere moments ago. At the sound, Baldwin lost his last shreds of patience.

"Count Guy," he rasped. "Put me down, brothers."

They lowered his bed to the ground, and the count came to stand in front of him, his voice respectful. "Did you call for me, my lord?"

"Do you think you can yet rule this kingdom, count?"

Guy did not answer for a moment. In that silence, Ramla snickered, and the count seemed to lose all sense of caution.

"I could do better than a nine year old boy," he sneered. "Or a blind cripple, for that matter."

The blood rushed to Baldwin's head. "I will make sure you never have the chance. And unless you'd like to answer to the High Court for felony, you'll keep your men from singing seditious songs."

He nodded to his attendants, signalling to them to pick him up and continue to his quarters. With that, Guy seemed to recall his wits.

"My lord," he said with a nervous rush of footsteps.

Baldwin heard the sound of—almost a blow, perhaps, as Ramla held him back. "Watch yourself, count."

"My lord, what of my wife's claim?"

Baldwin did not deign to reply, yet Guy persisted. "Sibylla is still my wife!"

The Leper King turned, baring what was left of his teeth. *"Not for long."*

The silence that followed was as violent as a blow to the jaw. Baldwin's words hung in the air like a spell. Anything might happen now.

Now I've said it, he thought. *Now I must see it through.*

God help me.

Guy's voice was a threadbare whisper. "What?"

"You heard." Ramla didn't even try to disguise his triumph.

The count floundered, his voice a mixture of terror and outrage. "Are you declaring me a felon? Are you going to kill me?"

"Saints, no." Ramla laughed. "Why commit murder when a divorce would do?"

"Ramla." Baldwin found his voice again. "Enough."

"A divorce?" Balian's voice cut in, aghast. "My lord, I withdrew that request!"

From Guy of Lusignan, there was no sound. Baldwin waved Balian away and said, "Count Guy, are you still here?"

"You must be joking." Guy's voice was bloodless and Baldwin imagined him staring, pale. "A divorce? Try it. I promise you, this kingdom will burn."

"Don't be foolish, man. Will you add crime to your folly?"

Guy laughed, short and sharp. "It's not *me* you should fear." He must have shoved his way clear of Ramla, because Baldwin heard the sharp sound of a scuffle and then footsteps rushing away across the courtyard.

"Set someone to watch him, Ramla," Baldwin said urgently. "If he sends a pigeon, I want it shot down and reported to me. What did he mean, the kingdom will burn? Ibelin?"

"I don't know, but I agree that it isn't him you should fear. If Marta is right—"

"Marta doesn't understand what it means to be a king," Baldwin growled as his attendants continued to carry him towards his quarters. "You were the one who first persuaded me to this, Ibelin!"

"Yet I thought better of it!" Balian hurried after him. "Did Marta tell you how she escaped the siege? That she stormed her way through Saladin's whole army?"

Baldwin had seen enough battles to know that sometimes, things that crazy actually worked, even without heavenly intervention. "Even if Marta does have the favour of God, she can't tell me how to rule my kingdom." Besides, he'd been a fool to try to please her, when she didn't care a button for him.

"It isn't *your* kingdom," Balian challenged.

The Lazarites carried him into his room, and Baldwin waved them away. "Leave me with Ibelin."

He felt half dead with exhaustion, but he had to be plain. "I am well aware that this is Christ's kingdom, Ibelin, of which I am only a caretaker. But the real sin would be to destroy it through sentimental weakness."

"You sound like your sister." Ibelin sounded unsettled. "You told Marta you would be content with cutting Guy from the succession. What changed?"

"I thought better of it." Baldwin echoed Balian's words coldly. "Guy still openly lusts for the throne."

"But you know him, my lord. He won't let go of her easily."

"So we split them up and get her remarried as soon as possible." Baldwin took a deep breath. "I haven't done this rashly. There's an Englishman coming to Jerusalem. I've already received letters of introduction from my cousin Plantagenet. This knight is a famous tourneyer, the son of a noble family, and Guy murdered his uncle. If anyone can take and hold my sister, he can."

Hasty footsteps approached and the lord of Ramla burst in on a cold breeze. "Ha! The game's afoot, my lord. Lusignan's running for it. He's passed word to his men that they're leaving."

Baldwin stiffened. Devil take it! Still, Guy would have learned of his plans for a divorce eventually. It might as well be now. "Where's he going?"

"No idea." Ramla seemed unconcerned. "He hasn't left yet. What's your will, my lord? Should I have him locked up?"

Baldwin put his maimed hands to his head. "For that we'd need Prince Reynald's co-operation—and Reynald is one of Guy's allies. We can't risk it."

"But you won't let him *go*, surely," Ramla said. "If I were the count, I'd collect Countess Sibylla from Jerusalem, head for Jaffa or Ascalon, and bar my gates. Then you'd have a war on your hands if you tried to do anything about it." Although Baldwin couldn't see him, Ramla's voice was intense, euphoric. "Let me saddle up and set an ambush in the hills!"

"*No*, Ramla! I don't want to start a war."

"Bit late for that."

Baldwin gritted his teeth. "In case you're wondering why I chose Guy of Lusignan over you, Baldwin of Ramla, this is why."

"I never pretended to be a saint." Ramla spoke contemptuously, and Baldwin's gut churned.

He forced himself to take a long breath and think of what he *could* do, which of the pieces on the board were still under his control. "Send a pigeon to Jerusalem and warn them not to let Sibylla leave. Wait," he added, as Ramla sprang into motion. "I emptied the palace. I can't send a lone rabble of Turcopoles to arrest my own sister." He beat his hand against his knee, full of nervous, painful energy. "Marta. It will have to be Marta. Balian, do you have a pigeon I can send?"

Balian was startled. "Yes, but *think* about this, my lord."

"I've thought too long, Ibelin. Now I act. Am I your king?"

Balian sighed. "Always, my lord."

He felt wretched asserting authority over Balian like this—let alone Marta and Sibylla. Yet the time had come to act. Baldwin could only pray that when she saw he was in earnest, Sibylla would agree to give up Guy rather than the kingdom.

"Prepare your bird, and send for my chaplain," he whispered. He'd get the man to write two letters—one to the garrison at the Tower of David, and the other to Marta. His heart was racing and he felt sick to the stomach. It was going to be a bad night.

* * *

Towards dawn, Baldwin dreamed of a terrible pain in his belly.

He lay on his back in the grass in the garden, and the pain intensified as though something had begun to grow there. A hard knot, a tumour. Whimpering, Baldwin pulled the linen hem of his shirt back and touched a soft tendril.

Something was pushing its way out of his navel.

Baldwin screamed.

The shoot grew, thickened, put out leaves. Threadlike roots plunged through his body, seeking soil. The young tree threw out branches, white with blossom. Its roots thickened, driving him into the dirt, smashing and burying him.

Golden oranges swung lazily in the sunlight above.

Chapter XL.

Marta took three steps to Persi and snatched the paper from her hand. She spun to the door, tilting the missive to catch the evening sun.

Baldwin, by the grace of God King of Jerusalem, to his beloved and faithful Marta Bessarion, greetings. It is my will to summon the count and countess of Jaffa before the High Court. Count Guy has already fled to his own fief. Bear my command to the Countess Sibylla to await my return in Jerusalem. It is her king and liege who commands. And if she will not obey her king, you may take charge of her body as felon. I have commanded the city garrison to assist you. I pray that you will on no account allow her to escape. Farewell.

Below the king's letter was an unsigned scribble in another hand.

He means to accuse their marriage.

That was all.

Oh Baldwin, Marta thought, her heart knotting under her breastbone. Was the hairy man already breaking into the kingdom? Was the king dying? A desperate urge took her to ride away to Kerak after all, to be with him at the end, but her forehead ached with remembered pain.

"You should go to Kerak. Speak to the king," Persi said. "He bears the seraph's kiss; the same burden as you. He's already so frail; a pain like this could kill him."

"There's no point," Marta said slowly. "It's too late; the damage is done."

"You have to do *something.*"

"I will. As soon as I think of something." Marta turned, looking at her loom, where Countess Sibylla's brocade waited with only a hand's-breadth left to weave. She sat down again, grabbing her shuttle. Compared to actually threading the loom, the weaving was fast, and she had the pattern memorised, her fingers flying with instinctive speed.

"If I allow her to leave Jerusalem, he'll declare her a felon," she said, working the fabric without really seeing it. She felt as though the whole weight of the kingdom was on her shoulders. "He'll be honour bound to make war on them both."

"*And* you," Persi pointed out. She shook the paper. "This is a royal command, not a friendly suggestion!"

She'd told Countess Sibylla that the king was like a brother to her. Marta sighed, wishing for the simpler days when she and her real brother, Lukas, had disagreed over the treatment of spiders, and whether younger siblings ought to be allowed on beach trips. "I could pretend we didn't get the message."

"The garrison will just go ahead and arrest her anyway," Persi said. "He says he's sent a message to them as well."

"Then the only way to keep him from divorcing them is to go to Jerusalem and warn her before the garrison can send for me." Finding that there was little room for her shuttle to pass, Marta reached automatically forward to wind the fabric on. But the loom resisted her. The cloth was done. She dropped her shuttle and straightened. "Maybe he'll listen to sense. Or maybe I can convince the countess to wait for his return."

"I don't like your chances there." Persi handed her a pair of shears.

Marta cut the cloth from the loom, running a hand over its pearly sheen. "I have to try."

"Tonight?"

It was about Nones, midway through the afternoon, but the early dusk of winter was already gathering, and the air whistling through the workroom's open door promised frost by morning. Marta straightened. "Tonight."

Persi looked at Marta with worried eyes. "Take your spear," she said. "And your armour. And…and me."

"*You?*" Marta blinked.

Persi's teeth flashed in a smile. "Well, *someone's* got to take care of you while you're saving the kingdom."

* * *

They rode fast, changing horses at Saint Gilles and Magna Mahumeria. By the time they reached Jerusalem five hours later, Marta's whole body ached and she could tell that Persi felt even worse. She pulled a fold of her mantle over her head, keeping her chin tucked as they rode in at Saint Stephen's Gate.

"Belated travellers from Caesarea!" Persi called in response to the porters' questioning. "No, we can't put up at the Asnerie hospice—we have pressing news for my lord's sister!"

A few moments later, she and Marta walked their tired mounts through streets slick with rain. "Do you think we fooled them?" she asked nervously.

Marta managed a smile. "If they've received the king's pigeon, they'll be on the lookout for Marta Bessarion of Nablus. I doubt they imagine I'd sneak in under Walter of Caesarea's name."

Unlike Marta, Persi had donned full armour for the journey with the goal of discouraging any highwaymen from interfering with them. Now, under her helmet, Persi's voice wrinkled in distaste. "Indeed. The less I have to do with Walter of Caesarea, the better."

"It's hard to warm to your own slaveowner," Marta agreed.

As they walked down the Spanish Street towards Countess Sibylla's house, Persi spoke abruptly. "What if we can't save the kingdom, Marta?"

"What do you mean?"

"I mean, what if the Leper King is right? What if doing the right thing really *does* destroy us?"

"But how could it? Have you Perceived something?"

"No; I'm just wondering." Persi sighed. "Maybe Jerusalem doesn't deserve to be saved. Maybe, once the slaves are freed and the other wrongs righted, there will be nothing left of us at all. Maybe we're supposed to dismantle the kingdom altogether. Have you thought of that?"

Marta's hands clenched on her reins. "But there's *good* in Jerusalem. Look at all the people of different religions who live in peace here. Look at us, able to walk in the street with our faces uncovered and converse with any men we please. The Franks aren't perfect, but I'd still rather live under them than under Saladin."

"You might think differently if you were still locked in that workshop in Cacho." Persi paused. "I just wonder, that's all. You're so focused on saving the kingdom. But a day might come when the right thing is to let it burn."

"Not if I can help it." Marta set her jaw. "I believe in this kingdom, Persi. I won't give up that easily."

The gate to Countess Sibylla's house was locked, but lights still burned quietly in the windows. Evidently, the countess had not yet received news from her husband. Handing the Bessarion Lance to Persi, Marta took the bolt of fabric from where it was strapped behind her saddle and knocked on the gate.

"I'm Marta the weaver," she told the porter. "I have the cloth Countess Sibylla ordered."

He unbolted the gate and pulled it open. "Are you expected?"

"No. But if you take her a message she will see me."

He whistled for a page to take them to the inner courtyard of the big house. Marta and Persi followed him to a vine-covered portico surrounding an open cistern and a garden that was drab with rain.

A door opened from the stables and footsteps hurried along the pavement. All of a sudden, Marta's heart jumped up her throat, and she ducked her chin, pulling her mantle further over her head. She prayed that it wasn't who she thought it was; prayed that if it was, he wouldn't recognise her.

"Marta?"

The sound of his voice stole the air from her lungs. Marta swallowed, frozen, like a rabbit in an eagle's sights. Tonight was already hard enough without *this.*

His footsteps hesitated, then rushed towards her. "Marta, is something wrong? Talk to me—"

Persi stepped between them, lowering her spear. In men's clothing, hidden behind the faceplate, she might have been a knight for all Miles knew. He pulled to a stop and stared at Marta. "Marta?"

A world of sadness echoed in his voice. Marta's own was a cracked whisper. "I don't *want* to talk to you, Miles."

Because if I do, I'm afraid I'll give in.

Persi stepped forward again, just as silent, just as threatening, and Miles threw his hands up and backed away.

"Sir Miles? Is something wrong?"

Marta started. Above, a warm stream of yellow lamplight streamed from an open door in the loggia. Countess Sibylla stood silhouetted against the light, her page by her side. How much had she seen?

Miles swallowed. "No, my lady. I was just going."

Looking up at the countess, Persi stiffened. "Marta," she whispered.

Sibylla turned to her page. "Remember what I told you," she said, and then came forward to the rail. "Sir Miles, I wonder if you'd go into the city for me and ask Master Nicolas for another of his draughts."

Miles looked startled to be asked to run a servant's errand, but he didn't argue. "As you wish, my lady."

"Marta," Persi whispered again, sidling closer. "Something's wrong with the countess."

Above, Countess Sibylla leaned over the rail, looking perfectly well. "Marta Bessarion? Come up. Tell your man to wait."

Persi yanked the helmet off, revealing a face drawn with worry. "No. Marta. Take me with you."

Her eyes slid sideways to the countess. Marta's blood ran cold. Neither of them understood exactly how Persi's gift of Perception worked, but her intuitions were never wrong. If she said something was wrong with Sibylla, Marta could trust her.

But the countess would never allow her to bring an armed companion to a private meeting, and Marta's only hope of saving the king from a terrible mistake was to warn her now.

She touched Persi's elbow. "Stick to the plan. Wait here and keep alert."

Persi's face tightened with worry. "Be very careful."

Countess Sibylla waited in the warm doorway of her own private

338

chamber. Inside, warmth and light glowed from the fire burning in the hearth. Marta scanned the whitewashed room, fully alert to danger. In the wall opposite the door, a narrow glazed window opened onto the street beyond. A volume of Averroes' commentary on Aristotle lay open on a reading-desk: Marta was not surprised to learn that the reclusive countess was something of a scholar.

She relaxed fractionally. "I have your cloth, my lady."

"What's the balance of the payment?" Sibylla flipped open the lid of a small money-casket, the same she had offered to Marta on her last visit. Compared to that last visit, the countess seemed aloof and taciturn. They might have been strangers.

Might have, but not quite. A stranger would have got her chamberlain to pay the weaver. A stranger would never have met her in person.

"Another thirty bezants, my lady." Marta laid the bundle on the foot of the countess' bed and unfolded it. In the firelight, the silver threads glinted like veins of fire themselves, and Marta couldn't help but feel a flicker of pride in her work. The cloth was beautiful.

Sibylla counted out the gold coins and handed them over. Marta dropped them into her purse, trying to figure out how to broach the all-important subject, but the countess beat her to it. "Was that all, or is there a reason you came from Nablus yourself?"

"I have bad news, my lady. I…"

Sibylla lifted a perfect black eyebrow at her, but even now, she couldn't find the words.

Instead, she dug into her pouch. "I got a pigeon this afternoon," she said, and handed over Baldwin's letter.

The countess held it to the lamp to read it. Her expression didn't change. "Have you brought the garrison, then?"

"No, my lady."

Sibylla smiled bitterly. "So. I do everything my brother asks of me. I renounce my throne at his pleasure, and *this* is how he repays me. By sending his *beloved and faithful* Syrian tirewoman to lock me away so that he can destroy my husband."

Marta swallowed. "I'm not going to arrest you."

"Such magnanimity!" The countess folded her arms. "Who are *you*, anyway, Marta Bessarion? A stranger. A servant. And yet it's to *you* that he turns, now that he wants his sister locked up." Sibylla's voice was cold and calm, frighteningly at odds with her words. "How have you bewitched him?"

"I haven't."

"Is he in love with you?"

Marta's mouth dropped open. Baldwin, the Leper King, in love with *her*? "Love? God forbid, my lady." The knot under her breastbone forced her to add: "I'd never wish him so much pain."

"Hmm." The countess sounded unconvinced, but to Marta's relief, she changed the subject, gesturing to the letter. "You've only just heard of this, then?"

"The pigeon arrived this afternoon." Something in Sibylla's words and manner triggered a suspicion. "Did you already know, my lady?"

"I am not *blind*." Sibylla's teeth bared in a grimace of rage. "Yes, I knew. I knew the same day he went to the Patriarch. I knew when the rumours began on the streets. I knew it all, *days* before they went to Kerak."

Marta blinked, unsure of her footing. This peaceful house. This open book. This bitter and seething rage confined silently in a little room. "If you knew, then why didn't you tell Count Guy?"

"Hmm," Sibylla said again, with a look into the fireplace. There was no sound for a heartbeat or two but the soft sputter of flame. "I'll answer that when you tell me why you have come to my house wearing armour."

Marta looked down at herself in alarm, but her mail wasn't visible beneath her plain gown.

Sibylla's eyes narrowed. "You're ringing like windchimes, child. Well? Why did you come?"

"To plead with you."

"And the armour? The man downstairs?"

"My friend Persi. We thought the garrison might try to stop us." Marta hesitated. "And we didn't know how you would react."

"You said you would not detain me."

"No longer than necessary to say my part."

"I suppose you are going to tell me to give him up." The countess walked to the hearth and stared into the fire, her face blank. "Guy is my weakness. The barons would accept me, but they refuse to accept him. I begin to wonder if I would be stronger without him, after all." She focused on Marta. "That's what you came to say, wasn't it?"

Marta stared. "No, my lady."

Baldwin would never thank her for this.

But Baldwin was not here.

"The kingdom," she blurted out. "Give up the kingdom, my lady! Live with honour, keep your oaths, be faithful to your love. But give up the kingdom."

Sibylla looked at her for a moment, and slowly, the blood rose in her face. Her voice thickened with rage.

"I *did* give up the kingdom. I let them pass me by and crown my son, so that I could keep my husband. Do you not remember? It was you who brokered that bargain. *Give up the kingdom, Sibylla, and your marriage will be safe.* Now I have no kingdom, but my brother is not satisfied."

It was true. And it was awful.

"You could leave, go to France. He'll never be able to reach you there."

"To *France?*" Sibylla spat. "What? Exile myself from my only birthright? Do you know it is the law there that a woman cannot rule?"

"But if it's a choice between that and war—"

"If that is the choice I would rather stay." Sibylla might have been grinding the words in a mortar. "I would stand like a stone and let the kingdom wreck itself." Her hands, her voice, were quivering with emotion. "Yes. That is what I will do. My brother may start a war if he likes. I am going to my husband." Sibylla was already throwing back the lid of a chest and yanking out a cloak.

"Why must you rule?" Marta burst out, at her wits' end. "No one in the kingdom wants Count Guy, and you can't force him down their throats. Can't you see? If you go to him, you will never be a queen, or a bailli, or

341

whatever it is you want." Marta wrung her hands. "This is madness. Give it up, my lady. *Please.*"

"You were never bred to rule, Marta Bessarion," Sibylla said in a voice of concentrated fury. She set enamelled bottles on a table and dipped into the chest again. "My great-grandfather was Baldwin the Second, and he had four daughters. The eldest was Melisende of Jerusalem. Thirty years she reigned as Queen, and she married the old count of Anjou. He was the greatest count of France; yet before she was out of her girlhood, Melisende taught him to fear her. The second was Alice of Antioch, who, because she had the will to rule, defied all her nobles and two kings of Jerusalem with full force of arms. The third was Hodierna of Tripoli. The old count of Tripoli got a son by her, but he persecuted her with his jealousy until she hired the Assassins to end him. The last and least of them was the abbess Iveta, who in the convent of Bethany taught me to rule. I am but the latest daughter of this house, and I wonder, Marta Bessarion, if you know what you are asking of me."

Marta thought of her own father, the Praetorian Prefect of Jerusalem, of the house that had once been her own and was now Lord Balian's. *I do know,* she thought.

"If you have nothing more to say, you had better go." Countess Sibylla crossed to the door and threw it open. Her face was pale, her lips white.

Marta had said everything she could. Sibylla was right about one thing at least: if a war began, it would be the king's fault, not her own.

She sighed. "Perhaps I can intercede with your brother for you, my lady."

"Perhaps you can leave my brother the hell alone." Sibylla's voice shook, and Marta was suddenly afraid to go to the door and walk past her.

Yet there was no other way out. Cautiously, she said: "Thank you for hearing me, my lady."

"Thank *you* for bringing my spear," said Sibylla.

Even as the countess spoke, Marta's heart stood still at the faint whisper of steel leaving a sheath. She flinched aside as Sibylla struck, but the whispering, razor-sharp knife's edge sliced through the skin on her unprotected neck, nicking the artery.

A hot tide broke against her skin, leaving her dizzy and light-headed. Marta clamped her hand to the wound, feeling her heart's jolt in the red stream running through her fingers.

She gasped in pure shock, staggering away and grabbing at the loggia's rail. In the garden below, Persi stared up at her across a sword's blade. The Nubian girl was on her knees, her hands pinned behind her back, the Bessarion Lance in the hands of one of the sergeants beside her.

Dazed, Marta turned to face the countess.

Sibylla lowered her bloody dagger, grimacing with disgust and fury. "What does he see in you, anyway?"

Marta could only try desperately to stem the flow of blood. She knew now why Miles had been sent away; what message the page had borne downstairs; the danger Persi had sensed, clouding the air around the countess.

Below, a knight raced for the stairs to the loggia, two sergeants close behind him. Despite her injuries, they were taking no chances with her.

Sibylla came closer, her blade ready. "You make me sick," she growled. "Always on your high horse. Always pretending to virtue. You aren't virtuous; you're *squeamish*. You've simply never wanted anything badly enough."

Marta was getting dizzier by the second, her gown and mantle a hot reeking slurry of her own blood.

Sibylla looked away. "Is the surgeon here yet? She's too valuable to lose."

Valuable. The word pierced Marta's fuzzy consciousness. Sibylla meant to keep her alive as some kind of hostage.

The armed men reached the loggia and turned towards her.

Time to act.

With her left hand, Marta grabbed a dry corner of her mantle and clamped it over the wound in her neck. With her right—slippery, hot, smelling of iron—she grabbed her own knife and swung wildly at Sibylla to dissuade her from following. She lurched into the countess' chamber, slamming and latching the door behind. The silver damask lay on the bed still in its wrappings. Marta grabbed the waxed silk that wrapped it,

343

careful even now to avoid getting the damask bloody, and staggered to the window opposite. She shoved the casement open, threw out the length of silk and, gathering all her strength, drove the dagger through it into the wooden sill.

If anyone was coming through the door behind her, Marta was too sick to notice. She wrapped the end of the silk around her one free hand, stepped onto the sill, and fell until the silk snapped taut, jolting her arm—then immediately fell again as the dagger yanked free of its moorings.

She hit the cobbled street in a cloud of silk and collapsed. Above, a pale face looked from the upper window. The whole house was full of running and shouting. She should get up, run for safety, but she couldn't. She was so tired, so dizzy, and she couldn't feel the pressure of her hand against her wound any more. A distant voice was calling her name, but she couldn't move.

All she could think was that Sibylla was going to war with the Leper King, and she would use the Bessarion Lance to do it.

The house, the face above, and the pale stars ran together and faded.

Chapter XLI.

Pain reached into the black murk where Marta floated and dragged her back into the world. Burning savagely, it lanced through her neck and Marta bucked against the arms that held her with an anguished scream. Voices, distorted with distance, hummed and crashed over her head. She couldn't move. She couldn't get away from the pain.

It lasted longer than she would have thought possible.

Overcome, Marta sank into the weary black murk again. Her last memory was of gentle hands dabbing at her wound, and of someone kissing her hair.

When she woke her head was pounding, her throat dry with thirst. Cold morning light pierced a shadowy vault overhead. Marta blinked and gradually focused on a wheel of lamplight, the wrought-iron fitting stirring recent memories.

The Hospital. She must be upstairs in the women's ward.

She felt weary, so weary. Marta lifted her right hand, crusted with blood, and went to touch the wound on her neck, but found thick bandages instead.

She was alive.

"Persi," she whispered.

A chair rattled on her right, and a wimpled face beamed into her own. One of the sisters. "Ah, you're awake! How do you feel?"

"Where's my friend?"

"Right beside you, m'love." The sister nodded towards the other side of the narrow bed, and Marta turned—feeling a twinge as the edges of her wound shifted—to see Miles sitting up from his place on the floor, blinking sleep out of his eyes.

"Marta," he croaked, seizing her hand. "God be thanked," and he buried his face against her bloody knuckles and his shoulders shook with sobs.

"Persi," Marta tried to croak again, but her throat was too dry. From the other side of the bed, an earthenware jug rattled against the lip of a cup, before the sister's arm snaked gently below her neck and shoulders.

"Drink this, m'love. It will help to restore your blood."

It was lukewarm salt-water, and the sister made her drink two beakers' worth of it before letting her speak. "We caught you in the nick of time," she said as Marta drank. "Your young man did well to bring you straight to us—our irons are always hot, and we were able to cauterise the wound immediately. You'll need a lot of rest, and a lot of red meat and salted broth, but a year from now you'll be sound as a bell."

"A *year?*" Marta spluttered.

"You've lost a lot of blood, m'love. We can't just snap our fingers and replace it." The sister patted her blankets. "I'll go in search of some broth. Keep her calm, m'lord."

As the sister walked away, Marta's eyes flickered to Miles where he knelt at her bedside.

"You're supposed to keep—"

Marta interrupted in a panicked whisper. *"Where is Persi, Miles?"*

He ran the tip of his tongue across his lips nervously. "I think the countess took her."

"Where?"

"To Ascalon, I think. I went back to the house after they'd managed to stop your bleeding. The countess was already gone, with all her knights and sergeants."

Marta stared at the ceiling, her gut churning. What did Sibylla want with Persi? With the Bessarion Lance? How did she even *know* about the Bessarion Lance? What was she going to do with it? *Oh God and Saint Martha and blessed Virgin Mary.*

"I should have seen this coming." Miles' voice was stiff, expressionless

346

as he stared at the blankets. "I should have realised she was just trying to get me out of the house. The apothecary wasn't even answering his door. I came back in time to see you fall from the window...." His voice shook. "This is what I feared."

She is too valuable to lose. Countess Sibylla had wanted Marta herself, not just the weapon.

"She has Persi. And the Spear." Marta clenched her teeth and rolled onto her side, digging an elbow into the mattress to lever herself up. Her head spun and black mist fogged her vision. Miles made a far-off sound of protest and caught her in his arms. When the room stopped moving, she was lying flat on her back again, and his face was a mask of worry hovering above. "For heaven's sake, Marta. There's nothing you can do in this state."

"I want Benjamin of Borca to lay hands on me," she gasped. "The Healer."

"I'm sorry Marta, he went to Kerak with the army."

The knot in Marta's gut pulled tighter; the army wouldn't return for weeks yet. Weeks in which Persi would be a prisoner, in which Sibylla could use the Bessarion Lance to do heaven knew what. The countess had been in a strange mood, fey and reckless, and whatever Persi had seen in the woman had frightened her.

Everyone else was with the army. There was no one she could turn to. No one but Miles.

"You helped me escape," she whispered. "Does she know? Did she see you?"

"I don't think so."

She hesitated a moment, then let herself look into his eyes; let the worry and the pain she found there wash through her. She was too weak to resist: tears came to her eyes and she gasped, "Can I trust you?"

He broke their gaze. "Marta..."

"If you knew this was coming, why did you vow to serve her? Why didn't you warn me?"

"I tried."

He wouldn't meet her gaze, so Marta took a deep breath and added, "What are you going to do now?"

"I hardly know." His voice shook. "Marta, I'm such a fool. Here's what I ought to have said that day: Without you, my wine is vinegar and my meat is dust. Every hope and thought sickens, and no matter how many fiefs I might hold, no matter how great a man I might ever be, it will all be for nothing if I don't have you. So, if the price of having you is all my hopes, whether in whole or part, I would pay it. I would pay it *gladly*." He smoothed her hair back from her forehead, a world of tenderness in his eyes, his touch, his voice. "I ought to have told you I'd be *honoured* to have you as my wife, Marta Bessarion. So if that's your question, this is my answer: I'll marry you, if you'll have me."

She didn't know what to say; she was too tired. She closed her eyes, savouring his words, his gentle touch on her hair, and a tear trickled free.

"Marta?" He leaned down, kissing her forehead, his lips warm and gentle. "Speak to me."

Her heart raced, making her feel faint despite her resting position. There was a treacherous relief in her weakness; she could not resist his caress.

Still.

"I can't answer now," she whispered. After all, she'd been wrong about him once before. How well did she really know him? All the adoration she'd poured out on him—was it really him she loved, or was it someone who existed only in her own mind? Marta sighed. She didn't have time for this, not now. "I meant, what are you going to do about the countess? Are you still her man?"

He drew back, running a hand through his fair hair. "I made an oath to the count."

"Could you go to Ascalon?" A dim and desperate plan formed in her mind. "Countess Sibylla's not in her right mind; she's ready to go to war with the king, and she's got the spear."

He looked alarmed. "What do you want me to do?"

"Just keep an eye on her and send word if anything happens. I'll stay here and get well, and when the Leper King comes home I'll speak to him, try to change his mind. You... you try to speak to Persi. Try to arrange her release. Do your best to keep the countess from doing anything rash, now that she has the spear."

Miles looked dubious. "I don't know, Marta. What am I to Sibylla, that she should take me into her counsels?"

"You're Miles of Plancy," she whispered. "You can talk yourself into anything."

A grin spread across his face. "True."

* * *

The Leper King returned to Jerusalem on the first day of Embertide, sooner than Marta expected. In the women's ward at the Hospital, Marta heard the news as it spread among the sisters and tried to get out of bed, but her head swam and her heart raced, forcing her to sit again. Although her wound had healed enough to allow her to sit up and do a little needlework, there was still not enough blood in her body to sustain sudden motion.

Fortunately, she didn't have to wait long. One of the servants of the Hospital ran to Temple Street with the news of Marta's whereabouts. Lord Balian and Queen Maria didn't even change their clothes before coming to see her.

As they entered the ward, the queen pushed her veil aside, revealing a worried face. "Marta? Thank God."

Lord Balian knelt beside her, lowering his voice. "The garrison sent to tell us that the countess had fled, taking a prisoner with her. I feared it was you."

"It was Persi." To Marta's horror, tears rose in her eyes. "I nearly got myself killed, I got Persi captured...and the *Bessarion Lance*. It's *gone*." She mouthed the words rather than saying them aloud, but Balian's eyes widened in horrified understanding.

Ever practical, Queen Maria beckoned her attendants into the room. "Can you walk downstairs? We have a litter waiting."

While Lord Balian helped Marta out of bed, the waiting women gathered up Marta's belongings. Marta thought with happiness of the sun on her face, the wind in her hair, the luxury of sleeping in her own bed—but she wasn't back in the game yet. She could hardly walk.

"Is the king still set on a divorce?" Marta whispered as they navigated the stairs, Lord Balian supporting her with an arm around her waist.

"I'm afraid so. He's already sent a summons to Ascalon."

"What?" Marta's blood froze. "Oh, strife." If Guy and Sibylla refused a direct summons from the king, they would become felons, and must forfeit their rank and fief. Even if Baldwin changed his mind about the divorce, no king could afford to overlook such defiance.

Prince Reynald will always win because he does what is clever and ruthless, instead of what is kind and good. Miles' words drifted back to her from that evening on the battlements of Kerak. She had tried to do the kind thing, and Sibylla had done the ruthless thing, and this was what it had come to. She had spent a week in the Hospital, while the king and his sister entrenched themselves ever deeper in conflict.

She hadn't been able to save Oliveta and her birth family, either. No matter how badly she'd wanted to.

In the Hospital courtyard, a small phalanx of knights waited to carry her litter. Marta stared as Lord Balian helped her across the pavement. Why, two of them were Arrabis, and as Marta settled into the cushions, Samuel Arrabi winked at her. Marta looked away in confusion, only to see the others smiling and nodding to her.

Lord Balian stepped away to speak to one of the Hospitaller brothers, promising a rich donation in gratitude for Marta's care and lodging. Marta tugged on Queen Maria's skirt. "I'm sorry I ran away from Kerak without telling you."

Queen Maria looked down on her, worried. "Balian takes you seriously. I just hope you know what you're doing, Marta."

Marta swallowed. "I hope so too."

Balian finished speaking with the brother, who came over to smile at her. "Goodbye, mademoiselle. The doctors say you must drink salted broth and eat red meat in plenty for at least six months. Don't come back!" To her surprise, he bowed, and not to Lord Balian.

To her.

Her knightly escort hoisted her litter to their shoulders. Marta lay back and thought of her next step. Ask the Healer to see her and lay hands on her. After that she must see Baldwin, find a way to persuade him. She wished Miles was still here to help her as he had with Countess Sibylla. Now she would have to do it by herself, and she'd never been good with words.

The knights carried her litter through the narrow passage that led from the Hospital compound to the Street of the Patriarch. As usual, people were gathered on the steps leading to the Patriarch's Baths opposite, and as Marta's litter emerged into the street, a hush fell. Heads turned. People stood and craned their necks, and Marta cringed, unsure of what made them all stare like this.

Someone cheered, and then the whole street erupted into applause. In front of the litter, Lord Balian and the queen waved. *Oh,* Marta thought in relief. *It's not me—*

"Bessarion! Bessarion!" someone yelled, and then the chant was taken up by the others.

A crowd followed them through the streets chanting her name. Stranded on the raised litter, Marta felt uncomfortably like an icon in a holy-day procession. People lifted up their children to look at her, and a flower-seller threw a red anemone into her lap.

By the time she was lowered to the ground in the privacy of their house on Temple Street, Marta was red-faced and mortified. Lord Balian turned to help her up, and laughed. "Why, Marta, what's the matter? You're a hero."

"Why?" she gasped. Had they all gone mad?

"You broke out of Kerak with Miles, remember?"

"But that was *weeks* ago. And all we did was run away."

"It was *preux.*" Lord Balian helped her up, and the Arrabis made a seat of their hands to carry her upstairs. "You forget half the minstrels in the kingdom were at Kerak for the wedding. By the time we arrived, they'd already made half a dozen songs about it. My favourite's the one in which you fought in single combat with Saladin himself, and overcame him with the merest glimpse of your beauty."

Marta's jaw sagged. "Oh no!"

Lord Balian was enjoying himself far too much to relent. "It's a good song. By now they're singing it in all the drinking-houses in Jerusalem."

"Oh *no!*" They carried her into her room and lowered her into a chair. Marta caught Lord Balian's sleeve. "Indeed, it's not true! Sir Martin, Sir Samuel, I thank you, but you mustn't believe it."

"You mean you *didn't* fight a single combat with the sultan?" Balian teased.

"No, of course not!" Marta buried her face in her hands, struggling to regain control. The Arrabis withdrew, leaving her alone with Balian and the queen, and with the closing of the door behind them, Marta's face crumpled into tears. "I'm not a hero," she sobbed. "I've ruined everything. I got myself stabbed like an idiot, and Persi captured, and I lost the Bessarion Lance, and Countess Sibylla will never forgive any of us for what we've done."

Lord Balian looked at Queen Maria. Neither of them said anything.

Marta sniffled. "It's all very well for them to cheer me in the streets, but I've failed everyone I've ever tried to help."

"Marta." Lord Balian crouched down to look into her eyes. "Dear Marta. Don't you remember? You're the one who showed us that with right on your side you could be stronger than a whole army. *That's* why they're cheering you in the streets. You didn't need the Bessarion Lance to get out of Kerak, and you don't need it to save the kingdom now."

"Save the kingdom?" Marta looked up at Balian with swimming eyes. "I can't ride, I can't fight. All I can do is plead with the king—and I can't even do that until I'm well enough."

"Then get well and *do* that." Balian grasped her hands. "Your strength was always in your pure heart and dauntless spirit, Marta. Not in your mortal body."

Chapter XLII.

At the end of Embertide, two messengers came to Ascalon.

Sara, the only one of her ladies Sibylla had brought with her from Jerusalem, looked into the countess' bower in the house she and Guy occupied near the citadel. Guy was strumming his lute, his head resting on her knee; Sibylla had her fingers woven through his hair. As everyone else turned against them, they had become all the more precious to each other. Sibylla didn't want to break this precious fragment of peace, but Sara's troubled face brought her reluctantly to the door.

"It's Kurosh," Sara whispered. "Remember the pottery merchant?"

Sibylla felt a cold premonition of danger and glanced towards her husband. "Kurosh?"

"He said something about a shipment of Fayyumi ware."

"One moment." Sibylla turned back to Guy. "Will you excuse me a while, my love? I think I should rest before dinner."

Tough and hale himself, her husband was always deeply ignorant of her frailty until she actually drew attention to it—and then he treated her like thin glass. He removed himself instantly and apologetically, and Sibylla waited for him to leave the house on a circuit of the town's defences before signalling Sara to bring Kurosh.

It was worse than she thought.

"My master knows you have the spear," he said as soon as Sara had closed the door, leaving them alone. "He asks why you have not yet sent it to him."

A chill ran down her spine, but Sibylla concealed it. "Your master knows a great deal."

353

"It is his business to know things. You never complained of it before."

"He never spied on me before." Sibylla leaned forward, gripping the arms of her chair. "Before I answer, I want to know how he gained this information."

"Out of the question."

Sibylla narrowed her eyes at the Saracen, her mind busy with possibilities. The Watchers had kept the Bessarion Lance a secret for decades; it was unlikely that they would break their silence to complain of its theft. If Kurosh knew she had the spear, he had not learned it from them.

She thought of the information Kurosh had given her in the past—things that only servants would know, those faceless, silent, invisible functionaries of any large household, who saw everything and knew everything.

The chill gripping her chest tightened. "One of my people is in your pay. Who?"

"My master owes you no favours. He requires his property, which you already agreed to return to him."

Sibylla reined in her retort. Now that she and Guy had defied the king, they were in need of allies. There was Guy's brother Aimery and her own Uncle Joscelin, besides Prince Reynald, all of whom could be trusted to support them in the High Court. If open war came, however, they'd sworn allegiance to the Leper King. When things inevitably came to the worst and Baldwin besieged Ascalon, she would need men and supplies, most likely from Egypt, and if Kurosh's master was as prominent in the sultan's court as Sibylla suspected, he could stop those shipments with a word.

As much as she wanted to, she could not yet afford to cut Kurosh loose, especially not while he had one of her servants in his employ. Another chill ran through Sibylla's body, and she fidgeted with her onyx ring. It was not unknown for the Saracens to plant agents in the households of their enemies years in advance. If the agent was an Assassin, he'd serve faithfully for years, keeping his knife sharp for the day when his orders finally reached him.

Almost any of her servants might be the spy, and trying to find out who would likely reveal her suspicions and provoke his master into deadly reprisals.

All she could do was buy time.

"Tell your master to have patience," she said. "As I understood it, he didn't only want the weapon; he wanted the girl as well. She slipped away from me with a wound in Jerusalem, but I've captured her associate, a Nubian weaver. She'll come to me of her own accord, for the sake of the spear, if not for her friend. When that happens, I'll hand both of them over to you."

Kurosh considered that. "Both of them, then," he agreed at last. "Remember: my master is always watching."

* * *

"I need to finish what I've started." In her dream, Sibylla stood atop Ascalon's Tower of Maidens beside her mother, overlooking the city's blue domes and honey-coloured streets. "And fast, before everyone turns against us."

"You need to make yourself queen," Agnes said.

Sibylla looked down at her hands. They seemed oddly naked; she unclosed her fist and there it was, the onyx ring, clasped in her right hand, although she did not remember removing it from her thumb.

"Baldwin," Agnes said. "Baldwin is the problem. He's always tried to control you."

A sick feeling of dread slithered down Sibylla's spine. It took her a couple of attempts to speak. "He's your son. I thought you loved him."

"You loved him too, once."

"Yes, but he's never tried to control *you*." Sibylla took a deep breath. The city was spread out before them and the land of Jerusalem beyond, vineyards and marshes, sand dunes and salt sea. Agnes stood beside her, but she couldn't turn; couldn't look at her mother directly.

"You're holding back." Agnes hissed with impatience. "You're as much of a coward as *he* is."

Sibylla clenched her hand on the ring. "I have to be sure."

* * *

The second messenger came the following day: Aimery himself, bearing a royal charter. Guy's brother barely spoke or greeted them as he held out the parchment with its dangling leaden seal. Sibylla glanced it over: she and Guy had been summoned to a meeting of the High Court on the feast day of Saint Thomas.

Aimery shifted, clearly uncomfortable. "What will you do?"

Sibylla folded the parchment again with a smile. "I will put it in a very safe place, believe me."

"But will you attend the Court?"

"We'll consider it." Guy's response was as they had discussed: Sibylla didn't believe in volunteering any more information than absolutely necessary.

Aimery's mouth firmed. "Guy, a word?"

Taking the hint, Sibylla retreated to the other end of the room and seated herself at her tapestry frame. Yet with her head bent over the coloured wool, it was easy to hear Aimery's words.

"Listen," he hissed, "you're just insulting the king further. No matter what they say, he isn't a saint. If you don't obey this summons, he *will* attack you."

"And if he does? Will you stand by us?"

"*Saints.*" Aimery ran a hand through his hair. "Look, my wife's an Ibelin. It's already hard enough having Ramla as a father-in-law."

Guy could be savage, too, when he wanted. "So I'm supposed to let the Leper break up my family for the sake of your domestic comfort?"

"I'm not saying that," Aimery hissed. "You know I'll be with you to the end. Together we rose, and together we'll fall. But for heaven's sake, you can still stop this. Obey the summons, humble yourself for *once* in your life, vow never to seek the regency or the throne, and you just *might* have a chance of getting out of this alive."

Across the room, Guy's eyes met hers, but Sibylla didn't speak.

"Remember where you came from," Aimery urged. "In Poitou you were a landless younger son. This county is the best thing that's ever happened to you. You've got two cities, a beautiful wife and daughter, a king for a stepson. I *beg* you, don't throw it all away on your damned ambitions."

"You think this is about ambition? If we appear before the council, they can do as they like with us. I can't risk it." Guy's voice became husky. "If they want my wife they'll have to fight for her."

Sibylla made no outward sign, but inside her a fiercely jubilant flame burned.

Aimery passed a hand across his chin, a gesture he only used when he was deeply worried. "Saint Thomas' Day is a little way off yet. Consider what I've said. A war will benefit no one."

As Aimery took his leave of them, Sibylla ran the tip of her tongue over her lips, knowing that she owed it to her brother to ask. "Do you have any message for *me*, my lord?"

Before leaving Jerusalem, she'd scribbled a hasty note and left it with Alix to be delivered to Baldwin when he returned from Kerak. Now, from the way Aimery's shoulders slumped, she knew that there was an answer—one that Aimery had hoped to leave without delivering.

Sibylla's gut twisted, and she became very aware of the weight of the onyx ring on her thumb.

Aimery crossed the wide audience-room to where she sat, twisting his gloves between his hands. "Yes, my lady. The Leper King says..." He swallowed. "The Leper King says, *I have not spared myself for the sake of the kingdom. Why should I spare my sister, who wishes to know what it is to be queen?*"

The cruel words took her breath away and left her staring numbly at him for a moment. It was true, then, what she had always suspected: that in Baldwin's eyes, her suffering was not enough to equip her for the throne.

Well. She had wanted to be sure, and now she was.

She forced herself to nod. "Thank you, brother."

Sibylla got through the leave-taking as quickly as she could, before hurrying into the room she used as a cabinet. Her hands shook as she slid the ring from her hand. She took a sheet of parchment, uncorked her

357

inkwell, and wrote a single sentence.

Baldwin, called the Leper, King of Jerusalem.

She looked at the words for a while, until they began to blur and run into each other. Startled, she blinked her vision clear, then folded the parchment shut around the ring and sealed it with hot wax. A courier waited outside her door and she called him in, handing him the packet.

"Take this to my mother in Jerusalem. She'll know what to do next. Do not lose it, on your life."

"On my life, my lady."

He left and Sibylla sat back in her chair, breathing deeply, but she couldn't relax. She tried to distract herself by calculating how long it would take the ring to complete its journey. How long before it took effect. Whether the Assassins already had an agent in her brother's service. Whether he would ever guess that it was *she* who had ordered his death.

Abruptly, Sibylla got up and drank down a dose of wine and hemlock. Not enough to put her to sleep; her dreams no longer provided rest. Only enough to dull her thoughts and bring her some small measure of peace.

She sank onto her bed and stared at the white ceiling, conscious of little but an unbearable sadness.

Chapter XLIII.

The Leper King was ill; the Leper King needed rest; the Leper King was busy meeting an embassy from his cousin, the king of England.

As Christmas approached, Jerusalem filled with pilgrims from as far afield as Cathay, Muscovy, and Iceland, and the influx of travellers brought increased work for everyone in the kingdom. Still, Marta found it difficult to escape the conclusion that Baldwin was avoiding her.

As Marta gradually regained strength, she kept herself busy weaving, embroidering, and seeing to the business. Persian and Indian merchants came to the kingdom with fine silk and linen fibre to sell, eager to connect with the Mediterranean trade. European merchants wanted finished cloth to take back to the markets of Italy, while knights from France or Germany were looking to turn their heavy gold into fine cloaks which could be re-sold at a profit in the north. The work tired her out, but it kept her from fretting: she could not charge into Ascalon and rescue Persi, but she could keep the business afloat for her.

Within a day or two of the army's return, Benjamin of Borca had been to lay hands on her. The Healer's prayers seemed to have been answered, and Marta's recovery progressed more quickly. By Saint Thomas' day, she was able to walk from one end of the city to the other without tiring.

"How is the king?" she asked Balian as he returned from the High Court meeting that afternoon.

Balian looked troubled. "Sicker than I've ever seen him."

He's killing himself, she thought. "Was Countess Sibylla there?"

"No. She and the count refused the summons. He's sent another for Holy

Innocents, a week from now."

"I doubt they'll come next time, either." Marta gnawed her lower lip. "If Baldwin won't agree to see me, then I'll have to sneak into the palace without his leave."

Balian choked on his mouthful of wine. *"No, Marta! What if you get caught?"*

That was a fair point; she might be up to walking through the city, but climbing and running still left her slightly breathless. Marta rubbed her forehead, but the seraph's kiss lay dormant. "Then I'll keep asking to see him. But if the countess doesn't appear at Holy Innocents, I'll find a way regardless."

Yet in the end she didn't have to. Holy Innocents came and went without the count or countess of Jaffa appearing in Jerusalem, and the Leper King's next summons arrived at the house on Temple Street for Marta herself.

He was resting in his chamber when she arrived that evening. Inside a gauzy curtain that protected his bed against flies, his attendants from the Order of Saint Lazarus rebandaged his arms and dabbed the sores with ointment. They nodded to her with friendly smiles, and motioned her towards a wooden chair that sat facing the bed.

"Is that you, Marta?" the Leper King whispered. He lay without moving, too weak to lift his head, and his breath hitched as one of the brothers dabbed a little more ointment into an ulcer on his arm. For the first time she could smell him—like rotting meat. Her heart wrung.

"Yes, my lord, it's me."

"Please sit," he whispered.

Marta sat and watched as the brothers finished bandaging his wasted arms. One of the misshapen hands lay near her on the coverlet.

Take it, her heart urged. *Touch him.*

She linked her fingers tightly and bent her head to look down at them through the tears that stood in her eyes. *No.*

Pain spiked through her head.

Ow! I can't very well touch him when he's told me not to!

To her surprise, the pain receded. Mystified, Marta wiped her eyes. *Why, though?*

No answer came. Instead, Baldwin spoke in a whisper. "I couldn't attend Court today. Too weak. Tripoli acted for me."

Marta swallowed. "You are dying."

"I have been dying since the moment I was born." Somehow, there was laughter lurking in his voice.

"Don't," she said. "You know what I mean. You're killing yourself. I warned you about it when Lord Balian wanted the divorce. You know in your heart this is wrong. Stop ignoring it."

"Is it, though?" he whispered. "I am only trying to keep the kingdom safe."

Marta leaned forward. "You can't. Not like this. You'll kill yourself, and then we will be left unprotected, as the Messenger prophesied."

"Stop it." Baldwin spat the words. "I *tried,* Marta. I tried doing it your way, but it didn't stop Guy. His men are still singing about how they'll make him king. He and Sibylla think the throne is theirs by right, an opportunity to gratify their own ambition. They don't see it as it truly is: a terrible, terrible duty." The king's breath rasped in his chest. "I always counted on Sibylla to replace me, but I can't give so much power to those who would only exploit it. I'm sick of reacting, sick of being caught off-balance all the time, sick of letting them set the pace. No more grace. It's time to deal with them both."

Marta felt immeasurably weary. Why did everyone think that goodness was something passive—a balance, a dance on a tightrope? In truth, it was more like plunging from a cliff and trusting the wind to catch you. The creature of love and fire she had met in the wilderness could not help consuming evil; that was its nature, and you survived it by leaping into the blaze, not by measuring out grainsworths of right and wrong.

He'd never tried it her way, not really.

She couldn't put it all into words, but she understood why he was afraid. "What are you going to do?"

"What else can I do, but declare Guy a felon and drive him from the kingdom? My sister will have to remarry, of course. I have chosen the

man. It only remains to complete the customary summons and seize them."
Baldwin took another rasping breath. "Our mother died yesterday. I think
it was this dispute between her children that killed her."

She'd heard that Countess Agnes had been ill. "Oh, Baldwin."

"I didn't ask you here to cry on your shoulder. Someone told me you
were the last to see Sibylla before she left the city."

Marta sighed. "Yes."

"Where does my sister stand? Did she go to Guy willingly?"

"Of course."

"His men didn't force her to ride to Ascalon?"

"She hesitated for a while, my lord. But in the end she went out of anger,
because she had given up the throne on the understanding that she would
be permitted to keep her husband, and despite this you chose to persecute
her anyway."

"Hm." Baldwin seemed unimpressed. "And what did *you* say to her?"

Marta tilted her chin defiantly. "I told her to go to him. You have no
right to part them."

"Devil take it, Marta! I could have you hanged for that."

He kept his tone light, but Marta sensed an undercurrent of truth. He
was angry with her.

Is he in love with you?

That was the real objection to Sibylla's question: you could not be friends,
or siblings, or lovers with someone who would say such a thing, from
someone with the power to control your life and death. To such, you could
give the cringing obedience of a slave, but never the love of a peer.

"I thought you wanted friendship from me, my lord. Would you have
me fear you, like a beaten dog?"

He caught his breath. "I would be obeyed as a king. Willingly—out of
love."

Marta gulped a long slow breath. "My love is my own to give. If you
want it rendered willingly, you cannot compel it. You must leave me free
to judge whether or not I owe it."

"That is not how kingship works."

362

"Then I pity you, for if that is so, a king can never be loved."

He was silent, then, for a while. Marta sat at the foot of his bed with her hands folded, and listened anxiously to his breathing. "Don't you want your sister to love you, my lord?" she added at last.

"Yes," he whispered. "But it's too late. She will never forgive me for this." He paused for a moment. "This knight of yours. He can be loved, I take it."

Marta shifted uncomfortably in her seat, torn between uncertainty at the king's question, and the fierce desire to keep her heart's wound secret. At last she cleared her throat and said, "Love and I are strangers, my lord. We met once in the street, but found we were travelling in different directions."

"If I were a different man, in a different life, I might be glad of it." There was a bitter twist in his voice. "But I am a king and incapable of love, I hear."

For an instant, Marta forgot to breathe.

Is he in love with you?

Strife. He was. He must have been trying to tell her for weeks.

"Forgive me." Baldwin's voice softened. "Sick and busy as I've been…I've missed you, Marta. This last week, I half expected you to come climbing in at my window."

She couldn't help smiling at that. "I would have, my lord, but I was sick, too."

"You were?" He sounded concerned. "What was it? Melancholy? Fever?"

"Loss of blood."

"What? You've been wounded? Who dared?"

Too late, Marta realised her mistake. "It was nothing, my lord. Just a—an unlucky scratch."

"Don't give me that," he growled. "Was it my sister?"

Strife, Marta thought.

"It was." For the first time, his voice rose above a whisper. "It was Sibylla, wasn't it? Devil take it, Marta! This was her revenge on *me.* Why didn't you tell me?"

"Because it had nothing to do with you," she erupted.

"Enough!" In the quiet room, it almost sounded like a shout. "My sister has defied my commands and attacked my people. I will *not* allow it." Baldwin swung his bandaged arm from his side, striking a bell that hung by his bed with such force that it jangled discordantly. "If she will not submit to me, I will end them both."

The door opened, letting in a stream of attendants. Marta jumped up and clung to the back of her seat, battling dizziness. "Please," she managed.

A squire turned to grab her arm, to steady her.

"That's all, Marta," the king rasped.

As the king whispered his orders to his attendants, the squire turned Marta about and marched her from the chamber. She made no resistance. Since the Leper King refused to hear her, she must save her strength for a different battle.

* * *

Two days later, the Leper King set off from Jerusalem. Most of the High Court followed his litter to witness the final summons that would make a felon of Guy of Lusignan. Before they left, Marta waited on Lord Balian in his cabinet.

"I've had another letter from Ascalon," she said.

Balian knew of her correspondence with Miles, and he eagerly took the folded paper, sealed with a blob of unsigned wax. The words were already branded on her memory like the dazzling afterimage of a candle flame in the dark.

Word has come that we may expect the king before our gates within days. We are ready to stand siege. Our allies are to be summoned, and no quarter asked.

"It will mean war," she murmured.

Lord Balian put a comforting hand on her shoulder. "You've done everything you can, Marta. Don't blame yourself."

"I *don't*," she said fiercely. "But I haven't done everything I can—not yet. I'm going to Ascalon to get Persi back. And my spear. If there's going to be a war, they aren't going to use the Bessarion Lance to fight it."

Lord Balian's eyes widened. "You can't possibly be well enough yet!"

"I've had a Healer touch me. I assure you, I feel impossibly well." She tired more easily than she used to, but she hadn't had a dizzy spell for a couple of days. "You must ride with the king. Perhaps he'll listen to you, if he wouldn't listen to me. Try to convince him to show grace."

"Grace? Saints, Marta. The countess *stabbed* you."

"That doesn't make the king *right*. There are laws against stabbing people, and none of them involve forcing the culprit to part from their spouse." She took a breath and let it out in a determined huff. "I'm not doing this for Countess Sibylla. Or even for the Leper King. I'm doing it for my family."

She had failed her siblings in Oliveta. She had failed Isabella. She was not going to fail Persi.

Lord Balian shook his head with a lopsided smile. "You never give up, do you?"

She returned the smile using all her teeth. "Not while I'm breathing."

Chapter XLIV.

Baldwin's litter lurched sharply to a halt. "Are we there?"

Brother John answered. "We've arrived at Ascalon, my lord. We're just beyond bowshot."

Baldwin listened, but the silence was broken only by the sighing of the salt-laden sea wind and the whispering of his barons. The customary law of the kingdom demanded that the High Court should attend him on this journey—from Chancellor William, who would have been very glad to see the back of Count Guy, to Uncle Joscelin, who was being very quiet but no doubt meant to keep an eye out for the Courtenay interests.

Their proximity was stifling, and Baldwin wished, not for the first time, that he was an ordinary man and could quarrel with his sister's husband in peace and quiet without a kingdom breathing down his neck.

"What's the view?" he asked his Lazarite attendants.

Lord Balian answered instead. "They're holding the gate shut against us, my lord, but they know we're here. The walls and towers are full of people."

"What are they doing?"

"Just…watching."

That was good, Baldwin thought. He wanted the people of Ascalon to bear witness, so that if war came, they would know it was Guy's fault.

Not that he could start a siege today, without a proper army. Today would be a bluffing game: which of them would flinch first?

Not me, Baldwin silently vowed. *I am the king.*

"Carry me closer to the gate," he whispered.

"My lord—" Balian began.

"*No,*" Baldwin rasped, as the litter jolted forward. "I've heard it all, Ibelin. You are here to bear witness, not to speak."

Next time the litter stopped, he felt the cold shadow of the massive Ascalon wall blocking the faint midwinter sun. Baldwin swallowed, hoping his voice would not fail him now.

I could do better than a blind cripple, Guy had said.

Baldwin took a deep breath, letting that rage lift him from his cushions.

"Guy, Count of Jaffa!" It hurt his throat to shout, but there was relief in the yell. "Twice we have summoned you to our High Court at Jerusalem, and twice you have failed to come! We solemnly command you, in the fidelity and love in which you are bound to us, that you will open this gate and let us enter!"

His words rang against the stones, and silence fell over Ascalon. Baldwin swayed a little, and Brother John reached out, cradling his shoulders to keep him sitting upright.

"Do you see the count above?" Baldwin whispered.

"He's there," Brother John replied.

"And my sister? Do you see her?"

"No, my lord."

Baldwin gritted his teeth and took another scratchy breath. "Well?" he shouted. "Why did you not obey our summons, *brother?*"

"I was ill." Guy's voice fell from the battlements above. "Cannot a man be ill without provoking all this fury?"

Baldwin felt momentarily staggered by the sheer audacity of the count's excuse. "Let me speak to my sister. Where is Sibylla?"

"Do you suppose the heiress of Jerusalem should patrol the walls like a common soldier?"

"Then I will wait for her to come." Despite Marta's testimony, despite her wound, he couldn't help clinging to the hope that it was Guy, not Sibylla, who had chosen this path. She was a woman of cold ambitions, after all. She *must* see that Guy was ruinous to all her hopes.

Guy's voice was ragged with fury. "Why should she come to you? Why should she obey you? You would tear her from her home and her children."

"It is so that other women may not be torn from their homes and their children that I do this. I have spared neither myself for the sake of the kingdom, nor our youngest sister, and she wishes me to spare *her?*" He straightened. "Once again we command: either open this gate and let us enter, or bid our sister come."

"Who am I to *bid* my lady come or go?"

"Then open the gate, or I will pronounce you felon, confiscate your properties and drive you into exile with force of arms."

"Do that and you will suffer for it!"

It was a childish taunt, and Baldwin only laughed. "Not half so much as—"

A metallic *clang* interrupted him, making him jolt almost out of his skin as something hit the road by his litter and rolled. His retinue shouted in alarm, and Baldwin heard the whisper of steel leaving sheaths, the clack of shields locking into place over him.

"Go on, you chickenhearts," Guy jeered from above. "Pick it up. Take a good look."

"It's a helmet, my lord," Brother John murmured into his ear. "The new kind, with a faceplate…"

That meant nothing to Baldwin. But there was a scuffle beside his litter and Lord Balian's voice spoke, tight with dread. "Give that to me."

"What is it, Ibelin?"

"It's Marta's," he breathed. "I last saw her put it on two days ago…"

"Guy!" Baldwin bellowed. "Guy!"

"He's gone," Brother John said.

"Devil take it," Baldwin spat. "Carry me to the gate. *Now!*"

They slid his litter from the horses and edged it forward. Baldwin reached out until the massive timbers of the city gate stopped his fist. Closed. Locked. Barred.

And Marta inside, dangled before him as a guarantee of his good behaviour.

"Open this gate!" Baldwin pounded on the door. Muffled in rags, his fists barely made a sound, but Baldwin knew all eyes were on him. "Open to the king! We, Baldwin the Fourth, command it!"

Above on the wall, no one responded. They dared not disobey their own count, even for their king. As stabbing pain and hot blood seeped through his bandages, Baldwin fell back into the cushions of his litter. "On your own heads be it!" he yelled.

Already his attendants carried him away from the wall. Hoofbeats fell into pace with him. Baldwin lay back, his heart racing, pain shooting up from his sodden hand. "Stop," he commanded faintly. "Balian. William. Uncle Joscelin. Whoever else is here. We call you to bear witness how Guy, Count of Jaffa has flouted us."

He did not suppose he would ever see Marta again. Sibylla had nearly killed her once already; perhaps had now done it indeed. Baldwin swallowed. He could not save her, but by heaven, he would avenge her.

"Now we summon you to Acre to announce the count's felony and declare war upon him."

Chapter XLV.

As the massive gate of Ascalon ground open, the knot in Marta's gut tightened. Without her spear, she felt naked. Yet she held her ground; only her hands clenched a little tighter on her horse's reins, ready to wheel and gallop if Count Guy didn't keep his word.

She'd reached the city about midday on the second day out of Jerusalem. One of the largest cities in the kingdom, Ascalon was surrounded by a semicircular wall built atop an artificial mound, a well-maintained moat at its foot. Its massive eastern gate was shut and doubtless barred against the Leper King's coming. Above, Count Guy's men watched from the battlements and the massive towers flanking the gate, their crossbows ready and trained on her.

Baldwin was still behind her, travelling more slowly with his larger retinue. Still, he'd arrive by the end of the day, and the garrison was understandably twitchy. The gate creaked open a little further, revealing Count Guy with a wall of men standing behind him. Although they had her spear, they were taking no chances.

Marta pulled off her helm and passed chilly fingers over the scar on her forehead. It didn't ache exactly; if anything, it was comfortingly warm, and as nervous as she was, Marta wasn't afraid.

She was exactly where she needed to be.

Count Guy looked at her and nodded curtly, snapping his fingers. The sergeants and knights flanking him shifted back as Miles pushed his way through the crowd, holding Persi by the elbow. Persi's mouth dropped open when she saw Marta, and her lips traced her friend's name in confusion.

From the shadow of the gate, Miles nodded to her curtly. He'd been in charge of the gate when Marta had arrived half an hour ago. *I should have known,* he'd said with resignation, but she could tell he was frightened for her.

In response to his nod, Marta kicked her foot from the stirrup and stepped down from the saddle, leaving her reins to trail on the ground. The animal nuzzled its way to the green grass by the roadside as she stepped onto the causeway spanning the moat. Miles and Persi advanced to meet her. As Persi realised what was happening, her eyes widened and she planted her feet, throwing her full weight against Miles.

"What have you done, Marta? What did you say to them?"

There was obviously no point in concealing it. Halfway across the causeway, Marta stopped and held out both her hands. "It's an exchange, Persi. You for me. You didn't seriously think I wouldn't come for you?"

Persi's eyes widened. "No, Marta. Don't do this." She tried to yank out of Miles' grip. "Unhand me, will you?"

"Hold her," Marta commanded, and Miles captured her friend's other arm and propelled her forward.

Persi looked at her with tears. "Please, Marta. Stop trying to be preux. Miles, tell her!"

"Miles knows better than to try. I have to get inside that city, and this is the only way."

Persi stilled in realisation. "You're going after that weapon?"

"I have to. I know what Sibylla will use it for."

"Don't. *Please.* Just let her have it. That spear can't bring us peace. That's not what peace *is.*"

"I'm sorry." Marta pulled her into a hug. "I already promised them I'd hand myself over if they let you go."

Behind Persi, Miles looked down at her with a crease between his brows. Troubled, but silent. Marta kissed Persi's cheek and let go. "Did they treat you well? Can you travel alone?"

"Did they treat *me* well—Marta, that woman stabbed you! There was so much blood…"

371

"It's all right. I'm healed, mostly. Take my horse. There are some weapons tethered to the saddle, but here on the coast you shouldn't need them. Ride to Ibelin; they're expecting you." Well, strictly speaking they were expecting Marta, but she'd always meant to send Persi back in her place. "If all goes well I'll join you there in a day or two. If not, get word to Lord Balian. All right?"

Persi shook her head. "Marta, you can't trust Countess Sibylla. She's being influenced by something terrible. I can see the shadows in the air around her—she'll act without reason, without pity."

"Is that what you Perceived, that last night in Jerusalem?"

"Yes, but it's grown worse since then. She's done something terrible, Marta. Opened herself up to it somehow. Be careful."

"I will. I promise." Marta signalled Miles to release her, and Persi turned on him with a snarl.

"You. Take care of my friend, Miles of Plancy. If I don't get her back in one piece, it's *your* head I'll collect."

Miles bowed to her with genuine deference. "For that, you can always rely on me."

Marta glanced towards the gate. "Hurry, Persi. Before they get tired of waiting."

Persi gave a sob and one last, fierce hug. Then she ran down the causeway and climbed shakily into the saddle. Marta stood her ground, watching as Persi urged the horse to a trot and made it out of bowshot from the wall. Then she turned to Miles, who looked down at her with those troubled eyes. He drew breath to say something, but Marta put a finger against his lips. "Later," she whispered. "Saint John's."

She turned and strode across the causeway, putting a swagger into her step that she didn't feel. What happened next depended entirely on her weakened body. She took a deep breath and fixed her eyes on Count Guy, praying that it would be enough.

As the gate ground shut again behind her, the count looked her up and down, his eyebrows lifting at the sight of her masculine clothing. "Search her."

"I'll do it." Miles stepped in front of her before the sergeants could touch her.

"Not you, Plancy."

A spot of red burned on Miles' cheekbones. Marta noticed it and wondered: clearly Count Guy put limited trust in Miles, but how limited was it? Did he know Miles was the one who'd carried Marta to the Hospital that night in Jerusalem?

"I understand, my lord, but this lady is gentle born. She should be treated with respect," Miles said stiffly.

Count Guy shrugged and turned, scanning the street. People were gathering to stare, and he crooked his finger at a middle-aged burgess-woman who was standing on her doorstep nearby. "You. Search this woman."

They took everything: helmet, hauberk, even a small eating-dagger—the only blade she'd brought into the city with her. Marta submitted in silence; what she lost in protection, she'd make up for in mobility. When the woman was done and Marta was shelled out of her armour, Count Guy had his sergeants tether her wrists together with a rope and fasten it to his saddle.

"Watch the gate, Plancy," he said shortly. "Send word to my house when the king approaches. Three of you sergeants, follow me and watch the prisoner."

Miles looked into Marta's eyes. His lips pressed together briefly, and she realised how worried he was. As he retreated to the gatehouse, Marta followed the count into the streets of Ascalon. They made an awkward little procession, the count riding ahead with Marta following like a puppet on a string. Behind, she was acutely conscious of the sergeants.

Well. She'd known this wouldn't be easy. At least the count hadn't demanded she give her parole.

As they turned south towards the Gaza Gate and the town's citadel, Marta quickened her pace, letting her tether slacken and testing the give in the ropes. She had spent years teasing the knots from threads as fine as hair. Now, she twisted her hands, dug her fingers into the knots, and pulled. A few quick tugs, and the ropes slackened.

It was not a market day, and the town was not busy, but Marta kept her eyes peeled for opportunity. She found it almost at once: ahead, a wagon waited outside an open warehouse, taking up half the narrow street and halting the traffic to a crawl. As the count slowed to push his way through, Marta acted.

She slid the rope from her wrists and threw herself sideways, hitting the street and rolling under the wagon. Behind her, the sergeants yelped in surprise, but they were caught in the traffic snarl and blocked by the wagon. Within heartbeats, Marta was on the other side of the wagon and up. The open door yawned before her. She caught a startled glimpse of the carter and ducked around him, into the dark warmth of a glassblower's shop. To the left, a furnace glowed. To the right, stairs led up into the living-quarters above. A wooden crate of glass beakers sat on the bench to Marta's right. She swept it to the floor as she passed, covering the floor behind with jagged shards.

The glassblower swore at her, but Marta kept moving. She pelted up the stairs to the door above and burst through into his living-quarters. A small child stared up at her with enormous brown eyes. At the hearth a woman froze, lips parted. Marta threw a handful of silver into a terracotta bowl beside her.

"For the broken glass," she gasped. In the opposite corner, a stairwell led up onto the house's flat roof. Marta flew up it and burst out into the raw January day.

Below, the house and street were a cacophony of shouts and running steps. An avenue of flat roofs stretched before her, and as Marta paused to catch her breath and her bearings, she couldn't help laughing aloud with jubilation. Despite her heart's quick tattoo, she felt better than she had in weeks.

Marta raced south along the rooftops, vaulting from one to the next. She collected a long woman's tunic and a sheet from the next washing-line she found, then used the latter to let herself down into a narrow alley before the Poitevins even made it onto the glassblower's roof.

Only once she was bent double in the alley, hands on her knees, did she feel a little dizzy with her efforts. Marta pulled the tunic over her trousers and gambeson, completing the outfit with a snowy linen wimple she'd carried folded in her bosom. Just like that, she was a respectable-looking burgess-woman.

She took one more deep breath before setting out for the town's central square and the great basilica of Saint John.

* * *

Evening had fallen, and the cold was eating into her bones by the time Miles came. Marta had managed to avoid telling the priest that she was here to claim sanctuary, since she didn't want him alerting Count Guy to her presence, but she still felt relieved when slow footsteps echoed in the nave and Miles softly called her name. She was waiting in a chapel, prostrated before the altar like one keeping a vigil; and Miles knelt beside her as she pulled herself shivering to her knees.

"You're cold," he murmured, whisking his cloak off his own shoulders and swinging it around hers. His hands lingered on her arms, rubbing gently to give her warmth. "I'm sorry. I was only just relieved from gate duty. Look, I brought you some food."

It was a small loaf sliced open with warm meat inside. Marta bit into the food hungrily. *Spiced lamb.* The taste took her back to that ghastly day in the pleasure garden of Jerusalem, and Marta's heart knotted at the memory. Had she been too hard on him? Just by being here, he was risking everything.

She swallowed. "Thank you, Miles."

There was a worried twist in his mouth. "Don't thank me until this is over."

In truth, she'd wondered if he was going to betray her. Before entering the basilica, she'd spent an hour on a neighbouring rooftop watching the city square in case he and Guy sent men to ambush her in the porch. She wanted so badly to trust him, but part of her still wondered. She didn't doubt he cared for her, but was it enough? She was so tired of distrusting him, aching for him. Exhausted from worry, Marta snuggled deeper into the warmth of his cloak and wished she could let go, fall into his arms and rest.

"I take it the Leper King has come?"

"This afternoon." He rubbed his chin, looking worried. "Count Guy refused him entrance."

"So it will be war," she said softly. The food was beginning to warm her. "Miles, do you know where they're keeping the Bessarion Lance?"

He stiffened a little. "Marta…"

"What?"

He swivelled onto his knee, facing her. "There's a small postern on the west side of the city, leading down onto the beach. You'll find it if you turn west at the house of Bertrand the Tanner. Locked, of course, but I managed to get my hands on a key. You could be out of this city inside a quarter of an hour, and I have a horse waiting at a farm just north of the marshes."

Marta stared at him, confused. He reached out, brushing the hair back from her face, his eyes dark with worry. "I'll give you the horse, Marta. Just *go*."

"Without the spear?"

"Devil take it, *yes*, without the spear!"

"Is it not in Ascalon?" As he hesitated, she swallowed the last of the bread and wiped her fingers on the napkin that had wrapped it. "You *know* I can't leave without it, Miles. No one is going to use *my* spear to fight this stupid war."

"I know you don't like it," he insisted. "But you can't afford to provoke Countess Sibylla. She doesn't fight clean; you of all people should know that. Last time you and she had a disagreement, I barely managed to save your life. What happens when your luck runs out?"

"That wasn't *luck*, Miles."

His shoulders slumped. "I just want to keep you safe."

"I know," she whispered. "But it's not just me at stake—it's the whole kingdom. Please, Miles. I'm not leaving this city without it."

He got to his feet and turned away from her, facing the chapel altar. She watched his shoulders lift and fall with a frustrated breath. After a moment he crossed himself and turned to her. "Then come with me, and I'll lead you to it."

"Thank you!" She sprang to her feet and hugged him. In the circle of her arms, his body stiffened, and he pulled away, not looking at her. The hair prickled on the back of Marta's neck. Something was wrong. Yet what else could she do? She needed the spear.

"Come quickly," he whispered, tugging the hood of her cloak over her head. "Keep your head covered."

Marta followed him cautiously into the town square. It was a clear evening with a nip of frost in the air, and the fading daylight revealed that the streets were nearly empty. Miles caught her hand and together they hurried south along the same road she'd travelled this morning.

The Ascalon citadel was a squat stone fortress on the south wall beside the Gaza Gate. The two high towers flanking the gate were black monoliths in the shadows of dusk, one of them bearing a square cupola. Miles reached into his pouch and withdrew a keyring, selecting one key with the utmost care to prevent their jingling. A wooden external staircase led to the second floor of the citadel, and Miles went up ahead, stepping lightly to keep the treads from creaking. At the top, Marta followed him into a dark room, but caught his arm as he moved to shut the door behind them. "Leave it open. We may be glad to see our way out."

She half thought he might object, but instead he grunted assent and led her on. After a moment's fumbling, he found the door leading up into the tower. Beyond was a small square room with streaks of light showing through the narrow slits in each wall. Miles pointed her to a wooden ladder, and Marta climbed steep wooden steps into the tower's topmost room: another dark stone box.

At the very top of the ladder, Marta felt a trapdoor, and heaved it up until its chain caught. Evening light flowed down on her, a crisp and fading lemon-yellow outlining the cupola's eight graceful pillars and the rippling black blade of the Bessarion Lance where it stood alone in a wooden rack at the tower's centre.

Relief washed over her. Marta erupted from the trapdoor into the fading light of evening, her hands already reaching for the weapon.

But she never touched it.

Hands clamped on her shoulders, yanking her to a standstill. Marta gave a strangled yelp and kicked. Her heel connected with an armoured shin, but to no effect. The soldiers yanked her aside and brought her face to pale face with a smiling Countess Sibylla.

"Marta Bessarion." Despite her triumph, the countess shivered inside her fur-lined cloak. "What a *delightful* surprise."

Chapter XLVI.

Miles climbed through the trapdoor, and despite the quickly-falling darkness, Marta saw the look on his face clearly. For an instant, her whole body went numb. "You *knew*," she whispered.

He swallowed, his face shuttering in iron-hard lines. "Don't reproach me. I tried to spare you."

She had no words. Since their meeting in the church, she'd been alert, watching for the moment he would betray her. Instead, he'd already done it. By the time he was in the church, offering her food, giving her his cloak, Sibylla was already waiting in the tower.

Miles captured her face between his hands. His breath trembled along her cheek, a promise of warmth. "There's still time," he whispered. Despite the strain in his face, his eyes begged, warm and liquid. "Don't break yourself against her. Tell her you'll marry me. Tell her you'll give up the spear. We could be so happy together."

It might have been a relief to cry, but Marta's eyes were dry, and her heart was hot. "I could never be happy with a man like you. Who do you love, Miles of Plancy? I thought it was me, but now I find it was something else entirely."

"Devil take it, Marta, do you *want* to die? She is too strong for you. Yield for just *once* in your life."

She would grieve later, but right now she was too angry. "If this is my death, sir, you make it very tedious."

"Enough, Plancy," said the countess. "No need to break your heart. When I come into my power, you will be great enough to buy and sell ten such

379

Syrian tirewomen and never know the difference."

Miles stepped back, his shoulders slumped in defeat. So that was the bargain he had made: he would hand Marta over to her enemy in exchange for the fief, the power and privilege he'd always wanted. Hadn't he *heard* Persi's warning?

Behind the countess stood Count Guy and a man in the robes and blue turban of a prosperous Saracen merchant. Sibylla turned to the Saracen and said, "Kurosh, this is Marta Bessarion. Do as you like with her. I only ask that she never returns to this kingdom."

Marta's heart almost stopped. Death she could face, but not servitude or imprisonment. *God in heaven,* she thought wildly, looking for some way to escape.

Perhaps, if she could throw herself from the tower, if she hit the citadel roof below and rolled—

Kurosh tilted his chin. "Aren't you forgetting something, countess?"

Sibylla's eyes flickered towards the spear. Marta touched her tongue to her lips, measuring the distance, counting the armed men between herself and the weapon. If not for Miles' treachery, she would have it even now; she would be invincible.

She looked at him with wordless reproach, but he just stared at his feet. So, he would look the other way as she was dragged down the tower and taken away God only knew where.

"Consider the Syrian a down payment, Kurosh." Sibylla's voice was cold and clipped. "I still have use for the weapon. My brother is about to declare the count a felon and an exile. Since we are to have a war, I mean to fight it with every weapon at my disposal."

She crossed to the rack and lifted the Bessarion Lance in both hands. "Come, Guy. God knows we didn't seek this battle, but let us be the ones to finish it. Take the spear."

"Do *not* take it." Kurosh stood his ground, glaring at Sibylla. "Heed my warning. That spear belongs to Khalil ibn Hassan, the Mighty."

The words jolted a sound of surprise from Marta's throat. Khalil—this man served Khalil.

380

Miles had sold her to Khalil.

"You have the girl in earnest of payment." Sibylla's voice was faintly audible over the roaring of blood in Marta's ears. "You will tell your master to have patience."

"We had an agreement," Kurosh growled.

"And I am altering it. Would you prefer me to end it altogether? Content yourself a little while longer, Kurosh." Sibylla turned to her husband. "Come, Guy. Take the spear and win yourself a kingdom."

"Jafar," Kurosh barked, "execute."

For an instant no one understood. Then the burly Syrian holding Marta's right elbow let go, snatching a knife from his belt. With one spring he caught the countess by the neck. The Bessarion Lance fell from her fingers, clattering to the floor.

An Assassin.

Marta's heart skipped a beat as she realised what she was seeing. She'd heard of the Saracen sect in the Syrian mountains, who planted spies in the households of counts and sultans, agents who might live as one of their enemies for years before finally being activated.

She'd never actually imagined she'd *see* one of them.

The Assassin's knife flashed in the air and Guy leaped forward to catch the Syrian's weapon hand as it arced towards Sibylla's side. The lance rolled under his foot, throwing him off-balance and sending the weapon clattering across the stones—away from Kurosh's grasping hand and straight towards Marta.

It was the opportunity she'd been looking for, and the sergeant on her left was, for the moment, stunned into immobility. Marta breathed a quick prayer of gratitude as she twisted from his grip, lunged to her knee, and snatched the Bessarion Lance from the stones. Strength poured into her at its touch. How right it felt in her hands! She snapped the butt around in a tight circle to her left. The invincible lance cracked against the guard's shins and he collapsed with a yell of pain.

The remaining guards were occupied with the Assassin. Guy clung to the man's knife-hand, while Sibylla clawed at the elbow that was crushing her neck. Miles stared at her from the opposite side of the trapdoor. Behind it, Kurosh reached out to her, his face a mask of fury.

The trapdoor yawned before her, open, waiting. She pivoted towards it on her forward knee.

Countess Sibylla gasped "Miles!" and pointed wildly at Marta, but she had already dropped through the opening, and slid down the steep ladder without even touching its treads. She landed below with a stagger.

Above, Miles' bulk blocked the trap as he climbed after her.

Marta pelted through the citadel's upper room, grabbing at unseen obstacles in the dark to throw them behind her. Halfway down the external stairs she heard the sound of a heavy fall, and groans of pain.

Alerted by the chaos in the tower, a knot of armed sergeants hurried out of the citadel to the foot of the stairs. Marta gesticulated to the tower's peak. "Assassin! Assassin! He's trying to murder the countess!"

They bolted past her without a word, not even seeing the Bessarion Lance in the dark. Above, Miles appeared in the doorway, only to be swept back into the citadel by the oncoming rush. Marta laughed outright to hear his protests, vaulted over the stair's railing and dropped the short way to the ground.

She could have kissed the earth to find herself standing on it again, but there wasn't time for that. Instead, she pelted east down the road that ran parallel to the city wall, then dodged sideways into an alley. Her forehead burned, but not painfully: she was a running flame, invincible. Back and forth she wove, deeper and deeper into Ascalon, losing herself in the alleys but always aiming for the western wall. Somewhere in the streets, the sound of hoofbeats blew towards her on the fitful wind. Miles was on her trail.

A beggar shivering in a doorway directed her to the house of Bertrand the tanner. Marta threw the man Miles' cloak—it would only hinder her escape—and within two minutes was standing at the head of a short cul-de-sac that ended in a small iron gate. Through it she glimpsed the sea's dappled silver and heard the constant wash of waves nibbling on the shore.

She had no key, but she did have a lance that nothing could resist. Poising the weapon, Marta strode towards the gate. Before she reached it, a slight noise alerted her and she stopped, letting the spear's tip sink to the pavement.

"I know you're there," she murmured.

Miles stepped out of the doorway in which he'd concealed himself, little more than a dark silhouette blocking the way out. He had a crossbow over his shoulder, and as he faced her, he levelled it at her heart.

"Hello, Marta." Miles' voice was weary, a pale shadow of itself. "Come closer. Three paces, and put the spear on the ground."

Marta stepped nearer as he commanded, but she couldn't bring herself to lay down the spear. "So you sold both of us." It seemed that nothing she said could get through to him, but she had to try. *"Why?"*

He looked down the shaft of the crossbow-bolt and into her eyes. "I sold myself because the price was right, and I have to find *some* way of living. I sold you because I love you and it was the only way I could find to save your life."

"I would have died anyway, Miles. That Saracen would have handed me over to Khalil ibn Hassan, who has already tried to kill me once. You sold me to my mortal enemy."

"The countess promised she wouldn't hurt you." He sounded shaken, but the crossbow didn't waver. "I love you; I couldn't stand by and let you provoke her."

"I know," she said. "You do love me. Just *not enough.*"

She didn't mean to be cruel, but he recoiled as though she'd struck him. "All right," he snapped, "what do I have to do to be *enough* for you?"

"Stop thinking I'll be happy with the dregs of a life. Giving up my spear to be used for evil. Sharing you with someone else."

He made a sound of frustration. "Oh, come off it, Marta! Nobody's perfect! Everyone takes paramours, even the Patriarch! The kingdom won't fall, just because you have a little fun for once in your life. No more than it'll stand, just because you have some high-minded ideals. That's the problem with you: you think life is a courtly romance, where all the virtuous end happily, and all the wicked die, according to the poet's will."

Frustrated, Marta shook her head. "Why do we read the romances, unless deep down we know they tell the truth?"

"How well has virtue worked out for you, anyway? Sibylla has beaten you at every turn because *she* is willing to do what *you* are not." He gripped the crossbow harder. "I'll only say it once more. *Put the spear down.*"

She was still too angry to think straight, and the words bubbled out of her heart, unstudied, rash:

"You had better shoot me."

His eyes narrowed. "Marta—"

She slung the spear across her shoulders and held out her hands. Defenceless. Angry. *Stupid,* a voice in the back of her mind told her. She paid it no attention.

"Shoot me, I dare you. For you I rode to Arabia. For you I fought an army." She stepped forward. "Go on, Miles of Plancy. Shoot me."

He ground his teeth. "If I let you go, it will make no difference. Sibylla will do whatever it takes. She will find you in the end and smash you like glass."

"But *you* won't." Another step.

His knuckles whitened on the crossbow. Marta took a deep breath, half expecting to feel the bolt smash through her ribs. She'd been wrong about him so often before; perhaps she'd misjudged him now.

"If you'd really meant to shoot me, you would have done it five minutes ago." Another step, and she stopped with the bolt tickling her breastbone. "Because you aren't *really* willing to do what it takes, are you? You keep telling me how strong the countess is, as though having rules makes me weak, as though my virtue is nothing but a chain holding me back. You fear her, so you try to appease her by serving her. Baldwin fears her, so he adopts her weapons and does injury to his conscience. But the one who fears God fears nothing else, and that's why I'm going to win. Because I really *am* willing to do what it takes."

She stepped forward, pushing against the crossbow-bolt, and Miles backed a step. Despite the frigid evening, sweat glistened on his forehead.

"People are always surprised by the lengths I go to. You of all people should know better. I didn't fear Arabia. I didn't fear Saladin or his whole army. Tell me, Miles of Plancy: why on earth should I fear *you?*"

His lips thinned. Marta's heart jumped and she braced herself for his shot.

Instead, he lifted his finger from the trigger and dropped the crossbow to his side. "What are you going to do?"

"Now that I have my spear back? I'm going to stop this war." She held out her hand. "Key."

He dug into his pouch, walked to the gate, and unlocked the barrel-lock.

"Go." He nodded towards the beach. "Might as well take the horse I have waiting out there, too. Ask for the farm of Hamid the olive-grower and give him the password *domina regnorum.*"

He'd yielded this far. Marta touched his shoulder. "As ruthless as she is, she cannot suck all the conscience out of you, Miles. Come with me. Don't ruin yourself alongside her."

With the last words, her voice trembled and broke. Miles dropped his crossbow to the stones with a clatter, and then he was kissing her hungrily, as though the world stood on the precipice of annihilation. As though it was the last kiss they would ever have.

Marta tasted salt, but whether they were his tears or hers, she didn't know.

He pulled back, and the cold sea wind rushed between them, stealing the warmth they had shared. He took a deep breath, and although the light was nearly gone she saw determination settle across his face again, the passion quenched from his eyes. When he spoke again, his voice was cold.

"Go, Marta."

Chapter XLVII.

"My lords, the need grows ever more pressing for us to consider the safety of the kingdom."

Baldwin found it almost impossible to focus on what Tripoli was saying. The bailli had already gone over the state of the kingdom's finances (good) and defences (vulnerable) in tedious detail. Now he was summarising the Ascalon situation: how Guy of Lusignan had retreated to the city with his wife and refused to budge; how Baldwin had personally summoned him and met with defiance; how from Ascalon the king had gone to Jaffa, confiscating the city's keys and installing a castellan of his own.

Now, in Acre, the High Court met to declare Guy felon.

Even with a fire crackling on every hearth, the king's house in Acre was chilly. Baldwin lay on his couch and let the count's voice wash over him, wondering why he was still exhausted from the journey, why no amount of rest seemed to do him good anymore.

Tripoli pointed out what all of them already know: Count Guy had broken his vows as a vassal of the crown. In any Frankish realm, his position, even his life, were forfeit. For the safety of the kingdom, he must be removed.

The room was full of attentive silence, broken only by an occasional cough or shuffle as the barons of the kingdom listened. Unable to concentrate, Baldwin's thoughts returned for the hundredth time to Marta Bessarion. Was she alive? If so, why hadn't Guy brought her to the gate in person? Saints, if he'd been a well man, he'd have done something to rescue her.

Lord Balian had refused when the king had suggested some kind of daring raid. "The best thing you can do for Marta," he'd said, "is admit Guy to your good graces again."

But Balian didn't know Sibylla like he did. In the pit of his gut Baldwin was sure he'd never see Marta again. He'd wounded his sister too deeply, and now she would strike out in anger, determined to make him bleed, no matter who she must destroy to do it.

You have no right to part them, Marta had said. If she died, it would be partly his own fault. The unguarded thought crept into his heart, and a shiver of pain ran through him.

No. *No.* He was the king. If he had no right to do it, then who did?

Tripoli had reached his summation: was the Leper King right to accept this dishonour? Would his vassals begin to safely defy him? Or was it time to declare the count a felon and proceed against him with decisive force?

Tripoli sat.

The first sound to break the silence was Patriarch Eraclius, clearing his throat. "My lord king." His slippered steps crossed the room, followed by two others. There was a rustle as he and his supporters—whoever they were—knelt before Baldwin's couch. "A boon. I ask this not for myself, but of your grace to Holy Church."

"As do I, on behalf of the Temple and Holy Church," another voice put in. The Master of the Templars.

"And I, my lord, for the Hospital and Holy Church." That was the Master of the Hospital.

Baldwin stiffened. The Patriarch was a member of his council, but the Masters of the great military Orders were present only in an advisory capacity. Their intrusion now was unwelcome. "Speak," he rasped.

"Behold how good and how pleasant it is, my lord, *for brethren to dwell together in unity,* as your lordship's predecessor has prophesied in the Psalms!" Eraclius' honeyed tones rolled through the council chamber, exquisitely measured, and Baldwin's doubts crystallised. Everything Eraclius said was a platitude. This could not just be brushed over because it was nice to live at peace.

The Patriarch was oblivious to the effect of his words. "It seems to us that if the count of Jaffa is not restored to your good graces, there will be war in the kingdom, most injurious to the cause of Christ and most debilitating to the cause of Holy Church. Therefore, if by any means we can do what the Church should always be most concerned to do, and make peace between Christian lords, we are prepared to persevere to that end."

Silence fell.

"How dare you?" Baldwin whispered.

"My lord?"

"You forget that I am a *king*, and I have been insulted and flouted and set at naught. Would you have me shame myself?"

"There need be no shame in admitting to having done wrong. Surely the count of Jaffa has the right to defend his wife against all the world."

The words were like acid poured on his smarting pride. Marta had said the same, but somehow it was easier to strangle his own doubts when Eraclius voiced them. "What! Will you speak to *me* of the sanctity of marriage? What of the draper's wife of Nablus? Where are your principles there?"

The Patriarch sputtered, but Baldwin barked him down. "And what of last month when you were so eager to find me grounds by which to accuse my sister's marriage? *Who paid you to sing this new tune?*"

Eraclius choked. "You forget the respect due to my station!"

"And you forget the basic duties of yours! What a thing it is, my lords, that the king should be chaste and the Patriarch lecherous! I ask you, was a greater marvel ever known?"

"My lord! Never in my life—" Eraclius sputtered. Someone in the council-chamber did not quite stifle a delighted bark of laughter—Ramla, most likely. As one of Countess Agnes' appointments, the Patriarch had never enjoyed Watcher support.

The Master of the Temple intervened. "My lord, truly—"

"I will not hear," Baldwin interrupted. His heart hammered from the effort of fighting them all, and he hoped he was not going to faint. "Get out of my hearing, before I say something you would find hard to forgive."

388

Eraclius' voice was thick with anger. "I can put the ban on you, my lord!"

"Enough," said the Master of the Temple, softly, and the Patriarch's voice stopped as though a door was closed on it. For a moment, the only sound in the room was Eraclius' laboured breath.

"I see the Church of God is unwelcome here," the Patriarch muttered, getting to his feet. His angry footsteps echoed across the polished floor, and a moment later the doors of the chamber snicked behind him.

Baldwin listened without repentance. As king, he was supposed to be Christ's knight, defender of the Sepulchre, the champion of Holy Church. But then, Eraclius was supposed to be Christ's bishop, holy and irreproachable. Neither of them was doing well today.

"Well? Does anyone else have any objections?" he snapped.

For the first time, Prince Reynald spoke. "My lords, you know I have always numbered the count of Jaffa among my friends. I know that his behaviour is not mere hauteur. Rather, if he shows defiance it is because he is faced with the prospect of being parted from his wife and stripped of his lands and title."

Baldwin gritted his teeth and signalled to Tripoli.

"Whether his defiance is understandable or not," his cousin said smoothly, "the count would have had the opportunity to make his case had he obeyed the king's summons and attended the court."

"Of course he disobeyed. Otherwise he would have delivered himself into the hands of his enemies." To his surprise, Reynald's words were greeted with murmured assent.

Worse, Lord Balian chose this moment to enter the lists. "With all respect, my lords, we can't afford to go to war over this. We're about to send an embassy to the West to ask for aid. Do you really think the lords of France and England will come east to fight in a family squabble? The Western Franks already think us soft, decadent and over-friendly with the Saracens. What will they think when they see us fighting amongst ourselves rather than confronting Saladin?"

This time the chorus of assent was louder. Baldwin opened his mouth to protest, but then Tripoli spoke, his voice pitched low to reach only the king's ear. "With all respect, my lord, Ibelin has a point."

"You too, Tripoli?" Baldwin said bitterly.

"We'll take a vote, my lord, but…"

But it was too late. Baldwin could complete his cousin's thought. He had gone too far. Eraclius and Reynald had shown that Guy was not without support in the High Court, and in the end, not even the Watchers were keen to involve themselves in an internecine war.

His anger bled out of him, leaving his heart racing as though he'd just run a mile. The voices in the room pressed in on him, their agitated rhythm making his heart race even faster.

"Brother John," he whispered. "I need silence. Take me out."

The Lazarites moved quickly, lifting his couch to bear it away. In the antechamber he got them to lower him to the floor again so that he could lie back and breathe. In through his nose, out through his mouth.

Gradually his heart began to slow—at least until the outer door of the antechamber burst open in a gust of argument and protest.

"I tell you," someone said, "the king must know—"

Both voices fell silent as they found themselves in the presence of the king himself.

Baldwin's heart was pounding again. "What is it?"

"My lord," the first speaker said. "We've just received a pigeon from the castellan at Darum. The count of Jaffa has attacked the Bedouins wintering in the pastures there."

Baldwin was motionless in shock. It wasn't just that Darum was part of the royal demesne: it was that the Bedouins given pasturage there were vital allies, his eyes and ears in Saladin's empire. A raid on them was close to suicidal. What on earth was Sibylla thinking?

The answer was evident: she *wasn't* thinking. She was lashing out at allies like Marta and the Bedouin purely for revenge on *him.*

Baldwin fell back on his cushions. Guy and Sibylla were already tearing the kingdom to pieces, and with the High Court keeping his hands tied, there was nothing he could do but watch.

Chapter XLVIII.

So far, everything had gone according to plan, and Miles of Plancy had never been sorrier.

He'd ridden with Count Guy to Darum with an idea of somehow getting ahead to warn al-Na'im, or of sabotaging the raid in some other way. When it came down to it, though, he hadn't had the opportunity to do anything.

The opportunity, a voice asked in the back of his mind, *or the guts?*

Black smoke belched from the Bedouin encampment and red flames licked the twilit sky. Around Miles, the screams and havoc of slaughter resounded. Some of the Franks had broken in among the camels and were herding them away, their laughter rising wildly above the squeals of beasts and the wails of frightened people.

How had he come to this?

He had lost Marta. He'd known that, even as he kissed her goodbye: she'd been cold and unresponsive in his arms, not the bright flame she'd been when they first embraced. He couldn't make her see reason, couldn't make her love him against her own inflexible principles, and so he had let her go. In her absence, he felt hollowed out, a numb shell of himself.

With Marta gone, the only thing he had left was his ambition.

When he had returned to the Ascalon citadel, the fight was over. Both Count Guy and Countess Sibylla were unhurt. The merchant Kurosh was in custody, but the Assassin had escaped into the city and the streets were full of search parties. It was then that the count had proposed a raid on the Bedouin.

"We don't need a magic spear," he'd said as they gathered in the upstairs chamber of the count's palace. "Let's light a fire under the king's seat. Show him we mean business."

"My lord, the Bedouin are our allies," Miles had protested. "You'll drive them into Saladin's camp and alienate the king as well. He promised them safe conduct."

Slumped wearily into a chair, Countess Sibylla had shot him a look of scorn. "Don't presume to advise us, Plancy. Be ready to ride by Vigils. Guy will need you for his raid."

Miles had stared at her. "My lady? Forgive me, but... It was the Bedouin who saved my life in Arabia."

At that, the countess had pulled herself upright, scorn crystallising into ice. "You remind me of my brother, Plancy. Always hedging your bets and pulling your punches in the hope of convincing yourself you're a good man. Make up your mind. You can leave my service, or you can ride to Darum."

He had already made up his mind. He had chosen Sibylla, and sent Marta away.

So he had ridden to Darum. And now he sat atop his horse in the midst of a burning camp, his spear dripping with blood and his ears ringing with the sounds of slaughter.

Miles slipped from his saddle and walked through the camp, past the motionless bodies that littered the ground. Until he reached the centre of the camp, he wasn't quite sure what he was looking for. And then he found it: the sheikh's tent.

Sweet Mother of God, don't let it be al-Na'im. Let it be some other tribe.

The sound of laboured breathing drew his attention to a man huddled on the ground, his hands clamped to a gash across his ribs. Miles approached with his heart in his mouth, stretching out the butt of his spear to prod the sufferer.

A lanky hand shot out and grabbed the end of the spear, the forearm gashed with sword-cuts: the Bedouin had had nothing but his own blood and bone with which to defend himself. He lifted his face and Miles stared, horrified, as his worst fear took shape.

"Sheikh al-Na'im," he choked.

"Miles of Plancy," the sheikh rasped, climbing to his knees. "Your king swore us protection."

"Saint George," Miles said helplessly. "I didn't know it was the Bani-Iaith…"

But I guessed.

Al-Na'im looked at him with disgust. "Spare me."

There had to be something he could do. "Get up. Take my horse," he hissed. "I couldn't save your people, but I can save you."

Grunting with pain, the sheikh took his arm and got unsteadily to his feet. Miles was still holding the stirrup for him when hoofbeats poured into the camp's central space.

Count Guy reined up beside them.

"M-my lord," Miles stammered.

The count's eyes glittered red in the firelight as he lifted his spear. "This is their leader."

"No!" Miles threw himself in front of al-Na'im and the spear thudded into his shield, splitting the wood in two. "I owe this man my life. I've sworn that he'll live."

Guy of Lusignan stared him down and Miles stared back, praying that the count would leave him this much self-respect, at least.

At last the count spat on the ground and snapped his fingers at his standard-bearer. "We have what we came for. Let's go."

The Frankish trumpet sounded, and the knights of Ascalon began making their way back to the rendezvous point outside the camp, loaded down with spoils and captives. With a sigh of relief, Miles turned back to al-Na'im. "I could not return your hospitality with injury, my friend."

Al-Na'im stared at him with frozen outrage. "You already have," he said, dangerously quiet. He pointed down at a body lying nearby. "That is my wife, Farah, God have mercy." His finger moved. "My son, Hamid. My brother, Abd al-Qadir. God have mercy on them all."

There was an awful silence.

Al-Na'im took a deep, shuddering breath. Words burst out of him as though breaking an ancient dam; a shred of poetry. *"I wonder, is despair a passing shadow or a companion for life…"*

Miles swallowed, his throat dry. "My friend…"

The sheikh's voice hardened to ragged fury. "I will accept my life at your hands, since God does not send me death today. But do not call yourself my friend, Miles of Plancy. I will make your people bleed for this."

There was nothing he could do or say to mend it. Miles had never thought of himself as a coward before, but as he turned away from the blood-soaked destruction, he knew he fled with dishonour.

Chapter XLIX.

It was the evening of Epiphany, and dusk was falling when Marta and Persi reached Acre.

Marta felt like one of the shadows herself as she slid stiffly from the saddle in the street before the palace gate. She'd paid the price for her adventures in Ascalon: following her escape, she'd reached Ibelin near a state of collapse, and Persi had forced her to spend a day resting before they followed the Leper King to Acre at a pace Marta found infuriatingly slow.

"Don't kill yourself with haste," Persi had scolded her. "Nothing terrible will happen before the king reaches Acre, and we're no more than a day or two behind."

Now, Marta reached out to knock at the gate but found it ajar and pushed through. Beyond, the rambling palace blazed with torches, but the courtyard itself was curiously lifeless. As she and Persi entered, the gatekeeper, who had stood with a knot of gossiping servants in a corner, wheeled around and ran to meet them. "Oi, you! Were you summoned?"

Marta threw an arm across her horse's withers for support. "My name is Marta Bessarion. May I see the king?"

"He can't see you tonight," the porter said shortly. "You had best go to the count of Tripoli instead."

"Baldwin will…" Marta caught herself, cheeks warming at the faux pas. She was so tired, she wasn't thinking properly. "The *king* will see me, I'm sure. If you'll only tell him it's me…"

"No one will see the king tonight," the porter insisted gruffly, "except maybe the Lord in heaven. Didn't you hear? King Baldwin lies at the point of death."

Marta stared at him, her well-built speeches tumbling down around her. "When did the crisis begin?"

Maybe he felt a sense of kinship with her distress, or maybe he enjoyed being the bearer of bad news. Either way, the porter was eager to share what he knew. "It happened at noon. He collapsed during the High Court's meeting, and now they say he's burning with fever. The barons are all in council."

The seraph's kiss. The sweat was cold on Marta's forehead, but under it, a steady ache had been building all day. Bearing such a thing was a constant burden, even for one who was alert to its promptings, but Baldwin had suppressed his for years. She couldn't imagine how much torment he must be in.

She nodded numbly, groping for a plan. "If the king is unable to see me, I'll wait for the count of Tripoli." The porter didn't object, and Marta turned to Persi. "Hold my spear?"

She wouldn't need it tonight. Marta took a deep breath and strode into the palace.

The stairs to the upper storey were inside the entrance-hall. Marta took them at a run. Upstairs, one empty echoing room led into another. If the barons were sitting in council, then who was with the king?

She found her way to an antechamber and got her answer. Two of the Lazarite attendants stood at a polite distance from one of the king's personal physicians, their voices low and worried till Marta's entrance silenced them.

Fear crossed their faces at the sight of her. Out of breath, clad in armour, she must be a wild sight. "I'm Marta Bessarion, and I can save him," she gasped, holding out her empty hands. "Please."

The lepers stepped in front of the door to block her way. "Who are you?"

She had no time to explain or apologise. "Think of me as his guardian angel." She swept up her sleeve, showing her Watcher's Mark. "Please, let me in."

They looked at each other and stood aside.

Beyond, the room was thick with silence and the scent of incense. Dozens of lamps burned around the bed, lighting Baldwin's motionless body. The only sound was the laboured rasping of his breath: the sound of approaching death.

He'd been touched by something holy, and because he denied it, it had been consuming him ever since.

She stole closer to the bed. "My lord, can you hear me?"

No sound came in response, just the labouring rasp of his breath.

I need a miracle, Marta thought.

His whole body was an open wound, the ulcers crawling across limbs and neck, even cracking open on his forehead. Yet there was no question what she must do.

She had known for weeks.

"Lord, have mercy," she whispered, digging deep into her memory for the liturgy. Hesitantly, she reached out and laid her hand on the Leper King's bandaged hand. *"You only are wonderful and You have pity on believers all. Therefore, O Christ, give Your grace from on high to those who are grievously sick."*

Her armour chimed as she climbed onto the bed. Carefully, gently, she stretched herself over his fragile form: hand to hand, chest to chest, face to face.

She felt the life in him, fragile and fluttering as his heart ticked weakly beneath her. She felt the destruction of his disease in the wasted limbs, the smell of pus and the burning heat of his fever.

Her own forehead blazed with painless heat. Marta took a deep breath and laid it against Baldwin's.

Their breath mingled. Burning pain washed through her, a knot of stabbing agony centred in her right arm. Marta jerked away, breaking contact with his skin, and the pain receded.

Baldwin's pain. Baldwin's burden.

Her forehead burned, reminding her of her task. Marta gritted her teeth and bent down again. Light and dark burst behind her eyelids. She was stretched over the king like a shield, and the pain beat against her like a storm.

With it came something else—grief, abandonment, a black cloud of emptiness that hung over her mind, leaching away her will to fight, to live. Yet that wasn't her own mind: it was Baldwin's.

"Give it to me," she whispered against his misshapen lips. "Let me in. Let me help you bear it."

She felt the room darken, and then, suddenly, she had the sensation of falling, until she dropped lightly onto her feet.

She opened her eyes. Darkness. A moment ago she'd been listening to Baldwin's breathing, and it was still going on somewhere beside her in the dark, quicker and rattled. Afraid.

"Baldwin?" From the way her voice echoed, Marta imagined they stood in a large chamber.

"Marta." For once, his voice didn't rasp or crack. It was soft, young, and more vulnerable than she'd ever known him. "I knew you'd come."

The ground quaked beneath a distant rumble. Marta gulped. "Where are we?"

He drew a quick breath. "I don't have much time left. You shouldn't be here."

Again, the room shook and reeled. A piece of the ceiling smashed to the floor, and in one wall cracks opened, glowing red with fire.

Marta lost her footing, tumbling to the floor.

"Marta, go!" Baldwin yelled.

The tremors faded. With the entrance of light, it was possible to see that she stood in a rich but empty palace room, its windows firmly bricked up. Footsteps echoed across the floor of polished marble, and a young man loomed over Marta, his hands out to bar her from the lines of fire in the wall beyond. Three or four years older than herself, he was fair-haired and fresh-complexioned, comely as an angel.

"Just go," he repeated. "Before the fire takes you. It won't be long now."

Speechless, Marta got to her feet.

It was Baldwin without his leprosy.

She had never wondered what he would be like without it, but still, she would never have imagined him looking like *this*. She stared in tongue-tied fascination, a hand wavering as she fought the urge to neaten her hair.

He grabbed her shoulders. "Marta! What's wrong?"

"Do you know you're beautiful?" she murmured.

His eyes widened in shock.

A rumble shook more dust from the ceiling. In the wall behind Baldwin, a brick fell from a sealed-off archway, letting in a ray of brilliant light. Beyond, Marta heard a roar, like a wild beast in pain.

"Just what is happening here, Baldwin?"

"I am falling to pieces. For the love of heaven—"

"No," she said, cutting him off. "It's more than that."

She tried to step around him, but he shifted to bar her way, eyes wide, hands trembling. "This is suicide."

"I just want to look."

"It'll kill you. Please."

"It can't hurt me." She ducked under his arm, evaded his grip and darted to the bricked-up arch. The light was blinding, but after a moment her sight adjusted.

The room beyond this one was just as large and fine, but in its centre stood a small iron cage. Confined within was a flaming dragon, smaller and less bright than the one she'd met in Arabia, golden rather than white. Cruelly packed into the cage, its tail and limbs protruded between the bars. As Marta watched, it made a convulsive attempt to get free, writhing against the bars and howling forth a stream of fire.

The room blazed and the palace shook. Bricks continued to fall, letting more light into the dark room where Baldwin had taken refuge. Behind, he gave a cry of pain and threw up his hands to shelter his eyes.

Marta's heart cramped. "Oh. You poor thing."

"I don't want your pity, I just want you to leave!"

"I didn't mean *you*," she retorted. One of the bricks moved under her hand. She shoved it. With a grind and clatter, it fell to the ground on the other side of the wall. "Help me!"

"What? No! Stop it!" He grabbed her wrist, trying to fight her away from the wall. "What are you *doing?*"

She faced him. "This is what's killing you."

"Yes! Thank you so much for pointing that out!"

Marta waited for him to calm a little, to look her in the eye. "You have to free it, Baldwin."

His hands clenched painfully on her wrist, but he didn't speak. She could see in his eyes that he knew she was right.

He swallowed and nodded, his skin slick with sweat and his eyes glassy with fear. Marta guided his hand to the bricks. Together, they pushed.

Mortar dissolved. The bricks tumbled, and light poured in on them.

Beyond, the dragon calmed and lay quiescent, its breath quick and shallow. Marta did not know if it even had room to breathe.

Marta stepped over the pile of fallen bricks. As she and Baldwin approached the caged creature, her foot landed on something shrivelled and hard: an old orange-skin.

Baldwin stared at the cage in horrified fascination. "It will burn me."

"Yes. That's what it does; it burns away everything false and leaves only the real you." She touched her free hand to her forehead. "Don't be afraid. I'm right here beside you."

His lips moved, repeating the Paternoster, and he held out a trembling hand to the dragon's nose. It breathed softly on him. Marta saw the Leper King's shape reflected in the beast's eye as he reached up and released the catch holding the cage together.

With a metallic shriek, the bars fell.

The dragon spilled out, its hide catching fire. White flame, bright as the sun, swallowed Marta's vision.

Then, slowly, she fell back into her own body and opened her own eyes. She was slumped over Baldwin's body, and his hands stirred below hers.

She jerked up onto her elbows to look down at his ravaged face. "Baldwin? Are you awake?"

"Dreaming, I assume," he croaked, "since there seems to be a girl on top of me." The faint tremor of humour faded from his voice. "Dear God, what have I done?"

Gently, so as not to hurt him, Marta disentangled herself and slid to the floor again. Her forehead was a little sticky from their close contact, but as she wiped it she found that the burn scar left by the seraph a year ago had vanished.

She stared at her sticky fingers. A spark of fire crawled across them, and the stickiness evaporated into steam and drifted away. The sparks faded. On an impulse, Marta touched her neck where Sibylla had stabbed her. That scar was gone, too.

In the bed, Baldwin moved. "Marta? Is everything all right? You—you touched me..."

"Yes," she managed at last. "I think everything will be...normal again."

There was a moment's silence. "You were right," Baldwin whispered. "I remembered months ago, but I didn't want to tell you. When I was a boy, I met a seraph, and it gave me a fruit to eat. Knowledge."

Marta took a deep breath, almost afraid to ask. "Do you..."

"Yes, I know what to do." He pushed himself to a sitting position, and although his head sagged a little with dizziness, his voice was stronger than it had been for months. "Deep down, I've always known."

Chapter L.

Water slapped the flanks of the gently rocking galley. In the aft cabin, Sibylla sat with Guy opposite her brother and waited for him to say something.

Baldwin sat in a high-backed wooden chair, wrapped with furs and propped up with cushions. A creature of bone and dwindling raw flesh, Sibylla was amazed that he'd regained the strength to sit. The last she'd heard from her spies, he was at death's door. Even if his sickness had not killed him, surely her onyx ring ought to have done its job by now?

Perhaps the same person who'd hired an Assassin to kill her on Kurosh's command had also made sure that her message went unanswered. Sibylla's skin crawled a little. That Assassin was still loose somewhere. Having failed in his task, he must now complete it or die. The only comfort was that she had hanged Kurosh this morning. Her arrangement with the merchant's unknown master was ended, as she had wished, with a modicum of inconvenience.

Leaving her alone to face Baldwin.

His messenger had come two days before the king's arrival by sea, with only a short verbal message to deliver: *Baldwin the Leper begs you to receive him for parley.*

Baldwin had arrived this morning by ship, and after Tripoli had sent one of his stepsons ashore as hostage, Guy and Sibylla had consented to be rowed aboard. The Leper King had them shown into this cabin, and now they sat facing him in expectant silence while he stared at his bandaged hands.

Beside Sibylla, Guy shifted uncomfortably in his seat.

Finally, Baldwin cleared his throat. "We are taking full responsibility for the raid on Darum," he said, using the regal plural. "We have sent Balian of Ibelin to repay the Bani-Iaith and resupply them with livestock. What you took from them, you took from us." There was a taut silence. "We do not require it at your hands."

Sibylla stared. "Is this supposed to be some handsome gesture?"

His voice was level, stronger than it had been for months. "We want you to know that what you did has cost us dearly. Darum is a royal possession, and the Saracens living there were under our personal guarantee. What you have done has cost us in gold, in livestock, and above all in honour." He paused. "We admit no obligation to shoulder the cost of your crimes. Yet what you did, you did because we drove you to it with an oppressive command that we should never have made."

Guy looked at her, and his eyebrows went up. Sibylla sat in frozen silence. With the possibility of an Egyptian alliance gone, she'd needed to get the barons on her side at once. She'd agreed to Guy's raid because as long as there was a chance of reconciliation, the barons would seek it, no matter what sacrifice that might impose on her. The raid was calculated to make them pick a side, to trigger *war.* Now Baldwin was here, making a song and dance of his magnanimity. What was the catch?

"This is a sudden change of course," she said at last.

"I believe that is the definition of repentance." He bowed his head towards her. "We were—no. *I* was afraid, Sibylla. I believed that only cruelty would safeguard this kingdom. I did what was expedient, not what was right. For that, I am sorry."

Sibylla was genuinely speechless.

Baldwin fumbled for the heavy key that lay on the table at his elbow, and pushed it towards them. "This is the key to Jaffa's gates. I've already told my viscount to surrender his office."

Hesitantly, Guy reached out and pocketed it. Sibylla's mind was a knot of questions. "Why?" she spat. "What are you trying to do, brother?"

"I am apologising." An awkward silence. "May I hope to be forgiven?"

Sibylla's lips tightened. "I want to be restored to the succession. Have me and Guy crowned, as Grandmother Melisende was together with her husband and son."

Baldwin was silent, and that silence told her that here, at last, was the catch.

"Your son is king," he said softly, "and Count Raymond of Tripoli is bailli until his majority. The boy is young. The barons will accept neither Tripoli nor your husband as king if he should die. Therefore I have recorded my will in the matter. If Baldwin the Fifth should die without issue, then the barons should choose themselves a new king from the West."

He paused. "I could not get the High Court to agree to any other plan."

In the numb silence that followed, Sibylla remembered the Messenger's words. *You hope for a great inheritance, my lady. They will take it away from you, and bestow it upon another.*

She had done everything to escape her fate, but still, her fate had come upon her. The prophecy was now fulfilled, and the future was once more a blank tablet, waiting for her to write upon it what she willed.

Sibylla's hand found the knife in her sleeve, and her muscles tensed. The cabin was silent, empty but for the king and one leper attendant. She was beyond caring. The Assassins had failed her, but she could make her own opportunity, and use their name to disguise her crime. With Baldwin dead, she could finally have her war. She could finally secure her inheritance.

"Did you know our mother is dead?" Baldwin said softly.

Sibylla blinked. "Yes."

"This was found among her things." Baldwin beckoned to his attendant. The Lazarite came forward, offering a small bowl.

Within it was the black onyx ring.

Sibylla picked it out of the bowl with a trembling hand. *How much did he know?*

Strike, her heart urged her. *He knows. Strike now and save your life.*

"She left a letter with it," Baldwin went on. "She told me that in the wrong hands, this ring could be dangerous. She counselled me to destroy it, but I know that whatever this is, you have guarded it safely for years.

404

You should keep it. Perhaps, one day, it will prevent someone from doing you a great injustice."

You should keep it. His words rang with sincerity, and Sibylla's armoured heart cracked. Against every inclination, she believed him, and the intensity of her relief shook her. He knew she'd tried to kill him, and he'd chosen to leave that power very literally in her hands.

He was her brother, and she'd loved him once. Perhaps she loved him still. She cleared her throat. "Since you asked my forgiveness, I must grant it, as I hope to be forgiven."

The words were chilly, but Baldwin bowed from the waist. "Thank you," he said softly, and she knew he understood how much that forgiveness had cost her.

Sibylla did not for an instant deceive herself. There were more battles to come, and she would never relinquish her claim to the throne. But today, it was enough just to survive.

After a somewhat uncomfortable meal, she and Guy returned to shore. Wanting to be alone, Sibylla took the citadel keys and climbed the tower where the Bessarion Lance had once been kept. Sea and coast lay before her, the kingdom that had her heart. Below, the king's galley slowly unfurled its sails and moved north, back to Acre. The city gates creaked open, signalling the end of hostilities. Down the Egypt road a smudge of mounted men travelled, Ibelin's delegation riding to soothe the Bedouin.

A voice broke in on her thoughts. *"All these things will I give thee, if thou wilt fall down and worship me."*

Sibylla whirled, hand to her heart. Beside her, dark hair ruffled by the breeze, stood Agnes of Courtenay. The smile on her lips was nothing like Sibylla had ever known.

She crossed herself and backed away until her back hit the rail. It took a couple of tries before she could speak. "You aren't my mother."

Still, that mad smile. "No."

Ice ran through her veins. Of course this wasn't her mother. It never had been, though it had masqueraded in Agnes' shape.

Saints, how could it haunt her like this, breathing out corruption—what was happening to her?

Trembling, Sibylla made the sign of the cross. "Go away. Leave me alone."
It didn't.

"It was a serious offer," the thing that wasn't Agnes said conversationally.
"I can give you this kingdom, if you like. I can help you destroy Saladin
and all his people. All I ask is regular feeding."

Not taking her eyes from the thing's face, Sibylla screamed for her guards.

"That was unnecessary," the thing commented. "I could only speak to
you in your dreams before. I should think this was more convenient for
both of us."

A guard clambered through the trapdoor and halted, scanning the room.
"My lady? Is something the matter?"

The thing smiled. "My dear, he can't see me. That privilege is reserved
only for you."

Sibylla swallowed, not taking her eyes off her visitor. "Everything is
perfectly all right, thank you. Wait for me below."

He bowed and started down the ladder. Sibylla waited for his footsteps
to fade before speaking. "Why me?"

"You made a blood offering." The tongue flicked out, touching red lips.
"My former allies have denied me food too long. I would have preferred it
to be the Leper King, of course, but those Bedouin at Darum did just as
well. We're bound now, you and me."

"I didn't know." Sibylla's voice was strained in her own ears. "I never
called upon you. I don't even know your name."

"It doesn't matter. You sacrificed innocent blood and I chose to accept
it. Now I'll always be with you." The creature moved forward, reaching
out to caress her cheek. Sibylla closed her eyes with a shudder; the hand
was cold, dead, inhuman. "If we're to be allies, you should know my name.
Call me Lilith."

Chapter LI.

In Damascus was a house that embraced the world. In the courtyard grew an orange-tree ringed by a reptilian mosaic, an endless pattern of waves and diamonds that almost but not quite resembled a serpent. On the second floor overlooking the courtyard was a loggia, carpeted and cushioned, lit by hanging glass lanterns. It was here, despite the January cold, that Khalil ibn Hassan met with the messenger from Ascalon.

"Kurosh is dead," he repeated, flatly. "Did you see it with your own eyes?"

"My master was hanged from the citadel," the old servant confirmed. "We saw it with our own eyes."

He wanted to ask about the spear, and the Bessarion woman who wielded it, but he dared not betray such secrets to a servant. "And nothing came from the city?"

"Nothing, my lord."

Khalil wanted to curse. Instead he rested his chin on his knuckles and thought. Kurosh, his eyes and ears in the kingdom of Jerusalem, was gone. Lilith was now his only hope of learning what had happened in Ascalon—and she hadn't shown her face in Damascus for three days now.

He would give her another hour before summoning her. Using a mortal spy had been too risky, anyway. If the sultan learned that Khalil had been trading information with the Franks...

Below the loggia, fists boomed on the door of the house. Khalil frowned as the noise cut through the city's evening murmur. During the three days of Eid, families gathered in the streets to feast and laugh. This could be anything; a gang of mischievous boys, perhaps.

407

The gate opened. Feet tramped through the lower entrance hall, weapons ringing. Khalil stood swiftly, grabbing Kurosh's servant by the shoulder and settling the blade of his knife against the man's ear. "Stand still. Don't speak."

His porter, a Turkish mamluk, raced up the stairs from the courtyard. "My lord, it's the sultan!"

Saladin himself. Perhaps things were worse than he had feared.

A door at the back of the loggia led to his own quarters. Khalil thrust his prisoner at the mamluk. "Lock this man in one of the storerooms. If he is seen or heard, he dies."

The porter bowed, grabbing the old servant by the scruff of his neck and hauling him through the door at the back of the loggia. Khalil stared into the glowing brazier at the centre of the reception area, took a deep breath and released it.

Composed, he strode to the wooden railing that overlooked the courtyard. "My lord, peace be upon you."

"And upon you, peace." The sultan and his mamluks were little more than shadows in the unlit courtyard below, their faces indistinct in the twilight.

"You see that I am unprepared for guests. Yet where there is wise and honourable company, even the humblest fare is exalted. Will you eat my bread and salt?"

That was the true test; Saladin was Kurdish, not Arab, but the rules of hospitality still dictated that one did not betray the trust of a man with whom one had eaten salt.

Khalil felt a tremor of guilt. *God be merciful. I do this for a righteous cause.*

"I came to ask your advice," the sultan said after a moment. "But I will eat with you, al-Aziz Khalil."

Khalil made sure his relief did not show on his face as Saladin ascended the stairs and settled cross-legged on the cushions at the low round table. Time and age had been kind to the sultan. Except for the grey that streaked his neatly-trimmed beard and the laugh lines spidering from the corners of his eyes, Saladin might have been much younger than his forty-six years.

A soldier's life had kept him lean and wiry, moving with the grace of an accomplished horseman. Once, before his own body was halted in a state of endless youth, Khalil would have hoped to age like this man.

Two of the sultan's mamluks followed him, standing to attention throughout the meal that followed; the others waited below in the courtyard. It was not until the servants had been sent away and they were filling in the gaps with fruit and nuts that Saladin came to business.

"I find myself at a crossroads," he admitted. "I promised that once the princes of Aleppo and north Syria had submitted, I would pursue the holy war."

Khalil's gut tightened with anticipation. "You will attack the Franks of the Coast?" Perhaps the Bessarion girl and the spear were not so far beyond his grasp after all.

But Saladin shook his head. "I don't know if it's the right time. So far, the Franks have had the upper hand."

"Do they still, my lord? We only had to abandon the siege of Kerak because Ramadan was approaching and the men were getting restless. As you said yourself, a wise general remembers that he is not a slave-driver."

"Flattery," Saladin said dryly.

"I respect you too well to resort to that, my lord." Khalil's voice was sincere. Saladin was ambitious, charismatic, kind to his friends and beloved by his men—the kind of man Khalil in his own long-distant youth would have followed and well-nigh worshipped.

He caught himself before that thought could go any further. No. He couldn't afford to think like that. Saladin was useful now, while Khalil was still fairly powerless, but there was no place for rival sultans in the empire he and Qeteb were building. If he served the sultan, it was only so that he might push Saladin from the throne and take it himself.

"Kerak was still a failure," the sultan said. "As was Galilee earlier in the autumn. The Franks presented an impenetrable defence, just by refusing to fight. If they continue such tactics, I will lose credibility anyway, and the prince of Mosul will be just as eager to profit from my weakness."

"It would put you in a stronger position to conquer Mosul first, *then* attack the Coast."

"I am in a cleft stick," Saladin admitted. "If I focus on consolidating the empire, I am criticised for failing to pursue the holy war. If I focus on the Franks and anything goes wrong, I give my enemies the opportunity to rebel." He leaned forward, the brazier flames flickering in his dark eyes. "I've received secret messages from two princes in Mosuli territory. If I march to Mesopotamia again this year, they'll fight for us. Say it succeeds this year; I could be preparing to attack the Coast next year at the latest."

"But say it fails?" Khalil pointed out. "The caliph has noticed your feud with Mosul, and he wants to make peace. If you fail again this year, he won't be in the mood for excuses."

Saladin looked thoughtful. "If I had the certainty of conquering the Coast, I would be in a stronger position to take Mosul, but the Frankish defences have been unassailable so far—and these Mosuli princes have offered to help us." He leaned forwards, his voice dropping. "What do you advise? What does fate have in store?"

Khalil took a deep breath, forcing himself to think rationally. Much as he wanted the spear, he was building something much bigger. It was because Islam was divided and weakened that the Franks had been able to gain a foothold on the Coast to begin with, and it was his mission to make sure that could never happen again.

He shouldn't jeopardise that, not even for the spear. Certainly not for revenge.

Abruptly, he stood up. "My lord, if you'll allow me to withdraw and consider this question for a moment?"

Saladin waved him away and Khalil withdrew to his own quarters, closing the wooden door behind him. With the snick of the latch, Qeteb appeared with a black bird of prey flapping and screaming in his fist. "Look what the cat dragged in," he snarled, throwing the bird at Khalil's feet, where it promptly transformed into a furious Lilith.

"I came of my own accord," she hissed.

"Three days is too long," Khalil told her. "We work *together*. You will report to us daily."

"So much fuss over nothing." Lilith ran her fingers through the feathers growing from the back of her arms. "I have the heiress of Jerusalem in my power, and this is all the thanks I get?"

"You have her?" Khalil echoed eagerly. "Where is my spear? What about the Bessarion girl?"

"That's the bad news. The little Bessarion creature took the spear and escaped. It also managed to pull the Leper King back from the brink of death somehow." Lilith jerked her head towards the door leading to the loggia. "What's happening out there?"

"Don't change the subject," Khalil growled. His fists knotted with frustration. It was *his* spear, and the Bessarions were only thieves. Yet time and again they appeared, as though from nowhere, to oppose him.

How many more of them would he have to kill?

"Where is she now? Nablus? That's only a quick raid across the Jordan."

Qeteb made a sound of disgust. "You don't seriously think to snatch the spear on a raid? Didn't you see what that Bessarion creature did to Lilith?"

Khalil swore at him, but Qeteb only snorted. "Face the facts, mortal. The Leper King is still living, and there's a Fiery One protecting the Bessarion. Try to reach it now, and you risk everything we've built."

The empire. The peace of his people. His chance for redemption. Khalil had committed many crimes in his long life; he could not let them be for nothing.

His thoughts must have shown in his face, because Qeteb grinned ferociously. "I knew you could not deny it."

Quickly, Khalil pulled resolve over his face like a mask. "The sultan is out there, asking whether he should attack the Coast next, or Mosul."

"The answer should be obvious."

"Chickenheart," Lilith muttered, but when Khalil turned to her, she only shrugged.

"The answer *is* obvious," Khalil said. "Lilith, return to the heiress and find others to corrupt. Report daily with what you learn. Qeteb, the caliph needs to be kept on Saladin's side. Try to subvert him, or failing that, someone he trusts. Leave Saladin to me."

411

They faded from sight, leaving him alone in the room. Khalil took a deep breath and pushed the doors open again.

"I have made my deliberations, my lord."

Saladin had been staring into the brazier. Now he glanced up, eager. "And?"

Khalil approached the fire slowly, letting the sultan's anticipation mount. "Mosul offers the most auspicious target. You should lend it your full attention."

Saladin's gaze returned to the flames. "And the Holy War? I have pledged myself, and would not be found faithless on the day of judgement."

"You fear for your soul?"

"I would keep my oaths."

Again, guilt assailed him. Khalil had committed terrible crimes, crimes he justified because they were in pursuit of God's will and the good of all true believers—crimes he fully intended to repeat.

But could he kill this man? Could he slip in the knife, let the blood, and tell himself *this* was for the good of all believers? After all, the Bessarions were thieves and infidels, but Saladin was not. Saladin was a brother.

Whoever kills a soul, it is as if he had killed mankind entirely. The verse drifted into Khalil's mind, raising a shudder. He'd found ways to justify his other crimes, but this...

Khalil shoved the doubts to the back of his mind. Far too late to turn back now. God was all-powerful, and if this wasn't God's will, then God would stop him.

"Mosul need not claim all your attention," he said. "You will have the time for at least one raid on the Coast this year. Why not Nablus?"

Chapter LII.

"Some things cannot be repaired," said the Leper King. "I am still dying, and my sister will never trust me again."

Marta looked up from her cup of fresh snowmelt, startled. "My lord, no! You're well, surely…the seraph healed you!"

"You can see for yourself that it didn't. Not completely."

Marta stared at him, heartsick. Baldwin sat before the fire, a Russian fur over his knees. Blind, lame, and covered with sores.

His face wrinkled in the closest thing he could give to a smile. "A wise woman told me once that this was not a curse but a blessing."

Her eyes prickled. "I wanted to save you."

"It isn't your part to save me from death, Marta." He held out his bandaged hand, almost as though he wanted her to take it. Then hesitated. "You're sure you'll be well? After…touching me?"

Marta knelt beside him and took the offered hand in her own, cradling it gently. "I'm sure, my lord—we had to do with angels and portents."

For a moment, it was enough to be silent together.

Outside, the winter sun was brilliant in a clear blue sky. Cold yet permeated the stone house, but despite the lingering chill, there was much to be thankful for. Baldwin had made peace with his sister and her husband. The kingdom was safe. She'd finally had the chance to tell him about her escape from Kerak with Miles. And Persi was waiting outside, eager to take her to inspect a weaver's workshop.

As for the seraph's kiss, it had vanished from her forehead, together with the aches and pains that it had caused. She didn't miss the pain, but doing

413

without it was like learning to walk again without a crutch. Good and evil were still the same: she knew she must not become complacent merely because her forehead no longer burned.

"May I ask you something?" There was something shy in the king's voice, and Marta braced herself, wondering if he was about to find the courage to say what he hadn't last time.

"Of course."

"Will you call me Baldwin? No one has, since I was small."

What a lonely life he must lead, Marta thought. *Baldwin.* Once she had told him that a king could never be loved, but she could have loved a Baldwin.

"I would be honoured, Baldwin," she said gently.

He smiled, and for a moment Marta glimpsed the Baldwin she'd seen in the crumbling house, hale and well. "Visit me again, when you can."

"I will. Soon."

She went out into the antechamber, pulling her mantle around her shoulders. Persi jumped up when she entered. "Are you ready?"

"One moment." Marta led the way into the palace courtyard, where a page waited with a beautiful grey war-horse bearing a full suit of armour. She stopped, blood rising in her cheeks.

Persi stared with eyes like coins. "Is all that for you?"

"King Baldwin wanted to thank me." She lifted a hand, allowing the gelding to sniff it. "He...I think this was *his* horse. His favourite."

"Oh," Persi said softly, but Marta found herself blinking back tears as she stroked the beast's glossy neck. To gain his reputation as a horseman, Baldwin must have spent hours in the saddle, training. Even when he could no longer ride, he'd still spent time with his horse in the garden. He hadn't just given Marta a horse: he'd entrusted her with a friend.

"I'll take good care of you, you beautiful boy," she whispered.

She gave the page directions to the house the Ibelins had rented, then prompted Persi to lead the way into the city. "Count Guy took most of my armour when I arrived at Ascalon, so I asked for replacements."

Persi whistled. "And there was Lord Balian trying to thank you by arranging a marriage with that nobleman's son from Tripoli."

Marta reddened. "He means well. Maybe…maybe in a few years."

Persi was silent for a moment, and Marta knew she was thinking of Miles. "He wasn't worthy of you, Marta."

Of course he wasn't worthy of her; that was why she had refused him. Still, knowing that didn't stop her heartache, or make her able to care for anyone else. Marta quickly changed the subject. "Tell me about this weaver."

"I discovered him at a small meeting of Watchers near the church of Saint Andrew last week. We didn't have the chance to speak much, but he says that his workers are all freedmen, and I gave him one of your designs to weave."

Acre was the largest city in the kingdom. If Jerusalem was the spiritual centre of the world, Acre was its trading centre, the rendezvous between luxuries from the east and buyers from the west. Untold quantities of gold, spices, sugar and silk flowed through its harbour each year.

It was in the direction of the harbour that Persi led her, but before they came in view of the sea she turned down a narrow alleyway barely wide enough for the two of them to walk abreast. When the alley opened into a small cul-de-sac, they followed the clacking of looms through a narrow doorway on their right and into a large room in the ground floor of a tenement. Inside to the right, a desk faced the doorway, groaning under an untidy pile of ledgers. To the left, the room was full of busy looms and flying shuttles.

Persi reached for the bell on the desk, but before she could touch it, a voice shouted her name.

"Mistress Persi! I have that sample you ordered!"

A young man left his loom and bustled to the desk, beaming from the depths of his dark beard. Marta guessed that he, like herself, was of Syrian extraction. He dove behind the counter, making nervous excuses for himself before bounding up and flinging a scrap of fabric onto the countertop. "Here we are!"

He paused, breathing rather hard and looking eagerly at Persi. Recognising the rather smitten look on his face, Marta inspected the young man more closely. He was about Persi's age, tall and well-kempt. As for Persi, her dark skin didn't show a blush well, but Marta could have sworn that she reddened.

She unrolled the scrap of fabric, and Marta recognised one of her most complicated designs, executed beautifully in crisp white and a vivid red the precise colour of a ripe strawberry.

Persi touched it. "It's very good. Did you make this yourself?"

"Well, no, actually. This was Mistress Anna's work." He waved a hand across the room; Marta didn't see exactly who he meant. "Once she'd set the loom, it took her less than a half-hour to make this."

Persi's eyebrows climbed. "That's *exceptional.* She must have a great deal of experience in double-weaving."

The weaver's teeth flashed white. "She was one of our first purchases—"

"Purchased?" Persi interrupted.

"Yes, that's how we find our workers." The weaver leaned his elbows on the counter. "We buy slaves skilled in textile work and give them their freedom, together with a job in the workshop and a bed in the dormitory if they want it. They owe us a debt amounting to ninety per cent of their purchase price, but they usually pay that off within a few years."

By now there were stars in Persi's eyes as well. "And how does it work from a business perspective?"

"It involves a little extra time and cost," he admitted. "My cousin keeps telling me we could run the business more efficiently without it."

"Don't listen to him," she said fervently.

He grinned. "I won't." He reached under the counter and brought out another sample—the same pattern, the same colours. "This is young Jouseph Bishara's work. It took him half an hour, a little longer, but you can see the weave's tighter. And this is mine. What do you think?"

Marta cleared her throat. "May I see?"

Persi didn't seem to hear. Instead, she ran her fingers down the stripes. "How long did this take you?"

"No trouble at all," he said incoherently.

Marta stared. She'd never felt more invisible.

"Well," Persi said, "if you can do work *this* exceptional so quickly, then the higher hourly rate is perfectly reasonable."

"For designs this beautiful," he said, staring deeply into Persi's eyes, "we would weave them for half the pay."

"Don't even think of it," Persi cooed. "We would be so honoured to support your work in any way we can."

As they left the narrow alley, Marta could no longer stifle her laughter. "*Strife*, Persi. Don't forget to invite me to the wedding, will you?"

"What?" Persi emerged from her daze rather snappishly. "Whose wedding? No one's getting married. Don't be ridiculous."

Marta swallowed her laughter, the jagged edges cutting at her heart on the way down. It wasn't Persi's fault that she was breaking her heart over Miles of Plancy, yet there seemed to be reminders everywhere. "Just remember that I'm depending on you to make clear-headed business decisions. Are you going to let me see those samples at all?"

"Didn't I?"

"Persi, you didn't even tell me his *name*."

"Oh. It's Zakar—Michael Zakar. Here, let's get out of the traffic and I'll show you the cloth."

They were in the middle of a street, a stream of pedestrians and the odd oxcart making it impossible to loiter, but a narrow lane to the left cut between two houses. Marta sidestepped into the cul-de-sac, and Persi handed her one of the lengths.

Even her critical eye could see that the samples were just as good, if not better, than what she could produce herself. If the weaver was telling the truth about how long it had taken them to do the work…

"It's excellent," she began.

Persi had been standing in the mouth of the alley to watch her reaction. Now, suddenly, someone shoved her aside. Persi staggered against the far wall with a yelp of surprise. Marta barely glanced up from the fabric before the man slammed into her.

Her back hit the alley wall. Marta gasped in pain as a forearm pinned her against the stones, and the blade of a knife nicked the skin at her throat.

The face snarling into hers was familiar, though it took her a moment to place it: the Assassin from the tower at Ascalon.

"Where is the Spear?" he snarled.

With a black eye and split lip, he looked terrible. Marta wasn't sure how he'd managed to escape, but Countess Sibylla's men had obviously done their best to stop him.

Marta fumbled between the folds of her skirt for the knife that hung there. "What spear?" she asked, wide-eyed.

"You know what spear!" the Assassin roared, spraying her face with saliva. "I saw you take it!"

It was her life or his: Marta freed her knife and punched it up into the soft belly just below his ribs. The Assassin gave a jerk and an ugly grunt, and a trickle of hot blood ran down her arm. As he recoiled, he drove a knee up and smashed her knife-hand against the wall. Marta shrieked with pain, dropping the blade.

He shoved her against the wall again, his knife-hand trembling. "Tell me where to find it!"

She didn't owe this man the truth. "Lord Balian has it." Where was Persi? Had he used his knife on her as well? Marta didn't dare look. "He's riding on a mission to Darum—the Bedouin are up in arms—"

An ice-and-strawberry cloth dropped over the Assassin's head and yanked, pulling him away from Marta. Instantly the Assassin lashed out with his knife, but Marta was already moving, throwing up her arms to parry. Bone jarred against bone as she slammed his arm up and away from her face. Then she ducked down and to the side, scooping up her knife in her uninjured left hand.

Persi had each end of the fabric bunched in each hand. As the Assassin staggered backwards, she pivoted, driving him against the wall opposite Marta with a sickly *thump*. The Assassin recoiled a step and fell to the ground with a groan.

Marta stared at her friend in astonishment, gasping for breath. "Did you have training?"

Persi shook her head. "Brothers."

"Ah."

The Assassin's knife had fallen from his hand as he hit the wall, and Persi, shaking slightly from the encounter, scooped it up and handed it to Marta. As the Assassin groaned and moved, Marta kicked him back to the ground and knelt on his chest, putting his knife to his own throat. "Who sent you? Was it Khalil ibn Hassan?"

Bleary eyes focused on her. "I admit nothing."

"You're an Assassin. A *failed* Assassin. What mercy will your people give you? Better to talk."

He showed bloody teeth. "You'd better kill me."

"On the contrary, I'd like to keep you alive."

The Assassin broke into a string of angry curses and Marta thumped his head, not too hard, against the pavement. "Language. Persi, get help."

He spat blood and stared up at her with dull hate. "Soon the Leper King will die and the help of God will be taken from the Franks. A hundred Saracens shall put a thousand Franks to flight. Al-Aziz, the Mighty One, will take back the spear that is his, and then the Coast will be swept clean of you all."

The Mighty One. That was what Kurosh had called Khalil. Marta swallowed nervously. She might have saved Baldwin's life for the moment, but he was still dying. The moment he did, Khalil would come for her.

Persi still stood watching them numbly. Marta turned to her. "Get help!"

In that moment the Assassin heaved with a strength she hadn't suspected he still had. Marta toppled from the Assassin's chest as he wrenched the knife from her hands.

"Marta!" Persi screamed.

The Assassin grinned. "The Mighty One is coming, and none can resist him!" He sank the blade into his stomach with a grunt, pulled it upward, and fell to his knees as his guts spilled into the alley.

* * *

"The Mighty One? What did he *mean?*" Queen Maria's voice was high-pitched with stress.

In the room she shared with Persi, Marta sat dabbing her sore wrist with comfrey salve. "Khalil ibn Hassan," she said quietly. "The Saracen sorcerer who nearly stopped me leaving Kerak."

Beside her, Persi stiffened. "The one who destroyed Oliveta?"

Marta stared at her wrist. The mottled red marks would soon turn to black bruises. *Saint Martha, protect me.* If she admitted the truth, she was terrified. She wanted to take her spear, ride out to find Khalil, and *deal* with the sorcerer once and for all—but even she knew it was madness. "It's true. He's alive, and he wants the Bessarion Lance."

"Saints and holy angels." The queen pressed the back of her hand against her mouth. "He knows you're here. He knows you've got the Spear. And he's coming for you?"

"So he says." Marta shrugged.

"He could send another Assassin. You should leave. We'll send you to Antioch, or Constantinople—somewhere you'll be safe."

If Khalil was still alive and causing trouble, then perhaps he too was part of her mission in this time. Marta flexed her fingers. "I'm not going anywhere. I'm not going to let him frighten me."

"What are you going to do?"

Marta looked from Persi's worried face to the queen's, and then to the papers that lay on her bed—grids picked out, waiting to be drawn and coloured. The ice-and-strawberry samplers were ruined, but she still had the original pattern, and many, many more in her mind, waiting to be made.

"What am I going to do?" She took a deep breath, forcing her heart to calm. She had nothing to fear. After all, she'd been kissed by a seraph. "My work, of course."

S.D.G.

Marta Bessarion will return in
The House of Mourning

Wondering what happened to the other Bessarions?

Read Rahel, Paulus, and Elisa's story in
Children of the Desolate
Available free at suzannahrowntree.site

Lukas' story began in
A Wind from the Wilderness
Available wherever ebooks are sold

John's story will begin in
A Day of Darkness
Coming soon!

Historical Note

It's my intention with the *Watchers of Outremer* series to include very few intentional historical inaccuracies. This book contains three.

First, the historian William of Tyre records that the axe-wielding knight who protected the townspeople's retreat into Kerak against intense Turkish attack was named Iven, not Miles. We know nothing else about him.

Second, Bernard Hamilton argues convincingly that, although many historians have recorded Guy of Lusignan's raid on the Bedouin at Darum as occurring in the first few weeks of 1184, in reality it must have occurred in the autumn of that year, several months later. This suggests that historically, Baldwin did *not* reconcile with his brother-in-law before his death (in 1185), although the High Court did indeed refuse to go to war against him.

Third, Baldwin and Sibylla's mother, Agnes of Courtenay, died sometime late in 1184—a year later than I have it. This is entirely my own fault, since I mistook the date in my notes, and did not double-check it until I had already hard-baked the wrong date into the story. Oops!

Apart from these inaccuracies, my hope has been to stick as close as I can to the historical record, embroidering upon rather than altering it, extrapolating personalities, motivations, and background detail therefrom. All historians do this to a limited extent; the dramatic novelist has a somewhat freer hand. Therefore, I did not invent Baldwin's attempts to have his sister divorced in the winter of 1183-84, nor did I invent the visit of the tourneyer William Marshal, the earl of Salisbury's nephew—later to become the most renowned knight of the medieval age—to Jerusalem early in 1184. I did, however, take the liberty of supposing that Baldwin might have seen him as a possible rival to, and even substitute for, Guy of

Lusignan.

Baldwin the Leper, Sibylla and Guy, Balian of Ibelin together with his brother Baldwin of Ramla and wife Maria Comnena, Princess Isabella, Reynald of Chatillon and his wife Stephanie of Milly, Humphrey of Toron, Agnes of Courtenay, Sultan Saladin and the Assassins were all real historical people. According to William of Tyre, who was his tutor as a boy, Baldwin "loved to talk", had a keen intellect, and until his disease attacked his face, resembled his unusually handsome father, Amalric. As both king and leper, despite the moral stigma some attached to the disease, Baldwin seems to have had a sort of semi-religious charisma about him: since both lepers and noblemen were expected to be lustful, the fact that he remained chaste was seen as evidence of unusual grace to some, while the Vulgate's translation of the Suffering Servant passage in Isaiah 53:3-4 contains a reference to leprosy, which led others to view the disease as a symbol of messianic suffering. Amidst all this reverence, Baldwin himself seems to have behaved and viewed himself as quite a normal, secular knight, fond of his horses and jealous of his throne. It amused me in this story to investigate the disconnect between how others saw Baldwin and how he saw himself.

We have less information on Sibylla's character and motivations: so little, in fact, that some have claimed she was little more than a pawn in the hands of more powerful players. However, we know for certain that at a pivotal moment in 1186, she had the courage to act swiftly, decisively, and boldly in the face of significant opposition. We can be equally certain that her marriage to Guy was a love match, and that Baldwin's attempts to separate them in late 1183 were frustrated when she fled to Guy at Ascalon rather than allow a divorce—another pivotal moment at which she demonstrated courage, daring, and resolve. It is, admittedly, historically unlikely that Sibylla was the sole intellect and driving force behind all the actions of both her mother Agnes and of her husband Guy, as I've depicted in this story for dramatic purposes, and her chronic ill-health is another invention of my own. However, too little attention has been paid to the fact that Frankish women in the crusader states enjoyed legal and social privileges far beyond what their cousins enjoyed in the West. Sibylla's family heritage on both sides contained strong autocratic women who ably ruled both kingdoms and counties, and she herself was raised in the convent at Bethany by two great-aunts, Hodierna and Yveta, who were themselves part of this tradition. At that stage in the history of Frankish Jerusalem, Sibylla would have had every reason to expect to inherit the throne, and the historical evidence suggests that she intended to wield the same power as her grandmother Melisende, who ruled the kingdom in her own right. The truth is probably somewhere in between pawn and chessmistress; but my version does make a good story.

If the only thing you know about Balian of Ibelin is what you learned watching the Ridley Scott film *Kingdom of Heaven* (2005), forget what you think you know. The historical Balian was born in the east to a knightly family that quickly rose to become one of the most powerful in the kingdom. Part of the reason for the Ibelins' rise was Balian's 1177 marriage to Maria Comnena, the queen dowager of Jerusalem and a scion of Byzantine royalty, who became Baldwin and Sibylla's stepmother after their father divorced Agnes of Courtenay. Balian's relationship with the Leper King was complicated by his involvement in the attempted coup of 1180, which was apparently designed to put Balian's elder brother Baldwin of Ramla on the throne as Sibylla's husband. Needless to say, at no point would Balian and Sibylla have contemplated a love affair: they were political opponents, Sibylla was devoted to Guy, and Balian was married to a powerful woman of much higher status than himself.

The story Balian tells Maria of his mother Helvis is an invention, as is the idea that Balian might have taught Maria and Isabella how to fight; however, when Saladin sacked Nablus in September 1184, historians presume that it was Maria who took charge of the defence, sheltering the town's citizens in the citadel until the sultan withdrew. The fifteenth century writer Christine de Pisan encouraged noblewomen to learn the use of arms for this precise purpose, and given the dangers of life in the Frankish kingdom of Jerusalem, it's not inconceivable that Maria might have received training. A few years later, during the Third Crusade, Muslim chroniclers would record Frankish ladies fighting as knights in full armour. No doubt a woman who fought would have been viewed as something alarming and unusual in this society, but it evidently wasn't unheard of.

Humphrey of Toron was later said by his enemies to be "cowardly and effeminate", but this was hostile propaganda and cannot be taken as evidence of homosexuality (as some have done). That was a dramatic choice on my part; the historical record on his sexuality is not conclusive.

Sultan Saladin, known to the Arab-speaking world as An-Nasir Salah ad-Din Yusuf ibn Ayyub, does not have a large role in this story, but it may be worthwhile to remark that, indeed, he was not on good terms with the Bedouin tribes that roamed between Arabia, Syria and the Coast. As independent entities within his empire who were not averse to working with the Franks, they were a thorn in his side. Additionally, at this stage in the sultan's career, he was often criticised for his wars against fellow Muslims and for his apparent lack of interest in removing the Christian Frankish regime in Palestine. This would, of course, change.

So much for the historical characters. My own inventions include Marta Bessarion, the Watchers' Council, Persi, Miles of Plancy, the Cacho weavers, Khalil ibn Hassan, Omar and Sheikh al-Na'im. Persi is in the story because the Christian kingdom in Nubia was a significant force in Egyptian politics at this time, and I wish we heard more about the magnificent civilisations of medieval Africa. Miles of Plancy is an invented character, but his father was not: a courtier of Queen Melisende's, the original Miles of Plancy was assassinated by political rivals in 1174.

Al-Na'im and Omar show some of the ways in which the Franks were able to cooperate with local Muslims (others lived in the kingdom as peasants or burgesses, and were able to settle disputes in their own courts, which likely applied a form of sharia law). On the other hand, I have no particular historical basis for placing a slave textile workshop in Cacho in the lordship of Caesarea, but we know that during this period, many textiles *were* produced by female slave labour across Christian Europe, and if anything I have failed to depict just how pervasive slavery was in the medieval crusader states: the traveller ibn Jubayr, while praising the Franks

425

for the justice shown to Muslim freemen in the kingdom, also recorded seeing both male and female chain gangs on the roads, many of them no doubt Muslim prisoners of war.

This book is close to my heart for a number of reasons, but one of those reasons is the opportunity to showcase what attracted me to this period of history in the first place. The crusaders have a deserved reputation for ferocity in warfare, but the Crusader States spent much of their nearly 200 year history at peace with their neighbours, and during this time they achieved some incredible cultural and social achievements: at one point Saladin marvelled that the Franks had transformed Jerusalem into "a garden of paradise." They carried out a massive building program to rebuild churches and shrines that had been destroyed during the Muslim occupation. They became a hub of trade for Asia and the Mediterranean. They pioneered care for the sick and poor in the Hospital of Saint John, the Order of Saint Lazarus, and other charitable institutions. The treaties they made with Muslim neighbours ensured protection for both Christians in Muslim territory and Muslims in Christian territory. They lived on good terms and intermarried with the indigenous Christian population (then still a majority in large areas of Palestine), creating a society that was, for its day, surprisingly multicultural. It is these peaceable achievements, flawed and incomplete as they were, that inspired this series.

As always, many people gave generously of their time and expertise to put this book into your hands. Most of all, I'm grateful for my beta readers: Peirce and Christina Baehr for all their encouragement and critique, as well as providing me with the most preux of goddaughters; Abigail Hartman, for the challenging emails which were exactly what this book needed; Stella Dorthwany, for giving me so much more excellent advice than I was able to take; Schuyler McConkey, for being the only one who was barracking for Miles; Leila Ammar, for ironing out the details of Muslim theology and telling me she'd follow Marta into battle; Courtney Gilliland, for helping me to believe my story wasn't crazy; and Deborah Cullins and Martha Rasmussen, for helping me understand what it's like to live with fibromyalgia. Finally, again I must thank my wonderful editor,

Lucy Holdsworth, and my cover designer, Jenny Zemanek, who has truly outdone herself. I'm so enormously privileged to work with all of you.

Suzannah Rowntree

October 2019

Further Reading

I read or consulted a wide range of historical sources in preparation for writing this book, but here are the most significant. Bernard Hamilton's *The Leper King and His Heirs* is the most important scholarly work on Baldwin IV's reign, and it has been my constant companion for several years. Malcolm Barber's *The Crusader States* is another magisterial work covering the history of this unique culture from its founding in 1099 until the Third Crusade in 1191. *Saladin: The Politics of Holy War* by Malcolm Cameron Lyons and D.E.P. Jackson is the premier scholarly biography of Salah ad-Din and provided the foundation for my take on Saladin, as well as essential details on medieval Nubia, Reynald of Chatillon's Red Sea raid of 1182-3, and the siege of Kerak later that year. Piers Mitchell's *Medicine in the Crusades* was a delightfully readable look at the surgical expertise displayed by doctors in the Crusader States, providing me with the details I needed to describe the various injuries in this book, along with their treatment. Malcolm Barber's *The New Knighthood*, and to a much greater extent, Jonathan Riley-Smith's *The Knights Hospitaller in the Levant, c1070-1309*, provided necessary detail regarding the military Orders, while Bernard Lewis' *The Assassins: A Radical Sect in Islam* provided the story of the real Assassins, who did not in fact spend their time in paradise gardens eating hashish but were still fascinating anyway. Riley-Smith also contributed *The Atlas of the Crusades*, an invaluable source containing beautifully-presented maps and diagrams. Adrian J Boas' *Crusader Archaeology: The Material Culture of the Latin East* contained fascinating details on the cities, villages, and household items of the time. Denis de Rougemont's *Love in the Western World* helped me understand the medieval courtly love phenomenon that lurks in the background of both Guy and Sibylla's, and Miles and Marta's relationships. Once again, I have consulted Christopher MacEvitt's *The Crusades and the Christian World of the East: Rough Tolerance* to get a handle on relations between the Franks and the native Christian population; John France's *Western Warfare in the Age of the Crusades* to help understand the military background; and Carl Stephenson's *Medieval Feudalism* and Marc Bloch's *Feudal Society* to understand Frankish social structures. Finally, as always, I have turned to van der Toorn, Becking, and van der Horst's *Dictionary of Deities and Demons in the Bible* for inspiration when it comes to writing Lilith, Qeteb, and the seraphim.

Geoffrey Hindley's *The Crusades* and Simon Sebag Montefiore's *Jerusalem: the Biography* are more readable popular works, the former containing some errors of fact, but a wonderful chapter on the status of women in the Crusader states. WB Bartlett's *Downfall of the Crusader Kingdom* is another very readable account of the events of the 1180s in Frankish Jerusalem, although it draws on some older scholarship, which Hamilton's *Leper King* has since challenged and superseded.

A wealth of scholarly articles have helped to complete the picture. I'm indebted to Bernard Hamilton's *The Elephant of Christ: Reynald of Chatillon* and Alex Mallett's *A Trip to the Red Sea with Reynald of Chatillon* for the background on Reynald and his Red Sea raid; M. R. Morgan's *The Meanings of Old French "Polain", Latin "Pullanus"*; Svetlana I. Luchitskaya's *Pictorial Sources, Coronation Ritual, and Daily Life in the Kingdom of Jerusalem* for the description of Baldwin V's coronation; Lila Abu-Lughod's *A Community of Secrets: The Separate World of Bedouin Women* and G. Cowan's *Nomadology in Architecture: Ephemerality, Movement and Collaboration* for some of the details on Bedouin life and culture; Benjamin Z Kedar's *The Subjected Muslims of the Frankish Levant*; Bernard Hamilton's *Women in the Crusader States: The Queens of Jerusalem (1100-1190)*; and Susan Mosher Stuard's *Ancillary Evidence for the Decline of Medieval Slavery*, which discusses the use of female slaves in textile workshops across medieval Europe. Finally, the Medieval Nubia Wiki at http://medievalnubia.info was helpful in fleshing out Persi's backstory.

As usual, no historical research is complete without consulting the histories and storytelling produced by the subjects themselves. Malcolm Barber's edition of *Letters from the East* contained useful commentary from the crusader nobility, and provided a model for the letters in this story. William of Tyre's *History of Deeds Done Beyond the Sea* is our main eyewitness source for this period, which I have supplemented with some materials from the Old French *Continuation of William of Tyre* and other sources as contained in Peter W Edbury's *The Conquest of Jerusalem and the Third Crusade.* Finally, Chretien de Troyes' Arthurian romances, written around the time this story takes place, inspired the strategem Sibylla uses to marry the man of her choice.

About the Author

Suzannah Rowntree lives in a big house in rural Australia with her awesome parents and siblings, reading academic histories of the Crusades and writing historical fantasy fiction that blends folklore and myth with historical fact.

You can connect with me on:
 https://suzannahrowntree.site

Subscribe to my newsletter:
 https://www.subscribepage.com/srauthor

Also by Suzannah Rowntree

The Fairy Tale Retold Series
The Rakshasa's Bride
The Prince of Fishes
The Bells of Paradise
Death Be Not Proud
Ten Thousand Thorns
The City Beyond the Glass

The Pendragon's Heir Trilogy
The Door to Camelot
The Quest for Carbonek
The Heir of Logres

The Watchers of Outremer Series
Children of the Desolate
A Wind from the Wilderness
The Lady of Kingdoms

Made in the USA
Middletown, DE
10 January 2020

82519305R00260